Phoenix Dragon

By

Howard Lycett

"Go out into the highways and hedges and compel them to come in."

Luke 14:23

IN HONOUR OF

BERNARD HUGH

MCMULLEN BEM

THE BRAVEST OF THE

BRAVE.

O.A.F.A.A.F.

CONTENTS

ACKNOWLEDGMENTS

I would like to thank a few people for helping and inspiring me to write this book.
Fellow author James Deegan for giving me sound advice and telling me that Squaddies can just about do anything they put their minds to.

Padraig Sweeney for his research at all hours day or night, and for the invaluable close target recce.

Paul Martin for the book's cover design.

To all my draft readers who had to read my earlier illiteracy before I sorted my grammar out. Charlie, Martin, George, Lee and Trish you are real stars.

To my long suffering wife Janet, wondering why I am in a bad mood because I've just killed off a leading character.

Finally to all the people who served or lived through Operation Banner or were affected by the troubles.

Authors Note

The subject of this book is but a minuscule snap of how complex and challenging the fight against terrorism in Northern Ireland was and continues to be.

Complexities and challenges that have in part been caused by the actions of foreign governments and the continued actions of dissident groups on both sides of the border pre and post signing of the Good Friday Agreement on the 10th April 1998 to date, not to mention the collapse of The Northern Ireland Executive on January 9th 2017.

However, these factors are not unique and can be historically attributed to the Island of Ireland dating back over several hundred years' two examples of this being:

In 1796 and 1798 Theobald Wolfe Tone Leader of United Irishmen/ Adjutant General French army and French Governments expeditions to support Rebellion in Ireland.

And for his part in planning the Easter Rising 1916, Sir Roger Casement member of the Irish Volunteers was executed in HM Prison Pentonville London:

Casement had an agreement with German Government to provide weapons and explosives and the release of willing Irish Prisoners captured in France to establish a fighting force to assist in Easter Rising, in return for the New Irish Government help in defeating British during 1914-1918 First World War.

Thankfully, both these plans failed, due to interventions not dissimilar to those stated in this book, that of Intelligence gathering, coordination between multiple agencies domestic and foreign and covert observation of individuals.

I hope the content of this book imparts readers with the broader implications that terrorist and criminal activities have on society and the determination of military and law enforcement agencies to work cohesively to endeavour that the rule of law and humanity will always endure over that which is unlawful and inhumane.

Howard Lycett

REFELECTIONS

The premise of the book was to predict what actions the Republican movement might have taken if they had access to a quantity of modern weapons enabling them to gain an upper hand albeit for a short period, and the reaction of the British state against such a dramatic threat.

I knew that at some stage during my research process I would need to return to the Province, to observe the ground which in memories from twenty-five years before.

I had visited Belfast many times since the troubles ended to see friends and delight at the progress of the great city and its citizens, but South Armagh was different, I had lost comrades because of the actions and expertise of the South Armagh Brigade, I therefore held a healthy respect for their ability to gather intelligence and mount successful operations at short notice. Even though it had been many years since I patrolled those fields and hid in the blackthorn bushes, I still held a nagging sense of vulnerability.

A voice from within told me not to go back, why take a risk when I could use Google Earth from the safety of my home, but the old soldier in me wanted to return. Like many veterans of Operation Banner, I needed to re-visit to give myself peace of mind and see for myself if my comrades and my actions had made any difference.

The Irish people are a proud and hardy race, they reflect on the past to adjust and develop to make a better future. I have found that this thinking can lead to violent reaction or overreaction at the slightest wrong word. A volatile nature and deep passion for any cause are inherent elements in the Irish psyche. No Irish person I know ever does anything by half. They evidence this in their buildings, culture, music and sport.

What I observed was pleasing, as in my memory the streets were dim and dirty, people hung around on street corners with no work to go to or chance of employment soon. There was only grime and dull colours which reflected the mood of a subdued people fighting to find a way to breakout of this world of deprivation and poverty.

I'm happy to say that their world has now moved on, people are smiling, moving with a purpose. Streets are clean and reflected an abundance of bright colours, gardens were tidy, hedges trimmed as if a newfound sense of local pride had lifted the former melancholy. The people I met in South Armagh were friendly and positive; they had also gained extra motivation.

We have spent considerable money on the infrastructure and I believe they have not wasted it as new housing, schools and businesses are growing. It's now up to the people to look at the young and focus on the future and say goodbye to the past.

INTRODUCTION

There was a rumour was in the air, one which nobody dared to whisper. Some wouldn't even contemplate its potential consequences.

Microscopic green shoots had appeared, as individuals with vision had nurtured the development which would hopefully create a pathway to peace.

The common people sought to grasp freedom from the paramilitaries that had consumed and controlled their daily lives.

The liberty to walk the streets without fear of being stopped and searched by forces of the crown carrying guns. Shops being blown to smithereens and being forced to donate their hard-earned money for a cause they longer cared, or supported.

Peace and reconciliation after over twenty-five years of violence and chaos. Could it be possible? The conflict had led to instability and uncertainty which stagnated growth and halted investment into an already impoverished society, bitterly divided along religious lines.

The fires of bigotry had created an unjust and unworkable one-sided culture of haves and have nots.

The old Thatcher hardliners had gone, substituted by a more forward-thinking government who soon grasped that war was expensive. The Republican movement had realised that the Armalite and the ballot box were more convincing to their supporters than the long war of attrition.

Caught in the headlights were the Unionists wanting to remain loyal to the British state and opposing every move towards 'Irishness.' How would this rumour of peace affect their vice-like grip of the Loyalist community?

With peace also brought division, the men of violence who could only see settlement by the total annihilation of the opposition. These men had a powerful voice within some alienated communities that refused to conform to any form of influence by a parliament sitting across the Irish Sea. Would these men vote for a ceasefire and return to their fields, businesses and trades?

It was a conundrum, discussion was the only way to resolve the impasse and appease the agitators.

In London, Belfast and Derry secret moves were afoot to further strengthen the green shoots, whilst in South Armagh the flames of war were being ever-increasingly being fanned, to create an unstoppable firestorm.

CHAPTER ONE

South Armagh Thursday 10th February 1994

Kelly Farm Complex Co Louth Republic of Ireland (Brevity Codename Alpha One)

Peewee opened his eyes; they were itchy and burning. The Shabben; known locally as the Forge Bar on Monascribe Road had been busy, filled with both heavy smokers and drinkers attending the South Armagh Martyrs celebration. His vision adjusted to the darkness, it embraced him; he felt safe.

He didn't enjoy attending functions, which drew a lot of attention to the Republican movement. They attracted Provisional Irish Republican Army wannabes who just wanted to rub shoulders with the present-day volunteers, old men blabbering on about how they fought the border war in the fifty's. There was even a chance of a spy sent by the Brits or the Irish government, trying to get a sniff of information or identify the next prospective informer.

It was partway through the evening when a small, raven haired beauty of a woman had introduced herself to him as Marie then gave him a full kiss, he was astonished when she clandestinely pushed a 'com' in his mouth with her tongue then turned on her heels and left. To those watching they would have assumed that she had desires on Peewee instead of passing the PIRA leader a message written in microscopic script on a Rizla cigarette paper and then wrapped in cling film.

The leader of the Jonesborough Active Service Unit was happy, only hours before his second in command had informed him that his team had been successful in murdering Dominic McGlinchey the former leader of the

Irish National Liberation Army in Drogheda. As the stricken man lay bleeding to death on the ground outside the phone box, he had been trying to use he cried out "Jesus, Mary, help me."

The four balaclava wearing men laughed, one of them Marty O'Hanlon had also been present when the big man's wife had been murdered whilst bathing her two young sons in their home in Dundalk, The leader Decers approached the dieing man and pointed the 9mm automatic pistol towards his blooded bald head.

"You calling for your fuckin dead wife Mary are yous Dom? Well, you will meet her." Decers whispered before finishing the attack with a with a coup de grâce. The four men casually walked back to their red Mazda before driving away, leaving a dead father on the street and a grieving son in the family car.

As he drove back to his isolated farmhouse, Peewee could just pick out the dark silhouettes of the British Army watchtowers which dominated the rolling drumlin hills overlooking the border with the 'Free State.' Occasionally he could see a faint light in the cloudy night sky as helicopters skimmed over the fields and hedgerows dropping off armed men with blackened faces or re-supplying the towers. He hated the Brits, the twenty-four-hour surveillance, the stopping and searching every time he drove to his father's farm in the north.

He yawned and stretched, hearing the cracks in his back and shoulders, as he tried to further accustom his eyes to the darkened bedroom. The farm complex and attached bungalow, which he had built himself, was in a considered location, one hundred meters inside the Republic of Ireland. Tucked in to the thickly wooded hillside of the Slievenabolear Hill it afforded excellent shelter from vision. The only hill in the north close enough to have any overview was the Carrickbroad and the only army watch tower was

Tievecrum Tower above Forkhill, three miles to the north west, too far away even for the latest Brit surveillance cameras.

Peewee had found the land by chance while looking for an alternative place to hide a consignment of Libyan rifles and Semtex explosive; he quickly decided it would be an ideal place away from the prying eyes of the Brits. He immediately visited the landowner and made him an offer he couldn't refuse.

"I'll give you a grand for the plot; if you want to haggle, I'll give the cash to your fucking widow." The man grudgingly accepted the money. Paul Patrick 'Peewee' Kelly was a republican like his father and forefathers, the biggest and best of all the bandits in bandit country.

The earlier heavy rain outside had abated, now the only noise was the steady drip of water on the windowsill, he turned to get out of the warm bed, the cold of the bedroom linoleum floor on his feet shocked him to rise.

"Where the fucks are you going?" moaned a bleary Eileen pulling the duvet up tight to her neck. The brunette's overlong hair cascaded over his now vacant pillow.

"Never yous mind, its business, my kind of business." He reassured his still drunken wife.

"Don't wake the fucking babies up. It's fucking three in the morning; if yous do, I'll fucking batter ya." She mumbled.

Even after seventeen years Eileen couldn't fully mask her Manchester accent, expletives flowed like a river, no matter who the company was. You could take the girl out of Wythenshawe, but not Wythenshawe out of the girl.

Peewee looked at the bedside clock it was three thirty and the babies were both teenagers, John Joseph 'JoJo' Kelly their sixteen-year-old eldest child had recently been out on his first military operation with his dad. Acting as a lookout for

British soldiers as his dad hid a milk churn of homemade explosives under a road culvert on the Kilnasaggart Road.

It was better not to argue with Eileen. The British army didn't scare him, but she did. How could one fucking blow job at the back of Vincent's Corner Pub in Benidorm get him into so much trouble? The memory brought a smile to his face as he pulled on his crumpled jeans and wandered barefoot towards the kitchen.

He took a peak into his daughter Máiréad's room; she lay peacefully with her arm cuddling a teddy bear. She was a honey blonde nine years old with the attitude of a teenager. Peewee put her brashness down to her mother's genes. He gently pulled the door shut,

Covert Observation Post (Nine Four Echo)

Less than a hundred meters from the farm's back door, two camouflaged men observed Kelly's movements.

Operation Warthog had been the first mission allocated to the newly arrived Close Observation Platoon of the Second Battalion Royal Regiment of Fusiliers. It had taken many months of planning and countless patrols until the Platoon Commander Captain Martin Jenkins and his Second Controller Sergeant Major Tommy Trainer had found the dominant position. The well-concealed position had been reporting the movements of Kelly, who was given the code of Bravo One, for over a year.

"Stand By, Stand By, we have lights illuminated in the kitchen of Alpha One. Yes, yes, that is a positive identification of the subject Bravo One. He appears to be smoking a cigarette and starring out of the kitchen window," whispered Sergeant Stu Taylor, into his personal radio. By Stu's side lay Mull, his wingman. Stu knew that Mull would be slowly framing the subject and correcting the focus of the brand-new Nikon N8008 SLR Digital Camera, which was on temporary loan to the Fusiliers Close Observation Platoon from the boffins at NISS[1].

"Peewee's up early this morning, Stu. Do you reckon he's shit the bed?" Mull whispered.

Corporal Eammon 'Mull' Mulready was an old hand in COP after previous tours in Belfast and Londonderry. Mulready, a Battalion boxer should have been a long-standing member of the Warrant Officer's and Sergeant's Mess, but a flippant tongue with officers and quick fists around people he disliked ensured that Mull would remain a junior rank, even if he was, in soldiering ability head and shoulders above his superiors.

Stu and Mull had been in the night standing observation post since crawling into the position from the main OP[2] an hour after darkness fell. It had taken an hour to crawl the half mile distance, constantly stopping to listen and ensuring they were not leaving any ground signs as they moved stealthily downhill. After a careful check for booby traps Mull lowered himself into a small ditch covered by overhanging bushes, then tied a sandbag on to the thickest branch which gave them both concealment whilst hiding. This was to be their home for the rest of the hours of darkness. Mull slowly extracted the manfrotto arm from his day sack, then cautiously tightened up the clamp on the sandbag, so broken bark wouldn't betray their position when they extracted. Stu, giving over watch of the rear of Kelly's farm, which had the code Alpha One, was testing the communications back up to Fusilier Jim 'MacGyver' Bennett in their primary position and to Zero Bravo the operations room back in Portadown.

The other four members of the patrol remained back in the main OP, using thermal imaged and low light video cameras to safeguard their two colleagues below. They had hidden the patrol in the thick woodland on the slopes of the

---

1 Northern Ireland Surveillance Section
2 Observation Post

Carrickbroad for ten days. The OP was subsurface with a tin roof supported by thick beams and sandbags. It had taken three days to construct and camouflage the position, under the watchful eye of 'MacGyver,' a former miner from Ashington. The OP gave a view of the front of the farm complex and Colonel's Road, which ran north to south. I had given each road junction a different colour code to aid quick descriptions of travel directions. Any vehicle heading north would be triggered by Nine Four Echo on to the COP soldiers manning the overt watch towers which lined the border and major arterial roads towards Newry.

"Vehicle lights Stu." Mull whispered.

"We have a dark saloon type vehicle from yellow one nine towards Alpha One, Nine Four Delta." The voice on Stu's radio was Fusilier Reeves Rawlinson high in the OP.

The early deluge had now passed, and a yard light brightly illuminated the rear of the Kelly complex. Both soldiers lay motionless, the only movement was their breath hitting the chilly night air as the temperature continued to drop. A spider unfazed about the presence of two humans continued to weave a complex fly trap on top of the bush they were concealed in.

Peewee heard the car as it drove on to the gravel path before parking at the side of the bungalow; not even Eileen's steady snoring could mask the noise. He rubbed the greying stubble on his chin and walked towards the door.

"I'm going inside to talk to this Culchie[3] Vic, you and Henry check around the area."

Aiden 'The Bird' Bonner looked much older than his thirty-four years. The limp was because of a British Army sniper from the roof of the Broadway nurses' home, the wide

---

3 Irish an unsophisticated country person

parting in his ginger hair, courtesy of a meat cleaver from a proddy bastard trying to burn an Ardoyne house in North Belfast.

The door was opened before he reached the step.

"Birdy, good to see you, I got a message from Padraig that we have a friend that wants to speak. Come on in, I'll put the kettle on."

"Thanks Peewee, it's been a long drive down, and the fuckin Peelers are stopping anything that moves tonight. We had to take a dozen detours. Luckily Henry is with me and he knows Dromintee like the back of his hand."

"Henry you say, Henry 'Bap' McConnell? That fuckin sleeveen₄ bastard, he's a chancer if you ask me. Keep him away from the boys in Cross, they hate that thieving bastard."

"I've got Secrillo with me. McSweeny insisted on that that bastard coming down to check security. That cold-blooded fucker gives me the shivers. I swear he's beat a confession out of more innocent volunteers than guilty ones. On the way down he was bragging about being judge, jury and executioner, a fuckin nut job in charge of the nutting squad." Bonner confessed.

Peewee chuckled, "I've met him a few times at General Headquarters meetings; he's in the Adjutant's pocket I tell you, he's a protected species if you ask me, I know the Army Council love him as he's always eager to please. He gets the job done and always gets a confession, so it pleases the Adjutant."

"Stand By, Stand By we have two male figures walking around the back of Alpha One, they appear to be conducting

---

4 Irish untrustworthy or cunning person.

a clearance patrol, wait good possible that a tall bald-headed male is carrying a short in his right hand. We have a further unknown male, tall, bulky, ginger-haired, in the kitchen with Bravo One, both appear to be conversation."

Operations Room TCG (S) Region Portadown

"Zero Bravo, yes. Acknowledge Nine Four Delta's sighting Nine Four Echo." replied Corporal Tony Boreman, the COP duty signaller. Movement at Alpha One in the early hours was unusual. Armed men in and around the bungalow was normal during the day, but not in the early hours. Tony used the buzzer to alert Ray Poad, the duty operations Sergeant who was asleep in the restroom.

"What's going on ball bag?" a sleepy Geordie voice whispered into the intercom.

"Ray the night standing OP has got two blokes mooching behind the bungalow, one is carrying a pistol, with a further bloke inside with Kelly." Tony explained.

"No dramas, inform Reeves in the over watch OP while I get my pants on, oh and put the kettle on while you're at it."

"Reeves has just been on the net and got the thermal image camera on. The blokes are not walking towards Stu or Mull; it looks like a clearance patrol or local security."

"OK, mate, give Del Delaney a buzz up at Romeo 21, he might trigger any movement coming north. I'll wake Herbie in the Special Branch office to see if he can give me a steer."

"Nice brew Peewee, now why have I been dragged all the way from a warm bed in Belfast for at this ungodly fuckin hour?"

"Fuck knows I was on the bevy when one of Padraig's lackeys gave me a com saying you and I would meet some guy. One of my fellas, Decers, has gone to collect him. I don't enjoy having a stranger visit my home, but apparently a matter of urgency."

"I'm just trying to get my noggin around why we in Belfast would need to come and support you South Armagh bandits." Bonner chuckled.

"I can't answer that, but when the IRA's Chief of the General Headquarters says you will meet someone, yous fucking meet him. End of story."

The Bird was impressed with Peewee; he was as wide as he was tall. Angry brooding eyes which scrutinised the very depths of a man's soul, windswept face from a lifetime of working outdoors. He was also a natural leader, confident of his own abilities. If he said things would be done, they got done. He spoke with clarity and authority, a man with experience and cunning. Peewee's reputation as a killer was unquestionable, roadside bombs, mortars, rocket attacks, sniper attacks, close quarter assassinations and kidnappings were all on his impressive terrorist CV, but his speciality was large scale coordinated attacks incorporating all methods of violence.

Under his stewardship the Jonesborough Volunteers had become the most dedicated and adaptable unit in the Province. It was little wonder that Special Branch Officers scrutinised their every movement as they had risen to the top of the most active list.

Kelly had rapidly climbed through the ranks of the PIRA. His leadership and planning capabilities were acknowledged by members of the seven members of the Army Council and rewarded with promotion to the role as Operations Officer in the General Headquarters.

Peewee had built a tight team of like-minded individuals around him, dependable men he could trust most of whom he had known since childhood, or men so terrified of him they would follow any order he gave them without question. He'd trained and tested them hard until they followed him with blind obedience.

Detective Sergeant Herbie Grey appeared at the door of the office with his ever-present coffee mug in his hand. Herbie was no oil painting; someone had once described him as having the face of an orangutan's ball bag, but he was an exceptional investigator.

"I've rung the other duty Special Branches and checked our register, there's no suggestion of anything going on tonight at the farm complex. I might get Big Joe out of bed and see what he thinks."

"Fuckin ell Herbie, wake up the big boss because two scroates are walking around with pistols, in a foreign land. Bit fuckin harsh mate?" Ray laughed.

"Big Joe never sleeps, plus he's got a sixth sense about these bastards."

The radio broke the banter again, bursting into life. "Stand By, Stand By, we have further vehicle lights towards Alpha One from the direction of yellow three seven. That vehicle has parked to the side of Alpha One and confirmation that the vehicle is Charlie Three, the black Volkswagen Golf BZG5917. That's a positive identification Bravo Three from the driver's door towards Alpha One, wait a further small male from the front passenger seat, also towards Alpha One. Bravo One remains in the kitchen in conversation with ginger unknown male."

Tony was busy scribbling notes on to the operations log as Ray explained to Herbie what had just happened in English.

"Our guys have now got two men wandering around Kelly's bungalow possibly carrying pistols, Kelly is inside talking to a thick-set ginger bloke in the kitchen area and Declan Taylor has just arrived in his black VW Golf with another male described as being small."

"Thank fuck you got all that, it was just a blabber to me."
Herbie confessed.

Peewee opened the door and amazed to find Decers stood
next to a small immaculately dress Chinese man. Before he
could open his mouth, the man thrust out his hand.

"Mr Kelly I presume, I asked our mutual friend Mr
McSweeny if I could meet you in person, my name is Steve
Ho."

Peewee looked him up and down as he shook his hand.
Judging by the firmness of the handshake, Mr Ho was not
just a businessman. Ho had several deep scars on his face,
his hands were heavily tattooed, but the tattoos could not
conceal the missing little finger of his right hand. Lost in an
inter-gang battle with the 14K, a rival triad group when they
had the audacity to attempt a takeover of the red-light areas
of Hong Kong possessed by Ho's Wo Shing Wo triad
organisation.

"Would you like a drink, Mr Ho? The kettles not long on."

"Whiskey and please call me Steve." Replied the now
beaming Mr Ho.

The Bird caught the look of bewilderment on Peewee's face
as he tried to remember where he had hidden his last bottle
of Jameson.

Peewee returned with the alcohol and filled up Ho's tumbler.
"Best whiskey on the island of Ireland, better than that
Bushmills Proddy shite. Now what can we do for you,
Steve?"

"Thank you for your kindness, I am here as an emissary for a
group of businessmen I represent. They are interested in
helping your organisation in return for you helping us

overcome a minor administration problem we have encountered." Ho explained.

"Steve we are not fucking businessmen, I am a simple farmer and Mr Bonner here is on the brew, unemployed because of the British Army trying to murder him."

"Peewee, may I take the liberty of calling you that? Let me get right to the point. Mr McSweeny knows the finer details of our long-term business strategy. As an act of goodwill my organisation has placed a shipment of weapons including rocket launchers and surface-to-air missiles, with a sizeable amount of ammunition on the west coast of your charming country."

Peewee looked across at the Bird, who was staring open-mouthed at the diminutive man. "Steve you can call me a bastard if you will bring us more weapons to assist in our struggle in the North of Ireland."

"Zero Bravo this is Nine Four Delta sitrep, Bravo one is in conversation with the tall ginger headed male. Ginger male described as thirty-five to forty years old, pale complexion, big powerful build, dark clothing, six feet plus, pale features, ginger hair with pronounced parting and appears to have a distinct limp. Second male is small, described as forty to fifty years old, dark complexion, small build, wearing a tweed suit, collar and tie, five-foot five max well-groomed black haired, wait one."

Stu rolled off the description, but something had caught his eye. "Mull, can you make out the new bloke's face? I think he's Oriental."

Mull carefully adjusted the lens, concentrating on a crisp, clear focus. The auto drive kicked in as it took a dozen pictures in a second.

Stu resumed his commentary "This guy, I would describe as

Chinese, and he's got tats on the hand he's holding the glass in." Mull nodded in agreement, now trying to get more details of the tattoos.

Back in the operations room Tony was glad of the brief respite from logging the last sighting from the OP.

The kitchen was silent; Mr Ho had his audiences' attention. "So, Mr Ho, err Steve, what can we do for you in return for your erm help?" The Bird muttered.

"Mr Bonner I am reliably informed that you are the head of your organisations Belfast operations, whereas I am a 438, the Vanguard in my organisation. I suppose you would liken my role to an operations officer, but I work internationally. My 489 or Dragon Leader has seen a business opportunity which could also benefit your cause." Ho explained, choosing his words carefully.

"So, what do you need from us Steve?" The Bird asked.

"Manpower and local knowledge, Mr Bonner. Belfast is a large and prosperous city, big enough for both our organisations to live, work and prosper together in harmony. Unfortunately for both of our sides it's full of, how do you call them Ulstermen? My people have had a few minor skirmishes with their paramilitary groups in Belfast who wish to take a share of our profits."

There were much deeper motives why a senior figure in the Wo Shing Wo wanted the Loyalist leadership dead but those would remain Ho's alone.

Peewee looked at The Bird, he wanted some clarification "I can understand why your 'organisation' is interested in taking over Belfast and I don't think it would be to provide electricity for the prods, but why do you need my boys involved if you will only require the Mr Bonner's teams?"

Ho's beaming smile returned. "Because Mr Peewee, I want to give you what you want. I want to give you a war."

"Hello, Boss, its Herbie is it ok to talk?" Herbie had known Chief Superintendent Joe Montgomery professionally for twenty years, but their history stretched back to a childhood brought up on Beechfield Street in the shadow of Belfast ship yard. The Short Strand was a mixed community until the troubles came. Joe and Herbie's family had long gone before they burned the protestant families out of their homes, and Loyalist defenders returned to gun down anyone walking along the street after darkness.

Herbie was the first-person Joe recognised when he opened his eye in the Ulster Hospital many years later. Herbie was at his dear friend's bedside to break the news that Joe had lost not only his right arm and eye but also his beloved wife, Caroline. The Provo's that planted the car bomb had expected Joe to be the driver, not the blonde-haired mother of three young children.

"Go on, you ugly bastard what is it, when you call me Boss, I know it's fucking trouble."

"It's Kelly; he's having a meeting with some tall ginger fella with a gammy leg and a Chinaman who arrived at the farm with one of the Taylor boys. The ginger guy arrived with two heavies who, according to the army, are tooled up." Herbie waited for the reaction.

"Thanks Herbie, a Chinaman, you say! Well, it's just a feeling in my bollocks, but we might need to look closer at this. Get the boys in the Towers awake and ring round the tasking group, get them into the briefing room at eight o'clock sharp. Oh, has the boys in the OP got any pictures to evidence what's happening?"

Joe was on immediately on automatic pilot, a thousand ideas formulating in his head, actions being raised, and further questions being articulated.

No sooner had Joe put the phone down than it was back at his ear. "Sebastian its Joe, is the South team still doing the covert search of the weapons hide in Mullaghbawn?"

"Joe! It's four in the fucking morning what's going down?" Captain Sebastian 'Seb' Alberti was on detachment to the Royal Ulster Constabulary's Southern Region Tasking and Co-ordination Group after two years as a Troop Commander with the Special Air Service, and a posting to the Sultan of Oman's Special Forces.

"Listen, Captain, I want the Bat Flight to over watch Kelly's Farm and make it pronto. Meet me in the office right away." Joe ordered before putting the phone down.

Seb lay back on the pillow and thought about his unsuccessful night at the Silver Birch Bar. He was losing his touch as he was alone in bed. I must dream up an alternative cover story, he thought. The line about being an airline pilot was wearing thin. Perhaps he should use the dolphin trainer story, which would be a good hook for the local women. His mind returned to the task in hand, Joe was a driven man with no comprehension of time. Rest was a dirty four-letter word in Joe's vocabulary. Seb picked up the phone and dialled the number. Almost immediately a clipped English accent replied, "Tim Operations."

Captain Tim Oliphant was the duty night watch keeper for the Special Surveillance Unit South Detachment, also known as the Victor Teams. Tim was a recent arrival at the unit's base in The Hanger in Fermanagh after just finishing the rigorous six-month selection process. Even after a brief time at the unit the seasoned operators had taken to calling him 'Slim Tim' because of his skeletal like body.

"Hi Tim, Seb here have your boys completed the hide search? I need to use Flight Nine from the 'Bat Flight' to go and over watch Kelly's farm. I will get a quick shower than get to the office to coordinate from there. Can you make that happen?"

"Flight Nine is waiting at the Mill so she should be on plot in about ten minutes if you need the top cover. Our search job is complete; the hide was empty so you can have her. I will phone Reg down at buzzard control and get them moving."

"Tim you're a lifesaver, make it happen big Joe is busting my balls, ciao."

The three detachments of the Special Surveillance Unit in Northern Ireland had a flight of Gazelle helicopters on call to support their missions. Each aircraft carried sophisticated surveillance equipment plus video and Forward Looking Infrared cameras. At least one operator would ride in the helicopter and follow suspects through the sighting system, usually loitering at around eight thousand feet, out of sight or sound of anyone below. Each aircraft also carried sensitive eavesdropping devices which could receive transmissions from covertly concealed devices on the ground. The 'Det' also could call on the services of 1 Flight Army Air Corps operating a fixed wing, Britten-Norman BN-2 Islander, to carry out photo reconnaissance work. The advantage of the fixed-wing aircraft was that they permitted it to cross over the South Armagh border up to one kilometre.

Seb sighed and ran his fingers through his thick mop of hair. He'd found Special Forces selection a huge mental and physical slog with an enormous amount of sleep deprivation thrown into the equation, but working with Chief Superintendent Joe Montgomery was worse. Resigning himself that a job was brewing, he shuffled towards the bathroom. "Sleep is overrated" he mumbled as he reached for the cold shower tap.

"Bob from Stu, they have detailed footage of the meeting, and the two males patrolling to the rear of Alpha One. He says it's evidential quality."

Immediately Bob's mind was in overdrive as the signaller

gave him the update from the OP. He knew that Stu was surreptitiously telling him that the footage was good, in fact so good that it needed to be immediately taken to Mahon Road for further assessment, and there in lay the first problem, the team on the ground Foxtrot Nine Four were not due to be relieved for another four nights. The replacement team Nine Two were still on leave and not due back in Ballykinler until the day before their deployment. Only members of the Nine Two patrol left in Ballykinler were the team commander and one of his Fusiliers, who were both living in married quarters.

The second dilemma was working out the logistics of trying to conduct a live letter box meeting to extract the images or even better a relief in line to extract Stu and Mull who would need to be fully debriefed. His primary worry was waking up the Second Controller Tommy 'Time Bomb' Trainor back in Ballykinler. The 'Time Bomb' was an exceptional soldier, but not an early morning person. He was permanently on the edge and likely to explode like his nickname at the slightest thing.

"So, Mr Ho what's your idea of a fucking war?" Peewee asked as he poured more whiskey into Ho's crystal glass tumbler.

"A brilliant man, Sun Tzu once said that warfare is based on deception. Hence, when we can attack, we must seem unable; when using our forces, we must appear inactive;" Ho looked around at the assembled faces to see if his words of wisdom had struck a chord, but all were blank.

"Who the fuck is this Sun Tzu, I take it he's one of your guys?" Bird laughed.

"Let me get this straight, you want us to be active by being inactive, even though you have provided us with the weapons we need to wage war." Peewee tried to comprehend.

Ho still smiling clarified what he wanted, "Mr Bonner my organisation has provided pistols and assault rifles, some are silenced. If you wanted hand grenades, we have supplied them for you. In return, we would like you to kill Charlie Wheeler and Billy Whitledge on our behalf. We would also have great gratitude if you could also dispose of the leaders of each UDA and UVF group in Belfast, as they are proving troublesome to my employees in the city."

Bonner contemplated the shock wave it would send through the protestant paramilitaries if the complete command structure destroyed overnight. He also considered that some secret local agreements between both sides would be gone forever.

The Protestant organisations had a formidable array of weapons hidden in deep hides throughout the city and rural Antrim; they also had an unknown element Tara, a shadowy organisation formed in the seventies in case of a doomsday scenario. Members of Tara were unknown to the Republican movement, unlike the leaders of the foolhardy UDA, UVF, and Red Hand Commandos. If you wanted to know who the leader of the Shankill UVF Battalion were you only needed to read a Sunday paper or ask anyone who stands outside the Rex Bar to find out. Tara however had infiltrated all of Ulster society, from politicians to bin men. They were an unseen enemy, unlike Wheeler and Whitledge who Bonner had met at clandestine meetings during his time as leader of Belfast PIRA.

"Look I'm not saying that we cannot achieve it, but there are a lot of elements which worries me. Families close to the peace line in north Belfast could be over ran and burned out. The peelers and Brits will come down on my boys like a ton of fucking bricks and finally where do I get the manpower from? You are talking about forty, maybe fifty fucking hits."

Ho thought about Bonner's comeback for a moment. "Mr Bonner, if you do your job quickly there will no enemies left to organise retaliation against your people. Mr McSweeny has assured me that help would be forthcoming from your associates in Tyrone, Derry and Dublin. As for the people you call peelers or army, this is where Mr Peewee's group fits in.

Mr Peewee will start a war in the countryside, a people's revolution which will draw security forces out of the city. This will be your diversion."

"Listen, Mr Ho everybody will tell you that nobody more than me wants to declare an all-out war on the fucking Brits, but they have helicopters, surveillance aircraft the fucking SAS. We appreciate the weapons you're giving us, but we need bigger and harder hitting stuff. To get the Brits down from Belfast, we would need to destroy their barracks and hilltop towers." Peewee declared.

"Mr Peewee, what do you want? Do you want surface-to-air missiles? Do you want anti-tank missiles? Do you want long range mortars? Heavy machine guns, rocket launchers, sniper rifles, even flame throwers? With this equipment, can you start a war?" Ho shouted, losing his cool for a moment.

Peewee looked him in the eye and held out his hand "Mr Ho if you provide me that equipment in sufficient quantity, I will win a fucking war."

"Stand by Stand By, it looks like the meeting is concluding, the two hoods are out of sight towards the front of Alpha One, Bravo Three has left the kitchen area and we have lights illuminated at the front of the premises." Stu calmly transmitted.

Seb burst into the operations room "Got a sitrep for me Bob, I have the Det's helicopter in bound about two minutes away."

"Fucking nick of time or what Boss, Yeh it looks like they are all saying their goodbyes." Bob explained.

"Mr Ho, Decers here will take you to wherever you need to go. I look forward to working for you and using your equipment." said Peewee as he gave Ho a firm handshake.

"Let your plans be dark and impenetrable as night, and when you move, fall like a thunderbolt." Laughed Ho "Another lesson from Sun Tzu, and no he does not work for our organisation, but we wish he did." With that parting shot, Ho left.

Kelly and Bonner remained silent until they heard the noise of the engine and the crunch of the wheels as they drove away the Chinaman from the farm.

"What do you make of that Birdy?" Peewee pulled a chair and sat at the kitchen table rubbing his craggy cheeks.

"To be honest, Peewee my heads in a fuckin spin. It looks like the fuckin prods have really upset Ho's plans and he wants their heads on a fuckin plate. The prods make a mint from drugs, prostitution and gambling all over Belfast apart from our home in the west and a few other estates in the north. If they lost all that revenue they'd be fucked. I know that a while back some Chinese kids died in an arson attack on a restaurant in East Belfast, but I don't know why that would piss Ho off so much. He really had the look of hate in his eyes when he mentioned Wheeler and Whitledge."

Peewee pulled on a tatty blue jumper "Do you know those two."

"I've come across them; they both have a fearsome reputation. Wheeler ran with the Butcher gang on the Shankill before most of them were locked up. Whitledge has killed more of his own people than we have by supplying drugs and dodgy alcohol made in a fuckin bath. They stay on their side of the city, and we stay on ours unless we need to sort something out."

"Perhaps you should have sorted them out years ago, Birdy,"

"Steady on Peewee, Belfast is not like South Armagh. You've never forced out of your own homes or had entire streets burned to the ground while the fuckin peelers stood there laughing. If you can cause a diversion big enough to get the Brits and those Black Bastards out of the city, it might just work, but I will need help from Ciaran in Derry and that fucking eejit Danny Roy up in Coalisland."

The two men shook hands as Peewee showed him to the door. Before he got to the car Peewee called him. "I just want to let you know before you hear it from anybody else. Last night my guys whacked McGlinchey, so the war with the INLA should be over."

The Bird smiled as he squeezed his sizeable frame into the front passenger seat of the waiting grey Ford Sierra. Secrillo was first to speak as the driver Henry 'Bap' McConnell turned on to Colonel's Road and headed North.

"What was all that about Birdy? Me and Bap are fuckin freezing and that fuckin yokel never offered us a drink or nothing."

Bonner sighed his mind was contemplating the job in hand and the repercussions not just to the Republican community, but also his illicit business enterprise with Wheeler and Whitledge. For years the three men had been raking in thousands of pounds from the very lucrative trade in drugs. A meeting had been arranged by Billy Fisher, a leading evangelical figure in Belfast to bring the sides together as a road to peace. The only thing that was agreed at the meeting was to meet up again at a place well away from the eyes and ears of the grandiose leaders of the organisations. It was fine for Gerry and Martin, spouting political shite while he was dodging police, army and prod bullets. What the fuck did they know about his life, six children to feed, alcoholic father and mother dying of cancer? They were off on their fancy trips to America or being hosted by the latest left-wing politician who wanted to rub shoulders with a has been terrorist. While they were away drinking pink gins and fucking high-class prostitutes, they left the policing of the movement to the Adjutant General and his civil administration unit, Republican zealots, who could quote the army green book's rules and regulations backwards.

Bonner had met his conspirators at the bar Altea in Alicante. The Bird had gone to inordinate lengths to conceal his identity and stayed in a cheap hotel in old Benidorm before travelling down the coast by train. The journey took a lifetime as The Bird jumped off and on trains to disrupt any surveillance mission by Special Branch followers. On arrival at the meeting The Bird couldn't believe that all his hard work was in vain. Charlie and Billy might as well have worn their orange sashes, Charlie sat swigging larger wearing his Glasgow Rangers shirt and baseball cap; whilst a shirtless Billy, his huge gut overhanging his football shorts had many loyalist tattoos all over his body. One tattoo over his right breast stood out to The Bird 'KILL A TAIG' he wondered how many times he had carried out that assignment.

Over a few beers they all decided that it was in their best interest to divide up the city, with a promise that no dealer would ever cross over the boundaries and that they would also come together to look after each other's problems.

"Aiden, we have a problem that you could fix for us. There's this young fella, Lawrence Dixon, lives up the top of the Springmartin Estate across from Ballymurphy. We could do with you doing a wee head job. In return, if you ever need us to return the favour, we'll do it. It shows the people we are still the guardians of our community and we get rid of a dirty wee shite into the bargain."

Bonner returned to Belfast, within a week he had two thousand pounds hidden away and the family of Lawrence Dixon were preparing the poor boys funeral which Wheeler and Whitledge both attended, telling the family they would avenge their son's sectarian murder.

A month later Adrian Martin was beaten to death by a loyalist punishment squad for 'anti-social behaviour.' His actual crime was that someone had spotted him selling weed on The Bird's patch.

The radio again broke into life again "Charlie Three South towards yellow three seven, I believe Bravo three is the driver with the Oriental looking male. A second vehicle, possibly a dark Ford Sierra saloon shape, is from Alpha One North towards yellow one nine. Bravo one appears to be up and working around the farm we will withdraw back up from our night standing position to Nine Four Echo's location."

Seb was about to comment when big Joe stuck his head around the door. "Everything OK boys, what's the update?"

"Well, you know all about the meeting Joe, just to keep you in the frame they have now split with Declan Taylor driving the Chinese guy South, luckily the rain has stopped and cloud cover is good so the Bat Flight is monitoring its movement towards Dundalk whilst the other vehicle has just crossed back into the north three up and being fed through the Dromintee bowl by the COP lads in the over watch towers. I can get a green team in Newry or a helibourne VCP on standby to do a stop?"

Joe had a quick think, "Very good Seb, well done everybody, but I think it's better to let the fucker run out of Newry. I don't want them to smell a rat when we're trying to catch one. I am ordering all units north of Newry to conduct VCP's to get some details about the occupants of that vehicle. Nothing to dramatic and don't draw attention to the stop, now get on with that. Bob, when are we going to see these photographs?"

"It's all in hand Sir, our 2I/C Sergeant Major Trainor will extract the two soldiers who witnessed the meeting and get them back here hopefully by ten hundred hours Sir."

"I bet Tommy time bomb was fuckin happy about you waking him up early son." Joe quipped as he exited the operations room.

Markethill

Bonner took a quick look in the rear-view mirror and looked into the cold unfeeling eyes of Victor Secrillo his nemeses, the head of security for PIRA General Headquarters or as he liked to declare, the head of the nutting squad. If Vic had any inkling of Bonner's other business, he would be lay dead in a ditch, eyes taped up to prevent them popping out when the bullet entered the back of his head. Blooded and bruised after a severe beating inflicted by Vic and his gang of thugs. Vic took great pride in his job, his record was faultless, and every one of his prisoners had admitted their guilt, even the innocent ones.

From his past days in the Belfast Civil Admin Unit, dropping breeze blocks on glue sniffers heads then perfecting 'six pack' kneecappings to ensure the victim would be in constant pain for the rest of their life; Vic took a sense of pride. Not only was Vic the principal henchman for Belfast Brigade, but he was also the chief executioner for the Adjutant General, James McElwaine, one of the controlling members of the Army Council; the day-to-day directors of the Republican movement.

"Was that a wee Chinaman cunt, me and Henry saw you with Birdy?" Vic's question broke Bonner's thoughts.

"It was, he's got us some erm merchandise, and I need you to get hold of Ciaran in Derry and Danny Roy up in Coalisland. I also need to see Mac D as I want the intelligence unit doing some stuff right away. Henry, get Fitzmartin to meet me in the Bee Hive tomorrow at five. Vic, can you speak to your friend Mr McSweeny and put him in touch with our quartermaster Ron McKeever? It looks like we will have a shipment coming our way and I want it safe."

"I can do better than that, I will put Ron in touch with James Fagan the Quarter-Master General."

Aiden Bonner bit his lip; Secrillo was name dropping leading members of the Army Headquarters to make himself look important.

Herbie stuck his head around the door, "Joe it's a quick update, the vehicle which came north has been identified by the army as a Ford Sierra AZF8713 which is a Belfast plate, no trace on Vengeful5 The other vehicle stopped a short while after leaving Kelly's Farm. The soldiers in the Jonesborough tower saw Declan Taylor return home alone. Judging by the time and distance plus the lights seen by the helicopter, we think they dropped Charlie Chan off by the Carrickdale Hotel just over the border."

Joe's eyes widened, "Get Johnny Nolan in here pronto Herbie."

"But you gave Johnny a week's leave to recuperate after his car crash, Joe!"

"Tell the bastard I don't give a shite; tell him to get his arse down to see that fat bird he was shagging last year, the one that's a manager at the Carrickdale Hotel."

Henry was making excellent time, even after using several quiet country roads to avoid Newry and the chance of bumping into an RUC road block. The journey from Jonesborough to West Belfast should have taken an hour and a quarter on a normal day, but even with Henry driving like a madman it would be at least two hours before they got on to the Falls Road. The mood had lightened within the vehicle as they finally reached a decent road from Loughgilly to Mullaghbrack which would take them to the west of Portadown and the motorway back to Belfast.

Vic was busy recounting how he had executed an informer in Derry on the orders of the Army Council. Bonner and Henry had heard the story before and suspected it was Vic's way of frightening them, emphasising that he had the power of life

---

5 Vehicle licencing database

and death. The car hit a wooded bend, and immediately Henry realised there was trouble ahead. The vehicle check point had been well sighted just beyond the bend and in a slight dip in the road. The lights of the pleasant village of Markethill were shining brightly to the left of the vehicle. It was a perfect ambush spot chosen by Corporal Phil Slinger, a farmer by day and soldier by night.

"Stay cool Henry I want no trouble." Bonner whispered.

"Give me the pistols Henry I will jettison them, quick now," Vic said casually from the rear seat.

In an instant, Secrillo dispatched the two pistols into a hedgerow.

The Sierra slowed in compliance to the hand signals given by the soldier stood in the road. The car rolled to a halt by the side of a green armoured Land Rover.

Secrillo chuckled as he read out the yellow stencilled sign on the side of the Land Rover "CONFIDENTIAL PHONELINE FREEPHONE 0800 666 999. Fuckin Tout line if you ask me; but at least they have the right number, 666 number of the feckin beast."

They were all chuckling as Henry rolled down the window.

"Pleasant Morning gentleman, can I see some ID please?" Big Phil's booming voice could have woken the soundest of sleepers in Markethill.

Henry handed over three forged driving licences, one of which matched the owner of the loaned vehicle from Belfast. "We're just on our way back from a fishing trip in Belleek sir; our tackle is in the boot if you want to check."

"All in good time Sir." Phil replied as he relayed the details on the cards by radio to the waiting intelligence staff at Drummad Barracks in Armagh city.

The three men were taken out of the car and searched by the

firm, but efficient members of the patrol from 6 Royal Irish Regiment. Upon searching the vehicle's boot, several fishing rods and bags were uncovered to verify Henry's story. After what seemed like an age the operator back at Drummad reported that the vehicle or men carried no subversive trace.

"Thank you for your cooperation gentleman you're free to go." Phil waved them off then strolled to back of the leading land rover. Inside the closed door sat Greenfinch6 Mary Williams. "Did you get them Mary?"

"I did Phil good clear video of them all." Mary had been using a small CCTV camera with a pinhole lens to film everyone that came into their check point that morning. The tape would be handed over to their intelligence cell at their debriefing and be analysed against the sighting reports made by the patrol.

"Three Belfast guys travelling back from Lough Erne this early in the morning, Phil? I don't believe that for one moment." Mary observed.

The big Corporal smiled "Two of them are Westies, Andersonstown or St James's if you ask me and the driver is a border boy, a strange mix. They are also well off track if they are coming from Belleek. Ah well, the vehicle check shows they are clean so let's wrap up here."

Phil gave the order to mount up and looked back down the road towards his cut-off man, young Alan Creedy. The junior soldier was new to the Regiment and as keen as they come.

"Phil bring the vehicles down here I think those fellas have thrown something from the car. I thought I heard something, but I can't be sure."
Just at the point that they were about to put it down to an inexperienced man's imagination Mary found the first pistol a 9mm Star Model BM not long after young Alan stood on the handle of a Colt.45. It looked like a museum piece, but in

---

6 Female UDR soldier

the right hands it was deadly.

Big Phil's eyes lit up a find, and a chance of catching some Provos out on a job. "Hello control this is X Ray One Four we have discovered two pistols by the roadside."

"X Ray One Four this is control return immediately to base with your find. No further transmissions please this is from Nine."

Phil was taken aback Nine was the Battalion's Commanding Officer, why was he involved at this early hour. The proper procedure was to get the RUC involved; they needed a scene of crime officer and a forensic team so they could preserve the evidence. Phil had seen too many RA bastards walk away from a prosecution on a technicality.

"X Ray One Four this is Nine, put your recoveries in an evidence bag and return immediately to base, confirm."

"Fuckin hell that's the big man himself Phil, what are we going to do?" asked Mary.

"We will carry out his orders, young lady. Nine, Roger Out." Phil threw the hand mike down and went to find a sterile bag and some gloves.

CHAPTER TWO

Friday 11th February 1994

Falls Road, Belfast

The first dull rays of light were piercing the dismal rain laden morning sky as Vic exited the Sierra outside the Rock Bar on the Falls Road. After a quick stop off in Donnelley's shop to get some fags, he walked to the corner of Beechview Park. Belfast was waking up, black taxis spewing out grey exhaust fumes, were taking commuters to their daily business adding further greyness to the hard-nationalist stronghold. Women hurried along the street to get back home after completing their early morning cleaning jobs at local schools, churches and offices. Vic took it all in as he looked down at the wooden bench by the dry-stone wall of the Beechmount leisure centre.

The weather-beaten bench was a memorial to Thomas O'Bray; a teenager who always stood on the corner waving at the passing black taxi's or buses. He used to wave at the army trucks until he received a punishment beating from Vic and his gang. Thomas was a Stook[7] he did nobody any harm, school children cruelly mocked him on their way home from school, but an overzealous member of Vic's squad went too far with a baseball bat. Thomas died from his head injuries after five days of intensive care in the Royal Victoria Hospital. By the time of his funeral Belfast PIRA had put word on the streets that O'Bray was an informer working for Special Branch and had been executed as a tout. The local people knew it was a lie and in defiance put a wooden bench on Thomas's corner. The plaque was always kept clean and flowers placed on it regularly, much to Secrillo's annoyance.

The bench also hid a secret; it was a communication medium

---

7 Irish Simpleton

between Vic and his British Army handlers. Vic sat on the bench taking the last drags on his cigarette and fumbled around his jacket pocket. Clutching the item, he reached behind the bench and nonchalantly made two marks in white chalk. Vic looked around. The volume of traffic was growing, and he felt tired and needed his bed. The chilly morning had bitten at his fingers, a bitter Belfast cold that always started in the bones and radiated outwards. Vic thought about which pieces of the night's events he would tell his handlers and which he would leave as insurance for a rainy day.

South Armagh

Stu and Mull lay in wait in the wood line hand railing the Carewamean Road; they had received orders as soon as they had arrived back at the main OP that they were to prepare for immediate extraction with a relief in line. A COP patrol led by the Platoon's second controller; Tommy 'Time Bomb' Trainor would patrol towards them and take cover in the woods. After ensuring they were not being observed by local dickers the patrol would set off again with Stu and Mull leaving the new OP commander Toots Dodge and his signaller Dick Pharaoh to make their way to the OP.

It was a cloudy morning, rain clouds were blowing in from the north-west which rustled what leaves still clung to the almost bare branches of the trees, whilst the green conifers danced in the gusts. A few meters up the track Tommy appeared and surveyed the road through his Susat sight on his rifle. Once satisfied that the area was clear he strode towards the fallen tree he knew his two soldiers would be awaiting his patrol's arrival.

"What's the score Tommy?" Stu asked breathlessly after living on his belt buckle for the last ten days.

"Bit of a flap at TCG8 after your sightings last night, Stu. Big

---

8 Tasking and Coordination Group

Joe smells something big is in the offing and you know he's like a fucking clairvoyant in all matters PIRA. They want you two back to Portadown ASAP and look at the product you got last night. Please tell me it's worth all this fucking hassle. I had Ray ring me up at sparrows fart this morning to tell me I needed to scramble a team down to the Mill to pick up your sorry arses."

"It gets you out of your scratcher and out into the cuds mate, you're also getting paid for it." Mull quipped.

Time Bomb gave him his distinctive withering look, "Fuck off, Mull. What's that fucking smell?"

Mull looked around at his Bergen "Sorry Tommy I drew the short straw so I'm carrying the turd bag, and I think it might have split."

TCG (S) Region Portadown

"Gentlemen can I call this meeting to order, as you all know we had some visitors at the Kelly residence in the early hours of this morning can I first ask Captain Martin Jenkins from the Fusiliers COP to give us some details about the situation."

Martin stretched his tall, gangly frame up from the plastic canteen chair. "Gentlemen at approximately 03:40 hours this morning a vehicle arrived at Alpha One the home of Bravo One, Paul Patrick Kelly. A saloon vehicle later identified as a grey Ford Sierra AZF8713 arrived after travelling south along the Ballynamona Road. This vehicle had three men on board, two of which were armed with pistols. They observed a large ginger haired male inside the premises in discussion with Bravo One. The two further males patrolled the complex. A few minutes later Charlie Three the black Volkswagen Golf BZG5917 driven by Bravo Three, Declan 'Decers' Taylor arrived with a further male described as a small Chinese male who described as being well dressed."

"Excuse me a moment Martin, did your boys get any photos of these guys." asked Alfie Luxholm, one of H Division's oldest and best agent handlers.

Martin took time to have a sip of his brew and wet his throat before he answered "Yes Alfie we did, as we speak Tommy is getting the guys off the ground. They will patrol into Romeo 23 and fly back here to Portadown for immediate debrief with the Intelligence Cell staff. They have been using a new-fangled piece of camera equipment which works well at low light and is also digital so there will be no need to wait for developing and they can enlarge the frames to quite a high degree losing no detail. The guys on the ground remarked that the meeting, which lasted only thirty minutes, was at points animated, and it was their interpretation that the oriental male led the discussion."

There was a perceptible oh! around the room.

"I don't believe that Peewee Kelly would take orders from a Chinaman." remarked Bill Preston the intelligence desk officer for the southern region.

"I can only tell you what my guys have expressed to me on the radio this morning, Bill. When the meeting broke up Bravo Three took the well-dressed gentleman to the area of the Carrickdale Hotel and the grey Ford Sierra travelled north tracked by members of my platoon in the overt watch towers through the Dromintee Bowl then towards Meigh away from Newry."

Joe rose to his feet and thanked Martin for his rundown of the events. "I have been told this morning that a patrol stopped the Ford Sierra just outside Markethill, after letting them on their way two pistols were found further down the roadside. Unfortunately, the vengeful check must have alerted somebody above our pay grade and the Colonel of 6 Royal Irish was told in no uncertain terms not to chase or apprehend the vehicle's occupants."

"So where are the guns Boss?"

"A good question Bill and one I would like somebody to answer. Apparently two 'Military Liaison Officers' turned up at Drummad and took the pistols within an hour of their discovery. Luckily though the Colonel, who is a close friend of mine forgot to mention a certain video tape which the patrol had made. This morning Herbie raced up to the barracks and got a copy. Kris, can you carry on?"

Sergeant Major Kris Derbyshire was the second in command to Seb; he was two years into his attachment to TCG South and a veteran of covert operations in Northern Ireland. For twelve years he had been in and out of the province working as an operator with the Special Surveillance Unit. Kris was now the Military Liaison Warrant Officer controlling all the covert surveillance teams in the southern region.

"Gentlemen can I please remind you all that this is a covered meeting nothing I say from now on in leaves this room." Kris's cynical eyes gazed at the assembled officers.

"I strongly believe that the weapons have been recovered by our colleagues in the Force Research Unit therefore there is a strong likelihood that somewhere along the line a covert asset is involved. I must stress the sensitivity of this information. Seb is busy on Bat Phone[9]" to try to resolve this matter at JCUNI[10] level. From the recovered video, I can tell you that the three males have not yet been formally identified.

Alfie spoke first "If, as you say we might have a snake at their bosom will your friends in the FRU give us access to the intelligence?"

"A few points on that Alfie, one I like your eloquence and two the Force Research Unit are nobody's friends. They provide good intelligence from the agents they run, and as we all

---

9 Encrypted telecommunications
10 Joint Communications Unit Northern Ireland

know human intelligence is vital in our world. However, some snippets they provide neither timely nor relevant. The motivations for their agents are Money, Ideology, Ego or because the FRU have compromised them and got them by the short and curlies. On the odd occasion some do it because of their Conscience."

Regardless of their motivation, they provide information at particular personal risk to themselves and their families. The problem we all have with FRU is they don't enjoy sharing information downwards. It has to go up before it comes down. They are like the school know it all that has to show the teacher his dazzling work before helping his classmates.

As I say Seb is trying to get some downward dissemination from them as we speak, but in my humble opinion don't hold your breath."

Hours after the meeting broke up Stu and Mull were still locked in the intelligence cell with Liam Salter an Intelligence Corps Staff Sergeant and his collator Corporal Francine 'Windy' Millar conducting a debrief. Each photograph was produced and discussed, the written operations log compared to their visual observations. The video retrieved from the pinhole camera of 6 UDA was also scrutinised against the images taken by Mulready. The examination was a long and monotonous process, it had to be accurate; the minutest of detail could unlock a whole new avenue of enquiry for the waiting Special Branch officers. It took a further two hours to get all the details down. Stu and Mull's eyes were reddening from the lack of sleep when Liam finally called a halt and arranged a flight back to Ballykinler.

Both soldiers were signing the evidence bags when Mull had a thought "Show me that Video again Windy." He became transfixed on the images taken by the Royal Irish. "I thought I recognised that guy, I remember him from my Belfast tour he's called Bonner; Aiden 'The Bird' Bonner."

By mid-afternoon a more detailed picture was emerging

from the previous night's activity. Joe had asked for a further meeting, but this time with only a few selected members of the team.

"Is that you, Johnny Nolan? And I thought you were on leave, boy."

"Thanks Boss, yes I'm well, but I think I will need more vitamin C after 'questioning' that colleen, I need frigging danger money."

"Stop your jibber Nolan you got a shag, and it was on double time is that ok with you now? So, what did that big auld heifer tell you?" Joe chuckled.

"Well, Boss, I have identified a Chinese male named as Sun Yee On, a sales rep from Fujian Province in China. He told my contact when he checked in that he was the European Manager for his company selling toys. Luckily the hotel makes a copy of all passport details and I have been in touch with the foreign liaison desk in Belfast, they will make discreet enquiries with the Garda. Now can I go back on leave I'm bolloxed Boss."

Big Joe laughed "You did a grand job now fuck off home you dirty wee bastard. Gentlemen, I've got a good contact in the Garda Síochána: Crime and Security Branch who might help this line of enquiry. Liam anymore from the OP boys?"

"No Sir, they are convinced that the oriental male was of extreme importance. He appeared to have several tattoos on his hands which I would say is inconsistent with a Chinese businessman; he also appears to have a digit missing and scars on his face. The pictures match the photocopy retrieved by Johnny Nolan at the hotel. I would add however that I was on the intelligence desk stationed in Hong Kong for two years and after examining the images of the tattoos I would comment that are consistent with Chinese gang culture."

"Do you mean Triads Liam?" asked one of the open-mouthed detectives.

"A Triad is one of many branches of Chinese organised crime. They have been around since the 18th Century so over time they have developed strongly in the south-east Asian countries and as a result forged criminal pathways into western society and become associated with local criminals."

"What! Fucking Charlie Chan 'a gangster' turns up on the doorstep of one of the most ruthless terrorists in Northern Ireland and lays down the law. What has he got to offer? You know South Armagh PIRA's attitude to drugs, they'd cut his bollox off in a heartbeat. There must be some other explanation. Get those tattoos blown up and analysed, I want some answers."

Seb raised his hands, "Ok Joe, I know what you're getting at. Tattoos can have a range of purposes in some cultures, and gang markings can indicate secret meanings like rank, criminal acts carried out and prison time. I will get Liam to push the pictures upwards and I will see if the Metropolitan Police can help as they still have a very busy Chinese desk. Let's not jump to conclusions just yet; it might be he is negotiating the building of the first Chinese takeaway in South Armagh."

"What! Paddy's China Garden, I suppose. Get me some answers and quick Seb." Joe shouted over his shoulder as he walked back to his office.

Belfast

Corporal Anthony Burke the McCrory Park CONCO[11] had briefed a twelve man multiple from the Black Watch and waited in line to load his rifle before running out of the heavy green gates of the camp on to the bustling Whiterock Road.

Every Army patrol were given specific intelligence missions to carry out during their time walking the streets. The tasks

---

11 Continuity Non-Commissioned Officer Local Army Intelligence gatherer

could range from carrying out personality checks, vehicle checks or house calls. On occasions they would conduct rummage searches of scrub land, gardens and allotments.

The multiple ran from the base using the front and back exits to keep PIRA observers or dickers as the soldiers called them, constantly on their toes. The patrol changed pace from slow to quick and back down to slow. The twelve men worked in three four men 'bricks' which was ideal for working in an urban environment. Sometimes they hard targeted using every available piece of available street furniture as a shield then walked normally amongst the pedestrians of the Lower Falls Road.

A vehicle check point was set up around the area of the Beechmount leisure centre. As the troops busied themselves covering their arcs of fire or stopping people and traffic, Burkey took a quick glance behind the bench.

It was an hour later when Burkey finally rang the number he had been given by two Military Liaison Officers several weeks before.

"Hello is Bernie or Andy around its Corporal Burke the CONCO at McCrory Park? We spoke a few weeks ago."

"Hello Tony, Bernie here, what have you got for me, mate?" Bernie's thick Manchester accent rasped down the secure line.

"There were two white chalk marks behind the bench you pointed out to me by the dry-stone wall of the Beechmount leisure centre. That was at eleven o'clock today."

"Thanks mate, keep your eye out for further marks from our friend. On your next patrol rub out those marks and put two red marks in place the way we showed you. Mind you're not being over watched." The secret 'bat phone,' went dead.

"Andy, Agent Lemon has been in touch he wants to meet tonight at area two. That young Corporal is leaving our reply."

Colour Sargent Bernie Hugh had been the agent handler for 'Agent Lemon' for two years. A seasoned member of the Force Research Unit, he had controlled many successful 'Covert Human Intelligence Sources' or CHIS as the unit referred to them. Bernie was in his last six months before returning to the Defence School of Intelligence to train the next generation of sources handlers. His partner Sergeant Andy Scriven had only been in the unit a few months but was developing steadily.

"Oh, so he is alive then, I don't know why we're paying him so much. People are getting killed on the streets and his information has dried up to a trickle. I'm sure he knows more than he's letting on to." Andy replied.

"Your right buddy, but he will get us a big gong and lots of fucking bodies. Wait till he hears what we have to tell him, I can't wait to see that fucking smile wiped from his smug face."

"He fucking owes us for getting him out of the shit last night. I might shove one of those pistols up his arse. It was a good job he dropped us that vehicle registration or we would be holding the meeting in Castlereagh interrogation centre."

"The one thing I've learned about Victor is he's a survivor who puts self-preservation above everything else. On occasions he won't tell you what he's up to and someone ends up dead then next he picks up the phone and he saves a life but the guy that told him that information ends up dead. It's been his way of moving through the upper echelons for years. Yes, we admonish him for not telling us about his latest nutting, but he says it adds to his cover. He's clever and cunning." Bernie explained.

"Well, I don't trust him one bit, he's devious, and he uses us to cover up his crimes. He's a murderer and should have been locked up." Scriven argued.

"Andy, trust none of our sources, remember if we only worked with good guys we wouldn't have any snitches would we. Yes, he's got blood and guts on his hand, but he gives us an insight into what's going on in his world. Remember, he's risking his life every day. One wrong word and he's dead, and not a pleasant death either. If you don't like it, you can always go back to the Monkeys,"

The Welshman Scriven nodded his head in acceptance. In his former profession as a detective with the Special Investigations Branch of Royal Military Police, he upheld the law. Now he was countersigning and encouraging the most heinous of crimes.

TCG (S) Region Portadown

Joe was looking through his old daybooks to locate the number of his top contact within the Garda. Superintendent Dan Currie was an old school copper like Joe; they were cut from the same cloth. Dan had been a member of the Special Detective Unit for many years and risen through the ranks. The SDU were still referred to as the Special Branch by most ill-informed sources; they superseded the Branch many years before and had even been given its own strike capability the Emergency Response Unit (ERU), a specialist armed tactical unit. The SDU and the ERU could now get into the ribs of any disaffected factor within its borders. If potential suspects fled abroad, the Army Ranger Wing (ARW) the Republic's very own Special Forces who had the skill and tenacity to kill or capture dangers to the state was available.

"Daniel is that you?"

"Arrah the only Ulsterman who ever calls me by my Sunday name, it's gotta be Big Joe Montgomery, how's you big fella, and mores to the point what do you want?" Currie's softly spoken Kerry accent had a rhythm, it was slow and methodical as if he was about to break into song at any moment.

Joe laughed, Dan knew him too well, and it was usually tickets for the rugby international he wanted. "No, my friend, I want you to keep your ear out as something might be in the wind. We've had some information about one of our boys talking to a Chinese fella that was staying in a hotel by the border. I don't suppose you have many dealings with the Far East, do you?"

Dan thought for a moment Joe was fishing for information, but it would not be given cheaply. "Arrah listen Joe I always fancied a day at the Bushmills distillery if we can arrange it for me and a few of the boys, can you do that?"

"Funny enough old son I will have the tickets and free accommodation for you all by tomorrow, as long as it's not the whole fuckin Garda Síochána."

"Arrah well how lucky am I, send me the details you have on the fella and the hotel and I will process it right away. I will tell you a bit of China gossip that is in the wind though; the only person I know to have visited China recently was Jimmy Fagan. He returned a few weeks ago, said he was buying toys for a new shop he will open in Westport."

"And has that chancer opened up the shop?"

"Has he shite, he's not even bought a feckin shop the eejit."

Joe roared with laughter. "Thanks, old son I will get the details to you right away, and lead the Bushmills tour myself."

Alpha One

Peewee was getting anxious; he had told Manny Holmes to pick him up at one o'clock sharp, and it was nearly three. Manny was a pleasant kid unless he was near booze or the bookies and one usually drove the other, but he was good in a tight spot. Only months before, he'd driven out of an army vehicle roadblock on the return from killing a judge in Richill. The judge, a man in his seventies and about to retire, was busy tending rose bushes in his ornate garden off the Mullaleish Road when Peewee executed him with a single bullet to the back of his neck.

In the distance Peewee could hear a vehicle rapidly approaching; Manny expertly performed a swinging turn at speed and stopped beside Peewee.

"And where the fucks have you been? We will be late to meet somebody who you never want to be late for." Peewee could barely control his anger.

"I'm err sorry Peewee, but the car had erm some problem, and I needed it looking at by err The Mechanic and err my Ma is ill, I didn't really want to leave her." Manny stuttered.

"What? Is your Ma in the Starry Plough Bar again, Manny? Yous smell like a fuckin brewery boy. And we are meeting The Mechanic on the fuckin way so I will ask him about the car. Now fuckin get me to Dungooly crossroad so the boys can follow on we have some stuff to pick up. It will be a long day and night. I will decide what to do with you later if you don't kill us both or get arrested by the fuckin Garda."

The over watch OP observed peewee's exit from the farm complex and the vehicle movement and passed via the secure Close Observation Platoon radio network. The net chatter was constant as Seb walked into the operations room.

"Anyone got a sitrep for me, guys?"

It was Martin who spoke first, rising from his chair in front of an enormous wall map which displayed the fifty-three mile South Armagh border.

"The OP has reported that Peewee has been picked up by B7 Emanuel Holmes who is driving a Maroon BMW 3 Series

IBE3243 at speed. My team at Golf Four Zero on Croslieve is reporting that the vehicle drove to Dungooly. Peewee jumped out of the vehicle and spoke to several blokes, then they all drove off in convoy. They describe eight vehicles in that convoy four as large box vans."

Seb rubbed the stubble on his chin. He was still tired. Even the ten-mile row he had just done in the gym hadn't shaken out his tiredness. "And they are still heading west on the opposite side of the border, you say?"

Martin pointed to a spot on the map "This is the position of 93 Bravo he's in a smaller overt tower once they go past the crossroads he's watching they will be from view. Have we had anything from the intelligence cell on their intentions?"

"Nothing at all, whatever Peewee's up to, we are blind to it. I'll get South Det on call in case we need an interdiction. It's probably just one of Peewee's little training exercises, but we can't take a chance."

"What about Ulster Troop." Martin enquired about the sixteen man SAS detachment on call.

"Fraid not, they are working up the Sperrin's with North Det, who believe they have found a QM's hide."

"Jesus the Sperrin Mountains in winter. I can think of better places to be Seb."

FRU Briefing Room Lisburn

Captain Peter Arnott was an unrecognisable man, bland features on top of a bland body, the perfect grey man. Arnott's role as the leader of the Force Research Unit "The Fishers of Men" as they liked to call themselves were far from grey; they were black, jet black. Arnott was chairing the weekly tasking and targeting meeting with his staff from each of the Brigade areas, who all sat around an enormous round table. Arnott liked to think of himself as a modern-day King Arthur, but no royalty could ever be so nondescript. In the middle of the table the FRU operators had placed pages of sighting reports and personality checks generated by the green troops patrolling daily throughout the province. The unit's collator Corporal Malcom Russo had painstakingly looked at every piece of intelligence to find links and associations.

"Anyone seen Arnott's personality report yet?" whispered the Geordie Staff Sergeant Vince Hill.

"No, he doesn't fuckin have a personality." laughed Corporal Rebecca Hamilton.

"Ladies and Gentlemen, excuse the absence of Bernie and Andy, but they are preparing for a meeting tonight so we will crack on first looking at the southern region please." Arnott was also grey when he talked and had sent his audience to sleep on many an occasion.

"Thanks Boss. One or two interesting snippets for the south desk, the first is a report from an overt observation tower in Dromintee which has identified Declan Taylor a member of the Jonesborough PIRA group visiting a caravan close to the Slieve Gullion country park. Not very interesting, you might think until you see the next sighting in which a female is later seen visiting him at the said caravan. The problem that 'Dirty Decers' has is that his wife Bridget Taylor is the sister of Paul Patrick 'Peewee' Kelly the head of PIRA operations at Army General HQ, so Decers is in the shit if we can prove he's messing around."

There were smiles all-round the table, sting operations were a favourite of the FRU. Catch somebody with their pants down and blackmail them into turning informer. The agents were more scared of their own comrades than they were of the crown forces.

"Boss put me and Bex on this case. I know Taylor and Bex has just completed the training package with the new eavesdropping kit." Gary Grimshaw volunteered. He was a Cumbrian farmer in his day, large calloused hands from farming and a wide flat nose from playing rugby for his local club Egremont.

"The sightings appear to be regular Gary, Tuesday and Thursday between 19:00 and 21:00. I have asked TC&G South for a support team possibly coming from the Fusiliers COP to lead you in for the task, is that OK Bex."

"Yes Malc, I will get my thermals ready and check the technical gear." Rebecca joked.

Malc continued "Another of the south Armagh crew Emanuel Holmes from Jonesborough was stopped and questioned by the RUC in Newry this week he had been visiting his sick mother in the Daisy Hill Hospital, she's got liver failure because of alcohol dependency. It seems that her son also likes the ale as well because he was drunk driving, it's his second offence so no more driving and a big fine. RUC have kept it quiet and passed it on up the chain were we intercepted it. I think we need to get into his face before Special Branch handlers try to bump him."

"Put the two Steve's' down for that one, we're down to work out of the Fathom Line patrol base and Romeo 15 vehicle check point for the rest of the week so we will try to engineer a pull on him." Sergeant Steve Morrow was on his second tour with the unit after a successful spell in Belfast. Steve was a likable Geordie who worked well with his cockney partner Sargent Steve Carter who always played the nasty guy with their agents whilst Morrow acted in a calm and friendly manner.

TCG (S) Region Portadown

"What!" Joe going into a meltdown "You now tell me that this bastard was on my parish last night, having a meeting with the most vicious terrorist in Northern Ireland?"

Liam Salter gulped and wished he had told Herbie the news rather than the boss himself.

"It's a positive identification of Aiden Bonner, the commander of Belfast. The pictures don't lie; it also ties in with the footage taken from the Royal Irish Regiment, and Corporal Mulready from the OP team also confirmed it. Bonner was travelling with his driver, Henry 'Bap' McConnell and Victor Secrillo who is assessed as Brigade civil administration unit. Henry McConnell was formally of Castleblayney Road, South Armagh, until he upset Sailor Murphy by shagging his daughter. After a few months on the run he ended up in Belfast driving Bonner about. So, we have a veritable nest of vipers."

"Victor Secrillo you say? He's head executioner; an evil bastard, let me tell you. I would say they are planning to execute somebody if Secrillo is there, unless he's monitoring The Bird. A few of the Boyos don't trust him; they say he's a rusty gun and not taking the war to the Loyalists in Belfast. McConnell was one of our players; part of the Crossmaglen group, but he's in the shit with them. The whisper in my ear was that he ran off with the cash from a Post Office robbery, after battering the poor auld Post Mistress who was a pensioner. Belfast must have taken him in, we thought he was hanging out in Dundalk with all the other 'On the runs,' and a right bunch of misfits that lot are I can tell you. I don't suppose you have any marvellous news for me, do you, Liam? No well leave me while I ring my counterpart Stan Lafferty head of Belfast T&CG."

Belfast

It was after five in the evening when Fitzmartin walked into the Beehive bar on the Falls Road to find Bonner stood at the bar with John 'Mc D' McDennis. Mc D was head of the Belfast intelligence cell, over the years he and his disparate team had provided accurate intelligence which led to the deaths of many off duty RUC officers, soldiers and Loyalists.

"Anthony thanks for coming, we need to find a quiet corner to have a chat." Bonner ushered the pair over to a cubicle. After a few minutes' of small talk, they got down to business. "Mc D I need you to get me a list of all the fuckin leaders and gunmen in the UDA, UVF and Red Hand Commandos, I also want you to find out as much as you can about Tara. Anthony will need targeting packs as his boys will whack them all."

"Fuckin what? Whack all the prods leadership; you know I have about twenty lads who I can trust in West Belfast and about a dozen in the North Birdy." Fitzmartin exclaimed.

"I've asked for reinforcements from Derry and East Tyrone, they will supply us with unfamiliar weapons silenced pistols and machine guns, assault rifles and grenades, so we will have the tools to do the job. Mc D look at places where these fuckers congregate so we can take out quite a few at once."

Mc D sat back in his chair and looked around the pub. After a swing of his larger he told them "The eleventh night."

"What do you mean? Fuckin eleventh night, explain yourself?" Bonner demanded.

"All the fucking Loyalist community will attend the bonfires on the eleventh night of July, so we can take them out then." Mc D explained.

Bonner shook his head, "Are you a fuckin mad man? All the leaders will be there, too, right, but their foot soldiers will surround them. It would be like the Brit red coats marching in lines to battle, and certain death. I'm not wanting my volunteers to go on a suicide mission Mc D, do you understand? Find where they live, drink and fuck their girlfriends."

"Boyfriends, knowing those proddy bastards Birdy." Wisecracked Fitzmartin.

"I will leave the fine details to you then. Anthony, I need some of your most trusted guys, the lookouts from the Fianna and girls from the Cumann na mBan to be ready to help bring a big shipment into the city. Ron McKeever is busy finding hides to stash it all. I've arranged for you to meet Ciaran Rock from Derry and Danny Roy from Coalisland to work out manpower. Tell them nothing, just that we are planning a colossal job soon and we want to know how many men they can provide. I don't fuckin trust Roy at all, he's a sound Republican, but a fuckin loon."

"Sounds like he's ideal for the job, Birdy." Fitzmartin laughed.

CHAPTER THREE

September 1993

Fujian, China

The bike and pan making Factory 394 in Donghuping was built high in the mountainous Broad-leaved evergreen forests of Fujian, above the meandering Jinjiang River which carried the complex's products down to the large seaport of Quanzhou. Thousand-year Old Camphor Trees intermixed with coniferous and deciduous trees framed the bamboo perimeter fence.

Factory 394 was one of the many industrial premises owned by CSC the China Supply Company a state-owned enterprise. CSC was under the control of the fifth ministry (Ministry for Ordinance) Factories in Beijing. From humble beginnings supplying cooking utensils to machinery parts, the company had steadily grown into the production of munitions and firearms.

CSC, because of its impeccable reputation with the government had also moved into petroleum & mineral resources development, international engineering contracting, optronic products, civilian explosives and chemical products. The move to diversify had led to the creation of many new complexes throughout mainland China and into Sino friendly countries in the Far East and Africa. Factory 394 was one of hundreds of industrial units owned by CSC, but 394 supplied a lot more than the bikes and pans constructed in the site's hanger three. The other seven warehouses developed and manufactured explosives, ammunitions, infantry small arms; infantry support weapons, Surface to Air Missiles, Communications equipment and military clothing, all for clandestine export to foreign governments.

Mr Han Wo, the factory supervisor, was a loyal red book carrying member of the communist party after a lengthy career in the People's Liberation Army. Han Wo loved his work almost as much as gambling, which had led him into the clutches of the San Ho Hui, a gang which was part of the Triple Union Society. The San Ho Hui ran gambling parlours, illicit drinking dens and brothels across Fujian province. It corrupted government officials and army commanders with bribes of cash or women. They also used blackmail as a leaver to extort goods or services required by the larger 'black societies' of mainland China. Many of the large Chinese organised crime groups, including the Wo Shing Wo triads had fled to British-controlled Hong Kong after being forced out during the Cultural Revolution.

The larger gangs had formed links to the USA and Europe, engaging in a variety of crimes, from fraud, extortion and money laundering to trafficking and prostitution. Many triads switched from opium to heroin, produced from opium plants in the Golden Triangle, refined into heroin in China and trafficked abroad. The Wo Shing Wo had remained in contact with the smaller enterprises in Mainland China like the San Ho Hui and acted as brokers for international marketing.

In return for a cancelation of Han Wo's gambling debts Factory 394 workers produced consignments of weapons and equipment for the San Ho Hui which were then shipped by sea to the associates of the Wo Shing Wo. The black societies controlled the transport infrastructure of trucks, boats and shipping. Local officials were coerced into signing the paperwork, Dockers loading the shipments were paid double by the gangs and even Da Xiao Wo Dang the local senior Colonel of the Peoples Liberation Army turned a blind eye to practices at the Factory during his snap inspections as long as he was supplied his cut and a constant supply of young prostitutes.

Dang's older brother was a leading member of the Big Circles organisation, a loose alliance of criminal gangs founded by former Red Guards after the Cultural Revolution. Big Circles were active in snakehead human trafficking and other criminal operations, including providing protection for the Factory and all illicit shipments to the ports.

In early 1993 an intermediary arranged a meeting between Lee Yip Wong the Dragon Head of the Wo Shing Wo and James Fagan the Quartermaster General from the Army Council of the Provisional Irish Republican Army. The middle man had met with an Irish Republican sympathiser at a Wo Shing Wo controlled restaurant in Manchester's China Town. The meeting led to Fagan travelling out to the legendary Hotel Lisboa. For decades, the twelve story tower hotel and its casino had an absolute monopoly on gambling in Macau.

Steve Ho, who had been at the introductory meeting, and hosted the get-together between Wong and Fagan, provided drinks, gambling chips and a secluded VIP area.

"Mr Wong, thank you for meeting me I have been hoping to discuss a business opportunity for both of our syndicates." Fagan began. I believe that your corporation has hit several international hurdles as has my own."

"Mr Fagan you have my time and my interest, how can we provide each other assistance?" Wong appeared to have a round face which blended into his neck.

"From one of my agents in the USA we have learned that the FBI are about to come down hard on some of your activities. An overt operation they have called Dragon Fire will impose new legislation to prohibit Chinese weapons, however, U.S. Customs agents are in the process of conducted a sting against your import organisation in Atlanta. I know this covert operation as Operation Black Dragon. You should also know that the Bureau of Alcohol, Tobacco, Firearms and Explosives are also sniffing around your business ventures."

Wong's eyes were wide open. The Irishman who sat across from him knew about a prime money-making scheme that was importing drugs and firearms into America and beyond. "Thank you for this information Mr Fagan and what do you want from me?" Wong had taken the bait "Please carry on Mr Fagan."

"My agent is in a position to continue reporting the activities of the American authorities against your business interests. After discussions with Mr Ho, I also believe that a resident of Belfast Liu Zhau and his girlfriend Yu Yan Wu were murdered by a gang called the Red Hand Commandos last month. I read in the local papers that they burned to death in their flat above the restaurant they worked in. I am reliably informed that it was the centre of a small drugs dealing enterprise supplying the protestant youths of the area."

Wong looked at the man across from him. The slim Irishman appeared cool, unflappable, a person who had seen adversity. "I know of you Mr Fagan; my people have done their research on you. You were the former commander of the IRA's Derry Brigade. They tell me you were ruthless and prepared to carryout daring attacks against the police and army. You cannot live in your homeland as you are wanted because of an informer in your ranks, so you live in the south and control the flow of weapons and ammunition to your brothers in the front line."

"Your researchers are as good as this fine Cognac Mr Wong. My organisation has recently had difficulty in procuring weapons. A loyal benefactor of ours in North Africa has also come to the attention of the Americans, but he has been bombed out of his many palaces. I am told that you can supply the weapons we require, and in vast amounts. In return we will pay a very good price plus clear the way for you to take over any nefarious activities you wish to undertake in Belfast and any other loyalist areas. We will also give you access to our friends in Scotland, which will link you into the whole of Great Britain."

Wong drummed the table and considered the Irishman's offer "You have made a very kind and generous offer; the American's action could mean we must stockpile quite a few of our products, so it is sensible that we look for fresh markets. The matter with your religious rivals displeases us as we believed we had come to a working agreement, but the murder of two of 49's or as you might say ordinary members has aggrieved us greatly. It is obvious to say that our members could not secretly carry out any revenge attacks against the formidable numbers of loyalist criminals, so your offer of help is very tempting. May I ask what weapons you are looking for exactly?" Wong sat back and admired the contents of his glass.

"In the past few years we have received several shipments from the Americas and North Africa. In these shipments we have received a negligible quantity of surface-to-air missiles, heavy machine guns, assault rifles and Semtex explosives. This weaponry has helped us to continue the struggle in the north." Fagan's speech was short and staccato as he fired off the tools he required to wage war.

"My European business manager Mr Ho is an expert on what firearms are available to export, he will make all the arrangements. You have my blessing on this relationship between our two parties, as a show of gratitude for your information about America we will provide you a taster shipment, as an act of good faith. Thank you and goodbye." Wong rose to his feet and shook the tall slim Irishman by the hand before taking Ho to one side. After a brief whispered conversation Ho returned and sat across from Fagan who was waiting in anticipation."

"Mr Wong has expressed his wishes that we will support your organisation by providing a number of shipments of the latest weapons, ammunition and explosives used by the Chinese army."

Fagan nodded his head in agreement. Ho rubbed his hands together unintentionally, looking for the severed little finger on his right hand, lost in a territorial street fight back in Hong Kong. Ho lost his digit and had deep lacerations on his face, but his opponents lost their lives. Back in those days' Ho was Sun Yee On a '426' Red Pole, an enforcer and an excellent one he was, as he quickly rose through the deadwood above him to be the gang's principal man in Europe.

"My role in the corporation is the Vanguard or as you might call it the operations officer. My portfolio covers the export of goods and commodities to Europe, in fact the unfortunate Mr Zhau and Miss Wu were my workers, so this matter has become very personable to me. I have read some books recently to study your conflict, and I think you require state-of-the-art equipment to fight against a modern British full-time army. I propose that we make several shipments to your country at a landing site of your choosing. You will need to construct a very large hide for the equipment we send plus the means and manpower to take these items off a ship at anchor. Is that understood, James?"

"Yes, Steve I already have a number of places to put the stuff, we refer to them as a QM's hide and we also have numerous smaller bunkers which stretch from the landing sites all the way to the war zones in the North."

"Very good you must have studied the Chinese revolution led by the Communist Party of China and Mao Zedong; he also battled much superior enemy with a peasant army. If I said I could supply the SAM missiles you requested would that help James?"

"Well, the Brits depend on helicopters to move around the southern regions of our country. It's this area that a popular revolt could start and light up the touch paper to kick the loyalists out of our land and make a united Ireland once again."

"Your revolution will require more than a few SAM rockets, I can also get anti-tank missiles, heavy machine guns, grenade launchers, flame throwers plus a full spectrum of infantry small arms and ammunition. I cannot provide Semtex, but China was the birthplace of explosives in the 9th century so we will supply TNT and the ammunition for all the weapon systems. My contacts can also provide a few experimental thermobaric weapons. I am told that this is a missile that uses oxygen from the surrounding air to generate a high-temperature explosion; the blast wave produced is significantly longer duration than that produced by a conventional condensed explosive. It will destroy soldiers hiding in trenches or fortifications." Ho looked across at Fagan, scrutinising his facial expressions as he reeled off the types and quantities of weapons available to export.

"James I would, as a personal favour, request that you dispose of the leaders of the Ulster Defence Association and Ulster Freedom Fighters. We had made a significant payment to these people to allow us freedom to trade peacefully in Belfast, before they betrayed our agreement. The exact numbers of weapons plus the time and place of the landing will be given to you shortly by one of my representatives. Sailing time dependent on route will take anything from forty to seventy days. So, my Captains will plan to arrive at the best tide and moon times for the unloading of the shipments. I must now arrange the production of your order; I have arranged for two of the best girls from our local pleasure house to meet you in your room. They will look after your every need, James." After a quick handshake, Ho was off into the night.

Glosh Beach, County Mayo

It had taken three long weeks and miles of driving before James Fagan had finally decided on the optimum landing site, the windswept beaches of the Mullet Peninsula in County Mayo. Dangling thirty kilometres into the cold Atlantic, the Mullet was a thinly populated Gaeltacht12

Irish-speaking isthmus which felt more cut off than many islands and had a similar sense of loneliness. The unspoiled beaches along the western shore and the cover provided by the Inishkea Islands made the site ideal for landing illegal weapons or any contraband. The Mullet populated by a sympathetic Republican community, though hardly any of them had ever stepped foot in North of Ireland or had any real idea about the latest 'Armed Struggle' they were willing to turn a blind eye to activities carried out by the 'Boys.'

The new site was well away from previous landings in Halvick Head in Waterford and Clogga Strand. The roads on the isthmus were narrow and often blocked by vast flocks of sheep which roamed the peninsula. The white tower at the highest point of Tower Road gave a good all-round view of the surrounding area and the hill on Inishkea South was an excellent vantage point for a lookout towards the incoming ships first marker point the Black Rock Lighthouse to the South.

Josephine Lanster, the overnight receptionist at the Talbot Hotel in Belmullet, had been pondering which Barbara Cartland novel to read next when she heard the rumble of a heavy truck passing outside on the Ballina Road. Heavy goods vehicles did occasionally pass through the compact fishing town, but when she heard the second followed by a third truck, she decided to investigate. By the time she had reached the door trucks four and five were passing heading towards the small bridge leading on to the peninsula. The flat bed lorries were each transporting red shipping containers, each about forty feet long.

Just as Josephine was about to return to the warmth of the reception truck six ambled through the village followed by a large white van which was followed by two yellow JCB diggers. Josephine had lived in Belmullet all of her adult life; she and her brothers walked the wild windswept coasts and hills every weekend. She made a mental note that on her next

---

12 Irish-speaking

walk she would find where the mysterious containers were going to.

It was three days later when Josephine and her brother Sean started their search of the peninsula, but they had buried in that time all six of the containers deep and concealed into the sand dunes of Glosh beach. The digger tracks had been camouflaged and sand placed over a newly built track leading from the local GAA club on to the white sands of the beach.

The camouflage and concealment of the containers was perfect using the natural undulating folds of the dunes and replanting the sharp marram grass on top.

The yellow JCB diggers had been stored in a nearby cow shed and the white van driven back to County Cavan with the dozen volunteers that had helped in the hides' construction.

By Fagan's side was Ignatius Flynn 'The Boatman' as his nickname suggested a seafarer all his life. The Boatman had advised Fagan about the tides, underwater dangers and navigation marks in microscopic detail. They would pass all of which on to the ship's Captain via Steve Ho.

A further three large shipping containers had been purchased and were on route with a team of volunteers to conceal them in the sand dunes on the route to the beach track South of Tiraun Point. The new containers would be given extra waterproofing and be used to store the expected heavy infantry weapons.

Networks of smaller hides were also in production in the Tristia Bog away from the Mullet Peninsula, thus reducing the risk of single interception and loss of all the stock in the large primary hides on the beach.

Three six-hundred-gallon oil drums had already been dug into sand dunes to separate the expected enormous volume of explosives. The empty hides only contained a stack of oil cloths, waiting to be wrapped around in incoming weapons to provide protection from the sea air.

The R313 was the only road in or out of the Mullet, at its narrowest point the isthmus was less than three hundred meters wide, a few men acting as piquet in the sand dunes at that point could give early warning of any suspect vehicles of Garda presence.

Happy that he would have the hides in place to receive the incoming shipment Fagan set off on the long drive to Galway and a meeting with Ho and McSweeny in P.J. Flaherty's a great Irish bar on the Lower Salthill Road, and boy did he need a pint.

China

Weapons Manufacture at Factory 394 in Donghuping had begun only a few hours after the meeting in Macau. The shipping arrangements had already been agreed with the Big Circles organisation moving the weapons from factory down the Jinjiang River to the container docks at Hutianjiao in the port city of Quanzhou. The convoys of trucks blended in well with the busy traffic carrying the new crop of rice and trucks from the Southern Geologic Survey Bureau of the Ministry of Nuclear Industry, carrying uranium ore.

There had been little trouble producing the required number of weapons and ammunition. The only fly in the ointment was Da Gao, a senior supervisor in Hanger Five, the production plant for Surface to Air Missiles. Da Gao, a bureaucratic man, who wallowed in his own self-importance, had questioned the order from Han Wo and been reticent in complying with his given directive. Wo had suspected he would encounter problems with the small rotund administrator and had made calls to his masters within the San Ho Hui.

Da Gao was sat sipping his second cup of green tea in the New Port Seafood Shop, by the banks of the river. It was the end of another interminable sweltering day; tomorrow he would again challenge the strange order from the factory manager. A shipment to Taiwanese rebels! Who did Wo think he was talking too? Did he think he was stupid? Yes, tomorrow he would confront Wo and tell him that he would report him to Colonel Wo Dang, who knows perhaps the company would see sense then and appoint him as the factory manager. He was happy with himself and the course which he planned to embark on. His mind wandered to the night's forthcoming events.

As he looked at the murky brown water flowing below the café's veranda, he sat back in anticipation of the arrival of Chao Bei, his fifteen-year-old lover. Da Gao had no vices; he neither smoked nor drank alcohol, his only parlance was a liking for young males. Young Chao Bei was his conquest; he had been providing a service for Da Gao for two years, since the supervisor found him begging for food outside the café. Food, clothing and presents had enticed the adolescent boy, grooming him slowly until Da Gao took his reimbursement. Chao Bei was proving his worth as he provided other younger street boys for Da Gao's pleasure, for which he paid a healthy reward.

Da Gao was shaken from his thoughts by the sound of a chair being moved; startled he looked up hoping to see a new boyish face with Chao Bei, but was shocked to see two very serious looking men wearing sharp suits and aviator sunglasses.

"Mr Da Gao, do you mind if we join you?" the taller man asked pleasantly.

Confused, Da Gao muttered yes and pointed towards the vacant chairs.

The second man, smaller, broad and menacing, took off his sunglasses and stirred at Da Gao. "Waiting for your little mài de13 you fucking pervert?"

Sweat ran down Da Gao's plump face like rain, the damp patches under the arms of his white cotton shirt were ballooning. He could smell himself and his two accusers could smell his fear.

The taller man smiled; he knew that Da Gao was like a rabbit caught in the headlights of a car just waiting to be crushed beneath the wheels.

"You know its shí bā jìn? Forbidden sex with a male child. Statutory rape the police call it, you will go to prison for a long time you depraved bastard."

"But I haven't" before Da Gao could finish his sentence, the smaller man started placing pictures of Da Gao and Chao Bei on the table.

Horrified, the overweight supervisor tried to scoop them up "No please there has been a mistake."

"Yes, your fucking mistake, Chao Bei will tell the police you have raped him and his eight-year-old brother. What will the community think about that, I doubt that you would ever make it to the police station before the angry mob cut your cock off and fucking hang you on the People's Square?"

Da Gao was now sobbing uncontrollably, "What can I do? What do you want?"

"Mr Da Gao we are not here to judge or condemn your little misdemeanours, we want you to get on with your task at Hanger Five and keep your fucking mouth shut. It would be very unfortunate if these pictures fell into the wrong hands. You can keep those snaps as a memento of our conversation today, and to remind you of our very generous offer. We have plenty more."

Both men rose together, smiling. The smaller man replaced his glasses on to the bridge of his nose, then put a firm hand on the shoulder of Da Gao. His hand was heavily tattooed, and his face menacing as he whispered into the ear of the quaking Da Gao.

"We will take it that your days as a paedophile are now over. It would be a great shame if we had to visit you again, Mr Da Gao, our negotiations might not be as pleasant. Goodbye."

Glosh Beach, Co Mayo

The first weapons shipment had taken five days to meander down the Jinjiang River to the enormous storage warehouse in Lian'an where the larger weapons were stripped down and packaged in non-descriptive containers. A local Junk Ship then moved the items over to
Shihu Port for loading on to a China Shipping Container Lines ship the Peng Hai. The twenty four-thousand-ton vessel was a bulker ship which either carried grain or ore. The grain carried on the Peng Hai was only to conceal the deadly cargo beneath. After a temporary stop in Hong Kong, the Peng Hai made the ten thousand nautical mile trip via Suez Canal in forty days.
Ignatius Flynn had first spotted the vessel from his prime vantage point on Inishkea South, arriving on the high tide on the moonless Wednesday 2nd February 1994.

The ship anchored in the deepest part of the narrow channel opposite Rusheen islet, approximately two kilometres offshore.

Flynn warned his waiting flotilla that it would be a long night. It was only a few hours into the unloading operation that James Fagan realised that he didn't have enough hides to conceal the amount of weapons, ammunition and explosives being delivered. The new hides in the Tristia Bog were quickly examined for suitability, quickly waterproofed and opened.

CHAPTER FOUR

Monday 14th February 1994

West Belfast

It was the early hours of the morning when the black Hackney cab pulled over to allow the two waiting passengers to enter. "Hello Vic, how's the taxi business going?"

"Very good all thanks to you fine gentleman. I thought I would return a favour if I could."

Andy and Bernie smiled at each other; it was their idea that Secrillo get a black cab to allow him free movement throughout West Belfast, and the ability to meet PIRA members all over the city.

"So how long have we got Vic and have you got anything good for us." Andy asked.

"First you can tell your cover car to stay back a bit, it looks like I'm being followed, and you have as long as it takes to get to the top end of the Glenn Road."

"Ok so what have you got to tell us?" Bernie pressed.

"I was ordered by Harry McFadden the Head of Northern Command to get a car and accompany Bonner who runs Belfast Brigade down to the South, He met some top jockey in South Armagh, Birdy called him Peewee. I couldn't go into the meeting, but a fuckin wee Chinaman turned up and went in. After we left Bonner didn't say much. He looked to me like he was brooding or something. Anyway, he then wanted a meet with Anthony Fitzmartin who is a top gun in the Belfast Active Service Unit, John McDennis; we call him Mc D he's the city's intelligence officer and Ron McKeever the quartermaster. I thought that was unusual then he asked to get the boss of Derry over Ciaran Rock and mad Danny Roy from East Tyrone, so something big is on the table, mark my words."

Secrillo deliberately underplayed his knowledge of Peewee, he knew full well just who Paul Patrick Kelly was and his role in the organisation, but if they were as clever as they claimed to be they could work it out for themselves.

"Why the out of towners?" Andy asked.

"I don't have a clue, but it's not good."

"What was the Chinese guy doing at the meeting? Can you ask McFadden what's going on?"

"Henry? No fuckin way, he'd smell a rat."

Bernie leaned close to Secrillo "Speaking of rats, perhaps you can tell Henry that he might have a rat in his midst."

"What do you mean?" Victor was worried.

"Your friend Bonner was seen talking to some very senior Loyalists. I bet you didn't know about that." Bernie enticed him. "If the Bird is in league with the other side, it might mean he will have to disappear, and maybe you would get further promotion up the chain of command."

Secrillo's devious mind was in overdrive, that fuckin shite in the pockets of the enemy. There had been rumours of Bonner dealing in drugs, but the accusers often died soon after, a number by the hand of Secrillo himself carrying out the orders of the 'Adjutant General', James McElwaine.

"If you had proof that the Bird did that, you would have been offering him your Queen's shilling and not talking to me."

"What if I told you we did, and he turned us down, so we thought you should know?" Bernie stretched out in the back of the cab, smirking. "Anything else for us, or has the cat got your tongue?" Scriven mocked.

"Just one thing we bumped into an army patrol and I threw

two guns out of the window. I think one might have a bit of history if you know what I mean."

"Don't worry Vic we have cleaned up your mess yet again, remember we are here to look after you. Bonner has been meeting his orange friends at the Crawford's Burn Country Park at least once a week. It would be interesting for us to find out why he's colluding with the other side Victor."

Bonner had grown too big for his boots; Victor now imagined what it would take to get a full 'confession' from the traitor. He would suffer, confession or not.

Andy and Bernie got out of the cab and walked back to the approaching cover car.

"Do you think that has whetted his appetite, Bernie?"

"Whet his appetite? We will be picking up pieces of Bonner for weeks after that mad bastard finished with him. Remember, only report what he told us on the contact sheet, no mention of our soon to be departed Mr Bonner." Bernie chuckled as he entered the waiting car.

"He should have taken up our offer to become an agent. I still don't trust that fucker Bernie; he knows full well who Peewee is and his importance. He's playing us, I'm telling you. And who's this Chinese bloke? It makes little sense." Andy lit up a fag as he opened the door of their pickup vehicle.

Bernie turned to his partner in the back "Remember what they told you on the entry course at Ashford, The enemy of my enemy is my friend."

Glosh beach, Co Mayo

It took hours of intense driving, using only back roads to arrive at the Mullet Peninsula. Manny was exhausted. The hours of intense concentration coupled with a monstrous headache was taking its toll. It didn't help that Peewee had not spoken a word throughout the journey. The tension within the vehicle was dense, Manny couldn't decide if Peewee's mood was because of his lateness or another purpose.

The convoy had been driving along desolate country roads for a while when they finally saw the village of Belmullet and the sea beyond. After crossing a small bridge, Peewee pointed out a sharp left-hand turn leading on to the Mullet Peninsula. Although the skies were cloudless, and the sun shone, it was a bitter day as a forceful westerly wind was blowing in, frothing up the white-tipped waves as they slammed into the shoreline.

"Pull over into the car park of the GAA club, tell the boys to have a stretch and a piss while I meet somebody." Peewee was out of the car and striding towards the sand dunes. Down on the beach Peewee saw McSweeny and Fagan deep in conversation with the Boatman.

"Fucking hell, gentlemen, if the Garda arrive how will we explain this lot, eh? Some of the most senior Republicans on the island of Ireland all by chance taking a stroll along a secluded beach together."

"It's not funny, Kelly." McSweeny cut in. "We have the largest ever weapons shipment in IRA history hidden all around us, in a few weeks' time another, even bigger consignment is due to arrive, followed by another twice the size of that. We need a bigger feckin beach, old son."

McSweeny led Peewee down through the elephant grass. On the beach men were busy covering up tracks while JCB diggers were digging in another large grey shipping container.

"Are all the weapons going in that container?" Peewee enquired.

"For your information that is the eleventh container we are hiding. There's also a few six-hundred-gallon oil drums filled with nothing but explosives, not to mention the Belfast weapons that we have moved to another fucking hide." Moaned the exasperated Fagan.

Expertly hidden beneath a concealed entrance was the gateway to Peewee's Aladdin's Cave. Fagan took Peewee to one side "There's about a hundred and fifty tonnes of equipment been brought ashore and let me tell you it took some shifting. Here's a list of what you're getting some of it I appreciate you will not be able to move tonight, but I suggest you put any operation you have in mind on hold and find someplace to store it all. Oh, I've noticed that some heavy weapons don't have mounting brackets so you will need to self-manufacture, if you want to put them on vehicles."

Peewee looked around the walls. There was no space left for another item. "I've got a superb mechanic that will build anything that I want. I've also got a few deep hides, but looking at this container alone I will need a lot more. After talking to that Chinaman, I'm going to put a stop to all our planned attacks. We will need time to move this lot and we're going to need to train everybody with the new weapons. I might get some young volunteers to start grinding up some of those fresh bags of fertiliser you got me Fagan, I'm thinking of throwing a few bunker busters into my attack plan."

"Well, it's all yours, once you get started, we will ask for Belfast to come and collect their gear. Get it moved as soon as you can, as I say I've got more stuff coming in. Before I forget you're going to a meeting with McSweeny, so you had better be off."

Pewee looked down at the handwritten list.

> 1000 Type 56-II 7.62mm Folding Stock assault rifles
> Type 56C Short-barrel rifles
> 200 M16 copy assault rifles
> 150 x Type 64 Suppressed Machine pistol
> 300 x Type 77 pistol
> A million rounds of ammunition;
> 12 x rocket-propelled grenade launchers;
> 12 Type 54 Anti-Aircraft Guns 12.7mm
> 12 x Type 87 35 mm automatic grenade launchers
> 20 x QW-1 Vanguard Surface to Air Missiles
> 20 x HN-5B Red Tasset Surface to Air Missiles
> 10 x HJ-8 Red Arrow wire guided anti-tank missile launchers
> 16 x Thermobaric warhead missiles
> 16 x HEAT missiles
> 6 x Type 87 82mm Mortar
> 2000 electric detonators and 4,700 fuses;
> 106 millimetre cannons;
> 30 x Type 80 GPMG 7.62mm
> 30 x Type 67 GPMG 7.62mm
> 200 x Type 59 grenades
> 150 x Type 67 Suppressed pistol
> Two tonnes of explosive plus detonators
> 70 x Body Armour with Ceramic plates
> Radios

Peewee exited the container with a broad grin. He noticed McSweeny cajoling one of the minions into helping redistribute the weapons.

"Padraig I believe you want to see me."

"Yes, we need to get out of here; we are going to meet to somebody at Campbell's in Westport so let's get a move on. I hope we can trust your driver to put his foot down."

Manny noticed a discernible change in Peewee's attitude when he got back to the car. He was jovial and grinning like the cat that had got the cream. After shouting out a few orders to the big fella Eammon Dore, he leapt into the car and told Manny to follow green VW Jetta. The ninety-minute drive flew by; Peewee was laughing and joking whilst he was doodling on a piece of paper. Occasionally he would stop and cross something out before starting again.

"How many watchtowers have we in South Armagh?" Peewee asked.

The nine overt Salient Towers had dominated the hillsides and border region for nearly ten years. The British Army had become sick of PIRA ambushes and bombs in the fields and narrow country roads. The recent additions of a super tower on Slieve Gullion and a small fortification on Aughanduff Mountains had made concealed movement in the area almost impossible.

Manny thought long and hard. Was it a trick question? "I don't know, too fuckin many I suppose Peewee."

Peewee laughed out loud, "What do you suppose we could do if the watchtowers weren't there?"

"Well, there would still be the helicopters though." Manny pointed out.

"Ha-ha yes the helicopters, well Manny, my friend let me sort those fuckin helicopters out once and for all." Peewee continued scribbling.

Westport

Campbell's was a favourite drop off for tourists visiting the local Great Famine National Monument; they served excellent food and cool beer. As Peewee and Manny entered the bar a Ceilidh band was about the start their first song of the evening.

"Manny here's some cash get yourself something to eat, no booze, if I smell anything on your breath you won't be seeing your Ma ever again, do you understand me?"

Manny looked into Peewee's menacing eyes. The fun and laughter of the car had long gone. Peewee was back on operations now, and to annoy him would be a gross act of stupidity. Manny thought Peewee was 'Cú Chulainn' an unrecognisable monster who knew neither friend nor foe.

Peewee turned and followed Padraig McSweeny to a table where a bald, hefty man was waiting. Harry McFadden had been the leader of Northern Command for five years. Some would say five years too long. McFadden was of a past generation, a sticky14 someone who thought waging war was a waste of time and the only solution was the ballot box.

"Mr Ho told me you want to start a war Peewee."

"No, Harry I want to win a war, and I think I know how to do it, if I get the right backing from the Army Council and the Executive."

"So, come on, what's the glorious plan then I'm all ears?"

Peewee rolled his eyes, he knew he would not get much backing from McFadden, a rusty gun who loved the kudos of sitting at the top table of the Army Council meetings but had never had the bottle to get his own hands dirty. McFadden had just stepped into dead men's shoes; a yes man who said whatever the political masters wanted him to say.

"After looking at the equipment we have received, I'm planning to take back South Armagh by attacking the Brits, I will then form several flying columns and push them back, forcing the Brits to deploy more troops to stop our advance. While they are so busy trying to deal with us Bonner and his

---

14 Stick in the mud

Belfast Boys can take on the prods."

"Are you fuckin mad you eejit?" McFadden erupted. "It's taken years to get to this political situation. The Brits are holding secret talks with the Army Executive; you could ruin everything, you dumb cunt. Those Chinese bastards have even given the Conservative government a substantial donation for party funds. It's all through legitimate companies, but they can then use this dark money to corrupt members of parliament. Get them to ask searching questions about those Unionists' sitting in the house. Get your head outta your arse and look at the big picture."

Peewee gave McFadden a withering look. "I don't take kindly to being labelled a fool especially by a has-been like you Harry. I often wonder who stopped me sending more bombs to the mainland, and who stopped me blowing up that member of the Royal Family, and who stopped me killing the RUC Chief Constable? I think it could only have been you. I think anyone looking closely might think you're a fuckin grass, a tout. Well, are ya's?"

McFadden tried to talk his way out of the situation. The younger man's allegations could lead him to a cruel death on a countryside road.

"I'm no fucking tout, retract that allegation immediately, I'm a close friend to both Gerry and Martin. Padraig put your wee snappy dog on a lead for Christ's sake."

"Shut your fuckin jabber Harry, I'm doing it my way, if I get to hear your opposing me I will send for Secrillo and tell him a few choice stories about your lifestyle, if you know what I mean, and I'm sure you know what I mean."

It scared McFadden; several extra martial affairs, drink, drugs and gambling had left him wide open to recruitment by the British security forces.

"Harry yous can fuck off now as I have proper business to discuss with Mr McSweeny the Chief of Staff here. Yes, your

Officer Commanding the North, but I'm the Operations Officer at Army HQ Padraig here has given me the task of conducting a large-scale attack and that's what I will do, so go fuck yourself."

After wiping the sweat off his balding head, McFadden stood, "You've not heard the last of this, you are a fucking chancer. I will tell the members of the Army Executive about this. The leadership only wants you to threaten the Brits, not stage a full-blown war."

"Yes, I have Harry heard the last of this, as long as you don't tell your Brit tout handler, I don't give a fuck. I'm told your fifteen-year-old daughter's child looks just like you, goodbye you incestuous cunt!"

McFadden stormed out of the bar.

"What the fuck was all that about Kelly?"

"I've been told that the police have been on to him for getting his daughter pregnant, now he's never been arrested, so somebody's protecting him along the line. Now Padraig, what do you want to know."

"Tell me what your actual plans are, and I will get rid of that fuckin fat problem. I will give McElwaine a call."

Enniskillen

It was four am when Brendan O'Malley finally drove the Volvo F727 thousand litre petroleum tanker out of the security gates of Emo Oil on Sligo Road in Enniskillen. A frosty window and poor wiper blades had all colluded to make him late for work. With time pressing, Brendan put his foot down as far as he could to make up the lost time.

As he accelerated along the dark wet Sligo Road, heading towards his first stop on the days schedule, O'Malley was unaware that a dark saloon carrying three balaclava wearing men had pulled out behind him from the car park of the Three Way Inn and was now tailing his vehicle.

To add insult to injury, the road taking him to the filling station on Moybrone Road was closed and a temporary diversion along the Swanlinbar Road in place. Feck thought O'Malley this is all I need.

Just prior to the junction of Oakfield Road the highway ran downhill towards a wooded nearside bend. It was only when the vehicle was on apex did O'Malley realise that he was driving into a vehicle checkpoint. A red torch light indicated that he slowed down. Is this day going to get any feckin worse, he thought as he fumbled in his jacket pocket to find his driving licence.

As the tanker rolled to a halt O'Malley noticed the black balaclavas worn by the men in the road. He immediately thought about his old Ulster Defence Regiment identity card he kept in his wallet as a reminder of his eight years' loyal service in defence of his homeland.

"Git down out of the cab, lay face down in the road." O'Malley was ordered, his mind now awash with potential outcomes of the ongoing event.

"We are taking your fucking truck and you will walk back to the depot to report it stolen. Do you understand me? Do not stop at a house or flag down a car. We will be watching you."

A few seconds later O'Malley heard his vehicle pull away and laughter from the hijackers. He sighed and vowed to burn his old identity card. Dying for a memento was not an option he would ever take again.

South Armagh Overt Tower G01

They had built golf Zero One amongst the grey jagged rocks of the scree fields on top of the imposing Slieve Gullion

Mountain, the highest in in County Armagh. There were many protests at the building because Sliabh gCuillinn, meaning 'mountain of the steep slope'. In Irish mythology they associate the mountain with the Cailleach, the divine hag who creates the weather and the heroes Fionn mac Cumhaill and Cú Chulainn. The mission of the soldiers manning the outpost was not just to observe and report the movements of the largely Nationalist supporting population, but also to guard the gigantic grey and silver rebroadcast masts, each of which had a dazzling array of antennas and microwave dishes.

Each of the mast boosted the radio signals power and eliminated any communication dead spots along the border; it also ensured that high speed covert messages could be transmitted to commanders anywhere within the Province. 15th Signal Regiment operators manned a dark compound in the centre of the camp. Their job was to intercept illegal transmissions and send the resultant product to JCU (NI) HQ in Lisburn for analysis and interpretation prior to dissemination and exploitation.

It was the hub of the British signals intelligence and communications in South Armagh.

"Let me just reiterate gentlemen, our analysts have told us that Decers has been meeting this unknown female on Tuesday and Thursday nights. Why those specific nights we don't know? All we are asking you to do is get Bex close to the caravan and she will do her magic. Any questions?"

Sergeant Brian Morton led the patrol out of the base, ensuring he didn't inadvertently hit any of the trip flares or PAD mine wires. The Projector Area Defence Mine was a smaller version of the infamous Claymore mine, but just as lethal. The PAD mines were woven into the razor wire and trip flares which surrounded the Golf and smaller Romeo towers picketing all the hills on the border.

Being lit up by the flares would be embarrassing, but six

hundred ball bearings flying into your arse was a different level of compromise. Morton stealthily led the team downhill beneath the silhouettes of the large radio masts until he reached the firebreak he had completed a close target recce on the night before.

At the end of the firebreak Morton made the hand signal for an emergency rendezvous. Everyone knelt down and waited in the darkness, scanning their individual arcs of responsibility to locate any movement or things out of the ordinary.

Leaving his second-in-command Dale Hollick in charge, Morton moved slowly forward towards the caravan, with Terry Wilton as his close support and Hamilton the FRU operator close behind. Morton had identified an entry point to get beneath the mobile home the previous evening and had worked out the layout of each room.

The team had only been in position for several minutes when a car hurtled out of the wood line.

"Standby, Standby a black Volkswagen Golf BZG5917 approaching I'm going mute, Dale you commentate?"

"Rodger that, we have a male in dark clothing, wait positive identification of B3 from the driver's door of the Golf carrying what appears to be a bottle. He's into the caravan."

Brian held his breath, unintentionally pushing himself further into the ground, an uncontrollable urge to be further away from the PIRA gunman whose footsteps could be clearly heard on the floor of the caravan above. He looked around at the camouflaged faces beside him, Terry training his SA80 rifle beyond the VW Golf towards the entrance road, and Bex busying herself putting together a small contraption which appeared to be a robust tape recorder attached to a small pole.

Bex reached out and held Brian's face; he looked into her deep green eyes as she mouthed "Bedroom?"

"Not now, it's too dangerous, besides I'm married." He whispered they all tried to hold in the laughter, he knew what Bex wanted and pointed further along the caravan. Slowly they inched along the length, ensuring they didn't make any unnecessary noises which would alert the man above them. Once in the correct area Bex probed at the wooden floor of the bedroom, trying to find a slight gap to get the microphone even closer.

The Lucerne Holiday Chalet had seen better days, the white vinyl coated galvanised steel was greying and in need of a good wash as green mould had formed on the twenty-four foot long frame. Decers had accepted the caravan in return for turning a blind eye to a minor smuggling setup a local farmer had been engaged in running. Jimbo O'Dawe had started an illegal fuel operation just to the south of the border. It was an insignificant business compared to some mega rich fuel barons living in and around South Armagh; the scam was so small that, in Decer's eyes, it wasn't even worth taxing for the cause. Jimbo made a bit of pocket money and in return Jimbo put one of his old caravans into a nice secluded field at the base of Slieve Gullion.

"Stand By, Stand By we have a further vehicle mid colour Range Rover IBM 8473 towards your location Bri, It's a vehicle from A1." Dale stopped his transmission. "It's a female from the car long hair, wearing a long coat, towards your location."

The three beneath the caravan again subconsciously held their breaths until the door of the caravan was closed. Brian looked towards Terry who was shaking his head; his face had a look of amazement. Brian was puzzled so crawled to be at his cover man's side. Terry whispered into his ear, "It's the wife of Bravo One, Eileen Kelly the Bitch." Both men were now grinning from ear to ear.

They had given Eileen the nickname 'The Bitch' because when stopped she acted like a complete loon. On some occasions the bitch would wear a short skirt and a low-cut blouse showing off her long slender legs and ample cleavage, more than a distraction to homesick soldiers, away from wives and girlfriends. She would smile and lick her lips as she handed over her driving licence, then launch into a full-blown tirade at all and sundry. Her foul mouth could make a sailor blush, with the odd allegation that "He's looking at my tits" or "Did you call me a fuckin wee whore? Ye spotty Brit bastard."

To the seasoned veterans it was amusing; yes they were watching her tits bounce up and down as she went her to one of her wild spasms of rage. Her behaviour only made the troops stop her even more, and get her into one of her mental moods, but what pissed them off was that they knew she also was a Brit. In their eyes she had sold out. A fucking traitor.

"I didn't think you were coming, what kept ya?" Decers asked as he opened up the newly bought bottle of Asti Spumante.

"Fuckin Peewee, he's been buzzing since that fuckin halfwit Manny dropped him off early this morning, he said he'd been to the seaside and that the old bastard McSweeny bought him a meal and a few drinks. He didn't want to go to the GAA practice tonight, I practically shoved him outta the fuckin door so I could get ready for yous my love."

Eileen Kelly had always liked Decers Taylor. He was funny and outgoing. The cause to him was like a game of cat and mouse against the authorities. Her husband Peewee however looked upon it as a personal crusade, a religious war. It consumed his every waking hour; nothing in his life came above the armed struggle, not his wife, family or future. When Peewee woke at dawn every morning he went out to wage war.

Decers was always flirting with the ladies, even in front of his despairing wife Bridget. Bridget was the prettiest girl in the class and Decers was the cock of the school in more ways than one. His dick nearly was his undoing at an early age when he got a local volunteer's daughter pregnant. It was only because his friend and ally Peewee got involved did he escape a beating.

Bridget was a stay at home mother, bringing up her children and keeping her house tidy. Decers always had a clean, pressed shirt to wear and a warm meal in his belly, but he couldn't help himself, it was the chase and the conquest, no matter what age, it was another game. 'The best swordsmen in County Louth' he would brag outside the earshot of his brother-in-law Peewee. On occasions he had pinched Eileen's arse or rubbed his cock up against her as she leaned over playing pool.

Eileen and Decers had first got together a year before, after Bridget had given birth to their third child. Because of complications with the child's birth mother and child had been moved from the Special Care Baby Unit at Daisy Hill Hospital up to the Neonatal Unit at the Royal Jubilee Maternity Hospital in Belfast. Being a good Auntie, Eileen had offered to look after the other children. After a day of chasing them round the farm Eileen had taken the kids to their own home, the tidy little semi-detached house in Forest Park. Decers had arrived back from Belfast late and sneaked into the house to find Eileen snoozing on the settee. He woke her by caressing her inner thighs. As she opened her eyes, she stared into the deep blue eyes of Declan 'Decers' Taylor. His unkempt black wavy hair framing his tanned features. Years of farm working lifting heavy machinery had kept him lean and muscular, unlike her husband. She felt warm and willing, so opened her legs. Decers didn't need further invitation soon his thumb was rubbing her clitoris through her jeans and she felt the old stirrings of an orgasm, something she hadn't experienced in several years with Peewee.

"Bed" Decers whispered in her ear, but the lust was too much and they ended up screwing on the stairs.

After a few minutes' rest, Decers led Eileen into the bedroom and started again. Slow, unhurried. He built her up to a climax then stopped, frustrating her, making her demand his cock and his fingers as they probed her intimately. He was an expert lover, warm and tender one minute then forceful and rough the next. She lost count at the number of times she climaxed.

TCG (S) Portadown

It was late in the evening when Big Joe received the phone call he had been waiting all day for; he snatched up the phone.

"Aar hello Joe, it's the Garda Síochána here the line for you."

"Fuck off Daniel, is this official or an unofficial call?" Joe replied;

"Well, my friend if it was official I couldn't tell you that a male with a Hong Kong passport in the name of Sun Yee On checked out of a hotel very close to the border with your country and flew from Dublin to Macau via Amsterdam. Mr Sun Yee On appears to be a frequent flyer according to an airline contact of mine. Perhaps you need to make enquiries with your masters at Box15."

Joe replaced the receiver; he needed to phone the duty Northern Ireland desk officer in Thames House, the headquarters of the Security Service.

"Thames Duty Desk Brad speaking, how can I help?" The voice of Brad Powell boomed down the line, Cornish to the core, a former officer in the Special Forces and veteran of the Northern Ireland campaign.

"Hi Brad, thank fuck it's you and not one of those schoolkids you've recently employed." Joe joked.

"Big fella, it's great to hear from you Joe, my old friend. How are things over your side of the water?"

"Well, not so good I suppose. I need you to do some digging with your friends across the river. I need to find out about a

---

15 MI5

guy calling himself Sun Yee On. I will fax you all I have on him and his travel. I might link him to an old acquaintance of yours, Paul Patrick Kelly."

"Peewee is no friend of mine as you well know fella, luck of the devil he has, had him in our sights a number of times and what did he do to thank us? He mortared the camp we were lying low in, stocky little fucker. Let me have the details and I will call those shits over the river, give them something to do. I'm coming over on a visit in the next few weeks so I will call on you Joseph."

"Make sure you do I will get a few bottles of the old stuff on standby."

Hong Kong

Suzanne Walker Johns arrived fashionably late to meet Lee Yung, a senior detective in the Hong Kong OCTB16 in Caffè Mamma, a trendy eatery a few blocks down Queens Road from Yung's office on the twenty third floor of the police headquarters in Arsenal House West Wing. It was always pleasant to meet up for a chat with Suzanne; she had a delightful smile and always wore clothing which enhanced her voluptuous figure and plunging cleavage, which he endeavoured to keep his gaze from, but never quite achieved.

"Suzanne how are you? How pleasurable it is that you call me. Let me order you a drink."

Suzanne had been working for the MI6 Hong Kong Station for two years. She had found it a refreshing change from her last role posing as a communications officer in Prague in the lead up to the Velvet Revolution. Hoping to entice a member of the Security Information Service to turn her, when in fact she would be cunningly extracting information from them. Prague, although a beautiful city, was hard work, a game of

16 Organised Crime & Triad Bureau

cat and mouse, plus the winters were long and extremely cold. Hong Kong was better, hot balmy nights. Things to do, places to see and plenty of Chinese officials easy to corrupt.

Yung ushered Suzanne to a small table in the corner, out of earshot to the busy customers. "Now how can I be of service to the British Foreign & Commonwealth Office Suzanne?"

Yung was an honorable man; he didn't want to embarrass her by declaring that he knew full well that she was an agent working for the British Secret Intelligence Service; he was a professional, and who knows she might even give him some little snippets of information which would help his own promotion ambitions.

Suzanne took a dainty drink of her latte, her lipstick smudging the cup's rim.

"Thank you for meeting me so quickly, it might be something and nothing, but if I need to get an answer, I know that you're the most reliable person in Hong Kong. Have you ever heard of a man called Sun Yee On? He sometimes calls himself Steve Ho. He has been to the United Kingdom frequently and we would like to know what his interests are."

Yung leaned back in his chair and rubbed a thinning patch on the back of his head "Sun Yee On you say, well that is a name I know well, a blast from the past as you would say, you have certainly come to the right man. Sun Yee On has murdered his way up the chain of command to become a senior member of the Wo Shing Wo the oldest of the Wo Group triad societies in Hong Kong. If my memory serves I believe reading that he is now 438 in the organisation this means he is in charge of all operations."

"438 what is that?"

"My dear lady Triads use numeric codes to distinguish ranks and positions within the organisation; the numbers are inspired by Chinese numerology and based on I Ching17. The

Mountain or Dragon Head is 489, 438 Sun Yee On is now on the verge of becoming the next Deputy Mountain Master.

The Wo Shing Wo are a part of China's black society, they are organisers of the smaller gangs, fixers for a gang to provide one commodity to a willing recipient, for whom the Wo Shing Wo take a healthy commission."

Suzanne thought for a moment. "So what commodity do you think this man would supply to the United Kingdom? What can his organisation get their hands on?"

"Practically anything, drugs would be my first guess, but I would need to ask my colleagues in our 'B' Department which monitors crime and security. In the OCTB we investigate complex and serious triad offences. We pool together resources and expertise from unique sources to tackle sophisticated and syndicated criminal activities. We also liaise with mainland and overseas law enforcement agencies for an exchange of intelligence to prevent and neutralise illegal activities. We have a wide net to collect intelligence, but the Triads are an embryonic organisation, they seek to grow out of their traditional homelands. Recent intelligence has shown links to the USA, Canada and the United Kingdom. They might encounter opposition from indigenous gangs in which they would endeavour to use another native syndicate to fight on their behalf."

"So it would be your belief then that Sun Yee On would organise drugs dealing on let us say a major scale to the United Kingdom?" Suzanne baited him.

"No not necessarily, as I say the triads can get their hands on practically anything. All people have a weakness, and triads' exploit that weakness so illegal shipments of tobacco, counterfeit goods even people could be being established. If there is a market, they will find the goods to trade or even create a market which was not there before."

---

17 An ancient Chinese divination text

Suzanne thought long and hard, "This next question is completely left field, what about Ireland?"

Yeung looked puzzled, "Are you talking about the murder of Liu Zhau and his girlfriend Yu Yan Wu?"

"I don't know, am I?" His immediate response surprised Suzanne.

"Zhau and Yu Yan Wu left Hong Kong about two years ago. Zhau was a 49, an ordinary member of Wo Shing Wo. I had to do some background work for your embassy after someone murdered them in Belfast. Now you mention it, they would look the murder of Zhau as a case of gross dishonour. I was not given the full circumstances of the attack just to get some history on the two victims."

"Do you think Sun Yee On would treat this matter as a case of disrespect towards him and his organisation?"

"Yes, of course, Sun Yee On is a very violent and dangerous individual. He is ambitious and calculating, somebody murdering his workers would be seen as contemptuous by his master, Lee Yip Wong the Dragon Head of the Wo Shing Wo. Sun Yee On stabbed a man thirty-five times and cut off his nose in revenge for a murder. He has never been back to Hong Kong since to my knowledge, I believe he works from Macau to stay out of our reach, but he does travel to Europe under the other name you gave me, Steve Ho and a hundred other false passport names."

The coffee cups were refilled, Yung looked at Suzanne, she was middle-aged, and a very attractive woman. He understood why the Secret Intelligence Service had recruited her. She made men feel at ease in her company; they wanted to talk to her, befriend her and eventually tell her their darkest secrets.

"Look Suzanne, I know of another strand of intelligence, I cannot say if we associate it to Sun Yee On, but a small gang in the Chinese province of Guangdong has been making a tidy profit from exporting arms to North America. If, and it is a big if, the Wo Shing Wo wanted to supply weapons it is a possibility they might use this gang and become the conduit for the end user. Maybe they are preparing to supply some pistols and rifles for criminals in Ireland. Hey it's a long shot, but Chinese nationals working in Ireland, come on they would stand out to the dumbest of flat foot I'm sure. I will send you a copy of Sun Yee On's file tomorrow."

"Mr Yung you have been a most charming man, now let me repay you by taking you for dinner in one of the best restaurants over in Kowloon, remember if I'm not in bed by ten you had better put me in a taxi home." Yeung gave a mischievous smile as he led Suzanne out of the coffee shop into the bustling streets of Hong Kong Island.

West Belfast

Vic looked down at the fuel gage of his cab. One more run along the Falls Road and he would fill up and call it a night. Takings had again been average, but it diverted the eye from his volunteer money plus the cash in hand from his handlers. It was by the New Felons club that the messenger got in, Vic had seen him a number of times before, young kid late teens did a lot of dicking and running around for the Andersonstown boys. After dropping off an old woman on Kennedy Way, they were free to talk. "I have a message about sorting out a fishing trip."

Vic nodded "That's fine son, here's your change." Vic reached back and handed the young man a fiver. "Now forget that message, do you understand?"

It took over an hour to find a call box which hadn't been vandalised or one he suspected of not being bugged.

"Hello, I'm after booking a fishing trip, when would the next package be available?"

The man's the voice on the other end of the line was dark and forbearing "No problems Sir, £500 quick fishing trip for one. The tackle is already down here in Dundalk waiting for you. See you tomorrow at seven."

So somebody was going to get whacked and five hundred quid was going to be in Vic's back pocket. Vic looked down at the fuel gage of his cab.

It took over an hour to find a call box which hadn't been vandalised or one he suspected of not being bugged.

So somebody was going to get whacked and five hundred quid would be in Vic's back pocket.

South Armagh

The three soldiers were cold and stiff when they finally crawled from beneath the caravan. They had waited an hour after Decers had finally cleaned up and driven off back home to his wife in Forest Park. Over the radio they heard from the OP watching Alpha One that the bitch had arrived back home. After reuniting with the over watch team, they slowly retraced their footsteps back up to the safety of the super sanger on top of Slieve Gullion.

"Well, what did you get Bex?" Grimshaw was eager for a result.

"I think they were holding an evangelical service because the amount of times she screamed Jesus and Oh God! He must have been blessing her." Brian exclaimed. "I even took some covert photos of the condoms he threw in the bin afterwards."

"So Decers is shagging his brother-in-law's wife, who happens to be his PIRA commander, oh this is fucking priceless. Listen, I warn you now this is very sensitive, in fact this job never happened you didn't leave camp tonight. I want that film and any notes you may have taken. This is a FRU only job, it's protecting yourself from any future repercussion, do you understand me guys?"

The COP lads had heard it all before, they called FRU operators Special Forces wannabes. They didn't enjoy spending the days and weeks out on the ground, but they would be in the bar tonight bragging on how they had been toe to toe with the enemy. Dirty war my arse, they thought, as they handed over their notes for destruction.

"So what next Gary, shall we bump him right away?"

Grimshaw the more experienced of the two operators thought long and hard about Rebecca's question.

"No, we don't have enough yet. When we get back to the office, I will give the technical people at NISS a call. We will need to get the love caravan fully wired for sound and vision. We need to make a little homemade porno movie to show Mr Taylor, and then we will have his bollocks in a vice."

Eileen was in bed when Peewee returned from football practice, he had been coaching the under 15's for a few years and they were developing well, perhaps an All-Ireland champion or two in his squad he dreamed. Eileen had left a message she'd a headache and his dinner was in the fucking dog, so he buttered some toast then thought about his future strategy to beat the Brits.

The Active Service Units around him were decent enough, but not up to the standard of his Jonesborough team. They trained hard around Carlingford Hill, a brief drive away, practicing patrolling and rudimentary tactics. Peewee had been given a stolen British Army Manual: Infantry Platoon Tactics. He had studied the document intently, so he had a good working knowledge of how his enemy would react. He was fascinated with the concept of firing weapons whilst manoeuvring his volunteers to better attacking positions, but could he teach the members of his unit to become proficient at these skills he pondered?

He would now need to make all the other units in South Armagh an image of his own. The first problem was finding an area big enough to train; he also wanted to practice shooting the unfamiliar weapons which would have been impossible to do at Carlingford Hill, without attracting the unwelcomed eye of Garda Jacobs the meddlesome old bastard. He would turn a blind eye to late night drinking, making illegal Poteen and smuggling cattle, but a bit of training in the hills and he was on the radio to his local Inspector. Peewee had thought about paying him a night time visit, but the people well respected the old fella. No, they needed another training ground; hopefully McSweeny would come up with a solution to the problem.

CHAPTER FIVE

Thursday 3rd March 1994

Alpha One

The next morning Eileen Kelly lay in the bath trying to ease her aching pussy, her dirty knickers still covered in Decers juices hidden at the bottom of the washing basket.

"What did you get up to last night?" Peewee asked as he burst into the bathroom to have a piss.

Eileen didn't bother to close her legs, Peewee wouldn't notice her swollen pussy if she put Christmas lights on it.

"Wee Martha's baby was sick, so I had a wee drink with her. Had a bit of a crac, you know." She lied, she always lied, her life was a lie. Eileen Kelly was not from Wythenshawe that was a lie even the name Eileen Kelly was a lie, her real name was Josephine Bridges from Wilmslow her only visit to Wythenshawe was a two-week stay to create her 'legend' a way of knowing the area, its people and eccentricities. Her family that came to her wedding were all undercover members of Greater Manchester Police Special Branch; one had even started a fight with an usher he was so convincing. The trips back to Manchester to visit sick relatives and the weekly phone calls to her sister were all lies, coded messages to her handlers on the mainland informing on Peewee and his activities.

It was a long way from her days at Churchill College Cambridge and her degree in Psychological and Behavioural Sciences. It was at Cambridge where she had been recruited by the Foreign and Commonwealth Office as a junior staff member at the head office on King Charles Street, London.

Within a year she was undertaking the MI6 entrance test at a discreet country manor on the Norfolk Broads. Josephine was now on a deep infiltration mission, married to a leading member of the IRA's General Army Headquarters. His role was the Operations Officer for Northern Command, which meant he was the most active and dangerous terrorist in the province. She had reported on his distrust of the political leadership within the Army Executive and his visits to meetings in the south. Some of her intelligence was so good that MI6 had bugged the meetings and picked up strategic information about the direction which the Provisional Irish Republican Army was intending to take. It had taken six months of research and training before she contacted her target, Paul Patrick Kelly. It was no chance meeting behind Vincent's Corner Pub in Benidorm; she also had to endure the mocking of her back-up team who had witnessed her clumsy attempt at felatio.

"I really must put you on attachment to some Soho sweat shop for a month Jo, they will really teach you how to use that pretty little mouth of yours." Exclaimed her team leader and principle case co-ordinator Samantha Arnold a veteran MI6 officer.

In the seventeen years they had been together Jo or as she now was Eileen had seen Peewee's meteoric rise through the ranks. It was her information that had stopped plots to bomb the UK mainland, attacks against members of the Royal Family and the creation of a 'Barrack Buster' mortar bomb that would have killed many soldiers sleeping in their unprotected Portacabins.

In the last few years, Peewee had become less talkative about his activities. Their lovemaking; if you could call it that was less frequent and over too quickly. Her husband was becoming more distant and seldom spoke about his 'work.' Decers was a different story; he now opened up new avenues of conversation. Decers was certainly not afraid of telling a tale or two, even if he rarely let the truth stand in the way of a splendid story.

Her handlers had thought long and hard about letting her embark on an affair which could lead to their agent being murdered. She was deep undercover with no back up apart from her training. If they compromised her, she faced a slow, violent death, with no prospect of rescue.

Dundalk

Victor Secrillo had left the hustle and bustle of Belfast at mid-day; he could see the smog hanging over the city in the rear-view mirror of the VW Golf as he climbed the Castlereagh Road to the east of the city. A shiver had run down his spine as he reached the junction with Ladas Drive, a road which lead to the Castlereagh police station, the infamous RUC interrogation centre. Seven long days and nights he had been held.

"Just sit on your hands and tell them nothing, they don't have any evidence against you." His army handlers had told him prior to his arrest.

Fuck, he should have run. What did they know about mental torture the bastards? It was a long route to get to his meeting, but the less chance of a roadblock on the way. After a quick cuppa in the seaside town of Newcastle, beneath the splendour of the Mourne Mountains it was off again following the coast through the fishing town of Kilkeel. It was an area that Vic knew well, summers spent with his father Antonio and his mistress at the South Point caravan park. Even in the height of summer the sea was fucking Baltic, but it gave him time to spend with his old Da.

He tried not to think about his father too often; he had always been a busy man, eventually finding his niche as a black taxi driver, a job he loved, but eventually led to his untimely death. It was late one November night; the pubs had been kicking out drunks when Antonio picked up the wrong fare. Two loyalists dragged him from his cab, and drove him away to a cellar or a 'romper room' as his abductors called it, where he was systematically beaten, tortured and burned. Antonio's body was found a few days later beside his burnt out taxi. A crude cardboard sign hung around his slashed neck with just one word 'TAIG' 18.

After turning South away from Newry Secrillo edged on to the Dublin Road before immediately turning off on to the narrow Omeath Road which hand railed the black waters of the Newry Canal. The Brits often patrolled the Fathom Line as it was locally known, but at least it avoided the vehicle check point at Cloughoge. A stop by the Brits could mean a lengthy delay and some explaining to his handlers Pinkie and Perky why he was back down in South Armagh.

It was early evening when Vic parked the car by Oriel Park football ground. He liked the car, its German engineering and reliability. He promised himself he would get some chocolates for Mrs Finnegan as well as the full tank of fuel when he returned it back to her after his 'fishing trip.'

Waiting around unnerved Secrillo, a time when his mind went idle and drifted into areas he didn't want it to go. Why was he being kept waiting? Was he being watched? Was he being led into a trap? Was his cover blown? It would take more than sitting on his hands for seven days to save his skin if the boys interrogated him, and he should know as he was the expert at beating a confession from a person be it man, women or child.

He hated his visits to Dundalk or 'El Paso' as it had been dubbed by the locals due to the amount of Gringos that had descended on the ancient town from over the border.

He saw the two youths approach in his rear-view mirror, with no pistol to protect himself he felt naked, he just had to trust McSweeny now and hope he wasn't the next for a head job.

He rolled down his window. "Victor?" the tallest youth enquired.

---

18 Offensive term used in reference to a catholic in Northern Ireland.

"I could be who wants to know?"

The young man hesitated, trying to remember his lines. "Erm if you want the tickets for fishing I'll take you. Leave your car here."

Dundalk's Lisdoo Arms was unusually busy for a Tuesday evening. There appeared to be a large gathering of men in the front bar. Vic ducked into the snug at the rear.

"A pint of Tennent's." He ordered.

The stern looking barman eyed him up and down. 'Slim' Tim Flynn had been a barman in Dundalk since his teens. He had seen his beloved town develop into a frontier settlement to hide northerners on the run from the law across the border. The northerners were brigands in his eyes. They brought trouble and unwanted attention from the Garda.

The Gringos would fight with the locals and with themselves. Several had been severely injured after being administered a punishment beating for sleeping with the wives and girlfriends of their imprisoned comrades.

There was nothing he could say against these thugs. They put lots of money over his bar, but the locals hated them. Beatings had been dished out to any local who spoke against their occupation of the town. Most of them had been given free housing on the Muirhevnamor Estate, which was slowly turning to Little Belfast.

"What's going on in the front room, big fella?" Vic asked.

"Something you had better not ask about and it's Harp or feck all, we don't serve Tennent's Scottish piss water. You might have missed the fact that you're in the Free State now, and this is the feckin home of the Harp brewery." Slim hissed.

"You're a real friendly fat cunt so yous are BIFFO[19]." Vic

19 BIFFO - big, ignorant fucker from Offaly.

spat back.

"I'll get that Vic, oh and a couple of Jameson's Slim bring them over to the corner." A voice ordered from behind Secrillo.

Vic spun around to see Padraig McSweeny, who was smiling like a Cheshire cat.

"Glad you could get down here so fast Vic, we have a slight problem we need you to solve for us tonight."

The raucous laughter and shouting was still coming from the main bar.

"Has somebody been married today or is it a wake?" Victor asked disturbed by the noise.

"No, it's our boys, but they will celebrate a wake soon, once you do your stuff. We are holding a recruitment drive in the front room. South Armagh need some men at arms for a colossal job and we thought we would use the 'On the run boys.' To be brutally honest, they are causing a fuckin menace, doing fuck all apart from drink, steal and fight so we've asked them to fight. They have no choice really, if they don't we'll stop their fuckin handouts and send them back to face the music in the North. They have been joined by sixty volunteers from the Dublin area so they are getting acquainted with each other."

Glasses were placed on the table. "Thanks Slim, would you do me a favour and shout the big ginger fella over, tell him we're ready for him." McSweeny politely asked.

"Yes, Mr McSweeny." Slim diligently shuffled off, sweating due to his twenty stone bulk.

"What's the script with the fat boy?" Vic asked.

"He's a sympathetic man, he doesn't ask questions, and he keeps what he sees and hears to himself. Any trouble in here with the northern boys and he keeps it in the house. I knew his father well, a good Republican back in the day. Sadly passed on, I'm afraid."

Secrillo was looking through the bottom of his whiskey glass when the tall ginger man arrived at their secluded booth. It took a few seconds to register the face of the wild-haired, fiery eyed man stood in front of him, and his heart skipped a beat.

"How's my Belfast Secrillo?" boomed Sean McLarty, no handshake or gesture of friendship was offered.

"Sean how good to see you again, I didn't err!" Vic stuttered.

McSweeny cut in "Victor I didn't know you knew the head of Northern Command, but I take it your paths have crossed back in Belfast."

"The head of Northern Command, what about Harry McFadden?" Vic stuttered.

"You will retire him tonight, give him the good news." McSweeny coldly told him.

"Make a fuckin expert job of it." It was another voice, a southern accent. He didn't recognise the voice, but certainly did the man Paul Patrick Kelly had walked into the snug behind McLarty.

"I want yous to shoot him in the fuckin face, no open coffin for that bastard, the fuckin grass. I've been also been reliably told that he had you carried out orders to murder my wee cousin Thomas O'Bray Victor. I will have a word with you about that order and who issued it when I get back to Belfast," McLarty menacingly told him.

Secrillo was lost for words McLarty of all fucking people, Mad McLarty the man who wanted to place a dozen car bombs on the Shankill and not give any warning.

"In fact shoot the bastard in the back of the head and blow his fuckin eyes out, do you hear me Secrillo, don't tape his face up that's an order right from the very top." McLarty continued.

"Erm do you want me to interrogate him as per the green book. Do you need a confession for the Adjutant General?" Secrillo asked.

"No, we want him dead, just shoot the cunt. Trust me, we have run this situation by James McElwaine and as Adjutant he has fully sanctioned this course of action. There will be a news bulletin tomorrow that the Provisional Irish Army executed a known paedophile who had raped one of his family members. We're not going to let the Brits know that we outed him as a tout, let them fuckin stew for a while." Peewee declared.

"But if he is a tout as you say, I can find out what damage he's done to the organisation." Secrillo explained.

"Are you listening to us? Just shoot the bastard."

McSweeny rose to his feet, "Gentlemen, I have made arrangements with my team to take Victor for his meeting with the soon to be deceased Mr McFadden. If you two would like to re-join our new volunteers, I will go over the finer details with our chief executioner." McLarty and Peewee walked towards the door, then hesitated.

"Don't fuck it up or we will be looking for a new head of the nutting squad. I will come to see you real soon Secrillo I want to know why my cousin was murdered." McLarty taunted Victor.

Victor was trying his best to hide his utter terror. Nobody had even whispered that Mad McLarty was due to be released from Portlaoise Prison, a maximum security prison built for the most dangerous in Irish society. The last time Secrillo had heard any mention of McLarty he was the commander of E Block, the Republican wing.

"Some of my boys will take you to McFadden place; he lives

in a caravan on his own behind his family's bungalow out on the New Road in Bellurgan. They will give you one of our new silenced pistols, its brand new still with grease on it so you might want to give it a clean first. Ciaran will take you to some woods so you can have a test fire before you blow his brains out." McSweeny told Victor.

The party next door had just started coming to scuffles and blows as Secrillo reached the door of the snug to meet his guide Ciaran. As he stopped to light up a cigarette as the rabble stopped fighting and broke out into singing 'The Crossmaglen Sniper.' The door to the main lounge opened and a tall slim boyish man exited followed by Peewee. The men stared at each other for a moment before Peewee made a pistol sign with his hand pointing towards Secrillo, he gestured the gun firing then blowing away the imaginary gun smoke, then followed the tall slim man towards a waiting maroon BMW.

Secrillo took the journey time out to the wood to compose himself and get into character. A large envelope by his side contained a Chinese Type 64 silenced pistol and a magazine with nine 7.65 mm rounds. He took out the weapon and checked it over, the brown Bakelite grip felt good in his hand; he felt in control again.

The last hour had been a nightmare, the appearance of Sean McLarty was the icing on the cake, how the fuck did he get released out of gaol without his knowing, he was bound to ask questions about Thomas O'Bray's execution. He was hatching a plan to drop all the blame on to Harry McFadden, Harry had been a good friend over the years and helped him rise through the ranks, but this was now life or death so McFadden would get the chop and take all of his secrets to the grave with him. How was he going to explain that a punishment beating carried out on the order of Bonner had gone badly wrong on his watch?

No way was McFadden a tout for the British, although the Adjutant General had long suspected there was an informant in the upper echelons of the movement, and even spoken to Victor at length about possible suspects, but nothing was substantial. The O'Bray killing was a different matter though. The rumour he'd heard was that the kid was in the wrong place at the wrong time, seeing a chance meeting of Bonner and his dealers parked up in a back street.

South Armagh

Peewee was in a jovial mood. On the way down he had been quiet, and deep in thought, but now he was alive, his brain racing.

"Manny I have a few errands I need you to do as quickly as possible." He asked.

Holmes looked across at his boss and nodded in acceptance.

"I need a lot of vehicles, if you steal them we will need false plates and have them repainted, do you understand? Talk to Pat Kehoe and find out how they made that big flame thrower they used to attack the Brit tower in Cross."

"Of course Peewee just give me a list."

"The boys in Cross have just stolen a petrol tanker. Tell Pat that I want to use it and if possible I need more, many more."

"McSweeny has come up trumps and got us a sizeable training area over in Drumreagh in County Leitrim. It's on the eastern banks of Lough Allen; we will then do some shooting at an old disused quarry on Corry Mountain in Bog County west of the Lough. We will be there for about a week so there will be no visiting your Ma in the hospital. I will write you down a list then give you a month to get the vehicles to Danny O'Hare's farm in Tullydonnel so the mechanic can start work on them."

Dundalk

Secrillo was happy with the pistol, the faint click of
the hammer hitting the firing pin before a 'Phat' of gas was
the only noise. It was close to midnight when he made his
approach to the caravan at the rear of the bungalow. The
flicker of a television was illuminating the inside, so he
chanced a peek. Harry was sitting alone, staring at the TV
screen. The knock on the door made him jump.

"Is that you Maureen?"

"No, it's fuckin not Harry, it's Vic. Let me in its blowing a
gale out here."

"What the fuck are yous doing here?"

As his eyes became accustomed to the light, Vic noticed
Harry's strange looking T-shirt.

"What the fuck is that thing you're wearing Harry?"

"It's a bulletproof vest with ceramic plates; I lifted off the
beach the other week when I watched the shipment being
unloaded. I heard that Mad McLarty was out and about, so I
thought I would be better off wearing it. Him and that
chancer Kelly fuckin hate me you know, I'm going off to see
the boys in the Executive in the morning and tell them he
will really fuck up the secret talks we're having with Major
and his government. The fuckin Army Headquarters are out
of control and need to be brought back in line immediately.
We need an extraordinary General Army Convention so we
can dismiss the lunatics in the HQ"

Secrillo was puzzled "What fuckin shipment and what talks
are these you're on about."

"Look our political masters are on the verge of a
breakthrough with the British Government, a political
solution to end the struggle. Last year they reached a secret
agreement at Downing Street. People at the top of the

organisation think the Brits are dragging their heels so we have been given a load of new weapons by a friendly benefactor. It could give us the muscle to force the Brits to agree to end this fucking war, once and for all. If they know we have re-armed, they will have to give us the concessions we require. Even the Taoiseach Albert Reynolds is involved Gerry and Martin thinks this will be a breakthrough as long as we don't start a fuckin war."

"So where did this weapons shipment get landed, Harry?" Secrillo asked.

"Oh, over on the west coast, loads of stuff, more than that fuckin Libyan clown ever sent us and more to come." McFadden hesitated

"I've probably said too much so don't go blabbing to anyone else, you understand. Anyway, what the fuck have you come to see me about Vic?"

"I'm sorry Harry it's only business; from orders by the Council I am here to relieve you of your position." Vic had drawn the pistol and was holding it in both hands.

"No, I've done nothing wrong, I can pay you, I will disappear, Victor please I'm begging you, we are friends, I know about your!"

Secrillo interrupted him "By order of the Army Council Chief of Staff Padraig McSweeny and the new head of Northern Command Sean McLarty I have been ordered to execute you in line with the rules of the Green Book that you Harry McFadden have been working as an agent for the crown forces."

"I demand re-trial with James McElwaine, the Adjutant General himself. What the fuck is Sean McLarty got to do with this? I beg you Vic for the people; our people please stop this madness before!"

'Phat!' the 7.62mm bullet smashed through the thumb of

McFadden's outstretched hand which was desperately trying to cover his face, at over a thousand feet per second the bullet severed the digit and hit him just below the nose, killing him instantly. Secrillo walked over to the motionless body and carefully removed the body armour, trying his best not to get any further blood on to the item. Secrillo then rolled McFadden's body over and pumped two more bullets into the back of his head, completely rupturing the cranium, causing a perforating wound and blowing out one of his victim's eyes in the process. After carefully retrieving the fired brass shells, he wiped down any surface he had touched and calmly exited the caravan carrying the body armour.

CHAPTER SIX

Sunday 20th March 1994

Newry

Emanuel Holmes had been busy all day, with most of the vehicles on Peewee's shopping list now hidden in and around Danny O'Hare's farm in Tullydonnel. His ear had been on the news all day, listening to the latest reports about the five mortar bombs falling on Heathrow Airport. He wondered if the attack had anything to do with the impromptu training camp which he had taken Peewee to in the Rossmore Colliery, situated in an isolated area six miles from Carlow Town. He remembered watching Peewee in discussion with two men from the Free State and Pat Kehoe, the head of Crossmaglen, whilst the mechanic Danny O'Hare was showing another man a red Nissan Micra and how to modify it. He smiled; at least that lengthy drive down to Carlow now appeared to be worth it.

It was soon time to visit his mother at the hospital, then get a few pints down his throat. The car park of the Daisy Hill Hospital was dark and gloomy; he had lost the green Vauxhall Astra that he thought had been following him since he drove through Camlough. He sat and waited, contemplating whether to have another fag before entering the ward. Just as Manny was reaching into his pocket he realised men were approaching his vehicle. The front passenger door and the rear driver's side door were snatched open and two men jumped in.

Manny immediately thought Peewee had sent some Newry boys to kill him, attend to yet another loose end. This was confirmed when he looked at the lap of the sizeable man now sat next to him as he saw he was holding a Browning pistol.

"I'm sorry; please tell Peewee I'm sorry for whatever he thinks I've done." Manny was sobbing, awaiting the shot to send him to his maker.

"Why would your boss want to kill you fella?" asked the man with a Geordie accent.

It bewildered Manny who were these men that had invaded his car.

"Listen, Manny, we have an offer which might be beneficial for you, your old mum and us. What do you think?" a Cockney voice behind him asked.

Manny realised that these were soldiers, and he was in big trouble.

"You're in trouble with the law, drinking and driving so the cops will take away your licence, no more visits to Mum and no money off Peewee so you're fucked." The cockney voice from behind taunted him.

"I'm no fuckin tout, I wouldn't be seeing my Ma if I was dead so fuck the pair of yous." Manny spit back.

"Look bonny lad we can make it all go away, police charges disappear, get the best treatment for your Mam. We could even get you some cash in hand. How does that sound?" asked Sergeant Steve Morrow, an experienced old FRU operator.

"No, I can't, Peewee would fuckin kill me." Manny cried.

"He will never know we just want you to visit your mum and leave us with the keys to your car for half an hour. If you have anything to tell us just speak up loud in your car and by magic, we will hear it. No police stations, or us visiting you. If what you tell us is good, we will leave cash in your Mam's bedside locker. Think about it, that woman in there is dying and you could save her, we could help her, but only if you help us. The cops will lock you up any day now and our deal will be off, and your Mam will be brown bread, fucking dead old son."

Manny couldn't control his emotions, weeks of driving Peewee around the country, threats to his life, stealing vehicles; it was all building up and then watching his mother turn yellow as her alcoholism destroyed her liver slowly sending her to an agonising death.

"She might need a new liver." Manny muttered.

"Yes, we know that; we might be able to get her to the top of a donor list." The cockney teased.

Manny rubbed his eyes "Look after my Ma you'll promise."

"Nee bother bonny lad, trust us. Now to start the ball rolling is there anything you want to tell us?"

Manny thumbed the steering wheel. They fucked him. "I took Peewee over to the West coast the other day. We took all the boys over so they could collect a load of guns that had been dropped off. I don't know whereabouts as Peewee directed me and I never saw or touched any guns because I had to take the Boss to Westport."

"Good lad, the first one is always the hardest. Here's fifty quid to help ease your soul, it will get easier in the coming months, don't go flashing the cash Bonny Lad."

Manny returned after thirty minutes at his mother's bedside. He held her hand and stroked her grey hair. She was his only family in the world. His father was long gone and his older brother Michael dead, blown to pieces when trying to mix homemade explosives for Peewee.

He looked around the car to find if any wires were showing or a strange extra item fitted beneath the seats. Nothing, the ashtray was still full, the radio on the same channel and sheep shit still on the car mats beneath his feet. What Manny didn't see was a Telplate recorder inserted into the steering column and tiny microphones covertly secreted throughout the vehicle. Two small black bleep boxes were also hidden under the car. These devices would enable all conversations recorded within the vehicle to be communicated as a burst transmission every time the car passed the two receiver stations hidden in the hedges either side of Manny's driveway or over flown by a Bat Flight helicopter. The car was now a mobile telephone booth, all Manny needed to do was talk and it would be chronicled.

Castleblayney

The grey pebble dashed walls of the non-descript house in Oliver Plunkett Park, Castleblayney had been vacated for the afternoon, the owners departing on a trip to Monaghan for the day, with a wad of cash given to them by Padraig McSweeny as they handed over their house keys. After a quick sweep of the house, McSweeny walked over to his waiting driver, Marie O'Hanlon. She was perfect cover for the operation. Marie had been associated to the movement since her teens joining the Cumann Na mBan20 first acting as a lookout and then later as a courier of weapons and messages. The fire of the republican movement was in her very soul, indoctrinated by her grandfather who was imprisoned after the Easter Uprising in 1916 then by her father who had been brutally beaten by a gang of Ulster Special Constabulary, commonly known as the B Specials whilst taking part in the civil rights movement march on Duke Street in Derry. Only four hundred marchers had turned up for the rally with a few hundred others just watching on as the procession tried to the protest about the unionist-controlled Londonderry Corporation, and its housing policy. The Northern Ireland government had banned the gathering the night before and a sizeable group of RUC and B Specials tasked to stop the proceedings.

The event went ahead, in defiance. Cheered on by a counter demonstration of Unionists, the police attacked the crowd with batons and then turned the water cannon on the

---

20 The Women's Council

marchers who were hemmed up between the River Foyle and the Waterside estate. Marie's father was left with severe head injuries and slurred speech for his remaining days.

"Right Marie, pick McLarty up from Sean's Bar, The Bird will be on the car park of the Coach Inn and Peewee will be at the Glencarn. Tell them to come on their own, no fuckin hangers on. Pick them up individually and then drop them off at the track I showed you on McGrath Road. Point them towards the estate and tell them to knock on number seven." McSweeny was taking no chances; his group of personnel henchmen had been watching the attendees of the meeting for thirty minutes to ensure there was no interference from the Garda SSU 21 or their 'Ghost Team 22 which conducted 'Black bag operations' from their headquarters in Phoenix Park.

It took over an hour to get all the participants together in the compact kitchen at the rear of the property.

McSweeny called them all to order. "Gentlemen, thanks for coming down. We have now had the first shipment and what a fucking consignment that was. Hopefully, you will now have most of the equipment within your own bunkers. A further delivery is imminent, so I wanted to get you all together to see how planning going for our repayment to our patrons. I can also tell you we have the sixty volunteers from Dublin ready to help Peewee's operation and thirty others that are hiding out in the County Donegal they will meet with the Derry boys at the White House in Buncranna then support you in Belfast Aiden."

All eyes turned to Peewee. Everybody knew his credentials were impeccable and the only one in the room that had constantly been at war with the Brits.

"Thanks Padraig I will get those guys to work right away. If any have bomb making experience, I will start them off

---

21 Special Surveillance Unit
22 Technical Surveillance Unit

grinding the ammonium nitrate and mixing the nitrobenzene to get the big bangs ready. I will need more coffee grinders so none of us will be visiting any coffee shops in the south for a while. I call the plan a Denial of Senses Strategy, to draw the Brits down to our killing grounds in South Armagh I need to be able to manoeuvre, and to do that I need to destroy their eyes, the watchtowers, their ears the listening posts and their mouth by blowing up all the radio towers. Before I can do any of that I need to stop those fuckin helicopters, so I'm forming flying columns like back in the historic days of the IRA in the twenties."

McLarty scoffed, "You're doing something from back when to beat the Brits?"

"No, Sean from a lot further back than the twenties. When I met Ho, he spoke about some guy called Sun Tzu, it turned out he wrote a book called Art of War and it details the type of revolutionary strategy which we will need to pull this off."

McSweeny looked around the now silent table. "Go on Peewee, carry on."

Peewee cleared his throat and continued. "I'm about to train the South Armagh flying columns. Over the last few weeks we have been gathering a fleet of pickup trucks, flat bed lorries and four by fours. We have modified these to fit a complete range of weapons from heavy machine guns to rocket and grenade launchers. We also have an armoured tractor which can pull a sprayer slurry tanker which we have turned into a huge flame thrower, that's sixteen hundred gallons of fire to scare them shitless. I've also got my engineers in Cross to build more barrack buster mortars to send gas cylinders filled with ninety pounds of homemade explosives over their walls."

"Fuckin Mad Max or what." McLarty butted in.

Peewee glared at his interrupter, "We will begin with a simultaneous operation on the helicopter base at Bessbrook by the Crossmaglen boys, at the same time some of my unit will attack Tievecrum Tower above Forkhill and moments later I will take the rest of my column to drive them out of their barracks in the village. The other groups from Cullyhanna and southern command will attack the towers at Glassdrumman, Drummakaval and Concession Road. With no eyes or ears we can push up through the Ring of Gullion through the Moyry Pass in the east and the Dorsey Enclosure between Belleeks & Cullyhanna in the west leaving the Brits at Crossmaglen Isolated. I have my boys sat out day and night watching the towers to give us an idea of just how many men are in each location and what observation and radio equipment is on each site. The bigger places we mortar the smaller ones we destroy completely then use the high ground as a lookout to spot and shoot the helicopters out of the sky."

"You're going to attack a company of Brits at the Forkhill Barracks? How many men are you going to get killed?" asked the beaming McLarty.

"Yes, I will attack B Company Royal Anglians, but it won't be a full company, as they provide soldiers for the towers, plus they won't be getting any reinforcements once we attack, because Bessbrook will be on fire by then. When have you ever cared about casualties Sean?"

McLarty sat back in his chair like a child who had been admonished by a teacher.

"So what can we expect after that?" asked McSweeny.

"Well, my first answer would be fuck knows, because it's never been done before. That said, in December 1989 I was directed by the then Chief of Staff to conduct an operation against a small fortified barracks in Derryard, North of Rosslea. We killed two Scottish soldiers, but before we could overrun their fort, another patrol outflanked us and we had to withdraw, but Derryard was tiny compared to Forkhill Barracks."

The assembled crowd looked at Peewee in admiration. So

this was the guy who pulled off the audacious attack in County Fermanagh.

"The Brits would need to relieve their soldiers in Crossmaglen; I don't know how long they could last in there or if we could starve them out like a big medieval siege, but their camp appears to be a real fortress, so apart from a few barrack busters over the walls I'm intend to leave them stewing there. I think firing three of those big bastards every day over their walls will get them screaming for help. They will try to bring troops and peelers in by helicopter probably over the Newry canal, that's why my second attack will be on the Fathom Line patrol base. That one is tough, but not impossible. We need that high ground to stop anything flying in from the east. Then of course there is the SAS who might try to sneak in using unmarked cars so we will blockade all the roads South of Newry. I would think within a week most of the British Army will be in Armagh getting ready to take back the South. Will that give you the time you need Birdy?"

"Fuck me Peewee, I don't think you will need the Belfast boys, you will be on our doorstep before we even fire a shot boy." exclaimed Bonner. "It's been done before gentlemen, the battle of Moyry Pass was in 1600 and only a few years ago an ASU 23 from Silverbridge held off an attack from a Brit Guards Regiment Included on the last shipment were grenade launchers, flamethrowers, anti-tank rockets and heavy machine guns it's possible to do it. Our friends have also sent along with the anti-aircraft rockets several new missiles called thermobaric. These things are hell on earth as it's a mixture of explosives, fuel and air. The blast wave is longer and more powerful than normal explosive. Watchtowers, armoured cars and soldiers in trenches can be blown to bits. We have a few long range sniper rifles to shoot out the cameras on their radio masts so they won't be able to see us forming up before the attacks. The only thing I don't trust is our CB radios, I'm sure the Brits hear every word that we say so I asked our Chinese friend if he could get us secure

23 Active Service Unit

radios. I've seen a few on the first shipment, but we'll need more on the next delivery."

"Well, it looks like you and your boys have been busy Peewee. What about Belfast, Aiden?"

The Bird scratched his head and rubbed his eyes. How was he going to beat Peewee? The D-Day landings sounded less well planned than his country colleague's scheme.

"We have mapped out most of the leadership of the Loyalist network and most of the places they live or visit regularly, but the gigantic problem is Tara it's like a fucking mythical organisation. All the Loyalists we have access to say it exists, but don't know anybody in it. We've been told they have a vast arsenal of weapons brought in from South Africa and have been put in hides across Antrim, but that's where the trail goes cold."

Sean McLarty cleared his throat, "The big Belfast attack will be on the eleventh night. I have a group of boys working for me in the South making bombs and gathering the materials we will need to make their bonfires go off with a fuckin bang." McLarty laughed at his own joke.

"In the next few weeks the prods will start making the bonfires so we've gathered hundreds of wooden pallets and old furniture to give them a start. What they won't know is that at the heart of their Loyalist effigy will be a ton of Republican explosives just ready to blow them to bits. We will also put flasks filled with nails and explosives in the old furniture so everybody will get a taste of the action."

Everybody around the table looked around, dumbstruck by McLarty and his wild plan.

"You do realise that hundreds of innocent men, women and children will be slaughtered?" McSweeny gasped.

"Have you been talking to Mc D? He told me something along the same lines a few weeks ago." Asked Bonner

115

incredulous.

"Mc D is an old ASU colleague of mine Bonner and don't worry, they are only fucking prods." McLarty grinned.

"Bird I've got a list of eight sites we will hit. I want your boys to snoop around and find out when they gather the wood and my team will go up and lay the base overnight with the bombs concealed in the centre. Two weeks later we will deliver the furniture. The prod hierarchy will be at the bonfires so we can take them and their fuckin families out in one go. I'm coming up to Belfast soon Bonner I want to talk to you about the killing of Tommy O'Bray, get Secrillo ready to talk to me as well I want to hear what he has to say."

Bonner was thinking about his two cohorts, Charlie Wheeler and Billy Whitledge. If they survived McLarty's planned carnage, they would soon plan a massive retaliation. They were Loyalists bigots, but not stupid. It wouldn't take them long to work out that their republican partner would have been fully aware of the impending atrocity. He had two choices, either tell his business partners or whack them both before they could retaliate. He was between a rock and a hard place. Bonner had another problem, his Intelligence Officer Mc D was the eyes and ears of McLarty, and his circle of trust was diminishing rapidly. He had to stop this crazy plan immediately.

"What about the Loyalists in Scotland, a sizeable loss of life would prompt them to come over in their thousands Sean?"

McLarty gave Bonner a look. "If they come, I will sink the fuckin ferries that carry the prod bastards. I will get Peewee's missiles to shoot any plane trying to land at Aldergrove."

Bonner rolled his eyes, but nodded in false agreement to Sean 'Mad' McLarty he was living up to his nickname.

"What happens in Belfast happens in Belfast. If you want to fight your war that way it's your choice, as long as the Chinese are happy and keep giving me the tools to push the

Brits out of our lands I don't give a fuck." Peewee exclaimed.

There was an edgy silence. The gravity of the last few statements had weighed heavily on the shoulders of the conspirators. McSweeny looked at the faces around the small Formica table. Peewee a driven man, a soldier and born leader. Then to McLarty wild, unpredictable and almost on the verge of losing control. Sat in between them Bonner looking like he was sitting on a track facing a runaway train.

As Army Council Chief of Staff, McSweeny had already predicted how the story would end. Many months before he and members of a secret Army Executive meeting had spoken about getting further concessions from the British Government, the armed struggle was faltering, and Brit spies had infiltrated the organisation to the very core, and the people had become dissatisfied with the war and the direction which the Provisionals were taking. Something needed to be done and done quickly. Shamus Donal, a Republican academic from Dublin University, had asked the others if they had ever heard of the Vietcong Tet offensive which took place in 1969. The other four men nodded that they had heard about it, but didn't know the whys or wherefores of the battle.

"In January 1969 General Nguyen Giap the North Vietnamese military commander ordered a series of coordinated attacks against a hundred targets all over Southern Vietnam. It was suicide, taking on a much superior force. The Americans were better equipped and had a vast intelligence network very much like the British in the North of Ireland, but what the Americans didn't have as with the Brits was the people. The offensive fermented a rebellion amongst the local population and encouraged the Americans to scale back its involvement in the Vietnam War. Though U.S. and South Vietnamese forces managed to hold off the attacks, news coverage of the massive offensive shocked the American public and eroded support for the war effort. Despite heavy casualties, North Vietnam achieved a strategic victory with the Tet Offensive, as the attacks marked a turning point in the Vietnam War and the beginning of the slow, painful American withdrawal from the region."

"So Professor Donal you are telling us we should have an all-out war with the Brits to get more support from the local community? How many volunteers do you think would sign up for certain death?" asked Joe Donaldson, the political advisor of the Republican movement.

"Tet was not an all-out war; it was a show of strength to both the Americans and the indigenous population. Giap gave the people of Vietnam and the world a statement that the struggle was not over and they were not about to go away. The Americans received the message, and within two years had left the country. What I am telling you is that the people of this country have become accustomed to the odd bomb here and there they have become disillusioned with the struggle which has no signs of success or end. They want a headline, a banner to get behind, dead heroes; who is the new Kevin Barry? For every dead martyr a hundred volunteers will come forward to take their place. For every dead Brit will be another stab in the heart of the people on the mainland. Death by a thousand cuts as they grow weary of seeing their sons and daughters slain whilst trying to repress the people of Ireland." Donal explained.

The rhetoric of Donal was not lost on McSweeny. Later in the evening he learned that Giap was a supreme military strategists who surrounded himself with loyal Generals who would carry out his orders to the letter. Many of the Generals Giap used were, to put it kindly overzealous or in the words of McSweeny "Murdering bastards." It was a combination which he liked and started the wheels in motion to link a military strategist with a madman. McSweeny was impressed with the talk given by the Professor; he knew that he didn't have to win just cause so much chaos that the Brits would become pissed off and over react causing colossal world revulsion. He envisaged that the martyrs would inspire a new generation on both sides of the border and lead to a renewed surge of Republicanism, sweeping the old guard away once and for all.

"Has the Army Council got the full backing from the Executive Padraig? If not, and we carry on with this mission, it's our own side that will kill us, not the fuckin Brits." Bonner asked.

McSweeny looked hard into the Belfast man's face. "Take it from me Bonner this has come right from the very top of the movement. You will free the six counties from the British occupation forces."

COBRA Downing Street London Monday 21st March 1994

"Sir Patrick, can you make any sense of these attacks on Heathrow? I thought we had made our position crystal clear that we are willing to negotiate a peace settlement. What more do these people want." The Prime Minister had called yet another emergency meeting in the COBRA office.

Sir Patrick Mayhew looked across the green baize table and cleared his throat. He studied the ornate fireplace behind the bespectacled leader of the UK and Northern Ireland. John Major had appeared to have aged over the recent days. He certainly was a different fish to Maggie, the former barrister thought.

"Prime Minister all I can add from the Northern Ireland Office and from a recent discussion with the Chief Constable Sir Hugh Annesley is that the twelve mortar rounds used in the attack in all probability is the work of a man named as Paul Patrick Kelly. Although Kelly was not in London, I am reliably informed that his finger, so to speak would have been firmly on the button to orchestrate the attacks."

"Northern 'Bloody' Ireland yet again, it's a weeping wound which just will not heal. How many more concessions do they require? The Irish Taoiseach Albert Reynolds was on the phone to me immediately after the first disgraceful attack, also asking the same question."

"The assessment over in the Province is that the Republicans are just sabre rattling to make us hurry our decision. I have spoken to John Hulme who has also spoken to Adams, whom as you might have guessed has no knowledge of any attacks. It might well be worth considering that these actions have been carried out without the knowledge of the Republican leadership."

Major took off his glasses and rubbed his reddening eyes. "Do you think Adams has got dissident factions within his organisation, Patrick?"

Mayhew looked around the room. Men in suits and uniforms were staring at him, waiting for his reply.

"Frankly, yes, Prime Minister. I would say that without any doubt Adams and his cohort McGuinness have upset quite a number of hardliners in South Armagh and a few of the leaders in Belfast. Some are merely disgruntled, others want to fight on, long war and all that nonsense. To support this theory, there is an intelligence strand from an Army source that there has been a recent weapon shipment landed in the South. The source is untested and the whereabouts, amounts and types of weaponry are as yet unknown, but it might indicate that one element of the Provisionals is not going with the tide. I will propose to Mr Adams a temporary cessation of hostilities, that way if any further attacks occur we can assume that there are other forces at work and that the Republican Movement may well have to do some housecleaning before coming back to the negotiating table."

South Armagh

Manny Holmes yawned loudly as he drove away from the farm in Tullydonnel after covering a Land Rover Discovery with a large tarpaulin. It was the last vehicle on Peewee's list.

"Ok so I have got a flatbed lorry, a tractor attached to a shit spreader, three Hiace vans and eight off-road vehicles which are a mixture of Land Rover, Mitsubishis and Toyotas. There is also an old petrol tanker which is parked inside a barn which is also full of wooden pallets, fence posts and old furniture. Are yous fuckers listening to me? There are loads of bits of iron and steel in the yard with fellas welding things on to the vehicles, hundreds of bags filled with sand and before you ask I don't know why and I won't be asking anyone because I will get a bullet in my napper." Just talking to himself helped ease the agony that he was betraying his team.

The sun was lying low on the horizon as Holmes turned on to his driveway. He would get in, open a can and then phone the hospital. Since the meeting in the car park his mother's treatment had improved, she had been moved to a private room and given better drugs to alleviate her condition. Unbeknown to him, his every sentence had been snatched from the recording device, ready to be sent to the waiting source handlers.

"Oh, before I go Peewee did a scribbled note he dropped in the car it says 1,000 x CASG Type 56 then QW-1 Vanguard and then HJ-8 Red Arrow. I don't know what it is, maybe some code, but he must have dropped it when we came back from the beach the other day."

As he closed the car door and walked towards his house, he wondered if the Brits had been playing tricks on him, fucking with his mind, anybody looking into the car would see a fuckin eejit speaking to himself. Then again, they were probably right.

Romeo 21 Jonesborough Hill

"Where the fuck is this wanker? Four fuckin hours he's been

at home." Rob 'The Bear,' Bare was under pressure.

"Every five minutes the ops room are on the net asking if Decers has left yet. I know my fuckin job Vinny." Beside the hulking Geordie was Fusilier Vince Andrew, another of the many north east natives in the Fusiliers COP.

"Get a brew Bear I will get eyes on." Vinny laughed.

"Wait! Stand By, Stand By positive identification B3 from the home address into C3 the black VW Golf mobile towards Meigh passing Yellow 32." The Bear let out a tremendous sigh of relief

"Got the bastard," he laughed.

Captain Alan Park was listening to the constant chatter on the COP radio net as soldiers in the overt towers dominating the Dromintee Bowl gave updates on the movement of the black Golf as it wormed its way along the back roads towards Meigh. He and the waiting quick reaction force had been sat on the helipad for hours waiting for a call from someone high in Army Intelligence. Just as Park thought they would abort the operation a runner gave him the thumbs up and within minutes the aircraft was airborne, heading south.

Park was trying to identify a suitable landing site for his Lynx helicopter so he could offload his passengers in the rear. He loved Eagle VCP's they broke up the monotony of flying in supplies to the watchtowers sited all over South Armagh or the glorified taxi service changing over troops at each location. Eagle VCP's were different, he was the bird of prey looking for its next meal, and this patrol was even better as he was working on a secret radio network listening to a voice from hidden soldiers, talking about a bad guy moving at speed around bandit country. He didn't know who he was speaking to, or who the dangerous guy was, but he would turn it into a great yarn when he was next on leave in the lively bars of his local town Uttoxeter. Yes, he was sure he could embellish the story enough so it would interest Old Jimmy and his daughter Emma the next time he saw them in the Old Swan.

Decers turned off the Ballintemple Road on to a narrow track locally known as Mourne Lane. The sound of a helicopter had been in his ears since he had turned off the Dromintee Road, but he hadn't chanced a sighting of it. One more bend and he would enter the top end of Meigh and a meeting in Murphy's Bar with a beautiful young barmaid. He had been working his way into Andrea's knickers for weeks. Perhaps tonight would be her first visit to the 'love caravan' since the night was young. What the fuck!

Decers daydreaming had weakened his sense of danger. As he rounded the corner he drove straight into a waiting army patrol. Fuck, it was that helicopter; he was cursing himself for not being more cautious.

"Good day officer can I help you." Decers began all sycophantic as he jumped out of the vehicle, to help get him through the checkpoint as quickly as possible.

"No Declan, we are here to help you old son." The soldier replied in a heavy Cumbrian accent.

Decers was taken aback; this soldier differed from all the others. No camouflage cream. His combat uniform appeared brand new and his boots were clean. Another soldier approached, again in a brand new uniform, but underneath the helmet was a flash of auburn hair which had come loose from her hair net.

"You've been a naughty boy Declan." Bex Hamilton teased.

"Who's the fuck are," Decers started.

"Get back in the car lover boy, you need to talk to us." Bex giggled.

Over the next ten minutes they showed Declan Taylor the edited highlights of his gymnastics with Eileen Kelly. He was sick to the pit of his stomach. Bex would repeatedly stop the small device to reply a segment followed by a flippant remark, but all banter was lost. All Decers could think about was the end of his miserable life. He knew what the game was. He either became a puppet for the Brits or a body on the edge of some godforsaken road on the border, hole in the head surrounded by booby traps and forever known as a tout.

"Think about your kids Declan, you know how violent Peewee can be he might even attack your wife and kids to make people think they were grasses." Gary Grimshaw asked.

"He's right, Declan; Peewee won't want the community to know that you've been shagging his wife so he might top everyone." The ginger hair girl was taunting him.

Taylor put his head down and sobbed uncontrollably, "You bastards, yous fuckin bastards." He roared.

"Hey big boy, or should I say little boy judging by the tape, don't fucking blame us, blame that maggot between your legs. Now you will work for us and we will make sure that this tape never sees the light of day. We are good employers, in fact we are even prepared to give you money for information you provide. Now what's your decision, Romeo?"

"What do you want me to do? I'm only doing this to save my wife and children." Taylor cried.

"Well, you're also doing it because you have put your bollocks in our vice and also your brother-in-law will cut the fuckers off if he finds out you're doing the dirty on him." Mocked Grimshaw.

"We know you're the second in command of the Dromintee and Jonesborough unit. Peewee is your boss, so we want to know who is in your unit, what weapons you have and what your boss is up to." Grimshaw passed the shaking Irishman a torch.

"To the naked eye this is a civilian torch, if you switch it on it doesn't appear to work, but it is in fact an infra-red torch and a powerful one at that. If you get any information, we want you to shine it towards Jonesborough Hill at midnight. The next day drive to this road and we will be here to talk to you. If it's an emergency drive to the permanent checkpoint on the Newry Road and tell the guard you are Agent Baboon and they will get you into the search garage away from prying eyes. Is there anything you want to get off your chest now? Get the ball rolling, so to speak?"

Decers thought long and hard. Pictures of his wife Bridget and their young children flashed into his mind. There was no escape.

"Look I'm not that important, I'm just a driver. Peewee doesn't tell me much. In fact, the other night when he met the Chinaman I had to wait outside in the fuckin car."

"Chinaman! What Chinaman?"

CHAPTER SEVEN

Saturday 9th April 1994

Glosh Beach, Co Mayo

The Jia Yia, a 67,000 ton dry bulk grainer had been at sea with its secreted load of Factory 394 made weapons, hidden under tarpaulins and covered in grain, for fifty-four days, after being loaded by members of the San Ho Hui 'Triple Union Society' in the bustling dock yard of Quanzhou on the northern banks on the Jìn River.

Quanzhou became infamous as an opium-smuggling centre in the 19th century and had always been under the influence of the Triads, who switched from opium to heroin, produced in the Golden Triangle, and trafficked on to North America and Europe, in the 1960s and 1970s.

With over two hundred ships, of all sizes and cargos entering, loading or departing the busy port, the dockyard officials not on the payroll of the organised crime syndicate had little chance to adequately supervise or fully check loading and export manifests.

The second landing via Cape of Good Hope had been arranged for 12th March to coincide with the moonless night; however, the landing would be complicated because of a typical eastern Atlantic storm.

The rain was lashing down and there was a large swell as Captain Chow Young Fat expertly manoeuvred his vessel to the east of the Black Rock Lighthouse, located on a rocky island seventy metres above sea level, hand railing the Mullet Peninsula. Ahead he knew was the inky shadow of Inishkea South and some protection from the power of the eastern Atlantic Ocean. The ocean floor would soon rise rapidly from the sixty meters around Black Rock to seventeen meters close to the coast.

Captain Chow Young Fat had learned his trade as a Shao Wei, an Ensign in the naval warfare branch of the People's Liberation Army, in the early 1960s. He had done well at the Naval Academy in Dalian, trained mostly by Soviet instructors. Chow Young Fat had been born across the Liaodong Bay in the Tianqiao Residential District of Huludao; his father was a 'White Paper Fan' administration officer in the Tianjin triad group

The Chinese Navy at the time was largely a riverine brown-water navy. Chow Young Fat had first seen action when naval forces were used to suppress a revolt in Wuhanin July 1967, the capital and largest city of the Chinese province of Hubei. Chow Young Fat's 5220 series 'motor torpedo boat' made in the USSR was used to blockade the Port of Wuhan located on the banks of the mighty Yangtze River, to prevent ferries moving two hostile groups who were fighting for control over the city at the height of the Cultural Revolution.

The two opposing forces the 'Million Heroes' and the 'Wuhan Workers' General Headquarters' killed about one thousand people with tens of thousands more injured, in Wuhan during the insurrection. They accused the Wuhan military establishment of supporting the wrong group in the preceding struggles in the city. General Chen Zaidao and his political commissar Zhong Hanhua were put on trial, but the shit ran a lot further downhill and Chow Young Fat was a casualty of the political recriminations that followed soon after.

After a few lean years working as an ordinary member a '49' with Tianjin triad group his father secured him a job as a second officer on a cargo ship sailing from Jinzhou Bay Port delivering steel to North Vietnam.

Captain Chow Young Fat was forever grateful to his father and the masters within the triad organisation.

The Captain was heading to a precise point almost a mile out at sea from the Peninsula in between two hazardous sandbanks. To the west, a narrow boat channel, the Rusheen islet, which separated the Inishkea Islands, was the marker for the ship to drop anchor. The predicted forecast showed a break in the weather for a few hours, which would allow the armada of small boats and fishing vessels to ferry the weapons on to the mainland.

As the anchor dropped into the clear blue waters of the channel Chow Young Fat sent a radio message to the Irish Marine Emergency Service at Blacksod Point, informing the local Coast Guard that the Jia Yia had an engine problem and he had diverted into the channel to escape the brunt of the storm from the eastern Atlantic Ocean.

The local Coast Guard, Jim Begg, relayed the message to the County Mayo Headquarters in Westport and told them he would drive down to the beach to ensure everything was in order. Upon getting a nonchalant reply, Begg rose and shook the man sleeping on the camp bed behind him.

"Mr McSweeny your ship has arrived."

McSweeny yawned and left the building, trying to get his eyes accustomed to the night. He approached a battered old blue Land Rover.

"Ignatius are you in there? The ships here get the boys to unload the gear."

For the next fourteen long hours, a flotilla of boats crossed from the mainland to the Jia Yia. Unlike the first shipment, James Fagan was well prepared with deep hides constructed and concealed in the many sand dunes between Aghleam and Tirraun. Weapons and ammunition were quickly identified and loaded into different containers. Several batches were immediately placed in vans and taken to the hides in the Tristia Bog waiting for onward movement to Belfast.

Peewee and his driver Manny Holmes arrived at the beach just after mid-day. Behind them Peewee had brought an assortment of vans, trucks and 4x4 vehicles towing trailers and horse boxes.

"Good to see you Peewee, thanks for getting your boys down at such brief notice. That ship heading off into the distance has just unloaded two hundred tonnes of guns, bullets and explosives. Fagan and his crew have done an impressive job. I know this looks like chaos at the moment, but he tells me it's organised chaos. Now this fella here is Albie McGlinn he will give you access to all the stuff you need. Albie will also show you the deep hides that they have made in Monaghan in case you can't fit everything into your own stores. I've written a list of what we've been delivered." A beaming McSweeny explained.

3 Type 78 recoilless guns 100 shells
6 Type 87 automatic grenade launchers with tripods
4 Anti-Aircraft Guns 14.5mm
4 Type 74 Flame Throwers
30 CASG Type 89 RPGs with 50 warheads
50 LAW rocket launchers
1000 x CASG - Type 56 rifles with fitted bayonets and folding stocks
500 x CASG - Type 56C Short-barrel rifles
Two million rounds of ammunition;
14 Type 54 Anti-Aircraft Gun
20 QW-1 Vanguard Surface to Air Missiles
40 CASG - Type 81 Light Machine Guns with 75-round drum magazines
14 CASG -NDM -86 sniper rifles
1PN51 night sight
20 Hytera Secure Radios BWT-133 & TBR 130/10
20 Type 823 & Type 884 VHF (Unsecure radios)
150 sets of Body Armour with Ceramic plates
20 CASG - Type 67 machine guns
Two tonnes of explosive.

"Peewee, I don't need to tell you to make sure you burn any boxes and leave no fucking trace at all, make sure you eat that list once you're happy." McSweeny jested.

"Don't worry Padraig we have it covered, we are going home via our training ranges over at Corry Mountain, so we will have an enormous bonfire to get rid of all the rubbish. We have also made a few hides in Drumkeerin for the bigger stuff as we don't want to get them to close to the border before we use them. I've brought our mechanic Danny O'Hare over to have a butcher at the equipment he will make brackets for. It's a busy time as I've sent Decers to have a look at the Dorsey Enclosure between Belleeks and Cullyhanna, then scout around Forkhill. Pat Kehoe the leader off the Crossmaglen boys is having a snoop around the helicopter base at Bessbrook and the rest of his boys are here with us or waiting for us at Corry Mountain."
"You don't waste any time do you Peewee." McSweeny declared.

"Most importantly, have the other radios arrived with this shipment?" Peewee asked.

"Fagan has put them to one side for you, he said some are normal radios and others are scrambled. There are loads of batteries and all the gubbins that go with them."

"I've got a war to plan and win fella." Peewee retorted as he marched back towards his waiting posse to get them working. "Manny put this list in the car and don't fuckin lose it."

"What the fuck is it?" Manny enquired.

"The full contents that the wee ship sailing over the horizon has delivered to us, son." He explained.

Manny watched Peewee barking orders at the rest of the group as they moved vehicles to various bunkers and tractors appeared to lift heavy weaponry into the trucks and trailers through the steamed up windscreen. He looked down at the list and carefully read out each item verbatim. Emphasising each letter "30 C A S G Type 89 R P G with 50 warheads." After finishing reading, Manny placed the list carefully into the glove compartment then went to help load the vast amount of weapons, ammunition and explosives."

Tobias Timbrenan, one of the Crossmaglen boys shouted Manny over to lend a hand lifting a huge green box into one of the many box bodied vans.

"What the fucks in here?" Manny asked.

"I don't know, but it's fucking heavy, the bastard!" wheezed Tobias.

A voice from behind them spoke up, "Guys be careful with that. Inside is a Red Arrow wire guided missile launcher that can blow up tanks and armoured cars. It can also destroy bunkers when you fire the thermobaric warhead." Danny O'Hare the mechanic was a bit of an anorak when it came to weapons and vehicles; they knew him to bore the pants off people drinking with him at the Three steps Inn in Dromintee.

"What the fuck is a thermobaric warhead." Asked Timbrenan.

The Dromintee boys all groaned in unison as they knew that O'Hare would go into a complete lesson on the weapon system.

Before O'Hare could start. Peewee shouted over, "It kills fuckin Brits, that's all they need to know you fuckin bookworm. Now get on with the loading, I want to be moving soon."

London

Steve Ho had been waiting for thirty minutes in the comfortable office within the Conservative Party headquarters on Smith Square in Westminster. He was relaxed, holding a bone china cup of Darjeeling tea whilst noting the very pleasant curves of the Chairman of the Conservative Party's secretary. A shapely woman whom he estimated was mid to late forties.

His developing erotic fantasy, in which the secretary would be the star, came crashing down when a loud buzzer sounded.

"Jeremy is ready to see you now Mr On, please follow me." The secretary smiled as she led Ho to a large ornate door. Two taps on the door and a voice could be heard within

"Enter"

"Jeremy, Mr Sun Yee On the European representative of China Worldwide your two PM appointment, you have a meeting with the Chief Whip at three Sir."

"Thank you Dulcie that will be all." Jeremy replied with a wry smile.

"Stephen how are you, and how is the wonderful Hotel Lisboa enterprise which you run so well."

"We are very busy, Jeremy as always."

"Whiskey? I have an array of fine malts I keep for special friends who take time to visit me Stephen." Jeremy interrupted. "How can I help you, my dear friend?"

Ho gratefully accepted the tumbler full of Scotland's finest. "It's what I can do for you, Jeremy. My business colleagues are looking to capitalise away from Far East and London could provide us with a great return for our future investments. The markets in China as you are well aware are unstable with the current regime and the impending handover of Hong Kong in 1997."

"Yes, Stephen I must agree with you Hong Kong will be a significant loss to UK PLC, but the truth is we cannot afford to stay there any longer, it's a tragedy. Look, if you want advice on investing in the capital I will put you in touch with the right people and organisations."

"Jeremy you are most kind and in return my fellow directors would like to donate to your party."

"That is a very kind thought Stephen, unfortunately our county's legislation does not permit any political party to be funded by overseas investors." Jeremy explained.

"I am well aware of your country's rules Jeremy; however, I have nearly ten thousand workers registered throughout the United Kingdom, each willing to donate say five hundred pounds each to your party. Let's not get bogged down with the minor details and amounts just yet, I have brought you an open-ended ticket for another 'cultural visit' to Macau. Perhaps you could bring your Prime Minister with you, without the wives of course." Both men broke out into raucous laughter.

South Armagh

It was after midnight when Manny finally pulled into the drive of his house. He was tired, sweaty, dirty and trying to find the words to describe to his unseen mentors what had happened over the last hours. After unloading the major haul of weapons in a large cellar under a deserted garage at the foot of Corry Mountain Peewee had been directed by Peewee to a field by the Carrickastricken Road just to the south of the Kilcurly border crossing point. After a brief walk over the wet grass Peewee pointed out a cattle trough at the junction of three fields which was to become a short term hide. Peewee and Manny placed two BWT-133 field portable secure radios, a 1PN51 night sight and two Type 64 Suppressed Machine pistol with four magazines of ammunition. Everything was waterproofed and the hide re-camouflaged. To finish, Peewee constructed a crude booby trap from a Type 77 Hand Grenade and wire to ensure the hide was not disturbed. The last act was to wrap a small wire noose around the gate post entry to each field. This was a warning marker to local farmers that the fields were out of bounds until further notice for both humans and animals, unless they were the unsuspecting British Army.

South Armagh had been using these local warnings for many years to prevent death and injury to the local population walking on to mines, IED's and booby traps.

Belfast

It had taken the best part of two weeks to move and hide the Belfast consignment of weapons around the city. The Belfast Quartermaster Ron McKeever had made use of the purpose-built hides constructed when the new estates of Poleglass and Twinbrook were developed. Many of the Poleglass residents were rehoused on the estate because of the demolition of parts of the Divis flats on the lower Falls. It was a hard republican area and volunteers were easy to find. From old age pensioners to pregnant mothers, all were willing to lend a hand for the cause.

The Falls Road Black taxi service was too obvious of a method to transport the weapons and explosives, so refuse carts, motorbikes, and private cars were used to move small numbers of the commodity to the front line in north Belfast. Women pushing prams and old women pulling shopping trolleys all helped move the equipment into local hides in the city's north.

The Active Service units were not involved in the movement and distribution as Mac D and The Bird had tasked them to create target packs on the known leaders of the Loyalist Paramilitary groups. The members spent hours getting to know their future victims' habits and locations they visited, building a detailed pattern of life.

Sean McLarty was also busy; he had handpicked a team of

four men from the Dundalk runaways to look at the proposed location of bonfires for the 11th night. Over seventeen hundred pallets had been acquired by Southern Command along with tyres and old furniture, the only items needed to complete the load was eight boxes containing homemade explosive, Semtex and small pieces of metal referred to by the bomb maker Jim Power as 'dockyard confetti.'

Jim was the Head of Engineering in Army HQ, an East Tyrone man with many successful operations under his belt. He had perfected the use of timers stripped from video recorders to give precise detonation times. They constructed bombs from evermore ingenious ways. Jim's latest project was hollowing out fence posts and the stringer panels on wooden pallets before inserting a mixture of explosives and metal fragments.

"What's on the list Gary?" asked Angel a six foot two former Ardoyne man who had been on the run since Long Kesh Great Escape in September 1983. Angel was one of the very few that remained at liberty. Of the thirty-eight escapees many had been caught within the first few hours, only eighteen had made it to the relative safety of south Armagh and transport across into 'The Free State' some had later travelled to America, but since been extradited back. Occasionally he would meet up with fellow escapees Gerard Fryers and Séamus Campbell, but they all remained in fear of their freedom.

This was the first time since the escape that Angel had crossed the border; not even his mother's funeral had tempted him back, but now it was different McLarty's speech at the Lisdoo Arms in Dundalk had rekindled the fire in his rebel heart. All the years of looking over his shoulder, not being able to open a door or jumping from his bed at the slightest whisper of a noise had finally broken him. Yes, Angel was free, but he was still on a life sentence. The stupid thing was that he probably would have been free if he had remained in prison as he would have made parole, the authorities would have escorted him to his beloved mother's funeral and he could prey at the very spot on the Crumlin Road where he murdered the poor Prison Officer driving home from work to see his wife and four children, four catholic children! He was never told the man's religion; he assumed he was a protestant.

"Right here goes Angel and remember this is in McLarty scribble. Fuck, there are loads to check." Gary Regan, a west Belfast man, had been born in the prefabricated housing area of the Westrocks. The 'Tin Town' housing had been built after the war as a temporary quick fix to get a roof over peoples head, but fifty years later the aluminium prefab houses remained. The 'Tin Town' kids were ridiculed at the local St Paul's school on Mica Drive, they were called amadans24 they were mocked for their appearance or told "Westrocks kids fuckin stink or Westrocks gives slums a terrible name." When his place of escape Pegasus Park was taken over by the British Army as a barracks Regan snapped and joined the Na Fianna Éireann the Provisional Irish Republican boy scouts.

Regan was eighteen when a booby trap bomb he was about to tie on to a hole in the fence of Corpus Christi College exploded prematurely. The Brits had been using the hole as a short cut to get into the Beechmounts. The first time he booby trapped the hole a stray dog walking with the patrol set off the device killing only the dog. A new unit the hated Parachute Regiment had arrived after and had used the cut through again, but this time it wasn't to be as the bomb lay at his feet the detonator exploded, but luckily for him not all the homemade explosives ignited: just enough to blow off Regan's lower leg and bollocks. Volunteers took Regan to a local doctor, then spirited over the border for proper medical attention. There was enough of Regan's DNA at the scene to convict him in absentia, so he remained in the south on the run.

---

24 fools, simpletons

"First, he's put Chobham Street in East Belfast anybody know that one?" Regan started.

"Just read the whole fuckin list out Gary, we can divvy up who goes where." Angel commanded.

"Ok keep you socks on fella there's Craiggyhill in County Antrim and the Ballycraig Housing Estate County Antrim, Moonrush in Cookstown."

"I know Moonrush, and the bastards that will build it. Leave that fucker to me." came a small soft voice from the back of the car. Thomas Dexter was from Cappagh, a fighter who was captured by the Ulster Defence Regiment at a vehicle checkpoint, but punched one soldier, snatching his rifle. Dexter shot three of the soldiers' one of them a female before himself being shot in the shoulder. With the adrenalin pumping, he ran over the fields to the village of Pomeroy. Although no lover of people from Cappagh, Dexter was given treatment and taken over the border to Donegal, to become yet another displaced terrorist.

"Ok Tommy, that's yours then. We have the Village in South Belfast which I know all too well then the Clooney Estate up in Derry, Ballykeel that's Ballymena I think, and Ballyduff in Newton Abby. Anywhere in Newtownards, what does he mean by that?"

"Some fucker from Newtownards stabbed McLarty at a football match, I think." Angel informed them.

"Oh, right well McLarty has an excellent point there then. The New Mossley Estate in Belfast I think that ones on Finvoy Street if my memory serves, and then the Cregagh Estate Belfast I know that one as well and the Avoniel by the leisure centre. He also says we have to look at Woodvale and Portadown." Regan mimicked a gasp as if out of breath at the exhaustive list.

"I know the Woodvale one Gary; it's fuckin huge. We need to get in quick as they will soon start building the base of that one." Angel declared.

"McLarty has all the equipment ready, and he's had some trucks done up with markings from Belfast, Derry and Antrim so when we offload it won't be any hassle." Dexter remarked.

"We need to be careful with the lorry drivers I take it they will be free-staters so they will need to keep their traps shut or we will all be on the fuckin bonfires." Angel quipped which rose a chuckle from the others in the car.

SDU HQ Dublin

The only office lit in the Garda Special Detective Unit at Harcourt Street in Dublin was being used by Superintendent Dan Curry he was hunched over a map of the country with one of his syndicate officers Inspector Joseph Guilfoyle.

"Aar have we got anyone on the west coast that we can trust to go snooping around Joey?"

"Over in the western region? Fuck they are mostly 'culchies' Dan, but I did a firearms course with a sergeant called Mark Harper, he's a real cute hoor25 but I'd trust him over there in 'Bennyvill.' Joey replied.

"I hope to god I'm not paying you two overtime at this late hour?" bellowed a voice from the doorway.

Both men looked around to see the imposing figure of Chief Superintendent Louis Range. A man mountain, former Ireland and Barbarian's second row forward with the scars on his nose and hands to prove he'd played, fought and drunk with some of the hardest rugby players on earth.

"We could ask the same about yous boss, what the feck are

25 Person who quietly engineers things to their own advantage

138

you doing at this late hour?" Dan laughed.

"I've been over at the CSB26 security meeting over at their headquarters in Phoenix Park. Put a cuppa tea on will ya Joey. Who in god's name has let that fuckin ejit Sean McLarty out of Portlaoise jail?" Range sighed as he rubbed arthritic left knee.

"Playing you up again, Louis?"

"Fuckin All Black hooker stamped all over it down in a test match in Dunedin the little bastard. Made it even more worthwhile when I broke his fuckin nose later in the game. I bet he had his nose straightened, but I'm still limping on this gammy leg, BASTARD!" he shouted.

"You're supposed to be the intelligence boys, tell me how Sean McLarty gets out of jail then within a week some cunt murders Harry McFadden the supposed IRA head of Northern Command, and before you start, I don't believe this crap in the papers that it was done because he was a fuckin Pedo! Anyway, that's why I am in late, what about you pair of bastards?"

Dan and Joey looked at each other. The junior man told the tale. "It was a nothing report Boss Coast Guard reporting that in Early February a ship was noted sailing very close to the Mullet Peninsula. Radar suggests that it may have diverted into the waters between the mainland and the Inishkea Islands, and then last week another vessel anchored in the same area after reporting they had engine problems."

"So what? Ships get engine problems." Louis scoffed.

Dan cleared his throat "Look I was speaking to Joe Montgomery he's the head of Special Branch in the Southern Region over the border an honourable man."

"Yes I know Joe, for an Orangeman he's good fella, and I'm

---

26 Crime and Security Branch

glad you've kept the back channels open for blokes like him Dan. So how does he come into the equation?"

"Well, back in February he told me that Peewee Kelly had a secret meeting with a Chinese male that we identified as a Mr Sun Yee On staying at the Carrickdale Hotel The male later flew from Dublin to Macau via Amsterdam. We also have a report that an old friend of ours James Fagan visited Macau last year. Now it might all be coincidence, but my big copper flat feet are tingling telling me something is going on. It could be shipments of illegal tobacco, drugs or weapons, I don't know but I bet it's bad fuckin news whatever it is."

"So it's a hunch that separate strands of reporting form some kind of grand felony, organised by Jimmy Fagan the former commander of the Derry Brigade?" Louis grumbled.

"As one of my criminal analysts would say, it's my hypothesis Boss. Look, all I need is that the next time you speak to the spooks at J2 just ask if they have heard any whispers on the international network."

The Directorate of Military Intelligence aka J2 was the military intelligence branch of the Irish Defence Forces. Although small in numbers the J2 branch had an unbelievable knack of producing top quality overseas intelligence.

"Ok I will ask. As it happens I have a meeting with the National Security Intelligence Section at Cork Harbour next week, they are responsible for dissemination of Naval Intelligence. Make a request to the Air Corps at Casement Aerodrome, to overfly the area; they have an intelligence section that can interpret air photos see if there are any hides on the Mullet. The Superintendent in the west is Johnny Berry, an old friend of mine and a good club rugby player in his day I will make a call."

"Shall I drop the word to Joe over in the north Louis?" Dan asked.

Louis pondered the question a moment "No let the fucker wait, see if you can put some truth into your 'hypothesis' before we blab to those fuckin Ulstermen."

CHAPTER EIGHT

Sunday 10th April 1994

County Leitrim

The Flying Column volunteers had arrived at a makeshift campsite set up in a large wooded area near Carnhill on a Sunday afternoon to be greeted by the commanders of each column. The days were getting longer as winter had retreated for the growing warmth of spring. Trees blossomed, and the grasslands slowly become drier.

Tents had been erected by the edge of the wood with a large tent in the middle to be used as a canteen and briefing area. Anyone flying over would swear that it was a very professional Boy Scouts encampment. What could not be seen were carefully camouflaged vehicles concealed in the wood line, armoured and weaponised tipper trucks, tractors, vans and four-wheel drive 4x4's. These 'technical vehicles27' gave the appearance of a Mad Max movie set. The Mechanic was still busy under the canopy of the trees adding more armour or fitting additional weapons brackets as the volunteers looked over their designated vehicles.

Peewee and some Jonesborough team were already out on the hills in Drumreagh Knockacullion. This part of County Leitrim edging down to the eastern banks of Lough Allen was rural, with farms lightly sprinkled across the rolling landscape.

From the Lough the hills steadily rose covered by a patchwork chequerboard of neatly groomed fields, which emitted a kaleidoscope of green shades which were interned by white and grey stone walls interconnected only by solitary

---

27 An open-backed civilian pickup truck or four-wheel drive vehicle mounting a heavy weapon, such as a machine gun

iron gates. In contrast, the heath lands above the managed fields were dark amber, bracken fought for space with dark green prickly gorse bushes all fed by a spider's web of small streams.

Men had visited most of the resident farmers claiming to be from the Irish Defence Forces explaining that the Defence Force were conducting special training in the area to get them ready to deploy on operations abroad.

The Monday morning started early with each volunteer being issued his own rifle and pistol. Each man also received an enormous canvas bag containing spare bullets and grenades. The remainder of the morning was taken up with target practice on a crudely constructed range set into a firebreak in the wood. The added incentive was that the four best shots would receive additional training and become a sniper using one of the imported NDM 86 sniper rifles.

Peewee had stood by two large cardboards handing out blue boiler suits and ceramic body armour to the volunteers.

"These vests could save your life so make sure you wear them when we're in action."

"Fuck me Peewee these are all in Chinaman sizes, no good to an Irish Maolán28 like myself."

"Tobias, we have all sizes, swop with Decers his vest covers his bollocks."

"Fuck Peewee sure Decers could do with his bollocks covering up."

There was silence and Decers gave Tobias a scornful look. Tobias immediately realised he was on thin ice mentioning the boss's brother-in-law's infidelity.

"It won't fit yous cos you're a fat fuck." Hissed Decers.

---

28 Warrior

"Hey Peewee with these dark overalls we'll look like the fuckin SAS." Joked another volunteer.

"Let's just hope we don't meet the SAS until we're good and ready. On our ground and on our terms." Peewee looked around at the assembled men. If one of them was a grass they were all fucked, if one of them had loose lips they were all fucked and if one of them had a dark problem which the Brits could utilise they were all fucked.

Peewee was conscious of keeping everything close to his chest, the targets, the tactics and especially the timings. The lessons of Loughgall and the dead volunteers from the East Tyrone Active Service Unit were not lost on him.

The SAS mounted Operation Judy in May 1987. It was the IRA's biggest loss of life in a single incident, and destroyed the most active IRA unit in the province at that time. Internal enquiries never rooted out the informer, which sent eight good and dedicated volunteers to their graves. The Loughgall Martyrs were an inspiration to young volunteers in East Tyrone, although Peewee had doubts about their operational planning, and cowboy like attitude.

After lunch Peewee introduced a British Army tactic, Fire and Manoeuvre, in which one man would put down suppressing fire whilst the other ran towards the target. Martin McLoughlin a member of the southern command volunteers had a close call when one bullet fired by his partner Albie McGlinn whisked through his boiler suit missing his calf by a fraction.

"Good job it wasn't auld 'Fat Legs Albie' his legs fill his pants unlike your chicken legs Marty." Peewee remarked.

As the week progressed the teams became proficient in firing an assortment of machine guns, grenade launchers, rocket-propelled grenades and anti-aircraft guns whilst both stationary and on the move in close proximity to each other.

Peewee introduced the trainees to the secure radios and then sent each column out across the area to test the communications. Mid-way through the week live firing moved to an old disused quarry up a grey gravelled track on Corry Mountain in Bog County west of Lough Allen. Peewee had placed out old vehicles and metal boxes to become targets. McSweeny had come up trumps by providing two old Portacabins stolen from a building site in Limerick and transported up by night to the quarry.

The move from Drumreagh to the quarry was an exercise in itself, as the columns had to discreetly travel through Drumshanbo and the ever busy Conway Bar by the T junction. The road into the village was narrow with plenty of choke points, Peewee used the speedy 4x4 trucks to scout ahead to ensure no nosy Garda vehicles were waiting along the route.

The only living soul to see the convoy was an old drunk staggering out of Conway's bar.

"Up the RA boyos!" he cheered. Obviously the cover story about the Defence Force didn't circulate down to his level, Peewee thought.

The high-sided tipper trucks belonging to the specialist column took an age manoeuvring through Drumshanbo, but with the scout vehicles reporting that the road ahead was clear Peewee instructed Pat Kehoe in the lead truck to take his time. The road from the village out to the quarry on Kilronan Mountain Bog was empty and the columns quickly made their way to the new campsite.

After a late start, the next phase of training began with the smoothbore recoilless guns and flame throwers being tested.

"I think you need to get more petrol Peewee, every fucker wants a go of them fire guns." Decers quipped.

"Shall we try one of those thermobaric missiles Peewee? It would be interesting to see what they can do." asked Manny.

Peewee thought for a moment, then decided to fire at a large square container. It resembled one of the boxes on the towers which littered every major hill in South Armagh. It would be an excellent test and a demonstration to the watching volunteers of the new firepower now at their disposal.

The honour of firing the first missile was given to Tobias Timbrenan, a farmer from Cullaville outside Crossmaglen. Tobias's older brother had been a volunteer until the day he tried to plant a bomb near to the phone exchange in Silverbridge. Waiting in the nearby undergrowth were soldiers from the SAS who ambushed the volunteer, killing him in a hail of bullets.

Tobias knelt at the side of the Red Arrow, making sure he didn't crack his knee on one of the tripod legs protruding from the base. His number two Bryan Gilgan grabbed one missile from the box and heard a clunk as the electrical plugs connected.

"It's ready Tob" Bryan said as he gave his boyhood friend a tap on the shoulder.

"Eye Gilly, here goes."

Tobias took an age acquiring the target and placing the pre-aiming mark on to the correct area.

As Tobias slowly squeezed the trigger it sent an electric current to the launch command of the missile, which immediately went into firing mode. A soft launch sequence began with the rocket motor pulling the rocket out of its protective sleeve and getting the warhead a safe distance from the firer. It was less than a second into its flight when the full propulsion of the rocket motor kicked in. The warhead zoomed towards its intended target, just at the point of contact the nose cone made a quick oblique adjustment so it struck the target at a right angle. The concave shaped charge in the warhead focused the effect of the explosive's energy, the metal liner compressed and squeezed forward, forming a white hot molten slug to penetrate the outer skin of the metal box. A millisecond later a vapour cloud exploded mixed with flammable dusts and droplets was injected into the hole and immediately combusted causing an intense shock wave which completely destroyed the box. A huge fireball escaped and was rising to the air.

At the firing point, all was quiet.

"Mother of god, what was that?" gasped Bryan Gilgan.

The clouds and mist had started to roll in over the windswept rust coloured heath land, when the guns finally stopped firing. The wind had picked up; it was late in the afternoon, Peewee was happy as the flying columns had worked in harmony. It had taken a few days for them to grasp the theory of firing accurately, moving whilst your partner fired and continuation of the momentum.

"The fuckin Brits do this in their sleep, FIRE and MANOUVRE it's easy to everybody, apart from you set of ejit Micks. They will cut us all to ribbons if you don't do this right." Peewee had barked and cajoled.

The Portacabins were attacked from a variety of angles with rooms systematically cleared. "This is how we practiced for Derryard." Peewee told Decers.

"How did you learn all this stuff?" Decers enquired.

"Some volunteer from Monaghan showed us. An ex Brit Para that was pissed off after Bloody Sunday and joined the cause. We never got as far as clearing the rooms in that attack, hopefully we will be luckier this time. He's the guy that gave me the Brit tactics book, Speed, momentum and aggression is what we will need."

At the end of the week the heavy weapons were removed from the brackets manufactured by The Mechanic. Sure he was a boring bastard, but he could fabricate anything you asked. The vehicles were scrubbed down and all traces of bullet cases removed. The last job was to clean the volunteers themselves and burn all the ammunition boxes and packaging. A disused cattle shed was set up as a cleansing station, with the sheep dip being utilised to get any lasting remnants of gunshot residue off their skins.

Peewee had formed five flying columns made up from the men supplied to him by southern command. Team one was mainly the boys from Dundalk with a few Dubliners mixed in under the command of Robert "The Italian" Hennessey. Spick as he was affectionately known was a happy go lucky chancer of a man. The only reason he was living over the border was he was hiding from his wife who caught him in bed with his next-door neighbour. Peewee considered the southern crew his weakest group. They were keen enough, but he wondered if they would stand and fight when the shit hit the fan.

He had no doubts about the second crew led by an old-time friend, Timothy "Fats" Inn. The Cullyhanna boys were well blooded in battle. On a number of occasions they had joined Peewee's own group and worked well and efficiently.

The third group were all Crossmaglen volunteers, led by an old gun Arthur O'Donnell; some claimed he was a 'rusty gun' as it had been a while since he had been in front line action, dedicating himself to making bigger and better mortars and bombs. It was good having an old hand like Arthur around as he would give sound advice.

The final two groups were Peewee's own team from the Dromintee and Jonesborough area. Peewee would lead one squad, the other by Decers' Taylor.

There was a fifth specialist group led by the commander of Crossmaglen Pat Kehoe. The 'specials' would control several shock weapons to support the primary force.

Each column had a Grenade Launcher, Heavy Machine Gun and Medium Machine Gun attached to one or more of its vehicles. An armoured van would follow the fighting vehicles carrying extra ammunition and six more men armed with either Type 56 rifles, light machine guns, and rocket-propelled grenades. Each of the men carried a pistol and grenades, attached to their ceramic body armour and all had a light armour rocket slung across their backs.

Peewee's columns also carried the Red Arrow anti-tank missile system. The Red Arrow also had a night vision device which for the first time would give the Provo's a surveillance capability during the hours of darkness. For too long the Brits had owned the night. Too many volunteers had lost their lives in ambushes by the crown forces. With the new night sight the Brits advantage had gone, at last they were on an even footing. Peewee also had two snipers on call to eradicate any stubborn problem areas and a team carrying a Type 74 Flame Thrower.

The real firepower was in with the specialist group, the Mechanic had spent hours creating attachments and armour for the four double axel tipper trucks. The trucks had been lined with a second metal skin and inlaid with sandbags to give the men in the tipper added protection. A 12.7mm Anti-Aircraft Gun was fixed to a stand above the driver's cab, and a General Purpose Machine Gun placed on a bracket in front of Kehoe in the front passenger seat of the lead truck.

The second truck was fitted with an 82mm Type 78 recoilless gun which was powerful enough to destroy a tank. The second vehicle was also fitted with a 35 mm automatic grenade launcher to give increased indirect firepower. Truck three had a heavily sandbagged base to protect the chassis and dampen the shock of an 82mm Mortar shell being fired. Truck four was fitted with a 14.5mm Anti-Aircraft Gun, a devastating weapon which could tear through defence walls and barricades.

The special team was supported by what appeared to most passers-by as an ordinary Massey Ferguson 390 tractor towing a Ruscon ST1500 Sprayer Slurry Tanker. This clever device was actually an improvised flame thrower, which could produce an immense wall of fire. The tractor could also pull any vehicles which became bogged down in a field or use its dozer blade to knock down hedges and walls around fields. The blade was also useful to protect the driver from incoming fire.

A large van was also part of the special team, the six men inside carried Qian Wei Vanguard Surface to Air Missiles, to provide top cover against helicopter reinforcements. A last item ordered by Peewee was that every vehicle should have a retractable armoured cover to protect the drivers and commanders once moving into battle.

Everything was ready equipment wise; Peewee did a last check of every vehicle and weapon before dispersing the convoy to various small barns and hides in the area around Tullydonnel. Each commander was given a large tarpaulin to cover up their vehicle. Speed, secrecy and surprise were vital elements in Peewee's plan, so nothing was left to chance. The secure radios had been tested on both sides of the border, lookouts had been on over watch to see if there was any reaction from the Brits, but there was nothing, just the usual administration run into a tower or base by a Lynx or a spotting patrol from a Gazelle. Both helicopters were seen daily basis flying over the killing fields of South Armagh. Patrols checked areas around their camps and guarded policemen as they tried to carry out their role of upholding the law in a show of normality in a completely un-normal situation.

Donaghadee, Co Down

Aiden Bonner had chosen the small seaside town of Donaghadee as a meeting place because it was well out of the way of preying eyes. It was also close enough to his impending drugs pick up in Bangor, which he needed to do once he had spoken to the madman McLarty.

He peered out of the large window of the chippy towards the white lighthouse on the harbour. The rain had stopped twenty minutes ago, but The Bird was drawn to the steady flow of water droplets colliding again and again, gaining more weight until they moved uncontrollably down the window taking other unsuspecting water droplets to their ultimate doom. Bird reflected, it was like his own life at the moment, and he had been sat in a relatively comfortable and safe position, then suddenly a chain of events above him and forced him on to an unstoppable spiral which, like the raindrop would only end in catastrophe.

Aiden's eyes became drawn to one particular rain drop midway down the window. It appeared to be holding on; other heavier drops falling towards it seemed to miraculously miss it by fractions. Bonner began to will the rain drop to survive, to live out its natural life and be dried up by the sun. As his hopes rose that the raindrop would endure a large hand rubbed the windowpane taking with it the rain drops last hope of survival.

"Is that you, Bonner? You daydreaming fuck!" the wild eyes, unkempt hair and rasping Belfast accent announced that McLarty had arrived.

McLarty swung the door open and surveyed the chip restaurant, a tidy and cosy family business, with red and white plastic table cloths giving the dining area a touch of colour.

"Why didn't we meet in a bar? I need a fuckin drink." McLarty's volume switch was permanently on loud.

"Because I didn't want to draw attention to ourselves Sean, like you are doing right now. This town is full of off duty Peelers, they live here they feel safe here so they won't expect two gentlemen of our nature to be having a chip dinner in their midst, will they?"

"Do they serve beer in here?"

"No, Sean, they don't serve fuckin beer here, they serve fuckin chips. You look like you need a good dinner and I will buy you one, now stop you're fuckin blathering."

Aiden approached the counter, and ordered two chip dinners. He looked back at McLarty slumped over the table, obviously still pissed from the session the night before. McLarty wore an old green parka jacket with a ripped right-hand pocket. Marks down the front of the jacket could have been last night's take away or puke, the jacket and McLarty stunk to high heaven. Who in their right mind had decided that he should become head of Northern Command? He was a time bomb primed to go off at any second and take anyone else in his vicinity with him.

Aiden returned to the table carrying two steaming mugs of coffee. "Do you want sugar Sean?"

"Nah sure I'm sweet enough, well at least that what that pretty colleen told me last night." He chuckled. "What have you got for me, Mr Birdman? And I want to know who ordered the murder of my cousin wee Thomas O'Bray."

"Ok, here goes. We have the leaders of the UDA, UVF RHC29 under control. We know where the fuckers live, drink, work and take a shit. We also have details on senior officers in the Ulster Defence Regiment and the Special Branch. Our fundamental problem is this fuckin Tara mob, they have changed their name to Ulster Resistance, and the other proddy gangs worship the fuckers. They are the Knights Templar of prods. They have access to a load of assault rifles, pistols, rocket launchers and grenades they got from Lebanon about five years ago which we think are hidden between Armagh and Portadown. They gave some stuff to the UDA and UVF muppets in Belfast, but they lost them almost straight away. Those fuckers are riddled with touts from top to bottom."

---

29 Ulster Defence Association, Ulster Volunteer Force and Red Hand Commandos

"So who's in charge of them Aiden?" McLarty now more hushed and considered in his tone.

Bonner looked through the steam of his coffee at the scruffy bastard sat across the table. He had aged considerably since Bonner had first clapped eyes on him on Dunville Street, a stone's throw from the Royal Victoria Hospital. McLarty had ambushed an off-duty policeman on his way home after visiting his wife and new-born daughter. The Bird had heard the staccato burst of shots, and then seen under the darkening Belfast skies, two men wearing black ski masks sprinting across the park.

"Here grab these; you know where to take them son now fuckin move." One of the masked men shouted as he jumped into the waiting getaway car.

As the green Ford sped off towards Lesson Street, the young Aiden Bonner calmly placed the two Colt 45 pistols into his school bag, He looked at the car speeding away and glimpsed for the first time the wry youth, wild eyes with unkempt greasy auburn hair he would later learn to be Sean McLarty, a rising superstar within Belfast PIRA. Bonner calmly walked through the narrow alleyways between the terraced houses on to the Lower Falls. It took over an hour of walking along the back streets and dodging army patrols until Bonner arrived at the safe house on Whitecliffe Crescent in the Ballymurphy estate.

An adolescent girl no more than seventeen years old opened the door. She immediately turned around to shout at an unseen figure.

"Uncle Paddy a wee man is at the door for you." Behind the girl appeared a smiling old man, dishevelled grey hair giving him the look of a mad scientist.

"Come in young man, you took your time, did you have any problems? Or should I ask, did anyone try to follow you?"

"No Sir, I did like I was told I used the back streets, and I stopped a few times to see if anyone was behind. I even walked back on myself through the Westrocks to make sure. There were a few Brit patrols out, but I easily got passed them Sir."

"Don't call me Sir, Call me Uncle Paddy, everyone does. Now here's a fiver for your trouble. I think you will go a long way in our organisation, son. Now did you like the young girl that let you in?"

"Er yes, she's beautiful Sir, I mean Uncle Paddy."

"Well, you wait on Rosie where are you my love?"

The girl re-appeared she reminded Aiden of the girl in the song 'Black Velvet Band'

'Her eyes they shone like diamonds, I thought her the queen of the land. And her hair, it hung over her shoulder tied up with a black velvet band.'

"There you are my lovely colleen; this young volunteer has been on his first, but certainly not his last mission for the cause. Take him upstairs and be gentle with him."

Rosy took Bonner's shaking hand and led him upstairs. He was in love with both the girl and the adrenalin rush from being on active service. Bonner would seek Rosie for comfort after many dangerous operations in the future.

"Well, who are their fuckin leaders?"

Bonner was suddenly back in the chippy, the warmth and smell of Rosie vaporised like the raindrop.

"They have a loose connection with the political parties, but unlike their city cousins this group are water tight. Everyone is tight-lipped. Nobody can confirm who runs them or who pays the bills. It's a ghost force. Throw in the Scotland Loyalists and we might have a major problem on our hands if we go down the doomsday route."

"What do you mean by that?" McLarty puzzled.

"What I mean Sean is that what if the Loyalists are more ready for doomsday than us? They could turn the tables and hit our communities hard. We could be back in the seventies with families burnt out and refugees heading for the safety of the Free State."

"Fuck what if! If you're not up for the fight let me know and I'll replace you. There are hundreds of volunteers that would stand up to replace you at the snap of my fingers."

"Hundreds of volunteers! What fuckin banana boat have you been on? We don't have hundreds, we have twenty or thirty trustworthy people. There are thousands of guys in the pubs and clubs in the city that say they are up for the fight, but they are all mouth and no action. We will fuck this country up for our children and grandchildren. We've had to bring people in from out of town to help us carry out this fuckin suicide mission."

"Your problem Bonner is you're a fuckin coward. I'm told you never lifted a finger to save poor Tommy O'Bray. You were OC Belfast."

Bonner had to think quickly, he had given the Civil Administration team the order to give O'Bray a punishment beating due to his 'anti-social behaviour.' In essence all the boy had done was to witness Bonner handing out drugs to one of his many street dealers. He had later told Secrillo that they had passed the authority down from McFadden. Never in the world did he realise that O'Bray was related to a psychopath.

"Yes, I was the commander of the city, but your fuckin grass should have informed you was that I was sat on my hands for seven days over at Castlereagh. The order to arrest Tommy bypassed me. When I got out I was told it came down from Harry McFadden to the head of the nutting squad, Vic Secrillo. None of my boys knew why Tommy got done. None of us believed he was a tout either, you should have asked

Harry, but no you had him nutted, and if you ask that cunt
Secrillo he will tell you Harry told him to get the job done
and we all know he likes to get the job done."

McLarty rose to his feet. His eyes glared at Bonner, "You had
better be like Secrillo and get the job done. If you don't,
expect a visit from Vic's crew and a black bag on the head."

A young waitress carrying the meal walked over, "Who's the
one having peas?" she innocently asked.

"Go fuck yourself you fuckin whore." McLarty spit at her as
he stormed out of the door.

As he entered the waiting BMW in the car park on Bow
Street, he was still foaming. He looked at the three men
waiting. "You fuckers want some action? Right go round to
that chippy on the front. When some gimpy legged bastard
wearing a black duffle coat and red curly hair comes out, give
him a beating and throw his head through the fuckin
window. That might liven him up."

The Hanger 1ˢᵗ June

Major Julian Clemont, the officer in charge of the Special
Surveillance Unit Southern Region sat impassive as the
orders group concluded. The entire process had taken nearly
two hours before Sergeant Major Colin Armstrong the
Operations warrant officer finally switched off the projector
and asked for questions.

"Yeh just one mate, what happens if that daft bastard can't
defuse the fuckin booby trap? You know how big Marky's
fingers are."

The rest of the team chuckled, a voice at the back "That fat
NAAFI bird at Aldergrove knows he has fat fingers." More
laughter

"And Marina" another joker shouted as the laughter rose.

"Fuck off I was pissed." Shouted a red-faced Marina Appleby one of the detachments few female operators.

"Calm down, you reprobates." Colin brought the meeting to order. "To answer your fuckin bone question Alf If Marky blows himself up you will see a lot more of him, all over the fields of South Armagh. The only person sad at his untimely demise will be the fat NAAFI bird, cos none of us will give a fuck. Remember, you are working in a foreign land so take your passports with you. Only joking do not get caught."

"So where has this information come from Colin?" Julian asked as the operators filed out to test their radios and load their weapons.

"It's come from the FRU, but as you can imagine they have redacted quite a bit of what this person has actually told them apart from there's a weapon hide just over the border with some interesting kit in it."

"It would be far easier if they gave us the full story, we are all security cleared."

"It's on a need to know basis you know that Boss. Anyway, they have the safety blanket of JCUNI30 backing them so it's a no go area. One thing I can tell you though is that Big Joe is not happy, and he's called for a meeting with Captain Peter Arnott from the FRU and the idiot has accepted the invitation. He will be walking into a lion's den."

South Armagh 2nd June

It was two in the morning when the team on the ground were happy that the area around the Kilcurly border crossing point was sterile and secure. Undetectable overhead was Flight 9 piloted by the Green Baron himself, Captain Rob Bailey with his dependable observer Reg Halford by his side

---

30 Joint Communications Unit Northern Ireland

looking for any movement approaching the surveillance box. Before the covert search of hide could begin Markey Roberts acting as entry man needed to photograph the area and then make safe the Type 77 Hand Grenade booby trap. Marky's wingman Alf Diggers was giving close support, looking out into the shadows using a set of passive night goggles. The G3 German made assault rifle carried by Alf tracked moved in unison with the tracking of the goggles.

Something hit the back of Alf's smock. "Fuck" Marky yelped.

"What is it?" a rather worried Alf asked.

"Fuckin fly off leaver has come off we've got five seconds."

Immediately Alf turned to look at his friend, trying to decide if he should dive on the deadly device.

"Wah! got you rubber dick!" Marky chuckled.

"Fuckin prick, get on with the job I fuckin hate bootys"31 Alf scolded.

"Right just a few more Infra-Red photos and then we can move the trough; the booby trap is made safe."

After carefully lifting the trough on to a rolled out ground sheet, Marky carefully opened the hide recording and photographing every move.

"Stand By, Stand By we have vehicle lights from Yellow 43 heading north on the Carrickastricken." was the call from Reg up in Flight Nine.

"All call signs hold firm." was called over the radio by Colin in the operations room.

Seconds which felt like hours slowly ticked by. On the wind Marky and Alf caught the faint noise of a car engine, then over the tops of the black thorn fence the unmistakable sway

---

31 Army slang for a Royal Marine

of the car's headlights. Both men were transfixed on to the gateway back on to the gateway leading to the Carrickastricken Road.

"If it's a gun team, we can bug out towards Major Road, at least we will be back in the north." Mikey whispered.

The car slowed down considerably as Marky and Alf looked at each other, convinced that the vehicle contained Peewee's gunmen. The car headlights suddenly disappeared and the noise of the engine faded. The two men held their breath, pushing themselves down into the damp ground.

"Stand By, Stand By that vehicle a 4x4 has turned east towards a farm complex. Wait, that vehicle is a stop, stop, stop. One male." The commentary briefly paused. When the commentary resumed Reg was chuckling "That's one male falling out of the vehicle and then staggering over to the farm. All lights are out."

Marky and Alf gave a huge sigh. Colin in the operations room waited a further five minutes 'soak time' before he was happy for the team to continue with the search.

"First item is wrapped in a waterproof bag, long barrel pistol wait, correction this is a Suppressed Machine pistol with four magazines of ammunition. There are two radios similar in appearance to the ones carried by our troops. There is also a small bag, something heavy within. Fuck, it's a night sight, and it looks like it has an infra-red capability." Marky's sentence immediately hit a chord back in the operations room.

"Did I hear that right Marky has found an infra-red, capable night sight?" asked Julian Clemont.

"Sounds like it wait one, I will get Marky to clarify."

"Ground team, give us some further details on what you have found." Colin calmly asked.

Alf answered the question "I've seen a sight like this before on a Russian sniper rifle. Markings on it are Chinese or Japanese, not Russian Cyrillic."

It's in a metal container with room for extra batteries, battery charger and the other accessories. An instruction book again in either Chinese or Japanese, in fact everything is written in that language apart from the word Hytera written on a plate on the radio and the letters CASG stamped on to the machine pistol."

Colin paused for a moment; he looked across at his boss Julian before deciding.

"Ok this is the plan, so we know that they have a night sight capable of seeing the flash from our equipment, chances are that they don't have any others, even if they did the intelligence from the OP and the towers is that Peewee and his merry men are tucked up warm in their scratchers. Alf and Marky I need everything and anything recording and photographing before you lift off. It is now extremely important that you leave no ground sign and you re- camouflage the hide perfectly. Do you understand the next phase?"

"Yes Wilko." Alf responded. "What the fuck is that Marky?"

TCG (S) Portadown 2 June 1994

Ray Poad surveyed the commotion from his perch on the steps leading to his Portakabin. Through the steam of his brew he watched as Special Branch officers loading cars with suitcases.

"Going on your holidays, boys?" he mocked.

"Get back to bed, Rip Van fucking Winkle, you sleepy bastard." Herbie shouted back. "We've got to get a helicopter over to Scotland, big intelligence meeting for the community.

Hush-hush is all you need to fuckin know."

"Must be a fucking important meeting with all those golf clubs you're cramming in the cars, Herbie." Bob observed.

"Well yes, there is the Nairn Golf Club just up the road from the conference, we might get a round in once we've finished."

Herbie chuckled,

"So who else is going on this jolly boys outing?"

Herbie scratched his head and looked up at the clear blue sky "Big Joe, Seb and Kris, a few of the desk jockeys and the agent handlers. All the other TCG's are sending guys over with the big bosses from Lisburn."

"I think I'll give it a miss mate, I have an import date with my bed seeing that I was on stag all last night. Don't worry about the troops you go and enjoy yourself, while we look after Peewee and his cronies."

"I fuckin will Rip Van fuckin Winkle."

It was mid-afternoon when the Southern Region convoy of cars passed through the checkpoint at RAF Aldergrove and were pointed towards a row of other high performance armoured saloons, parked in an immaculately straight line. An RAF Corporal snapped to attention and approached Joe as he stepped from the vehicle.

"Sir could your party kindly put their baggage on the waiting trolleys then proceed into the hanger. There's tea, coffee and biscuits inside. Your helicopter will be here shortly."

Joe shuffled his way inside and looked around the gathering number of faces, Billy Hanna his counterpart from the TCG in Londonderry was holding court with his team, explaining the necessity to follow through when striking a golf ball. Other small groups wearing tweed jackets and laughing loudly were members of the Military Intelligence community who each had variations of facial hair. Away from the major groups were two men in dark suits judging by their proximity and hushed tones Joe evaluated them to be members of MI5 'Box Boys' as Joe fondly called them. Joe had met many members of the British Security Service; he had frequently visited their headquarters by the side of the River Themes in London. They were talented people, very bright and very articulate, but he doubted if they really understood the genuine problems he faced on a daily basis in Ulster. Ten bombs in the province was one thing, but god forbid anything happening on their precious mainland.

"Joe, I need a word." A voice called.

Joe turned around to see the beetroot face of Superintendent Stan Lafferty, the boss of the Belfast TCG.

"Stanley my old friend, how about you? I take it we will have a few drams at the 19th hole later on?" Joe had known Lafferty for many years and had both worked together as detectives in the CID office at Corry Square in Newry.

"I'm not going over big man, I'm sending one of my boys over, but the rest I need in Belfast. All hell is breaking loose. Last night we've had two UVF commanders and a UDA senior guy shot dead. I've just been told that two guys from the Red Hand Commandos are missing."

Joe looked puzzled, "Is it a takeover of the loyalists commands? That guy Adair on the Shankill always fancied himself as a grand commander."

"Well, that's one line of enquiry, to be honest the prods don't know themselves, but what I know is that these assassinations were surgical very unlike what we normally get when one company declares a turf war. One of the bullet cases we found has come back as being from China, which is strange, but not as strange as finding Chinese silenced pistols, rifles and grenades in a hide in Poleglass last night. I've read your intelligence report this morning about a possibility that PIRA in your region have restocked their armouries with unknown weapons. Well, my friend, it looks like they have enough to pass on to their cousins in Belfast."

Joe rubbed his ears as if he didn't want the words to enter his head.

"There's another problem, Bonner the guy you told me was at a meeting with Peewee Kelly is at present in the Dundonald Hospital after being attacked outside a chip shop in Donaghadee yesterday. A couple of hoods gave him a real kicking and threw the bastard through the shop window."

"Is he ok?"

"Eye he'll live unfortunately, he put up a good fight and we think he did some damage back to his assailants as they were seen staggering back to their car. An off duty cop saw them speed off and swore that the car was being driven by that fucking nutcase McLarty. He got the vehicle number and I've just heard that it crossed over into the south via one of the illegal crossing points that we have a camera on."

"I was told about McLarty being active again by a contact over the border. It looks like he's had Harry McFadden done in and moved on to the Army Council, but I've no intelligence to prove it yet."

Stan shook his head and let out a low whistle. "That can only mean one thing my friend, trouble with a bit T. If McLarty is pulling the strings there will be a war. I'm going back to Belfast, have a good trip and sink a few drinks for me."

Stan's words were lost as the sounds of the incoming Chinook helicopter came closer. Joe looked out at the magnificent piece of engineering, two rotors synchronised in complete harmony. Then came the feelings, something unnatural in a sixth sense.

He had the same feeling on previous occasions. In the late 70s he had been patrolling with the army cross a field just outside Silverbridge, a gap in the fence was the easy way, but the felling said no. Joe fought his way through a blackthorn hedge. After a two-minute battle he was through, but the scratches on his hands and the rip in his waterproof jacket showed that the blackthorn had put up a tremendous fight. His next sensation was flying through the air then hitting the ground with a thump making him breathless. Chunks of mud rained down on his back and his ears whistled, temporarily deaf from the boom of the explosion.

The dampness of the field soaking through his trousers brought him back to reality, his back ached and his eyes burned. The smell of burning wood and ammonia hung heavy in the air. Joe sat up and realised that his precious flat hat was missing. He had worn the same hat on his passing out parade after completing his training at the police depot at Enniskillen. Still dazed, he felt around as the dust stated to settle. He picked up rocks, clods of mud, then a black leather boot. He peered into the boot, like a child inspecting a new toy. On looking inside, he saw that a foot remained within the confines. Shock hit him as he stumbled to his feet, staggering towards the gap in the fence which now appeared to be considerably bigger. The boot was the biggest part of Officer John Glynn's body that was recovered.

The sixth sense stayed with Joe frequently it acted as a guardian angel and steered him clear of trouble. The only time he didn't heed the warning was the time he let Caroline drive the new car he had recently bought for her birthday. Every day he asked himself why he didn't listen to his guardian angel. Perhaps Caroline would still be here.

The feeling was growing inside him, an immense sense of foreboding. Joe looked around at his team; many were family men, all close knit wonderful guys. "Go get your bags boys were going back to the office." He declared.

"What the fuck! Boss, it's an all-expense paid trip, an excellent chance for liaison with our colleagues from over the water." Ronnie' Corbett asked.

"If you want to play Golf, you can do it tomorrow, we're not getting on that helicopter we have work to do. Now back to the cars. Seb, get a message to that FRU idiot Peter Arnott. I want him to tell us all he knows at tonight briefing. I want the full works and I'm not taking no for an answer."

TCG (S) Portadown

Joe Montgomery was the last person to arrive in the briefing room. "I'm sorry I'm late, but I was talking to my counterpart in Belfast Chief Superintendent Stan Lafferty. I'll explain what Stan told me later, Seb, do you want to start us off?"

Seb cleared his throat. It was going to be quite a long briefing, and he knew his audience would ask questions even before he got to the end. He wished now he'd had a pee before Joe arrived.

"Before I begin, I would like to introduce you to Captain Peter Arnott from our colleagues at the Human Intelligence Unit. Peter is here to give you a classified overview of one of their covert operations. Peter,"

Arnott rose from his seat as grey as ever "Ladies and Gentlemen thank you for inviting me over" he began.

"Fuckin dragged you over." Grunted Alex 'Ronnie' Corbett one of the police source handlers.

"Yes perhaps. In recent weeks my unit has identified and establish several intelligence strands from sources linked to the Dromintee and Jonesborough grouping. From the intelligence we have received we can now disseminate to you that there is a possibility that PIRA has received one or maybe two large weapon shipments. I must say that this is only a single strand of reporting and we are endeavouring to parallel this information."

"So one guy has told you a story and you're looking for someone else to confirm it?"

"In a manner of words yes Ronnie, we also believe that the weapons are from CASG in China." Captain Arnott paused for effect "I sent a sanitised report to the weapons Intelligence Section in Lisburn, their analysts tell us that CASG is a perfectly reputable international arms manufacturer in China. It has a number of production plants throughout the country producing a wide range of products from bikes to bullets. The intelligence we have and I again stress that it is an untested source claims that PIRA have received heavy weaponry in the shape of anti-tank missiles, anti-aircraft guns, flame throwers and surface-to-air missiles."

There was a collective rumble around the room.

Joe stood up scratching his head, "Peter, are you telling me that those Provo bastards have got better weapons than us?"

Arnott raised his hands, "No, as I say our source is untried and the information they have given us is very raw. We are trying to re-establish communications with them, but it appears that most of the players have been off the grid for over a week which is unusual. There are concerns of course when last night's covert search by Sergeant Major Armstrong's detachment confirmed the presence of Chinese weaponry."

Colin stood up and looked around the room Armstrong was the total opposite of Arnott, big barrel chested his biceps could be seen taught against the cotton of his red checked shirt.

"Last night South Det working on intelligence provided Peter conducted a covert search in the area of the Kilcurly border crossing point. The items we found gave us some concern as they could lead to us changing our operational procedures. One item was a 1PN51 night sight made in China. This scope can pick out infra-red lights used by our vehicles and photographic equipment. For the first time in this conflict we would no longer own the night. We also found a 7.62mm

Type 64 Suppressed Machine pistol and two Hytera Secure Radios all made in China and all very sophisticated. At the bottom of the hide the guys uncovered a set of body armour with ceramic plates similar if not better than the equipment being worn by our own troops."

"Thank you Colin, which nicely brings me round to the telephone conversation I had with Stan Lafferty earlier. Stan has told me that last night the army searched a property in the Poleglass area of Belfast and found two Type 64 Suppressed Machine pistols, two Type 56C Short-barrel Kalashnikovs, silenced pistols, a box of grenades and sets of body armour with ceramic plates. Now Captain Arnott I will ask you again have we got a fuckin problem?"

Before Arnott could answer, Joe spoke again. "I think we can assume that the RA have indeed found an alternative source to provide weaponry, some of which has made its way into our country. We can also assume that Kelly, Bonner and our Chinese friend are all complicit in the equipment's distribution. My worry is that Kelly and his complete crew were missing for over a week, so the question is are they gun running or training. If they were training we must ask ourselves what are they training for and when is it likely going to happen? If they are gun running who have they distributed the weapons to?"

"Our assessment is that PIRA have stocked up on new weaponry to force the government's hand in the ongoing peace talks."

"What fuckin peace talks?" Joe cried.

"I am at liberty to add nothing further."

The room fell silent as each person reflected on the grave situation that the enemy had procured a state-of-the-art arsenal.

Ray Poad broke the silence bursting into the room.

"What's going on Ray is Peewee on the move?" Joe asked.

Ray looked at his feet, "No Boss, that helicopter you were supposed to be on has crashed in fog into a hillside on the Mull of Kintyre. They say that twenty-nine blokes are missing, presumed dead. Brigade just rang to ask who went on the trip from our region."

A shiver ran down Joe's back. His guardian angel had saved him yet again.

Forkhill, South Armagh 4th June

Arthur Regan had been ploughing the fields in and around South Armagh for over half a century. As a veteran of the border war, he had no love of the occupying crown forces. Even if they had reimbursed him handsomely for their use of his fields and hard standing area, which later became the Forkhill barracks. There was no particular need to be cutting the grass in the grounds surrounding the camp. The open fields had been left as fallow ground many for years. The only tracks across the pasture made by soldiers rushing from or to their safe haven.

To the untrained eye Regan was just an old farmer getting more forage grass for his herd of cattle, but Regan was under instruction to get the diameters of the field. Attached to the tractor was a trumeter measuring wheel to accurately check the distance of the outer camp walls. From the field entrance at the rear of the Church of St. Oliver Plunkett the old farmer drove towards Slieve Brac Park, then from Michael McCreesh Park to Fairview. At each turn he would jump down and pretend to check the height of the grass cutter and also record the distance.

On his last pass he drove along the wire, trying to spot any mines or flares interwoven into the coils of barbed wire which ringed the corrugated metal wall. Under each watchtower he took out the small camera given to him by

Peewee and took a picture of the area in which the soldier hidden above him could observe. Once his photographic mission was over the old man placed the camera into a small Tupperware box in between his cheese sandwiches and drove towards the gate by the church.

Just as he was closing the gate Regan noticed the approaching soldiers.

"Good morning sir, busy today?" asked the tall camouflaged soldier.

"No more than normal." His tone was brisk and offhand.

Corporal Hardiment had plenty of experience dealing with the folk of South Armagh, some were downright rude or like the old farmer sick of answering the same old questions.

"Is this your vehicle sir?" almost as he said it he knew the question was stupid.

Exasperated, the old farmer looked into the brown eyes of the soldier in front of him. "Who the fuck do you think owns this vehicle, you dumb cunt? You see me and stop me in it every fuckin day. Are you the brightest soldier in the barracks or has Forkhill been sent the biggest village ejit in England to annoy us?"

Hardiment's smile beneath his cam cream masked his feelings. "Thank you for your cooperation sir, no go forth and multiply."

Dundonald Hospital, Belfast

Bonner lay in his hospital bed, the pains in his head and back still hadn't dissipated. His left eye was completely closed; through the swelling on his right eye he could see the bandages on his hands, yes he was satisfied he'd put up a good fight.

The chip dinners had gone down well, even if the company was poor. He remembered leaving the diner knowing that he had to meet his two Loyalist associates to receive a fresh batch of drugs. As he looked towards the harbour, he spotted the two inexperienced men scurrying towards him. Hoods down, he couldn't see if they were a threat until the smaller one kicked him hard in the shin. The steel toe cap of the boot cracking his Tibia, the lightning shock of pain struck his brain as a gloved fist hit him square on the nose sending blood all over the window of the chip shop. Bonner's survival instincts immediately triggered, he knew that falling to the floor would have led to an even greater world of hurt. Luck was on his side as his flailing right hand grabbed the hood of the smaller attacker. Bonner pulled him on to his turning left elbow, smashing the cheekbone of the younger man. A shadow rapidly appeared as the taller man tried to head-butt Bonner, but Bonner dropped and tilted his head quickly so attacker's mouth hit Bonner's forehead, losing two teeth in the process. The pain in Bonner's left shin was unbearable, he got a few digs in but the young bucks were fitter and stronger. There was no chance he would be running away. The only option was to stand and fight in the hope somebody would phone the police.

The fight became a series of push and pulls until a third man appeared. Bonner's brain felt like someone had pushed it against his skull, glass shards from the bottle smashing over his head cut his face, nausea and numbness consumed his entire body. He tried to keep his eyes open, but the darkness was coming, before passing out he saw the cold angry eyes of McLarty who was grinning in his face. He was in darkness and had the feeling of floating before his skull received a second blow as they launched him through the plate-glass window.

It was all coming back to Bonner now; it was three attackers, not two, and McLarty had provided the final blow. Fuck, he was in danger; he needed to get out of the hospital quickly.

"Nurse! I need a…"

Bonner's shouts were quickly answered as a nurse burst through the door.

"Mr Bonner get back into bed." She scolded him.

"Listen Missus I need to get out real soon, and for your own safety you need to get me outta here."

"Well, lucky for us you have two friends waiting outside."

Bonner's heart dropped, McLarty's boys had returned to finish the job. He looked at his escape routes; the window was closed, and he appeared to be on an upper story.

"Birdy we've come to take yous home."

Bonner's head turned to see a shadow stood in the doorway. He wished he hadn't rotated his head so quickly as his neck and shoulders were in a world of pain. It was pointless anyway as his open right eye only gave him a blurred vision of the world.

"Birdy it's me! 'Bap' McConnell. Mac D is in the car we've come to get you outta here. Nurse, he's coming with me."

It took ten minutes of arguing with the hospital staff before Bap got Bonner to the waiting car.

"I don't need to ask you who did that job on you Birdy. McLarty can be very persuasive, I see." Mac D laughed.

"Go fuck yourself, but thanks for coming to get me."

"The nurse gave me a load of pain killers for your injuries, she said they crack your leg, but not broken they wanted to keep you in because your pissing blood." Bap explained.

"I want my family moving to a safe house." Bonner proclaimed.

Mac D looked over his shoulder at the broken man in the rear seat "No need, you don't have to be worried about

McLarty, in fact I think he was quite impressed with the fight you put up. He said you really fucked up those two young bucks he sent to give you a kicking. Anyway, he's happy now that the ASU's are doing their job."

"Job what job?"

"Calm down Birdy McLarty told us to let loose Fitzy's boys. They killed a few prods and they have two Commandos' in a garage on the Short Strand, he's on about taking a blowtorch to their bollocks."

"So the war he wants has started then?" Bonner was desolate. The blanket around his shoulders felt heavy.

"Not yet Birdy, we're just testing the water and the new gear. The word we've put out is that it's a vigilante group called Direct Action against Drugs; we'll then blame those fuckin ejits in the INLA32. The Peelers think it's in fighting amongst the prods and they've arrested a few of their leaders which is a shame as they are all on the hit list. No mind they will be released soon and we will be waiting."

South Armagh

Declan Taylor was up early; throughout the long drive back from Lough Allen he had been wrestling with his conscience. His lack of morals had led him into screwing the wife of his brother-in-law and into the long arms of the tout handlers. If he didn't report something to them soon, they would circulate the video they had taken of Eileen and himself in the caravan. He could just imaging walking into the Three Steps for a drink only to find all the boys laughing at him and his lover's sexual gymnastics. They wouldn't have been laughing once they recognised the naked shapely form of Paul Patrick Kelly's wife under his sweaty body. There would have been silence, then somebody would have seized the

---

32 Irish National Liberation Army

video and taken it to Peewee.

For the last few nights sleep had been fitful. He was sure that Bridget suspected that something was troubling him and if he didn't tell her, she would question her brother why her husband was so anxious.

He opened the boot of his car and reached to retrieve the broken torch. He flicked the switch on and off several times, nothing appeared to happen. Fuck it, he thought and faced towards Jonesborough Hill before again switching on the invisible signal. He was in a panic. Peewee had told him to check an area between Belleeks and Cullyhanna and then take a closer inspection of the barracks in Forkhill and the watchtower above the village on Tievecrom Hill. He knew his handlers would begin pulling at his chain and want answers to what he was doing. He decided to drip feed them information, make them interested enough so they wouldn't compromise his 'In flagrante' liaisons, but not enough so they would send the SAS in to kill him and his friends.

If the state wanted him to inform they would need to pay a good price because he had quality information in his head. The conclusion had struck him he was playing a treacherous game, but sure wasn't shagging his boss's wife even more traitorous.

Decers had spent an age after leaving his house traversing the narrow roads in the Dromintee bowl, to ensure he wasn't being followed. Finally satisfied, he turned on to Mourne Lane. He had heard no helicopters, so he prayed that the signal had worked and the torch really hadn't run out of batteries. Decers was almost on top of the soldier when he jumped out from a gap in the blackthorn hedge surrounding a field. The car sketched to a halt almost on the boots of the young squaddie.

"Speeding Sir!" a voice outside shouted.

Decers had broken out into an uncontrollable sweat; he tried to compose himself as he wound down the window.

"Hello Declan fancy meeting you here, be a good man and open up the boot of your vehicle. Might as well make it look like you're getting a proper search." Bex Hamilton told him. Flex of her auburn hair again protruding beneath the brim of her helmet.

Decers looked at her. She was pretty; the pale skin, cute freckles on her nose and deep green eyes were quite disarming. The combat suit didn't give much away about her figure, but he estimated that if he had a chance, he would defiantly try to ride her. A second thought flashed into his mind. Women, fucking women was the reason he was in the shit. Forget about her body and remember she was just using him.

"I need to talk, and talk quick, if I'm seen here I'm for the nut job. Do you understand?" He began.

"Look Decers we do this all the time, it's just a normal check point ok don't worry." She reassured him.

"Another vehicle on its way." Shouted a soldier hiding further down the road.

"Let it run into the VCP33 while I deal with this guy, give it a light touch." Bex ordered.

"Now get out of the car put your hands on the roof, make it look like you being searched."

Decers sweating was increasing; his mouth was dry as if his saliva had evaporated.

"Ok sir, you can go on your way." Decers heard the soldier.

"Go fuck yourself." Was the gruff reply.

Decers chanced a look behind to see who the remark came from, he immediately recognised Sammy Shandling an old farmer and Provo intelligence officer from Meigh.

---

33 Vehicle Check Point

"Let that poor wee boy go, ya bunch a cunts! Fuck em Decers son up the RA." Sammy shouted as he manoeuvred his trailer towing Volvo through the checkpoint.

The day was going from bad to worse.

"Fuck do you know who that bastard is? Sammy has a fuckin mouth on him like Portsmouth. People will want to know what I'm doing up here early like. If word gets back to Peewee, he will grill me, probably over a fucking fire."

"Stop being so melodramatic Decers, Shandling is an old gun. He was part of the border campaign in the 60s, but he's a piss head now. If you're so paranoid I can get the police to keep visiting so that your boys think he's an informer, perhaps slip his name into a few bars around the Bowl, you know what I mean?" Bex explained with a hint of mischief.

"So where have you been hiding, Mr Taylor? We've wanted to talk to you for a few days now. What have you got to tell me?"

"I've been on a training camp run by Peewee in County Leitrim, near Lough Allen. There was about fifty fellas there, some I know from Cross and Silverbridge, but others from over the border. They were a strange bunch because although they said they were from the south, most had Belfast or Derry accents. Look they gave us new guns I hid these to give you."

From under the carpet in the boot of the Golf Decers produced several shell casings.

"This is from the rifle, this is from a grenade launcher and this big fucker is from a machine gun which can shoot at planes. We also have rockets that can blow up tanks and buildings and an anti-helicopter rocket, but we didn't fire those."

The smile on Bex Hamilton's face had disappeared. Decers was on burst transmission as he detailed the weapons and vehicles.

"Look I've been gone too long you need to let me go. I'm going back to look at the Dorsey Enclosure for Peewee again." Decers mumbled as he got back into his car.

"What's the Dorsey Enclosure?" Bex asked.

"It's the road which runs from Fords Cross between Belleeks and Cullyhanna. You have towers that cover it. One has lots of radio antennas."

"Golf Zero One and Romeo Zero Nine, why is he interested in that area?" she asked.

"History, something about King William in 1690. I don't know."

"Is there an attack being planned?"

"Well, he's obviously planning stuff, but he's not telling anyone where, what or when. With all these Chinese weapons under his control we can put up a fight." Decers remarked, smiling for the first time.

"What Chinese weapons?" Bex asked incredulously.

"Those shells in your hand and the guns that fired them all came from China. The guys have been to some beach in Co Mayo and picked up loads of guns, ammunition and explosives. Peewee has organised all the local teams into individual groups he calls flying columns. Each of these columns has a variety of the weapons I told you. He's shown us something called fire and manoeuvre that one of your Paras showed him before he attacked Derryard."

"What Paul Patrick Kelly was one of the Derryard attackers?"

"No, he didn't just attack the place he organised and led it."

Bex looked down at the cases in her gloved hands. This will be some epic report writing, she pondered.

TCG (S) Portadown

Joe Montgomery sat back in his leather chair contemplating what his nemesis Paul Patrick Kelly was planning. He looked to the wall on his left filled with commendations and plaques from army and police units from all over the world.

"What the frig are yous up to Peewee?" he whispered under his breath. He was about to shout Herbie to see if he wanted a coffee when the phone rang.

"Aar Joe it's Dan Currie here my friend, look I'm not making this call from my office if you know what I mean, and I don't know where you got this information from. There is a strong possibility that two ships from China have dropped off shipments in the Mullet Peninsula we are sending a team down to have a look, and a plane to have a fly over."

"When did the landings happen Daniel?"

"A few weeks ago I'm afraid. Friday 4th February was the first one, then Saturday 12th March it took time getting the information from our Coast Guard service."

Joe looked down at the notes he'd scribbled down on his notepad. "That makes sense as we know that Peewee met the Chinaman on the 10th February and Peewee and his crew went missing just after the 13th March."

"Have you been told that Sean McLarty is out of jail and they murdered Harry McFadden?"

"Yes, I was told that Daniel. I know of McLarty, but don't know him well if you know what I mean. He's a bit of a looper and won't be sitting down at the peace table unlike the recently deceased Mr McFadden. Harry was a dirty low life incestuous pedo, fuckin his own daughter, but he had no heart for a fight and was willing to bring peace to this land. That's why we think PIRA has had a coup d'état and the lunatics are now running the asylum. While you're on, I might as well tell you we have found a few Chinese guns and equipment on my patch and up in Belfast. Also a number of Loyalist paramilitaries have been assassinated. That is also not for the press my friend as we are trying to keep it under wraps so we don't spook the locals. Thank you Danial I appreciate you going out on a limb for me."

South Armagh

"And where have you been so early? You didn't get home till late, you've not spoken to the children, what's going on Declan?" Bridget scolded.

He knew he was in the shit when Bridget used his birth name. She was a wee woman under five feet tall and very slender, but she could pack a punch. In the days when they were courting he was watching her arse under tight riding jodhpurs as she mucked out a stable. A large stallion old Mad Max made the unfortunate decision to take a bite out of her shapely behind. Bridget turned in a flash, slapping the poor creature around its muzzle, making it rapidly retreat into a corner to recover.

"I was told some cattle were out of the top field so I went to look, and as for last week I was out on business with your fuckin brother so don't give me any grief women."

"Well, I won't be giving you grief just yet because 'my fuckin brother' wants to see you, but when you get back, you will be getting more than grief. I'm hoping that you're not back to your old ways with some fuckin hoor!"

Decers thanked fuck his brother-in-law had given him an excuse to escape the wrath of a demented pigmy wife. He quickly grabbed his jacket and bolted out of the door. It then struck why he had been summoned to see Peewee. He'd been with him all the previous week and not mentioned anything. He had given him a full report about the areas he been checking, and there were no operations planned, unless! Fuck Sammy Shandling, that blabber mouth must have been on the South Armagh jungle drums. He was walking into an instant death sentence, as his mind raced to different conclusions.

He thought back to a guy that was executed years before. Decers was a kid, but he remembered a guy called Hennratty, big guy always in the Three Steps mouthing off. Someone knocked on his door and invited him to the bar. A week later they found his beaten and lifeless body on the Concession Road near the border. Black bag on his head and wires attached to bombs tied to his body. Decers asked Peewee why they didn't just shot him at home; get the job over and done with. Peewee explained that Hennratty was a big fella, and they wanted him to come without a struggle and be at ease. They didn't want to distress his family either, but they also wanted to send out a message to the rest of the community that touts would be tortured and murdered.

Hennratty's execution, he was told, was carried out by a Belfast man who took great pleasure in torturing his victim for hours until he confessed. The city man's speciality was that he could keep the man in agony, but not at the point of passing out. He gave his prisoners no respite until he shot them in the back of the head. Even at the point of execution he would fuck with their minds by pushing the pistol barrel into the back of their head then pulling the trigger only for the hammer to hit an empty chamber in his revolver. Some victims soiled themselves as the Belfast man and his team laughed loudly.

Belfast

"We need to talk immediately." It had taken an hour to track down the latest hiding place for Billy Whitledge. Bonner had been told by Mac D that his intelligence team were still trying to locate the burley Loyalist leader. It took a dozen phone calls all made from fresh call boxes until Aiden Bonner got to speak to his drug trafficking associate.

"You Finnian cunt! I thought we had an agreement?" Whitledge was scared and dangerous.

"Look Billy, we both have a problem and we need to meet alone. This is not a setup as I'm in the shit just as much as you and your people."

"Why the fuck should I trust you? Some of my commanders have been murdered by your Taig scum."

"Billy trust me I couldn't get word to you. For Christ's sake, the same people that have been whacking your guys also put me in the hospital. We are both being played, but with your help we can save many people, your people. You will be a hero in your community, but we must meet up before something terrible happens to us both."

Whitledge was unsure and feared a trap, but finally agreed to a meeting in a public place close to an RUC station.

"Ok I know a place we can meet; I'll arrange we don't have any prying eyes so get your Finnian arse to the Railway Bar in Holywood tomorrow at eight, and you had better have some fuckin wonderful excuses or you will visit a romper room on the Shankill."

Downing Street, London

"Prime Minister you have a call on the green phone from the Irish Taoiseach Mister Albert Reynolds." Announced John Major's Cabinet Secretary, Sir Robin Butler, the most senior civil servant in the country.

"Thank you, Sir Robin. Bertie good morning, I take it you are phoning to tell me you have found another error within the Downing Street Agreement." Major joked.

There was a wry laugh down the line "No Prime Minister I have some information from my Intelligence staff and I wanted to pass it on to you myself before you hear it from another channel. May I also send our condolences from the people of Ireland at the recent and tragic loss of life in the helicopter crash."

"Bertie, thank you for your kind words, we are trying to assess just how much we have lost in both personnel and intelligence. I'm sure you will be aware but Mr James Laine, our cross border connection sadly died along with a number of exemplary men. Right down to business, I'm intrigued, what have you got from me?"

"I have been informed that there has been some liaison at a grassroots level between the RUC and my Garda Síochána, which I am happy with. Some information provided by the RUC has shown that they have landed weapons in my country. Yesterday an air reconnaissance of a beach in County Mayo has highlighted the possibility that the information might have some substance. There are newly excavated areas in the place of concern. I am dispatching some covert assets to get conclusive proof of what exactly is going on in the area."

"Thank you Bertie, I have been made aware at a cabinet briefing yesterday that there have been a few firearms originating from China, found in Belfast. It is quite concerning that a separate string of intelligence informs me that the Provo's might have gained more than just small arms."

"John, this could get worse as my people have identified a possible third shipment. If our analysis is correct, the two earlier shipments were from the China Shipping Container Lines ship Peng Hai, which we think landed equipment on a beach in Co Mayo in February. They followed this by a second shipment from the Dairen in March; both were from Quanzhou Port in China, bound for Kollafjordur Harbour in the Faroe Islands via the Suez Canal. Our research has now identified a third vessel, the Tungting, which is due to enter Irish waters on Thursday 19th August."

"Reading between the lines Bertie, are you suggesting a joint operation between Dublin and London, to show the world we are both united in our fight against terrorism?"

"Well, that's one way of looking at it. The other is that your intelligence network and covert operations management is better tried and tested than my own. A joint working cell of My National Security Intelligence Section and your Intelligence Services coupled with your Special Forces and my Army Ranger Wing would be a very potent force. Your forces would work on Irish soil or seas so I must insist that we have primacy on all decision making."

"Bertie I concur with your judgement. The weapons that have been mentioned belong at the bottom of the sea, not on the streets of our countries. I will speak to Charles Chatterton from the Security Service and his opposite number Sir Richard Pottinger over the river at the Secret Intelligence Service to arrange a top level meeting with your Director of Military Intelligence; I take it that Simon O'Malley is still in the chair?"

"Yes, the Colonel is still in charge with his trusty deputy Berness Kerr, a fine figure of a woman. Finally John, do you know a man by the name of Sun Yee On? He also calls himself Steve Ho."

"No, I cannot recollect that name. Why do you ask?"

"It's a line of enquiry from my Special Detective Unit; this male may be the conduit of the weapons shipments. He is also thought to be speculating in the London property market on behalf of a Chinese organised crime syndicate."

The Prime Minister thanked the Taoiseach and replaced the receiver. Pushing his glasses to the top of his head he walked over to the door and opened it, rubbing his eyes he made his way over to the cherry red chesterfield sofa.

"Sir Robin can you get the COBRA team together ASAP and get the Chairman of the Conservative Party on standby, tell him it will be a meeting without bloody coffee."

Major stretched back, Albert Reynolds he deliberated; you're not a 'Country Bumpkin' after all.

Holywood, Co Down

Aiden Bonner was nearly twenty minutes late for his meeting at the Railway Bar in Holywood. Police checkpoints and the poor weather had culminated in forcing him off the Sydenham Bypass to make an unwanted division along the well-manicured tree lined Belmont Park.

As he drove down the hill towards the car park on Hibernia Street, he wished that he had brought a pistol with him. Hopefully, there might be a few off-duty soldiers or policemen wandering the area that could raise the alarm if his Loyalist conspirators turned nasty at the loss of their companions, but the heavy rain and high winds blowing off the seafront probably ensured that even the most hardy soldier remained in the nearby Palace Barracks. With no backup and no weapon, he was totally at the mercy of his drug dealing partner.

As he pushed open the big heavy oak door of the Railway Bar, he noticed two men stood talking to a thick-set barman wearing a white short-sleeved shirt. His arms were heavily tattooed, pictures of women, Union flags, names of people possibly his family and beneath the edge of his sleeve a big red hand of Ulster which was partially hidden, there was no doubting just where the barman's allegiance lay.

The bar was dimly lit; a sizeable man in the corner strode towards him.

"Put your fuckin arms up so I can search you." The voice was hard guttural West Belfast, Shankill Bonner imagined.

The man was overzealous in his manhandling, giving Bonner

a tap in his bollocks as he stood with arms stretched above his head. "He's clean Billy." The searcher shouted.

From one alcove appeared Billy Whitledge "Your fuckin late Bonner, have you been followed."

"No, Billy look we really need to get our heads together there's a fuckin storm coming from my people."

Before he could explain any further, the searcher dropped a thick polythene bag over his head. Another man appeared and tapped up the neck with electrical tape. Fear and panic consumed Bonner as he tried to rip the clinging plastic from his face.

"I know about the storm Bonner because an old friend has told me about it."

A man appeared from the alcove and stood by Whitledge's side. Even through the distorted plastic Bonner knew who the man was.

"You wanted to kill me and Charlie Wheeler so you can take over our business ye fucker. Kill a load of my boys and include us two to cover up your real motive."

The air being sucked into Bonner's lungs was getting hotter and fouler by the second. His captors had now tapped his wrists together and then stamped on his already fractured ribs.

"I guess you didn't know that I was in the Kesh with a friend of yours Sean McLarty. He ran the Republican wing, and I ran the Loyalists so you see we have done many favours for each other. When Sean comes and tells me you're a double crossing rat I believe him."

As the condensation of his breath began to make his vision even worse a head appeared close Bonner could see the mad eyes and flaming red unkempt mane of McLarty. The air was almost gone and Bonner was about to black out when he felt the excruciating pain as a pick axe angle hit him on his right knee. He tried to remember the words of the Act of Contrition 'O my God, I am heartily sorry for having offended Thee, and I detest all my sins because of thy just punishments, but most of' another blow this time to the left knee made him vomit filling the restrictive bag.

As he was about to die a silver flash appeared. Suddenly his hot burning face felt cold air, as the restrictive bag was slashed open. His lungs tried to suck in as much oxygen as they could, simultaneously ingesting some of his puke, causing him to him retch and cough. Bonner looked up to see his tormentor. Above him stood McLarty, holding a silver razor in his hand.

"Sean please no, stop the madness I didn't kill your cousin it was Secrillo. I don't know why he did it. Don't set those bombs." Bonner gaped but before he could finish his sentence McLarty carried out the ultimate betrayal and leaned down and expertly sliced through Bonner's exterior jugular vein and then the carotid artery.

Bonner was foggily aware of the narrowing world around him. An arterial spray of blood pumped in time with his weakening heart, then slowly faded as his blood pressure dropped.

"Excellent job Sean is that the way you dispatched Hughie Cullen in the Kesh?"

McLarty smiled and looked down at his handy work "Eye that's how I shived Cullen, another fuckin rat. Now let's talk about the 11th night which Bonfire will you be going in case I need to see you about our fresh arrangement?"

CHAPTER NINE

Thursday 23rd June 1994

Alpha One

Peewee was leaning on an old rusty red Massey Fergusson tractor talking to Old Arthur Regan, the farmer from Forkhill, when Decers arrived to pick up his boss. Peewee turned and nodded his acknowledgment of his arrival.

Decers couldn't judge his brother in laws demeanour. He wasn't smiling, but then again that was nothing new.

"Sure these pictures are brilliant Arthur, and these distances you've written down are accurate you say?"

"Yes Peewee, I used that wheel like you said and wrote down the numbers in the wee box that you showed me."

"Ah, you've done a grand job, Arthur. I won't forget it. Now don't be telling anyone else about this wee job, here's some cash to make you forget everything we've discussed."

The old man appeared weary as he mounted the tractor and drove back towards the border.

"What the fuck is that all about?" Decers asked then thought better of it.

"All in good time Declan, all will soon be revealed. I bumped into Sammy Shandling in Drumintee he said the Brits had pulled you."

A shiver ran down Decers spine.

"Er yes, the bastards came from nowhere I was out pretending to look for lost sheep while scouting towards

Meigh when the fuckers stopped me."

Peewee got into the car looking at his brother-in-law, Decers couldn't comprehend if they had raised his suspicions.

"As far up as Meigh you say? I told you Dorsey. We won't be liberating Meigh for another week or two." Peewee joked.

Decers gave a weak smile, "Where too?"

"Just drive and I will direct you, go towards Kilcurly." Peewee's voice was monotone and emotionless.

"What's going on Peewee?"

"The war is starting tonight, old son. A guy called Shakespeare once said 'Cry havoc and let slip the dogs of war' well havoc has just been called."

Decers felt like there was a tractor parked upon his chest and the driver sat upon it was the man in the passenger seat beside him. Immediately on pulling away, his senses had come become heightened. He looked out of the corner of his eye to see any untoward movements by his passenger.

"Pull over at Archie's field, I've some gear I need to pick up." Peewee ordered.

This was it, Decers thought, a bullet to the napper at Archie's field.

"Pull in through the gate and go round the other gates, take off the warning markers, then auld Archie can have his field back. If you hear a bang I've killed myself with me own feckin booby trap." Peewee nervously laughed as he marched off towards the cattle trough in the junction of the fields.

Decers wasn't laughing or even smiling, his mind was racing; Peewee was now in a jovial mood, not brooding or thinking about other matters. On the contrary, he was happy, buoyant and appeared to be the captain of his own destiny.

It took thirty minutes for Peewee to re appear carting a large heavy bag which he deposited in the Golf's rear.

"That's us, now over to the Mechanic's place and let's get ourselves a cuppa."

Decers survival instincts were now in overdrive. He was noticing things he had never done before. As he turned off the Concession Road on to the rutted boreen34 leading to the Mechanic's farm complex, he realised that even though it was less than a mile over the border it was located in a natural fold in the ground which hid the entire area from the watchtowers in the north. The thickly wooded area gave further cover and was a natural hiding place for the flying column vehicles from the air. Silver birch mixed with Alder and Ash trees provided a protective barrier from the preying eyes in the watchtowers and spy planes.

The yard was alive as Decers pulled the black VW Golf into the farmyard at Tullydonnel. Parking space was at a premium. The heavy weapons had been removed from the deep hides and were being cleaned and oiled before being mounted on the Flying Column's vehicles. Groups of men were sitting around in huddles loading bullets into empty magazines and preparing grenades.

Men rushed in and out of the many cattle sheds and barns scattered around the complex, lugging boxes of ammunition and heavy weapons towards the waiting vehicles. Most of the group were wearing the issued black boiler suits, which hadn't been worn since the training exercise at Lough Allen.

The stolen Volvo F727 thousand litre petroleum tanker had been reversed out its hiding place its contents used to fill a Sprayer Slurry Tanker, buckets of icing sugar were also being added to the lethal mix to make the flames 'stick' to anything it touched.

A further three tankers were parked undercover in a large

---

34 Small country road, barely a path

silver barn, one of which had large steel plates added to the sides.

"What the fuck is that." Asked Decers and then thought better of it.

Peewee laughed, "It's an added fuck off present for Bessbrook. I can't take the credit for it I only thought about pouring the petrol down the hill from Main Street on to Derrymore Road to make the Brit sentries uncomfortable, but the mechanic suggested that we roll the fuckin tanker down the road with bombs on the side. They have scored the armour plating on the inside so when the device goes off it will send shrapnel into both the guard post and the helicopter landing area."

In another corner two volunteers were listening intently to Pat Kehoe, they appeared to be holding long green drain pipes on their shoulders, but these drainpipes were deadly as they were part of the shipment of Qian Wei Vanguard Surface to Air Missiles.

A tarpaulin sheet had come loose under in one of the open barns, revealing stacks of pallets and fence posts. Each had been neatly drilled to leave a sizeable bore hole.

"Decers find us both a cuppa tea while I talk to the Mechanic." Peewee ordered as he pushed through the gathering of men and machines.

Decers finally saw a face he knew well, Crips O'Grady was an old school friend; they had spent many hours walking around the fields in Jonesborough after bunking off lessons.

"Hey Crips, how you doing? Show me where to get a cuppa."

"Fucked if I know Decers I'm just back here myself. I've been on the road all day and night dropping that wood off to a place up in Donegal."

It puzzled Decers "What wood?"

"The pallets and fence posts under the blue sheet. I spent three days drilling holes in the centre of the posts and each of the support beams of the pallets. It's Norwegian Spruce a bastard to drill. Once we had a full truckload, we had to drive them up to a farm complex in a wooded area off the Brae Road in Ballylawn. Some guy was waiting, a grumpy auld git Scully they called him. Loads of fellas working for him, he never even offered us a drink, just told us to bring the rest of the pallets and posts up tonight. I tell you I'm beat."

What Crips hadn't seen was the mass production of explosive devices made from aluminium filings, petroleum gel and nails: all wrapped around a core of Chinese explosive before being packed inside sealed cans. The cans were then linked in series with detonating cord before being carefully placed inside the fence posts and support rails of the pallets.

The improvised explosive devices were the invention of Professor Eammon Scully. The former chemistry lecturer at Belfast Queens University was a tall skinny recluse; his hobby had been making fireworks, which turned quickly into an obsession. Scully had been playing with ionisation smoke detectors. He hastily worked out that the constant electrical current that occurred between the two metal plates in the device could trigger a detonator. When smoke entered the aperture, it would disrupt the electrical current and causes the trigger sequence.

Jim Power, the head of engineering in PIRA's Army Headquarters, had recruited Scully. Power had shown Scully how to make small incendiary devices at a bomb factory close to the Professor's home village, Ardboe, on the western shore of Lough Neagh. Scully developed his trade and quickly perfected the original designs. Dozens of small devices concealed as tape cassettes were soon being smuggled over the lough and transported down to Belfast to wreak havoc in the city centre.

Scully rapidly became the go to man if the head of engineering encountered a problem or needed something special constructing.

Along with the stacks of wooden pallets were old settees. Concealed inside the lining were two vacuum flasks attached to the arms. The flasks contained three pounds of high explosive, surrounded by nails attached to a radio controlled triggering device. The blast bombs were designed to kill and mutilate anyone within fifty meters.

Curragh, Co Kildare

The drizzle, which had started when their staff car left McKee Barracks in Dublin, had turned into a downpour as Colonel Simon O'Malley and Major Berness Kerr showed their identity cards to Corporal manning the main gate of the Defence Forces Training Centre in Curragh, County Kildare. The fifty-minute drive along the M7 had given them both time to further study the air photographs which had been taken and interpreted by analysts from 105 Squadron of the Defence Forces Photographic Section. Red lines, arrows and circles were marked over black and white prints taken by the unit's Britten-Norman Defender aircraft.

"So it looks like the intelligence from the Garda and the North of Ireland is correct, there have been landings on our coast." Berness commented.

"It's not the landings that bother me, it's the amount. Look at all those areas of excavation; we need to get eyes on the ground to find out what's going on. This could be very embarrassing for our leaders in the Dáil."

"Can you sign in at the guardhouse, Sir?" The Corporal requested.

"No need we're visiting the compound today, lad." O'Malley informed the young soldier.

The name compound brought the Corporal up to attention.

He had seen the men from 'The Compound' enter the canteen at meal times. They all ran together, they ate together and left together.

"Very good Sir." The Corporal gave a smart salute and opened up the barrier.

O'Malley directed the driver of the staff car to the back of the training camp. Hidden from prying eyes by an enormous wall and green fence was a camp within the camp. Inside the walls were a few old Nissan huts, the accommodation of The Army Ranger Wing. The staff car approached the gates and O'Malley jumped out and spoke in to an intercom. Major Kerr couldn't hear a word because of the lashing wind and rain.

"You seem to know your way around here well Simon." exclaimed Berness Kerr who had recently been posted into her new role as head of intelligence with the Directorate of Military Intelligence.

"I was with the Rangers for seven years before moving over to the National Security Intelligence Section. In fact, some of the guys we've come to brief were in my assault team. I would trust them with my life; and frequently I have. I hope to god that when I've finished supporting the national security of Ireland, I can come back in some capacity. Driver pull into a space on the right when you get inside then stay with the car."

"I take it you don't want our driver to see anything of our Special Forces." Kerr asked.

O'Malley gave her a stern look "No Berness it's not that, I don't want to get anything robbed off the vehicle. These men are pirates, brigands, but I wouldn't change them for the world. Now let's get inside Major Danny Breverty the boss at the moment and Sergeant Major Albie Docherty are waiting for us inside. With a bit of luck they'll have the kettle on."

After brief introductions the visitors were ushered into a

brightly lit operations room by a small slim man with close-cropped hair, greying at the sides. Maps of Ireland covered one wall facing maps of Africa on the facing wall. Digital wall clocks showing the local time and Mogadishu time gave a hint as to where some Ranger teams were deployed. A large oak table surrounded by chairs was in the middle of the room.

The slim man introduced himself, "I'm Danny, the boss of this madhouse, it's Berness I believe? Simon here has spoken highly about you."

Berness blushed "I'm pleased to meet you, it's my first chance to meet with the Rangers, Colonel O'Malley was keen to bring me along."

"G2 Intelligence officers always welcome down here."

"Stop feckin flirting with the poor wee woman Danny." Came a booming voice from the doorway.

They turned around to see a giant filling the doorway. Sergeant Major Albie Docherty stooped to enter the room. Broad shoulders and narrow hips gave him a triangular look. A shining bald head was at odds with his thick blonde beard and bright blue eyes. Unlike the Major who was wearing camouflaged uniform, Albie was only dressed in a running vest and shorts.

"You're not telling me you've been out jogging in that downpour, Albie." O'Malley laughed.

"Jogging, what the feck is jogging? I only did ten miles Si and then Danny here tells me we have important visitors from Dublin so I can't go to the gym. If I'd known it was only you I'd have told you to feckin wait. Any how you're looking porky at the minute you will need me to run that offa you before you come back here." The accent was broad and defiantly from Cork.

O'Malley smiled as he grabbed one of the steaming mugs of

coffee from Albie's shovel like hands. "Go fuck yourself Sergeant Major; you did enough of running me into the ground over the tank tracks on the hill circuit during my selection. That's forty-five minutes of hell I don't want to revisit. Berness I should tell you that Albie is his nickname because he's the biggest fuckin Albino in the world." He chuckled before embracing the giant.

"Good to see you Si and this lovely lady, we don't get many women down here so you will have to excuse the profanity my love. Oh, and we all leave our rank at the gate so if you want respect you'd better frigging earn it." Albie joked, handing over another mug of coffee to the now bewildered Berness.

"You can lay out your briefing documents and maps on the table Berness. I've sent for Nat Heggerty and his Sergeant Johnny Elward they are on their way back from Blessington Bridge as its Friday the volunteers on selection 'we call it Kilo One' do life tests, and today is a forty foot jump off the bridge into the River Liffey, and to make sure they enjoy the test we make them do it twice."

As Danny Breverty continued talking two bedraggled strangers entered the room.

"Is that you putting the kettle on Albie?" asked the tallest of the strangers. He was tall, with boyish good looks. The mop of black hair cascaded from beneath his green beret.

"Captain or not, yous can make your own firkin brews Nat." Albie chuckled.

"Have you beaten my bench press record yet, Tiny?" taunted the second stranger.

The other man also dripping wet was much smaller than his officer, Captain Nathaniel Heggerty.

"Fuck you Johnny, you midget. It's not a record because you have no witnesses."

The smaller man laughed "Only because you intimidated half of Red Troop you big Culchie bastard."

Sergeant Johnny Elward was a Dubliner born and raised on the Finglas estate to the northwest of the city. Johnny, one of six brothers and two sisters, had seen many stabbings and shootings. The area was known for its love of weapons. Someone had stabbed one of his older brothers Rory to death in a gang feud. Two of his other brothers were serving lengthy sentences for exacting revenge for Rory's death.

Johnny had gained some notoriety as a bare knuckle fighter and was being drawn towards the local gangs to become an enforcer until his Grandfather took him to one side and told him to join the army before he became another Rory.

"Look fellas I need to get this initial meeting started as I want to get Nat and Johnny to prepare their team ASAP. We and it is the proverbial 'WE' have a colossal problem. The IRA has probably had two large shipments of weapons landed on the Mull Peninsula. I stopped the SDU from sending their guys up and alerting the locals because we need to get eyes on to find out what the fuck is going on." As the Colonel was speaking the door burst open.

"Sorry I'm late Simon, the trip from Kilworth has been a nightmare in this weather. Oh, I'd better introduce myself, I'm Major Mike Maguire Special Operations Maritime Task Unit."

"Typical of the boat boys to be late again." Ribbed Johnny Elward.

"Fuck off Johnny and all of your ice cream boys." Maguire hit back.

The Army Ranger Wing had two elements of which the Special Operations Task Unit Land and Air were considered the beloved sons with parachuting trips to southern France and the west coast of America following the sun to ensure maximum parachuting time hence the Ice Dream Boys nickname.

The bastard sons of the Rangers were the Special Operations Maritime Task Unit based in the middle of nowhere at Lynch camp in County Cork their training areas were the black water of Blessington Lake or the cold Atlantic Ocean.

"Mike good of you to join us, take a seat as we need to join up all the military dots on this before I plug any gaps with the Garda Special Surveillance Unit. We need to be sharp as I'm meeting the G2 Superintendent Johnny Berry and Inspector Jimmy Hardcastle from the Special Surveillance Unit at McKee Barracks back in Cabra later on today."

"Are the fuckin Shades involved in this party?" asked Albie.

"It's their intelligence we are working on my friend. It seems they have been giving our northern cousins a hand and found a problem on the beach at Glosh in County Mayo. The Mullet Peninsula is Gaeltacht therefore primarily an Irish-speaking region. As you can imagine, the population of around a thousand inhabitants would be supporters of the republican cause, maybe not strong supporters, but enough to turn a blind eye to any shenanigans happening on their beaches or the road by the side of the Glosh GAA 35 club." "I take it we're not parachuting in Simon." Nathaniel asked.

"No unfortunately not, the winds are very unpredictable and landing area tiny, so even with the Red Team's expertise we are not planning an air insertion. We are tasking Red Team to be deployed covertly by Mike Maguire's Boat Troop and then set up observation posts to report what the hell is going on in the area of the beach. If you see any potential areas of interest, we will ask you to conduct a close recce to confirm our suspicions. Anything you trigger will be passed to the Garda surveillance team to check where any known vehicles or people go to once they are off the peninsula."

"What's the action on compromise? If the locals see a few

---

35 Gaelic Athletic Association

camouflaged soldiers hiding in the dunes, they might think we're the British SAS that have got lost."

It was an old joke in Ireland as the famous SAS renowned for their map reading skills had been caught driving along the border regions by the Garda in the late seventies. On being questioned their leader claimed he had got lost, but could not explain why a second SAS patrol had made the same map reading error an hour later.

"Good question and answer one would be don't get caught and answer two is if you get caught don't let fuckin Phelam O'Grady talk, he was an Irish Guardsman before he completed Ranger selection and has a better cockney accent than Michael Caine."

It took a further hour to carry out a detailed survey of the maps and air photographs before a rough plan of action and set of standing operational procedures were agreed.

As the meeting broke up O'Malley emphasised the importance of the mission in hand. "Gentlemen you are directly under the command of the Chief of Staff at Defence Forces Headquarters. He will monitor every facet of this job> you will be glad to know that I got the short straw, so I have to brief the Taoiseach first hand. There is a distinct possibility that the Provos will have better and more powerful weapons than the Red Team soldiers. The only nearby soldiers will be a squad of Boat Troop hiding over on Inishkea North island, that's four kilometres away across the sea so your best defence is your concealment."

CHAPTER TEN

Friday 24th June 1994

The Mechanic's Farm, Tullydonnel, Co Louth

Peewee stood on some bales of hay and cleared his throat. The assembled men didn't need to be told to lower their voices, just the sight of Kelly raised above them brought silence. He had a presence, an aura about him; it was the reason volunteers loved him and were willing to follow him without question.

"Over the last few weeks I have been riding you hard. During training everyone got a bollocking. The Mechanic's team also took a lashing as I was insistent that they sort out and make modifications to vehicles. Finally, I pushed my brother-in-law to get details of the Dorey and the areas around Forkhill and its protective towers. I thank you all because nobody ever quizzed my reasons so tonight you will find out what you have been training for."

The gathering looked around at each other in anticipation.

"In an hour the Flying Column led by Pat Kehoe will move out to Bessbrook. Now you probably think the towers and helicopters will pick them up as soon as they cross the border, but hopefully this won't happen as I have a convoy of cars driven by some Free State volunteers forming up at the Dungooly Cross Roads. The Brit towers will see this and fingers crossed will take the bait. The dummy convoy will slowly drive south of the border towards Crossmaglen, then up towards the Lakes. They will have their lights off and try to act as suspicious as they can be."

The crowd began nodding in appreciation that Peewee had put plenty of thought into the plan.

"Pat's boys will go over the border near Altnamackan. The route has been checked, and they have fixed the hole and the barrier the Brits put at the crossing point. Once they get in position, they will wait for me to give the order to attack."

"So you will blow up the helicopter base tonight, Peewee?" shouted one volunteer.

"No, Alex when Pat gets his column in position your brother Declan will lead a team up the Tievecrom Hill to destroy the Forkhill over watch tower while my team attack the Barracks. Then and only then will Pat destroy the helicopters."

The crowd shuffled around and for the first time murmur.

"We're going to attack a Brit fort? They have hundreds of well-armed soldiers and land mines in and around them." Albie McGlinn began.

"They don't have hundreds of soldiers Albie; some will be manning the towers and others asleep in their shelters after watching the World Cup football. If we do as we've practiced go in quick and hard the Brit's won't know what hit them."

Peewee described each aim for the Flying Columns. Southern Command attacking Creevekeeran Hill south of Crossmaglen. The Cullyhanna team's operation was the Drummakaval Tower whilst the remaining Crossmaglen team took on the Glassdrumman OP. In reserve, Peewee had kept three teams armed with heavy mortars. The job of these teams was to drop smoke and high explosive 82mm shells on to the three hundred and eight meters high summit of Croslieve which had a massive surveillance camera and a sizeable amount of radio masts.

"Once we start the attack on the barracks and Tievecrom Hill, I will get Pat to attack the helicopter base and destroy as much as he can. Once phase one of the operation is over, each of your columns will block the roads to stop any reinforcements coming in, or stop the fuckers escaping. The Dorsey Enclosure between Belleeks and Cullyhanna is a deep glen so we can hide a check point there as it's likely that the

Brits will try to infiltrate the SAS in there or on the on the Ballynamadda Road from Dromintee."

"Are you sure they will send the fuckin SAS in Peewee?"

"Not at first as they will be blind as to where I will position us. There will be missiles on a number of hills around the area to stop helicopter flying in troops from over the Newry Canal and from the north. We have sent some missiles to the Belfast boys who will try to shoot down any helicopters travelling down from Aldergrove. They will operate in and around Long Kesh as we don't want to show our hand in Belfast just yet."

"Why, what's going on in Belfast?" it was McGlinn again who was instantly punched in the back by Decers.

"The man said we don't want to show our hand, you dumb bastard."

"Now I know most of you don't read any history."

"Some of these dummies can't read at all." Someone shouted.

Peewee began again "The Dorsey Enclosure's proper name is Gleann Dubh. The historical term refers to the road between Faughart Shrine and Kilnasaggart Bridge. It has always been one of the most strategic assets in Ireland. Back in 1690, King William stayed three days in Newry while patrols scouted up around the area. Such was the reputation of the Gap. King Billy was too scared to leave his safe area, and it's safe to say that the Brits will do the same while they gather their forces, look for more intelligence and lick their wounds."

"When we've taken Forkhill, I will despatch teams to lay siege to Crossmaglen and two of the mortar teams will bombard the tower on Slieve Gullion to destroy the radio masts."

Peewee jumped down from the bails to the sounds of loud

200

cheering.

SDU HQ, Dublin

Dan Currie had just picked up his coffee cup to make another drink when his phone rang.

"Danial it's Joe I need another favour."

"Aar do you want me to come north and show you what a proper policeman does?"

"Ha that's funny lad, but you can come and be one of my probationers if you get this job right. It seems that Peewee and all of his trusted Lieutenants have gone missing again."

"Have your agent handlers contacted their sources? And what sightings have you had from the observation towers?"

"That's the problem Daniel, they have all gone. It happened a few weeks ago, and we then found out they were training and moving the equipment forward, but they've gone yet again."

"What I can tell you is that the Defence Force think they have located the landing spot and they are putting some covert soldiers to over watch. Superintendent Johnny Berry, our man in the west, is coordinating between the Army and the Garda. If anything moves, our surveillance teams will follow it. If Peewee and his gang turn up, I will let you know."

"Thanks for that Dan; I've got a nasty feeling about all of this."

"Aar I take it your government has told you about the Tungting Joe."

"No, what the fuck is the Tungting?"

"It's the third shipment due to enter Irish waters on the high tide of Thursday 19th August. That's another reason it involves the Defence Force."

Belfast

The four removals lorries had spent all night delivering and laying the bases for the Loyalist bonfires. Each pallet had been painted red, white and blue to conceal any signs of the pallets supports stringers being hollowed and replaced with six pounds of high explosives and shrapnel.

The crews had stated to strike up a rapport with the loyalist building the bomb fires. The initial delivery had started in early April with the provision of a large wooden crate, which when opened and displayed to the local lads showed Celtic, Clintonville and Derry football shirts. Concealed from the observers was a further box containing twenty kilograms of Chinese manufactured high explosives surrounded by an array of nuts and bolts.

From the initial reconnaissance they had chosen eight prime sites to be supplied with the boxes and pallets with a further five locations to be secondary attacks which only received fence posts. The final delivery of old furniture and tyres would be dropped off on the 10th July, the day before the celebrations were due to begin. As arrangements were being made between the bonfire constructors and Angel Murnane back in his workshop Eammon Scully was putting the final touches of his tyre bombs together.

Nails had been arranged to line the treads of each tyre, then painted over while the inner liner was packed with high explosive which was then concealed under a rubber strip. The tyre bombs had an electric detonator pushed into the explosive. The Chinese detonators made with mercury fulminate as the primary, and mixed with potassium chlorate were very volatile. Scully estimated that gripping one of the small silver devices for a matter of seconds could ignite them. Just to be on the safe side and to act as a secondary means of detonation Scully added blasting caps which would react to the heat of the bonfire to ensure each bomb exploded.

Tandragee, Co Armagh

Charlie Wheeler had been very nervous throughout his journey from the Shankill down to the small cottage facing the Tandragee Presbyterian Church. The UDA had been surprised when a clergyman the Reverend Owen Morgan had walked into the Shore Bar and requested his presence at a meeting. It was an invitation he couldn't refuse as the offer had been made by a John Dawson, a leading member of Ulster Resistance.

An old lady answered the door. She had a warm smile. The woman ushered Wheeler into an enormous reception room overlooking the church. A bearded man, wearing a tweed suit, sat on an expensive- looking leather chair leapt to his feet.

"Mr Wheeler I presume." the accent was mid-Ulster, the handshake firm and the look of a person with authority.

"Call me Charlie, are you Mr Dawson?"

"No, unfortunately Mr Dawson has other matters to attend to but be well assured I speak for the whole of Ulster Resistance. We are monitoring the situation in the border areas and also the recent attacks against your organisations in the city."

"It's nothing we cannot handle Sir, a renegade unit of taigs trying their hand. We are working on plans to take the war back to them."

"Excuse me if I differ Mr Wheeler, but my organisation not only keeps our eyes on the Republican Movement but also our own. I am reliably informed that Mr Whitledge, and yourself have strayed away from your primary roles as figureheads of the organisations which claim to be defenders of our community. I also know about your racketeering and drugs supply in collusion with the recently deceased head of Belfast PIRA."

The man sat across from Wheeler was well informed, though lighter and smaller he held a presence. His lean frame beneath his tweed was athletic, his eyes dark and piercing.

"Yes, that Finnian was executed by the Third Battalion of the UVF in East Belfast Sir."

"You just don't see the big picture do you Mr Wheeler? These attacks are not the work of some disgruntled member of the Nationalist community using his cause to mask taking over your inherently ugly drugs market. This is a definite challenge to the Loyalist community by destroying the command structures of three organisations."

Wheeler tried to challenge his accuser, but before he could form any words tweed man spoke again.

"Get back to Belfast and warn all of your members of the imminent danger. We at Ulster Resistance have been given information from a good authority that this is the beginning of the 'Doomsday scenario' which we had envisaged many years ago. Weapons will be supplied to the UDA, UVF and the Commandos from our deep hides. All the weapons have been well maintained and are in pristine order. We are also sending one of our intelligence officers Mr Woodrow, a former Royal Marine to conduct an appraisal of the situation prior to conducting compact training packages for selected members of each organisation. When you get back to the City get the commanders to choose their best and brightest, so Mr Woodrow doesn't have to sort out the chaff, so no cowboys have a go hero's or suicide jockeys. Also, Mr Wheeler none of your drug dealers or substance users. Do I make myself clear?"

"Crystal Sir." Wheeler muttered.

"Don't worry about the groups in Mid Ulster or Londonderry I have already been in touch with them to provide a reserve force should we need it."

"Just one question Sir, what's the situation in the border areas?"

"We have been informed that the Republicans have received a substantial weapons shipment, hence we are putting all of our organisations on a war footing. Good day Mr Wheeler."

From nowhere, the old lady reappeared and showed Wheeler to the door.

Once the heavy wooden door slammed shut a tall grey-haired man entered the room shaking his head, his cold blue eyes looked at the man in tweed.

"What do you think Graham?"

Tweed shock his head then looked out of the window to watch the irritated leader of Belfast UDA trudge head bowed back towards his car.

"What do I think, Ian? I think we have recruited a bunch of gangsters and imbeciles, most of which have risen to command level. These idiots have alienated half of the people they were supposed to protect and provided the other half with narcotics or the chance to sell the damn stuff. It's my humble opinion that we should execute ever last one of them, not training them."

"I'm afraid I must agree with you Graham, but as the clouds are gathering, we must use these fools to protect Ulster, even if we use them just as cannon fodder to protect the better members of our society. Tell Woodrow to make a note of who could become our future leaders and also the cannon fodder we can later throw under a bus."

"I will do Ian; he's no fool after twelve years in the Marines he knows the type of people we require. Are you categorically sure about this 'Doomsday' intelligence?"

"Of that I am certain Graham; The Minister was sitting beside Mr Major at the cabinet meeting when the latest situation was discussed. I will put the word out to our associates in Scotland. If push comes to shove, we might need some extra hands."

Bessbrook Mill

Kehoe looked down at his watch, it was four o'clock in the morning and the armoured fuel tanker had only just arrived at the junction of Main Street and Derrymore Road, Kehoe flung open the cab door. He had been hiding in the bushes behind the gospel hall for thirty minutes listening to Peewee's growing annoyance at the Flying Columns lack of promptness to get into their start positions. In less than an hour the first light of day would be upon them.

The sound of Love Is All Around by Wet Wet Wet was playing in the tanker's cab.

"Switch that fuckin din off you fuckin ejit Gilly, now quickly reverse the tanker like we planned then get ready to open the sluices. Once you hear us start the job, send the petrol downhill, prime the bomb then let the fuckin thing roll towards the Mill."

Kehoe ran back to his original position where Bryan Gilgan and Tobias Timbrenan lay behind a 40mm grenade launcher. The remainder of the team were positioned behind bushes and a dry stone wall on the Millyvale Road with an 82mm mortar.

The helicopter base had been quiet for over an hour, occasionally an English voice could be heard and they could see moths fluttering into the security halogen floodlights which lined the perimeter of the camp.

Romeo 23, Tievecrom Hill, Forkhill

The radio crackled in Peewee's ear, "Tievecrom in position."
It was Decers breathless voice. He'd found that the walk up
the steep slope of Tievecrom Hill much more difficult in the
dark carrying a rifle, ammunition and extra rockets for the
attack.

Peewee knew that Taylor had now got his men into the wood
line, only one hundred meters short of the Romeo tower the
Brits called R23. Slightly south and lower than Decers
assault team were Graham Walker and Neil O'Halloran
laying behind a Red Arrow 120mm wire guided anti-tank
weapon, with the crosshairs of the infra-red sight aimed at
the aperture of the box on top of the tower.

The other commanders of the Flying Columns reported back
that they were in position and ready to start the assault.

"Mortar team south, fire smoke bombs at Croslieve, once
you've fired ten give them ten explosives bombs." Peewee
ordered before turning to Manny and pointed at the gate
which led from the car park of St Oliver Plunkett's school
into the open fields which was the start line of the attack on
to the British barracks at Forkhill.

TCG (S) Portadown

The previous evening had been a rush of activity for the
members of southern region Special Branch as the towers at
R23 and G40 high on Croslieve had reported the movement
of a large convoy of vehicles moving from Dungooly
Crossroads then heading west. Big Joe had immediately put
everybody in the south region on high alert as the convoy
pepper potted along the country lanes hand railing the
border. G30 at Glassdrumman was the next to report the
suspicious convoy quickly followed by the isolated outpost
G20 at Drummakaval.

"Could be Crossmaglen they are going to attack." reasoned Herbie

"The analysis doesn't suggest an attack on XMG and the chatter on their CB radios suggests that it's a training exercise." Argued the Intelligence Corps Staff Sergeant Liam Salter.

"Can you confirm if Peewee is with this convoy, Liam?"

"I'm afraid not Joe, in fact we can't recognise any of the voices. According to one of our Irish experts in the signals intelligence unit, he's saying that the accents are a mixture of southern Irish and Belfast. Some of them are from the extreme south of the country."

The convoy stopped for several minutes close to the G10 at Creevekeeran near the Cullaville Road before moving off in a North West direction again hugging the border, but never crossing it. As the vehicles moved on their progress was being relayed back to Portadown via the small Gazelle helicopter of Bat Flight. Unseen to the towers and Bat Flight were the two men over watch teams hiding in roadside ditches after being dropped off by the convoy. Ten minutes after their departure the man would come out from their hiding positions and begin surveillance on the watchtowers.

It was one in the morning when Joe had seen and heard enough. The convoy was last seen driving towards Monaghan. One of Joe's officers suggested that it was a stag party picking up people on the way to an immense piss up on Dublin Street in the lively town. Bat Flight and Victor One team of the Special Surveillance Unit, which had been shadowing the convoy's movements north of the border had turned around and were quickly making their way back to the Phoenix Bar inside the Hanger for a quick pint before bed.

Forkhill

Paddy Key. Chris Price and Liam Dooley started preparing the first batch of ten smoke bombs and high explosive bombs which would start the assault.

"Manny go and wake up Sammy" Peewee shook Manny from his daydream.

"Why, What does that auld hoor want with us when we're getting ready to fight?" Manny was grumpy after being awoken abruptly.

"Because she will distract those soldiers on guard in the towers. We have warned her about doing her anti-social behaviour before, but I sent word around for her to give her best display ever. She's even got a cucumber to use in her act." Peewee explained.

"I don't want to know what she's up to, what I know is that she's got three children and one is black so she must have been diddling with the Brits. Call me a thick Mick, but I can't see any other black people in South Armagh apart from the soldiers."

Peewee laughed, "Sure she got a beating for that, and her husband left her, but trust me she's useful to us just now. Pally is just hiding in the treeline over there with the sniper rifle once the tractor goes to work he will shoot out the big cameras on the mast."

"Are you going to fire them rockets at the towers like we did in training? Sure they'd be in a world of hell."

"No, Manny, all the towers have little fences around them like screens so we will blast the lot away with the anti-tank gun. I'm reckoning it will take the fuckin lot out in one go."

Peewee had spent hours studying the pictures taken by the old farmer and calculating the amount of explosives required to send a two hundred and twenty pound mortar over the thirty foot fence surrounding Forkhill Barracks. Peewee had also been monitoring the recent movements of army vehicles along the closely guarded road leading into Crossmaglen. Thousands of soldiers had dug trenches to piquet the high ground. It was a tempting target, but he decided to best to save his resources for the big attack.

Some towers had received extra layers of protection. Watchers reporting back to Peewee had described seeing Engineers welding mesh screens and mending twisted wriggly tin walls before leaving.

Only a few miles away from Peewee's farm, four of his young helpers had been busy grinding up Ammonium nitrate from fertiliser granules, then mixing the fine grey powder with fuel oil. They had broken a dozen grinders in the process, so they had sent word out to members of Southern Command to steal more. The consequence was that half of the coffee shops in the Dublin and Dundalk areas had become victim to burglars, who stole their coffee grinders along with cash and cigarettes.

The residue not packed into the gas cylinders would pack out the two twenty-four foot long compartments, cunningly concealed in a stolen white Leyland Freighter flat-bed which was covered under a tarpaulin in one of Peewee's many barns. Once loaded the vehicle was to be driven by a volunteer from Sligo, who had been chosen for his clean record. They would load the lorry on to a ferry in Larne bound for Heysham where it would be collected by sleeper agents on the mainland. A war on many levels across many battlefields will keep the Brits on their toes, reasoned Kelly.

Forkhill Camp

"Sutty come up to Sanger One ASAP Sammy's up early and she's putting on a show with a green dildo or something."

Private John Hunter was supposed to be observing his arcs

high in Sanger One, but had trained his binoculars on the bedroom of 'Sanger Slut Sammy' who for years had been entertaining the troops in Forkhill.

"I'll let Ginge know in Sanger Two; he can see her bedroom from his position."

"Don't tell Ginge, he will have his pants down cracking one off, the dirty bastard. I hate going on stag after him, he's a hygiene nightmare."

Corporal Dean Sutton the guard commander left his second-in-command Dave Walsh in the hut by the main gate and hurried off to see the delights of Sammy.

CHAPTER ELEVEN

Saturday 25th June 1994

R23 Tievecrom Hill, Forkhill

Corporal Chico Hamilton was sick of revising; he was only a month away from leaving the province and getting back to Catterick to start his Education for Promotion Certificate. The EPC exam was his last hurdle in becoming a Sergeant.

At twenty-nine years old Chico was no flyer, but he was an excellent soldier after settling down. His early years Chico had shown great promise and enjoyed quick promotions, after excellent results on the Section Commander's Battle Course at Brecon, and the Jungle Warfare Instructors Course. Flush with his success came a move from A Company 2 Royal Anglian Regiment to C Company where he had fallen in with a group of fellow Corporals' led by Nick Adams, an outstanding soldier, but a disastrous personality.

The binge drinking sessions which had started on Friday evenings till Sunday afternoons had quickly moved to Thursday nights till Monday mornings. Younger Corporals had overtaken Chico and he and Nick became bitter and twisted, leading to even longer 'crib' sessions in the local bars around Colchester. The final nail in the coffin was the posting to Berlin, the city which never sleeps and always had a welcoming open bar.

A combination of fighting, drinking and general poor performance had led to Hamilton being reduced to Private soldier and Adams thrown out, services no longer required stamped on to his conduct sheet.

Whilst on leave Chico looked at his options, he either carried on his road to Armageddon or he cleaned his act up. His sister Rebecca was just about to leave college and was also set on a career in the Army. What kind of example was he giving her?

It was a late night after leaving a pub when his world changed. He remembered finishing his last pint and deciding to go to Flicks nightclub. It was Thursday 'grab a granny night' with plenty of older divorcees and married women out looking for a bit of fun. That was his last thought for the next week.

When Chico awoke, a nurse explained that a car had hit him as he crossed Southgate towards the booming music. The car failed to stop, leaving Chico with a fractured skull and broken fibula. Because of the severity of his injuries, Hamilton had been moved to the Lincoln County Hospital whilst in an induced coma.

Nurse Mandy Sharples became Chico's primary carer as her shifts on the ward seemed to coincide with his waking hours. After his discharge, the relationship developed until Chico limped down the aisle six months after his discharge from hospital.

Six years on Mandy was living with their three children in a married quarter in Catterick preparing for Hamilton number four, and Chico was living in a green steel box studying hard after successfully passing the Platoon Sergeants Battle Course this time with a creditable distinction.

Chico adjusted his glasses and looked over to the young Private soldier fiddling with the night sight the "Brendog what are you looking at?"

Private Brendon McGing was fresh out of training, a depot sprog with only nine months experience. The South Armagh tour was his first trip away from home, but in the time he had been working with Corporal Hamilton he had developed well and become the spotter in his four man 'brick' commanded by Chico.

"I'm just looking through the Thermal Image cameras; there are some hot spots just further down the hill. I'm trying to focus the camera in better." The junior man explained.

"Anything else?"

"Well, yes, as you mention it, there's a tractor and trailer just drove into Forkhill, a bit suspicious at this time in the morning. I mean we've been up here two weeks Chico and I've never seen a local farmer moving this early."

Chico smiled at the junior soldier's enthusiasm. He thought back to when he first joined the Battalion; he was just as keen. "It won't be our problem in a minute, buddy. Go and make a brew, then get Legs and Petty out of their scratchers."

McGing carefully made his way down through the narrow trap door and weaved his way along the labyrinth of fortified corridors until he reached the kitchen. The defence complex smelt stale and damp, which added to the aroma of sweaty men feeding on Army compo rations for weeks at a time.

As he was waiting for the kettle to boil McGing pushed open the heavy black metal door to let in some fresh air. As his eyes became accustomed to the darkness, he could pick out the silhouette of the nearby wood line. Down in the valley below all appeared to be still until a strange 'thump' sound followed by a second one.

He looked down the darkened hill towards the grey wriggly tin fence surrounding the barracks in Forkhill on the lower slopes of Croslieve. They illuminated the perimeter by powerful white security lights turned the surrounding fields into day contrasting with the orange glow from the streetlights in the sleeping village.

Chico removed his green skull cap and yawned; he looked down at his now closed text book. Yes, he was confident that he would pass his education and be ready for the next promotions board. Down below in the village of Forkhill something caught his eye. Reaching for the large Swarovski ships binoculars Hamilton swung them in the direction of the sodium-vapour street lights of Shean Road. The Brendog was right, there was a tractor pulling what looked like a slurry trailer parked near the junction Fairview Park and two dark figures appeared to be working on the trailer.

Thump! Thump! Even through the thick armoured glass Chico could hear the sounds. The noise reminded him of the last attack at Brecon as he led his men into an attack supported by mortar fire. He quickly jumped off his stool and lifted the heavy ships binoculars so he could get a better view towards the south. As he put the weight down an ever growing red flame was hurtling towards the sanger.

Brendon was enjoying the cool breeze on his face. It made a change to the claustrophobic corridors of the watchtower. On the wind he could hear dull footsteps on the grass outside the protective wire, then the faint clink but distinctive sound of metal upon metal. The only visitors they ever received on foot was from the COP team transiting the tower to hitch a lift on the next helicopter back to the Mill, but they were always warned off about any arrivals in case they thought it was an attack and fired off a PAD mine.

McGing cupped his ears and concentrated hard as they had taught him in basic training when operating at night. Faint voices whispering, getting steadily louder, then a whoosh as a flaming red shooting star flew to his right towards his Corporal's position high above him in the watchtower. It was becoming a surreal situation which gravitated further as an unseen fist hit him square in the solar plexus. Brendon's body catapulted back into the shelter, hitting the white wall of the corridor. Darkness was drowning McGing he looked up at the once white wall which immediately stained with his blood. It was then that the blast wave hit him.

Hamilton had turned to see the anti-tank missile hurtling towards his position his only escape was the trapdoor, but as he stooped to reach for the handle the 120mm wire guided rocket hit the steel plating just below the armoured glass causing instant heat and over-pressure. Hamilton's body was struck by a stress wave causing a cerebral arterial gas embolism. Razor sharp super-heated shards of the sangers inner wall ricocheted around the small metal box, several of which hit the still flying Corporal. As the internal pressure continued to rise within the small metal box, the corner welds fractured as the structure buckled then popped like an over inflated balloon.

Black figures had reached the wire perimeter as the two off-duty soldiers Private Dave Pettit and Lance Corporal Legs Greenwood jumped out of their sleeping bags on top bunk beds. In the darkness they fumbled to find their SA80 rifles and chest rigs containing ammunition.

A blast from a flame thrower pumped a mixture of diesel and gasoline thirty feet into the doorway of the structure, setting light to the wreathing McGing in his death throes. A second blast of compressed nitrogen gas propellant set aflame the grass in and around the razor wire defences, also igniting a trip flare.

"Hit the wire again in case they've got any traps." Yelled a voice from the darkness.

A third spray of the flammable liquid enveloped the boundary setting off a PAD mine immediately firing hundreds of ball bearings out in an arc. Miraculously only two of the deadly objects hit a target with Eammon Dore getting a graze to his arm and Alfie McGaught being hit in the centre of his ceramic chest plated body armour.

The overwhelming smell of burning flesh hit the nostrils of Pettit and Greenwood as they tried to get a fire position by the doorway. A blacked sticky mess was lay against the wall.

"It's Brendog I can't get his feet out of the way to close the door." Pettit shouted just as the last blast from the flame thrower hit the doorway. Both men died of asphyxiation before they could advance any further.

Decers and his men had been waiting in the treeline for a lifetime when they eventually got the call from Peewee to make their assault on the tower. They were glad to be on the move as the early morning chill had been soaking into their bones. Walker did his final check to ensure that the warhead was correctly fitted to the firing platform and tapped the firer Neil O'Halloran on the shoulder.

"Ready to fire." He whispered.

Over to the west Liam Dooley was dropping the first of the ten prepared 82mm smoke bombs into the mortar.

O'Halloran waited until he had heard the second mortar round head off towards the towers on top of Croslieve. His point of aim was the southern facing green window of the box on top of the tower. A faint light was just radiating from inside as the trigger was slowly squeezed, starting the soft launch.

Eammon Dore grabbed Decers by the arm, "Look, there's a Brit at the door." He whispered. The sound of Dore's 7.62mm ammunition belts hanging from his Type 80 machine gun clinking and drawing the attention of the drab figure in the doorway.

Without order Sean Gilgan carrying a sniper rifle fired one shot at the centre mass of the dark shape. The 7.62mm bullet fired from an NDM -86 sniper rifle travelling at eight hundred and thirty meters a second, hitting the soldier square in the chest causing a colossal kinetic energy wave to rip through his body destroying his heart and lungs, breaking his spine before embedding into the wall behind.

"Hit the wire with the flamethrower." Ordered Decers.

Dennis O'Neil gladly obliged. He was sick of carrying the cumbersome tanks on his back.

"Hit the wire again in case they've got any traps." Screamed Decers above the gunfire.

As the grass burned hidden munitions exploded, one producing a ball of bright white light which shone for nearly a minute. The second explosion sent shrapnel towards the attackers, but caused no series injury although they all heard the hot ball bearings flying past them into the treeline.

O'Neil, partially blinded by the fierce white light, fired off a third blast of flames towards the doorway. His face was black from the smoke produced by the flamethrower.

Forkhill Barracks

The operations room buzzer activated, waking the duty signaller from his catnap.

"Operations, this is Hunter in Sanger One I can hear mortar shells being fired from the direction of Oliver Plunkett Church." Private Hunter shouted over the intercom.

Company Sergeant Major Jim Cunningham standing in as the duty night watch keeper immediately dropped his paper and hit the red mortar alarm button on the desk. Quickly scrabbling for the handset to warn everyone in camp to expect an immediate attack.

"Stay under cover until the bombardment has ceased." He commanded. Fuck, I need to ring the Battalion watch keeper and get a quick reaction force up in the air immediately, he thought.

"Sir, it's Hunter again. He says that 23 is being attacked and has just seen a ball of flames." The duty signaller Private John Ahmed relayed.

"Get on the net to 23; find out what the fuck is going on up there while I ring the Mill." The Sergeant Major coolly instructed.

The buzzer went again "Sanger Two I have just seen a ball of flames directed at Sanger One, it's ablaze."

After hearing the mortars being fired, Dennis Dinley and his partner Connor Johnson had cautiously moved the tractor towing a large slurry trailer forward along the Shean Road until it forked with Slieve Brac Park. An enormous explosion from the top of the Tievecrom Hill temporarily distracted the pair as they looked up to their right and saw a fireball rising from the tower. Conner kicked the small jockey motor which would power the pump to project a blanket of molten liquid towards the front gate and sentry tower of the barracks.

The soldier on duty was momentarily distracted, watching the attack up on the hill and did not realise the developing danger. At fifty meters Johnson aimed the spray gun and fired a ten second burst of flame which stuck to all surfaces of the observation tower. The flammable mixture with added icing sugar acted like napalm, some of which entered through the open metal aperture of Sanger One.

A shot rang out from the treeline, and then the crash of glass and metal as the first of the large tower cameras was smashed to smithereens. Moments later a second shot destroyed the second camera. A darkened face moved into the square frame of the open window of the North West facing Sanger Three.

Pally noticed the movement. The face although camouflaged could still be clearly seen. A quick range estimation and adjustment to the elevation drum, and the sniper was ready. The face reappeared as Pally controlled his breathing and took up the first pressure on the trigger, then squeezed. The face disappeared in a haze of crimson mist.

In the meantime Peewee had manoeuvred the rest of his forces into a bush line to the west of the barracks, on his order an 82 mm high explosive shell fired from a Type 78 smoothbore recoilless gun fired at the western tower Sanger Two missing it by a few millimetres.

"Reload and fire again quickly." Peewee ordered

Lance Corporal Ginge Bonsell immediately recognised the threat and fired a General Purpose Machine Gun towards the flash, some rounds hitting the armoured windshield and armour sides of the 4x4 carrying the recoilless gun.

Seconds later a high explosive anti-tank shell hit Bonsell's tower, instantly killing the Lance Corporal.

From Peewee's vehicle a grenade launcher began pumping 35 mm bomblets over the wriggly tin fence. Other vehicles within the flying column opened up with 14.5mm anti-aircraft machine guns.

Sanger Four was silent. A ranging shot fired by the sniper had been slightly low and had hit the lip of the metal-framed window, causing the bullet to rise and spin. Private Harvey McGovern had backed away from into the darkness when the round hit him just below the left cheek, bursting his eyeball and tumbling through his sinus until it lodged into his brain.

Major Michael Hammond, the Officer Commanding B Company 2 Royal Anglian Regiment, had hastily made his way to the operations room. His boots were unlaced and shirt open.

"What the fucks going on Jim?"

"We've lost comms with 23 and the Sangers, I've been in touch with Battalion."

Jim was stopped as the sounds of a machine gun being fired could be clearly heard.

"That's Sanger Two!"

BOOM! The shock wave from the blast reverberated around the room.

The first Barrack Buster mortar hit the grey corrugated steel fence only halfway up, tearing two panels away before the homemade explosive detonated, destroying the outer breeze block wall and sending shards of masonry and metal into the camp. The second mortar was slightly more successful hitting inside the barracks and rupturing the fuel tanks of the camps butane gas tanks which erupted like a rocket on take-off. The third and final round remained fizzing within its tube before gasping its last breath and exploding in its tube smashing windows in the nearby estate.

Peewee did a quick calculation of why the mortars didn't fly into the centre of the camp. He quickly concluded that the Farmer had overestimated the barbed wire depth and fence heights during his triangulation.

"Paddy stop firing at Croslieve and get Liam to put five explosive bombs into the barracks, the Buster didn't do the trick." Peewee shouted over the radio.

Bessbrook Mill

Pat Kehoe looked around the corner of Bessbrook Gospel Hall on Main Street and looked out towards the fence surrounding the helicopter landing area.

"I can hear a few shouts from the landing pad and people running, set the sluices going Gilly. Mortar team fire now." Ordered Pat then tapped Tobias Timbrenan on the shoulder. Ten 35 mm grenades were immediately pumped over the wall towards the grounded helicopters, joined a moment later by an 82mm high explosive mortar shell.

Bryan Gilgan at the rear of the armoured tanker had originally struggled to turn the large red dial to open the sluices on the tanker, but after a few seconds puffing and panting the petrol was flowing down the hill like a burst dam. Gilgan pulled two dowel pins acting as safety pins on the timing devices and quickly jumped back into the cab of the vehicle and started the engine, once the wheels were in motion and on the downward angle of the slope the tanker had enough momentum for Gilgan to leap from the vehicle, allowing it to free wheel towards the main gates of the mill.

Within the perimeter fence the flying grenades had been accurately sending slivers of air bursting piano wire in wide-ranging arcs. The mortar was not as precise with the first round flying high over the compound and landing by the metal fence in front of the primary gate.

"Drop your fire by one hundred yards." Yelled Kehoe on the radio.

The Crossmaglen mortar team were used to firing improvised devices, landing a bomb within two hundred yards of a camp was an achievement, but off the shelf military equipment was precise and could, if used correctly hit the same area every time. They had practiced hard at Lough Allen, trying to adjust fire from one target to a secondary one and make corrections to the fall of shot. The mortar men made the adjustments, dials were moved and the angle of the barrel altered accordingly.

The next three mortars hit the centre of the helipad, destroying a Lynx parked by the side of the control room. The next burst of rounds peppered the tanks of the fuel bowsers waiting to refuel aircraft. Aviation fuel vapour filled the air, the smell of kerosene was now prominent indicating to the hiding ground crew that their situation was critical.

A bund wall made from breeze blocks protected the south of the helipad. Dug into a pit was the bulk fuel area where several black bladder tanks containing the aviation fuel for the site. The walls had taken some damage from shrapnel, but done the job of stopping any penetration of the rubber tanks.

As the vapours from the aviation fuel reached the burning Lynx, the nocuous cocktail reached flash point and ignited in a spectacular flash of orange, yellow, red and blue. The control room was immediately engulfed in flames.

More mortar rounds landed, one splitting a hosepipe connected to a three quarter full Air Portable Fuel Container. Over a ton of fuel began spitting out its contents.

"A vehicle is approaching the gate from the direction of Main

Street." Private Tom Poole informed the guard commander of Bessbrook Mill. Tom had remained calm and gave good and clear situation reports when he heard a number of bangs going off from the direction of the airfield. The detonation of a mortar round landing just feet away from his armoured outpost pressed him into the rear wall, but he remained relatively calm.

Tom could smell petrol, it was intense; he assumed that the smell was emanating from the helipad and the flash and subsequent explosion seemed to confirm his idea. Now he could hear a vehicle slowly moving down the road. Fighting against the immense heat originating from across the road, he looked up the hill towards the small village of Bessbrook. A large ominous shadow was approaching at an ever increasing speed down the hill towards him. The fires from the helipad appeared to be reflected in the puddles on the street. The puddles! The thought hit Tom like a sledgehammer as the door of his lookout post opened.

Corporal Jim Loan the Quick Reaction Force commander appeared. "What's all this water Poole?"

"It's not water Jim, run just fuckin run."

The tanker was almost level with the primary gate when one of the rear wheels dropped into the shell hole caused by the first mortar. PIRA could not have planned it better as it had stopped the vehicle from rolling away from its intended target.

The soldiers from the QRF along with Tom Poole just made the cover of the blast wall when the parkway timer initiated the explosive devices on the tanker. The armour on either side split into large fragments, completely destroying the defences around the surrounding area. Splinters burst the bladder tanks, two gazelle and a Puma helicopter were enveloped in the blast and immediately caught fire acting as a catalyst to ignite the aviation fuel vapours from the newly ruptured bladders.

"Fuckin perfect firestorm, it looks like Dresden, the Crown Forces are beat. Now let's be like a Shepard and get the flock out of here." Kehoe shouted over the radio.

Forkhill Barracks

The assault in Forkhill was hard and aggressive, as mortars, grenades and heavy machine guns laid down protective fire. Dismounted men advanced towards the sizeable holes in the camp's perimeter.

"We've lost Sanger Two and I can't get a reply from Three and Four either." Sutton informed the Sergeant Major over the intercom.

"Where's the QRF Jim?" Asked B Company's OC

"Corporal Hardiment has got a team from 1 Platoon ready and waiting by the entrance to the accommodation."

"Sir you need to hear this now." Ahmed took off his headphones and switched the Battalion radio network on to a loudspeaker. The chatter was incessant. Radio discipline was totally lost as different locations broke in to give contact and situation reports. The simultaneous attacks had been vicious and unrelenting. Then suddenly the chatter ended.

"Ahmed, get the radio back on, immediately." The OC demanded.

"Fuck all wrong with the radio Boss, they must have hit the relay station at Golf 40 Cameras are down and only the gate is communicating we're now deaf and dumb."

Before the OC could make any plans, the building was shaken as anti–aircraft rounds blasted through the tin fence and inner breeze block walls before ricocheting around the camps confines.

Private Russell rushed into the operations room, "Sir from Corporal Hardiment he's looking out through what's left of the perimeter fence and he says there's a convoy of enemy vehicles all weaponed up like advancing towards us from the southwest. Our section has suffered two casualties and one dead."

"Jim, gather what men we have and get them by the back gate. Ahmed ask Sanger Five if he's seen any movement to our north. If we're surrounded we're fucked."

"Are you thinking what I'm thinking, Boss?" Jim asked.

"Fighting withdrawal? They appear to have more firepower and have gained the initiative. What about 23 can we get to the high ground?"

"Negative 23 is gone and with Battalion QRF tied up in their own battle at the Mill A Company won't be coming to our rescue soon."

"This is another Derryard they will be in the walls soon."

Outside the onslaught continued as at attackers now supported by the mortar manned by Paddy Key, Price and Dooley. Five high explosive rounds landed in quick succession, one of which ignited the second propane fuel tank, sending a colossal fireball harmlessly into the dawning sky.

The dropping shells were bursting and sending metal fragments mixed with pieces of breeze block and shale in a ninety meter killing radius. Voices could be heard outside the perimeter as shadows ran towards the razor wire. Someone was shouting and directing the bodies towards a specific break in the fence. A 120mm shell first flew through the gap impacting on to the wall of the hardened accommodation block followed by a hail of red and green tracer rounds fired from heavy and medium machine guns.

"The break in battle is beginning." Hardiment told his ever

decreasing number of men.

"The first fucker through the fence gets a burst from the Gimpy Stan, you all right with that." Hardiment's Norfolk drawl was aimed at his wingman, Private Stan Ridgway, who was nervously aiming the General Purpose Machine Gun at the gap in the fence. Ridgeway suddenly realised and pointed at a further gap.

"Hardy, where's Sanger Two?"

An intense blast of flame and heat burst through the gap followed by a volley of rocket-propelled grenades, one of which hit the wall next to Hardiment's section. Dust and grit were in his eyes as the Corporal tried to regain his composure.

"Give them a burst Stan, Stan!" but Ridgway failed to acknowledge.

Hardiment looked down at his decapitated fallen colleague hit in the throat by the tail fin of one rocket.

Sergeant Chris Nifton had quickly returned to the accommodation to ensure they left behind nobody. In the darkness of the Chef's room he saw movement, a big black shape.

"Louie is that you?" he called

"Yes Nif what the fucks going on? I'm shitting myself here."

"Grab your rifle bud, all hands to the wheel."

"But I'm a fuckin Chef mate, I can't fight."

"You'd have more chance of killing someone with your cooking you fuckin slop jockey, but no time to make a cake, get your rifle and get outside pronto."

More mortar shells rained down on the beleaguered camp, impacting on the hardened roofs of the living accommodation. Red and green tracer rounds zipped through the fence like angry hornets. The cries of injured men were mixed with the shouts of the advancing attack force.

A blast at the base of the fence sent one of the green support beams flick flacking backwards towards the defending soldiers.

"Corporal Hardiment, move your section to the back gate and secure it for extraction."

Hardiment looked through all the dust and debris to see the Company Sergeant Major Jim Cunningham running towards him.

"Where's Sergeant Nifton?"

"He's trying to gather all the remaining men, Sir. Some of my guys have already moved the injured and dead to the back gate. When's the QRF getting here?"

Cunningham rested his hand on the young Corporal's shoulder. He was a talented lad, a farmer's boy and strong as an ox, yes he dished out a dig or two when his troops fucked up, but he wasn't a bully and his section always performed well.

Hardiment's eyes were red, Cunningham couldn't decide if it was because of the dust or loss of his comrades.

"Section, look to your front, gap in the wall rapid fire!" Hardiment's target indication and fire control order brought an instant reaction from his remaining men. A volley of shots rang out, aimed at shadows now entering through what was left of the breeze block wall.

One of the figures appeared to be thrown back by the hammer blow of a round hitting him in the chest. "Holy shit that guy is back on his feet." Hardiment said in amazement.

In retaliation, two 66mm rockets flew through the smoke,

knocking the defenders off their feet.

"Hardy, move your guys to the back gate, it's time to bug out."

Hardiment looked up at his Sergeant Major and realised that this was damage limitation.

"Where's the OC?"

"The boss went to find Lieutenant Norcross at the front gate and I'm hearing on the radio that it's being nailed with RPG's and grenades. Colour Sergeant Noone and his multiple are checking outside the back gate. Maybe PIRA are giving us a chance to escape. Once we have destroyed all the confidential stuff and radio crypto Major Hammond wants us to withdraw and break contact."

"Where are we going to?" Hardiment asked as he fired a few more shots at the inky silhouettes.

"Up to Golf Zero One. It's a tab, but I haven't heard any contact reports from them, only a mortar attack. It's about five kilometres so plenty of scope for these bastards to have another pop at us on route so tell your guys to stay switched on."

"What about the dead? I've lost two good blokes and fuck knows about the other platoons or the sentries in the towers."

"Carry them to the back gate and cover them with a poncho. I'm afraid we won't have the manpower to extract them. Now let's get moving. Let's hope they respect the dead."

TCG (S) Portadown

"So the convoy was a decoy, and we bought Peewee's deception. FUCK," Joe Montgomery was seething with rage.

"The army started getting reports of being attacked all along the border, then all radios went off apart from the COP network. They work on a unique set of rebroadcast masts so they can still communicate." Herbie Grey reported to his boss.

"So the COP is the only ones with any eyes on the border?"

"Yes Joe, from what we've been told so far all the towers along the border have been destroyed or took a hell of a beating. The camp at Forkhill has been overrun, and the soldiers were withdrawing to Slieve Gullion, but worst of all they lost the helicopters at Bessbrook Mill."

"So let me get this straight Crossmaglen, Fathom Line Patrol Base, Jonesborough Hill and six COP soldiers are the only defenders we have to stop the RA driving into Newry?"

"Well, we still have a few smaller hilltop sites covering the Dromintee Bowl and Dorsey Enclosure."

"What's the army doing?"

"Sending in soldiers from Drummad and Ballykinler, once they can scramble some Chinooks from Aldergrove."

"Is that wise, we've been told that they might also have surface-to-air missiles. I know they've not used them yet, but perhaps they have them ready?"

"The army wants to take the initiative back ASAP,"

"Why didn't we get some warning from the Signals people, we listen in to their CB transmissions and they must have been in radio contact to carry out the attacks simultaneously?"

"The radio boys were tracking the convoy on the other side of the border, but nothing else. Perhaps they have new radios working on a frequency we don't know about."

"It's a possibility Herbie, maybe the Chinese gave them

radios as well. I'll get Liam to speak to Signals Intelligence to make an assessment. The big question now is what will Peewee do next, will he run for cover of the border or wait until we go to him? Half of the Army will mobilise and the Chief Constable is sending us manpower from Belfast and Londonderry to our Major Incident Room."

"One snippet we got was that two vehicles which must have been damaged by the Army limped back over the border then went out of sight in the Tullydonnel area. The radar from the tower on Croslieve tracked it. The operator stayed in the tower even while being mortared and tracked them to a mile square over the border."

"Why have they both gone the same place?" Joe's mind had dropped into gear. PIRA would usually dump and burn out operational vehicles to cover any forensic evidence that may have been inadvertently left behind. Such was the power of forensic evidence that PIRA had destroyed the RUC's forensic laboratory at Belvoir Park in south Belfast with a three thousand pound bomb, which was believed to have been made and delivered with precise accuracy by Peewee and his men.

"Herbie ask our military colleagues about this movement towards Tullydonnel and if there is any way of getting a closer look at the area."

Crossmaglen

It had been an hour since the last mortar round had landed in the confined area of Crossmaglen Police Station. The base had received an initial bombardment of 82mm mortars at precisely the same time that B Company had been attacked in Forkhill eight miles away. Twenty minutes prior to the attack Corporal Chris Becket, the commander of the ~~watchtower Borucki Sanger~~36 (Golf Five Zero) had reported

36 Corporal James 'Snook' Borucki 3 para was murdered in Crossmaglen 8th

230

several civilians leaving their homes and walking across the market square away from the area of the security force base.

The dark two-tier structure was placed on the junction of the Dundalk and Concession Roads giving an unrestricted view of the square and the crossroads. The tower had only recently been refortified by members of the Royal Engineers as part of Operation Rectify in which they had delivered tons of building materials along picketed roads to enhance the protection of Crossmaglen and its protective satellite Borucki Sanger.

The white walls of the village houses were in direct contrast to the dark green of the tower and its surrounding black metal cage and mesh, which had been fitted to disrupt incoming rocket attack.

The first two mortar shells fired from a hedgerow by the side of the Blaney Road had overflown their intended target and exploded on the centre of the GAA pitch to the southeast of the camp, but the third round had been corrected and landed on the roof of the hardened accommodation block. Over the next hour they hit the camp with a further twenty high explosive rounds and five smoke rounds.

A sniper prowled around the perimeter of the base, taking the occasional pot-shot at the exposed surveillance cameras and bulletproof glass in the watchtowers. Within an hour the camp was blind.

The troops within the camp remained in their protective underground bunker which they had christened 'The Submarine.'

Pat Kehoe had hurried back to Crossmaglen from the successful attack on the heliport at Bessbrook to oversee the assault on the police station in his home village. Arthur O'Donnell and his men had pressed on from Glassdrumman August 1976 by a remote controlled IED when a parcel left on a bicycle was detonated by PIRA.

after seeing the tall green tower move to an angle similar to the Leaning Tower of Pizza, to meet the rushing Kehoe behind the library.

"How did it go Pat?"

Kehoe had a beaming smile, "Do you need to ask Arthur? It was the best bonfire I've ever seen. We have burnt those Brits, and their helicopters to a fuckin crisp. There won't be any flying from there in a long while, I can promise you."

"I've done as you'd asked; Paddy Lennon and his team have the barrack buster bomb set up on a tractor in the field behind the houses on the Cullaville Road. Once you give the order he will fire that and I will tell Spud Murphy to move forward with the giant flame thrower to melt the Brit tower on the Square."

"That's good; just reassure me that Padraig has shot all the cameras from their mast and towers?"

"He has Pat, and he's also shot plenty of bullets into the glass of the towers so they will probably look through a kaleidoscope now."

"Ok, that's me happy then. Tell them to start their attack, then we will withdraw."

"Withdraw! Are we not going to storm the place like Peewee has done in Forkhill?"

"No, he's adamant we shouldn't go in just hold them in a siege, and then kill any bastard that comes down the Newry Road. The soldiers in the barracks are just a big worm and the rescuers are the salmon that will be on our line soon enough."

Within thirty minutes Crossmaglen Barracks was a smouldering mess, with gaping holes in the grey corrugated fence, the main gate hanging askew after the top brackets had buckled and broken. The main mast had fallen on to the fence by the side of the GAA pitch, leaving the living quarters in plain view of the residents of the Lismore Estate. The force of the blast had shattered the internal breeze block wall sending large shrapnel omnidirectional through the fence, some fragments hitting local houses smashing windows and roof tiles.

Casualties amongst the troops were light as most were sheltered in the safety of the submarine. Soldiers manning the Sangers had suffered cuts, abrasions and concussion, but had miraculously escaped the blast from the exploding two hundred and twenty pounds of homemade explosive packed tightly inside the orange Kosangas' gas cylinder.

The large command tower on the north-west corner of the barracks had been stripped of its green skirt and rocket netting. The rickety ladders which once gave access to the viewing platform lay amongst the other debris on the Cullaville Road.

Borucki Sanger was a blacked mess after being doused in flame for what seemed to the occupants an eternity. Only quick thinking by the commander Chris Becket, moving his troops down to the hardened accommodation had saved them.

Kehoe viewed the devastation. He had achieved his goal, but at what cost. His old Aunt's shop was ablaze on the Market Square; His Cousin Imelda's house had large parts of the roof missing and most of the residents living close to the barracks would return to a home with no windows.

Holding his head in his hands, he reflected on his role as the saviour of his people. The Brits hadn't caused their suffering; it was him, and he felt sick to the pit of his stomach.

"Somebody get on the radio to Peewee and tell him that the jobs been done as he asked." He shouted as he turned away from his still burning village, which no longer had white walls.

Drummad Barracks, Armagh

Major Dan Cairns had been summoned to Drummad Barracks in Armagh city thirty minutes after the initial contact report from Forkhill. Dan was the Officer Commanding A Company which was the Brigade standby company, awaiting orders for rapid deployment anywhere within the Brigade area at a moment's notice.

"Hi Dan, it looks like the shit has hit the fan in enormous lumps. Somehow the intelligence boys in G2 have missed a trick and PIRA has hit us down on the border, and I'm afraid to say we've received a very bloody nose."

Dan looked at the cavalry officer who spoke with a plum in his mouth. Major Crispin Gault, Blues and Royals now the Brigade Major for 3rd Infantry Brigade whose tactical area of operational responsibility included the hot spots of East Tyrone and South Armagh.

Crispin a blond, six foot plus old Etonian was destined for greater things, married to a General's daughter his next posting, which was only weeks away was to be an aide-de-camp to a member of the Royal Household would probably be accompanied with an OBE at the very least.

"Dan we have little time and the Brigade Commander is speaking on the secret line to General Wheeler at the moment so the plan is that we fly your company into the Patrol Base on the Fathom Line from where you will conduct aggressive patrols towards Forkhill. Be aware that we are also flying in Right Flank Company Grenadier Guards to a landing spot just North of Crossmaglen in order to relieve the garrison and break the siege."

Cairns looked puzzled. "I'm sorry Crispin can we backtrack a little the message I received this morning was that there had been a skirmish down on the border and that Forkhill camp had been mortared, what the hell is going on?"

Gault sighed and ran his long-manicured fingers through his mane of thick blonde hair.

"Please forgive me I thought they had apprised you of the current situation which I must stress is fluid to say the least. In the early hours of this morning simultaneous attacks were mounted on the helicopter pad at Bessbrook Mill, which is why we have moved all helicopter operations down here to Drummad, and further assaults along the border knocking out or severely damaging most of our Golf and Romeo towers. The communications towers at Golf 40 and Golf Zero One on the Slieve Gullion feature have been irreparably damaged by mortar fire. Oh, and Forkhill was attacked and overrun."

"Overrun! Christ Crispin how the hell did PIRA managed to carry out these actions without us knowing?"

"Please let me finish Dan, and I warn you it doesn't get much better. They overran Forkhill as I said; B Company 2 Royal Anglian fought a rear-guard action back to Golf Zero One. The latest estimates are that at least twenty-six soldiers lost their lives or at this present moment unaccounted for. PIRA we now know have been re-supplied with a large weapon shipment which included heavy support weapon systems like anti-tank missiles, anti-tank guns, mortars and anti-aircraft machine guns. To sum it up, we are blind on the situation north of Forkhill."

"You mentioned Crossmaglen." Cairns reminded the Brigade Major.

"Ah yes XMG as we call it, well basically it's under siege by a bombardment of mortars and sporadic gunfire and missile attacks. The troops within the base are fairly safe for the time being as the accommodation is subterranean, but that can't be said for the section holed up in the tower overlooking the market square who have not been heard since being hit by a fusillade of rocket fire and a flamethrower."

"A bloody flame thrower, what next a T72 tank?" Dan said as

his anger rose.

"Is there any intelligence to suggest they have any surface-to-air missiles? Because if they have, I could be flying my men into a world of hurt."

"At this present time G2 do does not know, but I'm convinced that somebody on the dark side probably knows a great deal more than we do."

Abercorn Barrack Ballykinler

On the drill square, A Company Sergeant Major Dennis Samways walked along the ranks of his men waiting for an incoming Chinook. Dennis had recently returned to the Fusiliers after two years teaching officers at the prestigious Royal Military Academy in Sandhurst.

"Smith what are you doing?"

"Sir, I'm just checking the gas parts of my Gimpy."

"Put the split collars back and tighten up the gas regulator before you lose the fucking things." Before he could impart any more information, the distant sound of 'wokka wokka' could be heard, the familiar sound made by the rotor blades of an incoming Chinook helicopter.

"Platoon Sergeants get your troops ready to emplane once we get the thumbs up from the loadmaster." Samways ordered as the troops lifted heavy Bergens on to their shoulders.

Five minutes later fifty-five Fusiliers crammed into the hull of the Chinook were flying westwards over Ballykinler ranges towards the Mountains of Mourne.

CHAPTER TWELVE

Sunday 26th June 1994

The Mechanic's Farm, Tullydonnel, Co Louth

Peewee held the mug to his lips, all around him men laughing and joking, they had fought well. The attacks had gone far better than he had envisaged, with very few casualties. Most of the observation towers ruined or so damaged that could no longer pose a threat to his marauding teams. The large radio masts on Slieve Gullion were bent and twisted by the incessant volleys of mortar shells.

Kelly was most proud of his Jonesborough men, who had destroyed the lookout tower on Tievecrom Hill before mounting the auditions attack on the barracks in Forkhill village. His observers had reported seeing lengthy lines of soldiers retreating from the base back towards the camp on Slieve Gullion.

The Mechanic and his team were busy fixing the beat up vehicles, which had become a focus for the defenders shooting. Bullets or shrapnel had injured some men, but none seriously. The Chinese body armour had literally been a lifesaver. The most badly wounded was a volunteer from the Free State who had placed the barrel of his rifle on his boot and accidently shot his big toe off.

Peewee had briefly gone inside the vacated barracks. Some men took weapons, ammunition, helmets and discarded pieces of uniform, but Peewee ordered that there was to be no looting of personal items, jewellery or money. Bodies found amongst the debris were laid with their comrades by the back gate.

"What now Peewee?"

Kelly was shaken from his thoughts by Decers. His brother-in-law looked tired.

"Good question. I think we tell the boys to sleep and get ready for tonight. I've ordered the guys with the missiles to man their blocking positions, so that should stop any reinforcements flying in by helicopter. When we are all rested and fed we will go to our ambush positions and wait."

"Wait for what?"

"The SAS." Peewee smiled.

Cullyhanna

As the Fusilier's Chinook approached fast from the east of the Fathom Line taking a nap-of-the-earth low-altitude flight course, dodging through the valleys of the Mourne Mountains then hedge hopping over fields South of Newry, the helicopter's sister aircraft carrying the Grenadier Guards was conducting the same manoeuvres as it raced over the sleepy village of Cullyhanna at one hundred and fifty-five miles an hour towards its intended landing zone, a farmer's field on the northern side of the Newry Road between Creggan and Crossmaglen.

Major Dirk Calvert the Officer Commanding Right Flank Company of the Grenadier Guards threw off his headset and turned to the fifty heavily laden soldiers who were crammed into the red netting benches which the RAF laughingly called seats or sprawled on the silver aluminium floor. "Two minutes to land guys." He screamed, his voice battling with the constant whoop of the tandem rotors and the roar of the twin 4,733-horsepower Honeywell engines.

The troops immediately fidgeted with webbing straps and began checking their personal weapons.

Anthony 'Donald' Pleasance and Liam Crossen had been sat by the driveway into St Patrick's Church on the Tullynavall Road for an age. Crossen looked out of the window of the stolen transit van towards the grey stone tower and green solid oak door of the church. He had strong ties to the building, he had been baptised in its font, as had his four children. He was married at its alter and made the Sacrament of Penance in the confessional box. His parents and grandparents were buried in the graveyard to the rear.

"Liam can I just nip to my Ma's and get a refill for the flask and maybe a sandwich for us both?" Anthony was a restless teenager who had been given the name Donald because of his premature baldness caused by alopecia and the slight scar on his cheek from a stray Ash hurling stick which gave him the appearance of a young Donald Pleasance. 'Donald' was happy with his nickname as he enjoyed being cast as an evil guy and super villain.

Crossen was an old hand in the Cullyhanna gun team, he had fired the teams M60 and Browning .5 machine guns at the security forces on many operations, but his new weapon really exited him.

In the back of the van wrapped in a bedspread was Chinese made Vanguard Surface to Air Missile, over five foot long and weighing a hefty thirty-six pounds. The leader of the Cullyhanna team Timothy 'Fats' Inn had christened him 'Liam the SAM man' a title he relished.

Liam turned his attention away from the church and his next confession of "Bless me Father, for I have sinned. It has been a week since my last confession. I would like to confess that I shot down a Brit helicopter and killed lots of soldiers."

"Donald I told you before Fats said to wait here and stop any Brit trying to reinforce the barracks at Cross, so we follow his orders is that clear son?"

"But my Ma's house is just over the fields on Drumalt Road. I can practically see her door from where we're sat, and she makes a fine sandwich Liam."

"Shut your jabber before you taste the back of my hand. I'm

getting out for a piss."

Liam was in mid-flow when he first heard the sound on the wind. He turned his head to ensure his mind wasn't playing tricks on him, then the realisation stuck him like a thunderbolt. His enemy was approaching him at over a hundred miles an hour and he was stood with his dick out pissing on a bunch of nettles.

"Donald, grab the fuckin rocket the bastards are coming."

The beat of the composite rotor blades was constantly getting louder and appeared to be coming from beyond the hill by the Post Office to the north of the village so Liam estimated it was following the Cullyhanna Road and using the low hills as cover.

Donald was at the back of the van in an instant, pulling the rocket out of its protective blue quilted bedspread.

"Shall I switch it on Liam?"

"No, not yet. The Mechanic said that it only has fifty seconds of battery life so I will wait until I see it before I switch it on."

"Where do you think it is?"

"It's following Cully Road and will pass over the estate soon, I reckon."

Liam heaved the long green tube on to his shoulder and flicked up the sights

An alarming thought came into Donald's mind "If you shoot the helicopter down over the village it might crash into my Ma's house Liam."

"Don't be an ejit son; I'm hardly likely to want to destroy my own village, am I?"

It was then that the noise of the rotors became louder as it passed over Cooey's Hill, the final obstacle obscuring the

Chinook's flight path.

Liam flicked the small green button and immediately the firing display came to life. A green circle appeared in the centre of the screen as he turned to acquire his target. The infra-red homing seeker in the rocket's nose quickly picked up the heat signature of the approaching aircraft as it twisted and turned over the village and out over the fields.

"I'm ready." Liam shouted as Donald quickly moved to his side and removed the end caps from the front and back of the launcher.

Time froze; Liam could pick out the details of the Chinooks Olive Drab fuselage and a glint of sunshine reflected from the cockpit windows. The rear door was partially open and the head of a crewman could be clearly seen. There was a faint aroma of aviation fuel and a heat haze from the silver exhausts as the aircraft raced south.

"Fire." Donald shouted above the roar of the engines.

Liam concentrated hard trying to keep the helicopter in the centre of the green circle then partially depressed the trigger, to activate the electronics battery and open the coolant bottle, cooling the seeker to operating temperature. Seconds passed, then a red flashing light, and a beep gave Liam the signal that the warhead had identified the target and was ready to fire.

Slowly Liam took up the second pressure and squeezed the trigger fully back.

Both Liam and Donald were initially shocked at the very tame nature of the rocket's launch as the missile fizzed then appeared to jump five feet into the air. The launcher on Liam's shoulder was now twenty-three pounds lighter. The fizzing sound was then replaced with a roar as the solid fuel booster and solid fuel sustainer rocket motor kicked in after the soft launch. Within a second the rocket was darting at six hundred meters per second towards its prey.

Flight Lieutenant Andy Bigsby caught a brief glance at a flash and smoke out of his port side window, he immediately knew that his and his passengers' lives were in mortal danger, but before he could shout out a warning one and a half pounds of high explosive packed into the fragmenting warhead impacted on the aft rotor assembly sending red hot shrapnel through the engine casing and into the exposed cargo deck.

Bigsby tried in vain to control the ten ton aircraft. Flying at over one hundred and fifty miles an hour at less than a hundred feet from terra firma, his task was impossible. As the rear engines caught fire, the intermeshed rotor blades lost symmetry and clipped on each rapid rotation sending more fragments into the screaming soldiers in the hold.

The pilot soon lost all control as the Chinook began to auto rotate and smash sideways into a field before bursting into flames.

Glosh Beach, Co Mayo

Red Team of the Army Ranger Wing had spent the second night of their mission conducting close target reconnaissance amongst the sand dunes along the Mullet Peninsula. Their insertion by Boat Troop the previous night to the North of Port Glosh Beach, using the cover of the Rusheen islet had gone well and given Nathan and his handpicked team ample time to locate and construct an excellent observation post.

The misty morning caused by the warm temperature and rolling sea mist had initially hampered the team observation with the only movement being grazing rabbits. The OP in the five thousand year old sand dunes were trying to observe the T junction of Caislean Road next to Our Lady of Lourdes Church, but after a long discussion with his second-in-command Sergeant Johnny Elward it was decided that a second OP on Termon Hill above St Deirbhile's Holy Well might be needed dependent on the findings of the impending night time ground recce.

As the mist cleared at mid-morning, the Rangers logged numbers of work parties walking into the sand dunes and vehicles disappearing along a narrow track towards the windswept beach.

It was in the early hours when the patrol led by Elward found a disturbed piece of ground amongst the marram grass. Within a few minutes Ranger Phelam O'Grady had discovered a trapdoor.

"Johnny look here! I've stood on this sand and it gave in a wee bit so I scratched around and it feels like a square door. Do you want me to de-turf around it?" Phelam whispered to his patrol commander.

"Wait let's just check for booby traps first, but well done." Beneath his cam cream Johnny was beaming at the success.

It took a further thirty minutes to painstakingly fingertip search the area, then uncover the entrance into what looked like an Aladdin's Cave.

Johnny searched through his chest rig and pulled out the newly issued digital video camera allotted to his squad. Within an hour Colonel Simon O'Malley sat at the ARW headquarters was being shown the footage of the team's night work.

O'Malley rubbed the stubble on his chin and looked over at the ARW Sergeant Major Albie Docherty "I'd better make a few phone calls then get a shave Albie. I think I will have a long day explaining this to the Garda."

"It won't just be the guards you'll be talking to, this will reverberate right to the very top my friend. I take it you don't want a crusty old soldier to come and watch your back."

"No Albie, I can deal with the politicians, even when you're telling them something they don't want to hear. In private they will want a scalp, but they will also want to keep the find discrete after the events of last night in the north."

"Anything you need me to do while you're fighting off the bureaucrats?"

"Just tell Nathan to get as much details as he can about the numbers of people working down there, and any descriptions of vehicles. I will get permission for the Blue team to move up to thirty minutes notice to move as the Reds will probably need back up if this goes the way I'm thinking it's headed. Give Mike Maguire a ring down at Boat Troop and tell him his boys are going to get their feet wet again."

Newry Canal

Chinook Six was rapidly approaching Warrenpoint and about to take a sharp drop and left-hand turn to follow the Newry Canal when Co-Pilot Jim Noaks spotted the orange flash illuminating the skyline above the Fathom Line "Incoming!"

Without hesitation the pilot Flight Lieutenant Bryan Scott dropped his aircraft down towards the canal then performed a banking turn left towards the cold waters of Carlingford Lock, making the pursuing missile twist and turn, burning its precious fuel at every rotation. The Fusiliers in the rear were thrown about like washing in a tumble dryer as the airframe flipped one way then the other.

"I can't outrun the damn thing or out fly it, but I can out fool it, well at least I think I can. Start counting Jim." Bryan remarked as he threw his aircraft into a series of banking manoeuvres.

"What?" the wide-eyed Co-Pilot screamed.

"These missiles have about eighteen seconds of fuel, so fucking count."

Just as Jim was about to call fourteen, the SAM self-destructed after reaching the end of its life, thirty meters from the rear of the Chinook fuselage. Shards of metal were sucked into the engine intakes, causing the turbines to cough and splutter.

"I need to drop the crate down quickly we've been lucky that the bastards fired front on and you saw it Jim. Look I've got an oil warning light on now call mayday and I will get us a landing spot I don't fancy a swim and neither will the boys in the back, especially their Sergeant Major he looks a big bastard."

Chinook Six narrowly avoided a copse of trees before coming to a skidding halt in a muddy cow field off Drumsesk Road near Rostrevor. The aircrew immediately began shouting orders for the Fusiliers to evacuate as the pilot and Co-pilot began closing down the engines.

"Stay calm, man! There's no need to panic." Samways boomed as he picked up his shaken Fusiliers.

"Form an orderly file and get off the aircraft and get into all round defence one hundred meters around the chopper. Platoon Sergeant's report to me with your casualty states. Corporal Young get me some communication back to Battalion."

Samways strode off the aircraft as if he'd been walking down the promenade on a sunny summer's day.

TCG Portadown

The Tasking Group South's morning meeting had been rescheduled from its usual eight o'clock start back to ten. Joe had been in his office since they had passed word to him of the attacks in South Armagh. In the hours that passed, Joe had phoned every one of his agent handlers to get them to contact their assets to try to get some information. If this was the work of South Armagh Brigade, they must have had help. He was sure who the head organiser had been, but such manpower, where had it come from? The weaponry used and the amount of it was staggering, added to the homemade bunker busters and flame thrower tractors had been decisive in routing the soldiers from Forkhill Barracks.

Unanswered questions were whirling in Joe's head. How did they get the volunteers over the border with the amount of surveillance towers covering the crossing points? Where did they hide the weapons, who had taught them new tactics and had they trained for the assault, then the big two? Why hadn't any of the informants under control of his handlers spoke about a forthcoming attack and what was Peewee going to do next?

"Joe I think you'd better come down to the operations room straight away." It was Herbie's voice on the phone, but he sounded distant, disconnected.

"I take it's not splendid news." The phone line went dead.

Joe opened the door of the operations room and blinked at the brightness of the large space. An illuminated map board with blue china graph markings stretched along the wall to his right. Air photographs were strewn on the desk in between the radio sets. Three soldiers wearing headphones sat at the long desk which resembled a shop counter. Plastic sheets covered the top to protect sheets of phone numbers and code words. On the far wall the magnolia painted wall was covered with large television monitors showing live feeds in black and white, colour and thermal images of various aspects of Alpha One the Kelly household. They had pinned montages of faces to a large cork board on his left along with a large-scale map of South Armagh. In the corner was a tall table which was surrounded by Joe's senior officers along with Seb, Kris and Martin.

Nobody had noticed Joe's arrival; all were transfixed to a large television high on the wall. The image was a burning field and twisted metal. Firemen in their black tunics and bright yellow trousers were trying in vain to saturate the roaring fire.

"What's going on?" Joe asked.

Seb looked away from the carnage, "They've shot down a Chinook trying to get troops into Cross. It looks like they are all dead, Joe."

"Christ, no!"

"Before you ask Joe, a request has been made to the director of Special Forces in London to deploy a full squadron, but it might take some time as we have a B Squadron out in the Middle East assisting a government at the behest of UKPLC, D Squadron with our American friends monitoring the developing situation in the Balkans and obviously the rest of Ulster Troop which at this moment is A Squadron are the standby anti-terrorist unit held back in Hereford. We are pinning our hope that G Squadron are called back from their annual Norway exercise to lend a hand. The sixteen guys from Ulster Troop have been withdrawn from supporting 39 Brigade in Belfast and will be here shortly."

Joe leaned back against the door and sighed. Two years from retirement, a line days ago he wasn't looking forward to crossing, but days like this made it so tantalising.

"Look Joe, I know Cedric, the Director of Special Forces, he was my CO in the Regiment he's a good guy and he will move heaven and earth to get as many guys over here as possible. I spoke to his aide a few minutes ago, but he's been called to COBR37 meeting in Whitehall."

There was a sombre mood in the room when all the participants took their seats around the table. Joe paid no attention to the opening intelligence briefing being delivered by Liam Salter; he was pre-occupied looking at a list of the dead soldiers. There had been gasps as Liam had mentioned attack sites and the numbers of dead and injured. As he

37 The Cabinet Office Briefing Rooms

finished all eyes turned to Joe. He looked around the room as if looking for support. His eyes were moist.

"We have a company of soldiers under siege in Crossmaglen, missing men in Forkhill, six men from the Fusiliers COP cut off from safety and destroyed surveillance towers and radio mast still smouldering on the hills overlooking the border. I need to know what's going on down there and quickly, so the floor is open to you."

Julian Clemont a former cavalry officer, small and pale was the Commanding Officer of South Det, was in complete contrast to Seb who appeared to be perm tanned after a two-year secondment with the Sultan of Oman's Special Forces and standing six foot three in his stocking feet.

"Seb and I have been looking at the situation Joe, and we both feel it would be best suited if my guys did a drive down with our Gazelle Helicopter in support. It's what the green army would call an advance to contact."

Kris Derbyshire made a coughing sound.

"Sorry to piss on your chips boss, but there is a total ban on all flights and that's from the head shed in Brigade. Losing Bessbrook means that all air support will move to Drummad until the sappers can sort out what's left of the mill. So if you want to do a Charge of the Light Brigade down south, you won't have any top cover."

Julian remained resolute "Look Joe I held a Chinese parliament with my teams this morning; probably a terrible choice of terminology in the present climate I know, but all of them want to give it a go. Victor One will take a central route in between Silverbridge and Mullaghbawn Victor Two will handrail the Fathom Line to the east and Victor Three will take the west from Newtownhamilton towards Creggan. Each team will be mobile in four vehicles and we are up gunning them to three operators in three of the smaller cars and four operators in the larger Trojan command cars. A motorcycle will lead each team as they are fast and agile. I will brief all teams to avoid contact if possible to carry out a search and rescue mission and also assess the collateral damage. The teams are ready to move once we get your blessing, Joe."

Joe thought long and hard about the proposal which had been put to him so eloquently.

His concentration was broken by one of the Special Branch officers entering the room.

"Sorry to break in boss but we've just been told that the fire service have found two survivors who were thrown from the Chinook in Cullyhanna a crewman and a Grenadier Guard's Corporal. It's a miracle they survived and also that the Republicans didn't find them. The Firemen have hidden them in their vehicles and will get them to safety. Also Golf Zero One is reporting that it has observed soldiers in the area of the Glenmore Road north of Silverbridge. It is possible that it's some troops from Forkhill that have got disorientated during the evacuation. They have had stragglers make it back to Slieve Gullion all morning."

Joe nodded, his mind made up.

"Julian you do realise that we have no coverage once your guys get south of Newry. God knows how far Peewee has pushed his pawns up onto the table. They have anti-tank guns and rockets, not to mention heavy machine guns. They could probably ride into the gates of hell. Once you have briefed them to remind them of the words of Alfred, Lord Tennyson *'All in the valley of Death rode the six hundred. Forward, the Light Brigade! Charge for the guns!'* I will forward mount teams from the Mobile Support Unit to act as your cavalry should you need it, but remember that they aren't as agile as your troops so it might take a while before they arrive, but it's better than nothing."

"Theirs's not to reason why, theirs's but to do and die. Into the valley of Death rode the six hundred." replied Colin Armstrong shaking his head.

Belfast

The removals lorry dropped off its last load of the day. Wooden pallets, fence posts and settees were left at the rapidly rising Bonfire site at Finvoy Street in Belfast. The deliverers had been happy to see that all the sites they had visited were now boasting red, white and blue beacons at least fifteen feet high and flourishing.

The local youths who had been guarding the area had been more than happy to help unload the cargo, which unbeknown to them hid concealed explosive devices.

It had been a long and demanding week for the delivery crew since the deliveries had begun. Seventeen hundred wooden pallets had been delivered to fourteen different Loyalist sites throughout Ulster. They had taken the eight large wooden boxes containing twenty kilograms of high explosive surrounded by nuts and bolts to the areas most likely to attract sizeable crowds.

Five hundred fence posts, each one concealing a thirty inch plastic explosive sausage packed into welded tins surrounded by bolts and nails, had also been dropped off at each location. The last items to be delivered just before the attack were the old sofas, containing pipe bombs made from vacuum flasks consisting of aluminium dust mixed with a gelling agent made from cooking jell and aviation fuel linked to a remote-controlled detonator.

Eammon Scully came to the door of his bomb making factory off the Brae Road and watched as the lorry reversed into the cover of the large hay shed.

"Is that you boys done then?" he shouted as the four members of the delivery team stretched and groaned as they jumped out of the cab.

"They are just waiting for the stuff we will drop off on the

10th Scully. Will the furniture be ready on time, because a certain big ginger fella is busting our bollocks to get everything in place?" asked Angel.

"Don't you worry everything will be ready to go bang on time." Scully appeared to be elated with the news that his deadly devices were getting put in place in ever-increasing numbers. After a large stretch returned his thick glasses from his unkempt bushy hair back on to the bridge of his nose and turned on his heels to return to his work.

TCG (S) Portadown

Seb had been contemplating going to the gym and for an hour on the rowing machine leaving everything to his sidekick Kris when he received an unexpected call from the commander of the Force Research Unit.

"Hi Seb, it's Peter Arnott here, I want to run something by you can we go green?"

Seb leaned over and flicked the switch on the phone to talk over an encrypted line.

"Ok Peter before we start I'd better let you know that Big Joe and his staff are not thrilled with you or your unit. They think you have been sat on intelligence which might have prevented last night's fiasco."

"Now look here old boy I can understand Joe being a fathom perplexed about the situation but."

"Listen, you pompous Harrovian tosser, its taken years to build up a level of trust between us and the Special Branch down here. Joe isn't perplexed, he's pissed off because nobody let him into your dirty little secrets. Now give me some answers because I've got an irate one armed Superintendent that wants me to parade you on."

"Parade me on what the hell is that?"

"It's police speak for you marching into Joe's office in your best bib and tucker and explaining why you have withheld vital information which may have cost the lives of many soldiers and four constables over the last 24 hours. I'm sure he would relish questioning you under caution."

The voice on the other end of the line was now not as clear or mannered. "He can't do that I'm an officer, plus I sent all of our reports back up the chain to JCUNI as per standing operational procedures."

"Peter you are digging yourself into a hole and the only escape is to give me answers quickly."

Seb knocked on Joe's door; it was unusual that it was closed. It had become quite an embuggerance to the SAS Captain that he had to sneak by the office to get to the gym during work hours. He heard a muffled "Come in" and entered.

Joe was on the encrypted phone deep in conversation making a copious of notes in one of his famous day books. These day books were full of scribblings in a hand which only Joe could decipher. Some pages were covered in highlighter ink and others had loose pages stapled to them. Each one had been meticulously referenced and indexed. During meetings a name would be mentioned which would send Joe scurrying off to his secure filing cabinet to retrieve one of his old day books.

"Thanks Brad I will let you know when the document arrives. I've just got Seb in the office now so I will brief him and the COP officer later."

Joe replaced the handset and leaned back in his chair, looking at the ceiling for divine inspiration. "You know Seb I thought I knew everything there was to know about the people and events of my parish, but over the last few hours my eyes have been widened significantly. What can I do for you?"

"Well, I've just had Peter Arnott on the bat phone trying to make some excuses for the 'intelligence void' his terms not mine. One of their assets might be very close to Peewee, the problem is he's gone to ground, but they have come with a cunning plan to get him to visit his sick mother in the Newry Hospital then have a word with him about what's going on."

"That disrespectful posh bastard did you tell him I want him to parade on? Sick mother, you say, so who could that be?"

"Anyway, I passed on your threats which seemed to spur him on to offer to send a courier down here with the agent contact sheets. They will all be anonymised because he doesn't want your handlers sniffing round offering them a better deal."

"Ha-ha good man and I take it you had to explain what I was meaning, the thick fucker. Emanuel Holmes that's the name I was looking for, his mother Martha is an alcoholic and at death's door last I heard he will be their man. To be fair, that's exemplary work as he's Peewee's driver. Look while you're here I need to tell you something which is highly classified, it's been passed to us by Brad Powell at Box."

"I know Brad; he was D Squadron second in command when I passed selection. The last time I bumped into him he was over here as a civilian working for the Security Service as their Military Liaison Officer. He's a good egg and phenomenal when he's on the booze; the troops loved him."

"Well, he still keeps his fatherly eye on our little patch and he's now MI5 liaison with the other lot across the river. For many years they have also had an agent close to Peewee. He's coming over in a few days so you will meet up with him and discuss old times."

Seb couldn't believe the name that Joe had spoken. He smiled as he shook his head.

"Fuck me Joe my flabber has never been so gasted, MI6 has been running his own wife Eileen Kelly against him for years."

"No, she's not an agent, she's an undercover officer, been living a lie since they day she met him."

"So why tell us now, Joe?"

"Her team are getting worried about her safety and want us to make some contingency plans to get her and the kids out if the shit hits the fan."

Seb thought about the problem for a moment.

"The obvious solution would be to get Ulster Troop down, sneak over the border and have her away. Our guys have done it in the past, yes we got our knuckles rapped a few times, but in the current climate her closest help lies only a few hundred yards away with the Fusiliers COP observation boys. They have an added advantage that after six months in position they know the farm complex and the routes in and out better than Peewee himself."

"That was my conclusion. I want you to make an extraction plan which will be held in a sealed envelope in the operations room in case we get the green to go. Only brief Martin about the job. The code word to open the envelope will be Backlash."

Tandragee, Co Armagh

"Thank you for coming to see us Mr Woodrow we want to enquire about the level of the students you are training and how well they are progressing."

Woodrow was not his actual name, but standing at well over six feet tall, with broad shoulders, angry brooding eyes and bald head, nobody would question his proper title.

The former Royal Marine instructor sat upright in the hard-backed chair. The bone china cup held daintily in his huge hand seemed out of scale even though he was holding his little finger out at an angle.

His wide large brown moustache, elegantly groomed and windswept face gave away that he was a man of the outdoors.

Though he was dressed smartly dressed in a dark blazer and grey slacks crisp white shirt and 42 Commando tie, green tie with silver Fairburn Sykes daggers, topped off with highly polished shoes, the tattoos of swallows on the webs of his thumbs showed that he may not be the gentleman which he liked to portray himself to be.

Woodrow had left the family farm in Ballymena to become a commando. A thrusting Marine, destined for greater things until he was blown up by a land mine in East Tyrone, he was lucky to survive unlike the three others in the Portee lightweight Land Rover alongside him.

After months of surgery Woodrow took up the post of Training Instructor at the Royal Marines Depot in Lympstone. After five years of shouting at Nods, named after the nodding heads of the sleep-deprived trainees the allegations of bullying began culminating in Woodrow punching his Troop Commander after a course "Run Ashore" whilst dressed as vicars, which had been the chosen theme of the night. It really was quite a sight to the bewildered civilians witnessing what appeared to be two clergymen fighting outside the Ship Inn, which happened to be facing Exeter Cathedral.

After leaving the Corps Woodrow described himself as a Security Professional on his CV, which was just another way of saying Mercenary. He travelled extensively through Africa and the Middle East working for anyone with an open chequebook willing to pay a gun for hire; until he returned to his native father's dairy farm in Ballee outside Ballymena and his Presbyterian roots. Woodrow became the local scout master and advisor to the parish minister and soon came to the attention of Ulster Resistance.

When asked questions about his service life he embellished

his achievements and also included a twelve year career in the Special Boat Service when the closest he'd even been to the SBS was acting as enemy forces for one of their exercises on Dartmoor.

Mr Woodrow cleared his throat and placed the cup on the saucer waiting on the white-laced table cloth.

"Gentlemen some people I have been sent are at best imbeciles. Some show signs of substance abuse and others are mentally and physically unfit to carry on."

"My god, is that the level of our volunteers?"

"No, I'm glad to report that I have whittled them down to six very good and determined combatants. They are proficient at shooting all of our available weapons, construction of small explosive devices, covert communication methods and anti-surveillance techniques. Tomorrow I will run a final assessment for them in the hills above Antrim if you would like to come and see for yourselves."

"I am afraid that because of our positions in our community we would prefer to remain in the background away from the foot soldiers. Have you given any thought to possible venues to attack?"

Woodrow leaned back in the chair they don't want anyone to recognise them and tell the police he thought as he looked at the clergyman and local Politician sat opposite him.

"Well, my first suggestion is the Rock Bar on the Falls Road, a popular meeting place for Republicans. I had aimed off for your question so last week I asked the six competent students to conduct a recce of some likely operations areas and they came back with not only with the best target but also a sound plan of attack."

"Impressive Mr Woodrow, when will they be able to strike?"

"I will assess their performance tomorrow, if they are up to the standards I want them to be at I will let them off the leash and hopefully they will begin the operation on Friday night. One of the team is quite a steady fellow from Crossgar he suggested a bar called the Heights Bar in Loughinisland it will be a lot easier than an attack on the Falls Road plus most of the 'Micks' will watch the world cup football as the Finnian's are playing the Italians so dependent on how well tomorrow goes they will hit Belfast or Co Down. Are you happy with that arrangement, gentleman?"

"More than happy Mr Woodrow, please carry on."

Downing Street, London

"Thank you for your condolences Albert, I'm afraid it's been a recurring theme over the last few weeks and really throwing spanners into the cogs of a route to any peace settlement. I'm afraid to say that the perpetrators of the attacks last night are still at large and possibly using the border as a bolt hole to avoid the security forces."

The Prime Minister of the United Kingdom was looking drawn and tired. John Major had received news of the attacks whilst flying back from yet another tedious European Union meeting in Corfu. Instead of facing questions on Britain's rejection of the attempt by President of the European Commission Jean-Luc Dehaene to assert a stronger influence on the direction Europe in the next five years, he exited the aircraft to a maelstrom of questions about the security of Northern Ireland.

"I understand the situation you are in John; I can also inform you that we have found the landing ground for the recent arms shipments on the west coast."

"That's wonderful news Albert I take it you are conducting further police and military operations against that site?"

"That is correct, and I am about to authorise the disclosure of all of our intelligence to your security service."

"My intelligence staff are asking about our joint venture to apprehend the vessel containing the third shipment. The Tungting, a twenty thousand ton bulk carrier, will enter your territorial waters on Thursday the 19th August. We are monitoring its progress; it might be an idea that we form a joint naval task force when the vessel enters the Bay of Biscay on route to your coastline. It's travelling via Cape Horn so we have time to plan a shared response with maybe with the combined strength of your Rangers and our Special Boat Service."

"It's very kind of you to extend your help by inviting us to a joint working relationship however I must remind you that all decisions made whilst in our waters or on our sovereign lands are made by myself and my ministers. As you are aware the Irish Defence Force is relatively small in comparison to your own military. We also lack certain equipment and expertise in many areas so could I ask that liaison begins immediately to overcome my countries deficiencies."

"That is not a problem, my military Chief of Staff will make formal contact within the hour, but there is one last request I have and I know it will be a thorny one with you and the elected members of the Dáil. Analysis of movement prior to the attacks has indicated the possibility of a staging area just inside your borders at a place I am reliably informed is called Tullydonnel. My intelligence staff would like to have a look in the area and as aircraft flights in the area have been curtailed I was wondering how we could come to an agreement about this problem?"

"Well John you are right to bring this matter to my attention and I must stress that neither I nor any of my ministers allow any incursion into the Republic of Ireland. That said, if my Garda and Defence Force were withdrawn two miles away from the border in order to not inflame the growing situation in the north I am sure it would create a vacuum for say two days, but I would also request that anything you find must be shared with my intelligence service. Oh, and for god's sake don't get caught or we will both be in the mire."

"Mr Taoiseach I look forward to this enhanced joint working relationship, thank you for your assistance in this matter."

Reynolds picked up the phone again; his personal secretary answered it. "Clive can you find out where the President is today and book me a place in her diary I need to have an urgent discussion with Mary and I don't think it will be comfortable for either of us."

TCG (S) Portadown

It was almost dusk when Seb was summoned back into Joe's office. The desk was now a mass of files and old day books as Joe tried to recollect every aspect of Paul Patrick Kelly's career and his rise through PIRA ranks.

"I see you've binned the clear desk policy then Joe."

"Go fuck yourself. Listen, I know that the Victor teams are almost ready to go, but I need another team to do a covert search at Tullydonnel. I've just been told that Reynolds has given permission for the use of covert forces to cross the border for a limited distance and duration, basically it's a 'North of Ireland problem' I will also need the plane from Aldergrove to fly over the border in the west and follow it down to South Armagh to get some photos of that farm complex. Can you sort that out?"

Seb thought about the task he had been given.

"Have we got written authority to invade the south?"

"Don't be so fuckin stupid, what politician puts his name to any clandestine activity, its political suicide. He's moved his police and army back a few miles to give us a chance to get in and out so no compromise and defiantly no shoot outs, do you understand?"

"Wilko that Joe, I will see if I can get Charlie Team down from Londonderry. JCUNI has put them on standby to assist with any tasking over and above our current workload. I will give their operations Sergeant Major a ring, I know Stan well and his guys will be glad to get down into the fields. The Victor teams have just finished briefing so I expect they will start the advance once it gets dark o'clock."

Joe looked at the tall Captain, "Come on Seb, spit it out."

"Well, it's regarding the move of the Victor teams, I'm still not at ease with Julian's plan, so I've just been talking to Tommy Trainor about the possibility of Nine Four Delta doing a night standing observation on the northern side of the hill they are occupying. They should be able to cover the approach of the team using the route out of Newry; they will also have cover from the tower on Jonesborough Hill, which hasn't suffered too much damage to their surveillance capability. We will still have eyes on Peewee's farm to at least report his movements, should he return home"

"I'm also thinking along those lines; those boys are on a collision course and without the helicopters to see for them I fear the worst."

Seb's idea was sound but entailed that the key observation post would have fewer men to observe the farm complex, and the troops would get even less sleep than their usual four hours between shifts. The detached position would use the latest thermal imaged and night vision equipment to warn and report any unwanted activity in the Dromintee Bowl.

The Hanger

The light was rapidly fading as the operators checked their weapons and began walking towards their vehicles. Test messages were being sent from radio body sets and shouts of

'See you in Dundalk' as the operators began their banter and mickey tacking.

"Guys on me." Sergeant Major Colin Armstrong, the Operations Warrant Officer for South Det called everyone in.

Ops Col as he liked to be called stood in silence and eyeballed every one of his team. There was stillness. Calm had returned from the previous disorder. In the background the sounds of further radio checks by the signallers in the operations room could be heard escaping from the open Q car doors.

"Before you deploy, I want to have my twopenath. Julian has given you his tallyho plan, and it's given you all fuckin hard ons! Well, gentlemen and ladies; Sarah and Denise be fucking careful. If you ask me, it's a job for the Rottweilers from Hereford, not the thinkers like us, and I want you to think and remain switched on. Bikers make sure you keep a bound in front of the team; your job unfortunately is to act as a sandbag. The first sign of trouble on the road you turn tail and get back to safety."

East Belfast

"How many are in there Mac D?" asked Anthony Fitzmartin.

Mac D had been sat outside the Bunch of Grapes Bar on the Beersbridge Road for nearly an hour.

"My boys have been following the twins that run the prods in the north of the city. They both went into the door on Kenbaan Street, less than five minutes later the Brigade commander of the eastern mob rocked up."

"Are you sure it's him?"

"You cannot mistake Doris Day Fitzy. He has so much gold on him he looks like a wobbling jewellery shop. It must be important as he has posted two of his heavy's on the side door they entered. They've checked a few people going in quite a few they appeared to know and pay reverence too."

Fitzmartin rubbed his black beard. "The Brigadier of Bling, eh! What a target. My team are just around the corner with the gear, but I need you to fuck off as I need to put a car in this very spot."

"That's fine by me, I'm off to look for that wee baldy bastard from Boundary Way on the Shankill."

The red Ford Escort driven by the stunning blonde did a U turn at the end of the cul-de-sac. The headlights of the stolen vehicle illuminated the loyalist memorial, and the draped Union Jack as she manoeuvred the vehicle to a parking spot directly opposite the side entrance of the bar.

The doorman looked with interest towards the recent arrival as she ducked down as if to retrieve a bag. The blonde switched on the signal receiver to the primed Mark 12 horizontally fired mortar hidden on the rear passenger seats, before opening the door.

A long slender leg appeared first from the driver's door.

"Hey doll, do you need a date for the evening? Don't break my heart and tell me you're looking for somebody else." Rick White, chief bodyguard of the Brigadier, shouted across the street.

Bridgette closed the car door and locked it. Tall, lean with flowing blonde hair over her shoulders. Her make up perfect with the focus on her red shinning lips. "I'm just away up the road to do a few messages. If you look after my car I'll let you buy me a drink later." She laughed as she walked back towards Castlereagh Road and from view.

"I will ride that hoor like a fuckin Grand National winner tonight, Chester."

Chester Potts was twenty years younger than White and in many ways much better at his role as a bodyguard.

"Well, she might be fit, but it looks like she's shit driver. Look at the damage on the panelling on the rear door."

"Well, she can drive me any.....!"

The blinding camera flash from the end of the street stopped White finishing his sentence as the seventy-five centimetre projectile activated and flew through the red-painted paper which had been concealing the aperture of the mortar.

Before Potts could turn to face the sound of the explosion, the rocket was passing through his lower abdomen, cutting him in half before hitting the heavy metal door of the bar. The two-and-a-half kilograms of Semtex ignited within its copper surroundings turning the head into a shaped charge inverting the copper dome and sending a molten slug through the entrance, killing a further three men standing by the bar.

A raging fire caused by the heat of the blast and fuelled by the broken liquor bottles started. Survivors jumped over bodies to get to the safety of the front exit on Beersbridge Road. Just as the first survivor breathed in the smoke free air he was flung back inside as if by a giant invisible fly swot. Masked men appeared through the doorway and sprayed all and sunder with machine gun fire.

"Where the fucks are they?" the lead man shouted.

"Look for an upstairs." Replied Fitzmartin over the cracking of the flames as the upholstery and curtains caught a flame.

"I can't get in any further Fitz, the fire has taken hold."

"Throw in a few grenades and let the fuckers' burn then."

The four masked men retreated out of the blacked former white walled pub, with its flags above the door ablaze, and jumped into the waiting Ford Cortina driven by a beautiful blonde.

West Belfast

"Not you again! Your trouble, I will ban you from riding in my taxi." Secrillo pulled his flat cap over his bald head.

"It's urgent Mister, you've got to go to Cable Street right away."

"Do you mean Cable Close off the Newtownards Road?"

"No Cable Street in Derry." The denim-clad youth replied as he jumped out of the taxi, not even waiting for his usual tip.

South Armagh

"Stand By, Stand By, we have a vehicle towards Alpha One." Toots Dodge was steadily focusing both the thermal and night time cameras on the approaching vehicle.

All the other OP locations immediately stopped sending messages to allow the encircled observation post primacy of the airwaves. "It's a four by four with three men on board. One man from the front passenger seat towards Alpha One. It's a good possible for Bravo One." Toots was joined by Fusilier Derm Randell.

"I'll do the cameras, you do the commentary mate."

"No dramas, thanks. Try to zoom into that vehicle to get a registration."

"Yes, that's Peewee Toots I could recognise that walk in my sleep mate, he's got another person with him and it looks like the Bitch is giving him a real ear bashing."

"Nine Four Delta giving a positive identification of Bravo One he's with a further male from the address...... Oh fuck!"

"What's going on Nine Four Delta?" The Operations room signaller asked.

"Did I just see that Derm?"

"Yes, mate Peewee has just clocked her, a fuckin good un it was right on the chin she's down. I think the other guy is the son, and Peewee is taking him with him."

"Do you think he will blood his son?"

"I wouldn't put it past him, the horrible bastard."

"Nine Four Delta, Bravo One has punched Foxtrot One and left with the eldest child, we think. The vehicle they are in is a dark four by four with a large weapon on the roof possibly a grenade launcher and a machine gun out of the passenger window."

Seb pulled the listening Joe to one side. "Do you think we should call Backlash yet?"

"No, Peewee appears to have left, so she's in no immediate danger, but I'd better ring Brad to contact her handlers and you had better brief the COP controller about a rapid escape plan including a quick visit to the Republic."

TCG (S) Portadown

The unremitting chatter on the COP radio channel had disturbed Joe. Reports of armed men stopping vehicles in the Dromintee Bowl had brought him to the conclusion that Victor Team's task was a fool's errand.

"How bad is it Seb?"

"Bad, Joe the night standing Nine Four Echo is using a thermal image sight, and it's picking up movement in the bowl and even along the Fathom Line almost as far up as the patrol base. I'm just going to ring up Julian and get them to pull back."

"Good call; I take it they are still a distance away?"

"Yes, Victor Two is just approaching Newry and Victor Three is north of Newtown. Victor One was making excellent progress, but comms are an issue with the masts at Golf Zero One in tatters. Kris is trying to get an accurate location for me."

"That's fine, stand them down and tell them to have a rethink about how we get in there. I need to find out where all these bandits have appeared from."

Vauxhall Cross, London

"London duty operator speaking how can I help?" It was the tenth call that Maxine Jackson had received that night at the headquarters of MI6, the Secret Intelligence Services who's offices over watched the rising and falling tides of the River Thames.

"Hi Maxine, It's James again from the Doughnut in Cheltenham, we've picked up some chatter about a potential meeting between Green Eight One and Green Seven tomorrow in Dublin at Doheny & Nessbit. Our research has found premises of that name at 5 Baggot Street in Dublin."

"Thanks James I will pass that on to the case officer for immediate action."

Numbers and code words, Maxine shook her head it looked like the quick trip out from her desk at Babylon-on-Thames to visit one of the new trendy eateries opening up in the railway archways on Albert Embankment would have to be put on temporary hold.

She leaned across for her glasses and looked through the lists of the subjects hidden by code words on the intelligence database. Once Maxine had found the actual names she cross-referenced them to ongoing operations until she found the name of the desk officer then realised that she had seen Freddy in the breakout room just minutes before.

She visited his office just along the corridor. It would give her a chance to pass on the information and do a bit of flirting at the same time.

South Armagh

"Manny pull up in the car park of the church in Aughanduff. The rest of the guys are there."

Manny screeched the vehicle to a halt. Within the car park were ten other vehicles all stolen by Manny over the last few months, but since falling into his hands they had changed dramatically. Machine guns, anti-tank rockets and grenade launchers now festooned their bodyworks.

After the last twenty-four hours, Manny was dog tired, he pulled up the ski goggles that had been protecting his eyes due to the absence of a windscreen, which had been shot out during the battle in Forkhill. He looked like a negative picture of a giant panda, black face from the dust of the road, gun oil and cordite in contrast to large white eyes. He rested his head on the steering wheel and tried to sleep.

Peewee had shouted over Decers to the front of the vehicle, well within earshot of Manny's resting head.

"Ok Decers what's our position?"

"I've sent up a few guys to place out the traps on the road you wanted. They've found some Brit bodies they will use as a distraction. The fellas have put on Brit uniforms and helmets which we looted from the barracks. Once they get back, I was going to put the vehicles in a blocking position on the Glenmore and Silverbridge road junctions, then take an ambush squad up to the bend at McLees derelict barn."

"You look done in Decers, so I want you to have a break from this battle and have a sniff around the camp up the Fathom Line. I want to hit that one next. You did an outstanding job blowing up the tower on Tievecrom Hill."

Peewee put a supporting hand on his brother-in-law's shoulder. Hours ago Decers was convinced that the man in front of him would put a bullet in his brain now they were best friends.

"Just take your vehicle crew with you and tell no one else about our next attack."

Manny heard it all.

"It was hell up there Peewee, those soldier's burnt bodies stunk like hell. Do you want me to call in on Eileen and tell her your fine?"

"Nah let her fuckin rot. I just nipped in to get young Joseph and she had a go at me, which didn't go down to well for her at least."

"What happened, did you have a big bust up?"

"Bit worse than that, I lost my rag, and she ended up getting a punch in the face. Fuck her anyway. JoJo's out here where he belongs, fighting Brits with his Da."

"Are you sure he's ready for it, Peewee? I mean no disrespect, but he's only just turned fifteen."

"Decers, look you can't run with the big dogs if you piss like a pup! I planted my first bomb when I was his age and weeks later me and my Da were taking sniping at a Brit patrol in Meigh. Now off you go and scout that place, tell the rest of the boys to get their stuff together and follow me up the road. It's just getting dusk and those Brits will be on their way down, and I we be ready."

"Why do you think they will use this road Peewee?"

"The blind bend at the derelict is a natural choke point; they will be dead before they know it. What the Brit won't know is that this is the Dorsey Gap."

Decers turned to walk away, then stopped. He looked towards his nephew Joseph and threw him a heavy item. "Here JoJo, make sure you wear this it might help keep your head attached to your skinny wee shoulders." He mocked.

JoJo placed the helmet on his head. It was too big and wobbled, but he vowed never to take it off.

The Dorsey Gap, South Armagh

"Denise have you got comms with Colin back in the hanger yet?"

"That's a negative Brian comms are fucked, probably because of the damage to the masts on Slieve Gullion and this valley we are following. I'm only getting you on direct mode so don't get too far ahead of the convoy." Denise Higham was trying her best to relax in the front passenger seat of the lead 'Q' car. A tactical bound in front was Brian on a black and purple Honda CBR600F2 which the Operators had nicknamed the flying bruise.

To the rear were two saloon cars carrying three operators each. Following up at the rear was the Trojan, a people carrier with six heavily armed SSU operators.

"Victor One Alpha approaching a nearside bend, high banks and a derelict barn to my offside. Somebody has put a homemade sign up. Welcome to the Dorsey Gap."

"Roger that Alpha." Denise answered.

She turned to her driver Marky "Dorsey Gap was mentioned on the briefing, wasn't it?"

"Alpha looks like there's a body on the wire above the hi...." The radio became silent, the running commentary suddenly cut off.

"Go on, Alpha?" Denise prompted.

The leading Q car, a black Ford Sierra, was quickly approaching the bend. The driver Sergeant Marky Roberts scanned the road in front as the vehicle's headlights illuminated the derelict barn and sign described by Brian.

"Look for the bodies Bri saw, they should be on the bank to our left. Christ!" Marky jammed his foot on the break as the horizontal flying bruise came into view in the middle of the road.

Marky skilfully avoided hitting the bike and the headless driver still holding onto the handlebars, but not the razor wire trap strung tightly over the road, which hit the windscreen of the Sierra cracking the windscreen and cutting into the window frame before snapping. With nowhere else to manoeuvre, the car hit the bank of the road and flipped on to its roof, spinning and twisting before coming to a halt.

Battered and bleeding in the front, Marky shouted to Denise. Both remained upside down, restrained by their seatbelts. Dave Playfair in the rear was not so lucky as he was not wearing a seat belt and had catapulted in between the front seats and smashed face first into the windscreen and out on to the road, breaking his neck in the process. All motion had ceased. There was an eerie silence. A powerful smell of petrol filled their nostrils.

"Denise we've got to get the fuck out of here. Move" Marky screamed to spur Denise into action, but in that moment the entire world became drenched in the headlights of the second Q car, a Vauxhall Astra. Before either could move the Astra slammed into the upside down Sierra.

"Ambush left!" Screamed the Astra's vehicle commander Corporal Alf Diggers reaching for the Heckler Koch 53 compact assault rifle in the car bag at his feet.

Shots started raining in along the Astra's left side, bright orange muzzle flashes could been seen coming from the top of the steep bank.

"Hit the flash bangs." Norm Taylor shouted from the rear.

It dazed the vehicle driver, Marina Appleby; the impact had sent her head crashing into the steering wheel, breaking her nose. Through dazed eyes she surveyed the scene in front of her then immediately had a range of senses overloading her muddled brain. It was the smell which alerted her.

"Alfie no" she tried to warn her commander, but Diggers was already pulling the leaver which released two G60 stun grenades from their concealed compartment under the vehicle. A blinding flash of light of around 300,000 candlepower and the bang of 160 decibels distracted both attackers and defenders. The resultant flash also ignited the petrol leaking from the destroyed Sierras fuel pump. Within seconds, both cars were engulfed in flames.

The attackers soon resumed the onslaught, firing bullet after bullet into the retreating shadows, trying to flee the carnage.

The third vehicle in the convoy slowed as the firefight from less than a hundred meters up the road intensified. The vehicle commander was about to jump out of the car when the roadside bomb exploded less than an arm's length away from the stationary Vauxhall Senator. Nuts and bolts from the improvised claymore shredded both vehicle and human alike.

The Trojan sped past a slow moving Vauxhall Nova on a blind bend, the driver Ms McGochan, a teacher at Oliver Plunkett infant school in Forkhill was tutting as yet another vehicle passed, almost pushing her into a roadside ditch.

"Victor One, this is Trojan come in. Pull over Duke." Corporal Lee 'Mez' Mereday, the commander of the Trojan vehicle ordered. Mereday and his driver Eddie "Duke" Hazzard had simultaneously seen the flash as it spectacularly illuminated the landscape. Seconds later the large orange fireball appeared, silhouetting the bushes and banks which encompassed their path.

"Mez there's movement up ahead on the road. It might be the lead crews' bomb bursting back."

"Fuck off Duke they would need to be travelling at the speed of a thousand gazelles mate. That explosion was at least a click in front. Pull over."

Mez thought hard, then gave the order to debus from their vehicle. As he was about the close the passenger door a whooshing noise was getting louder, he turned to see a silver flash as the head of a light armour rocket hit the front grill of the Mercedes-Benz G Wagon sending him crashing into a small ditch at the side of the road and peppering his arse in red hot chunks of steel.

Fuck! he cried as he reached behind to feel the warm sticky liquid soaking his jeans. I've just bought these fuckin Levis, he thought. He was about to shout out to check if there had been any further casualties when a fusillade of fire came bouncing up the road. Most of the shots were aimed toward the stricken G Wagon.

"Prepare to move." Mez screamed for all he was worth, hoping that the rest of his team had extracted themselves from the now burning mess.

On the far side of the vehicle he heard pop, pop as an Operator started shooting back down the road with a pistol. Limping back, Mez caught sight of one of his men still trapped within the vehicle. Despite the flames, he wrapped his arms around his comrade's shoulders and drag him out into the night air.

"Jacko is that you?"

Dale Jackson, a twenty-one-year-old sailor, was the youngest member of the detachment. He had flown through selection, because of his immense fitness, stamina and quick thinking.

"I've lost my leg, Mez." He cried.

"You don't need one, I'm carrying you bud." Mez looked down at the vacant space a size nine boot used to be. The foot had been amputated by flying metal from the engine block."

More shots were incoming and shouts and screams could be heard as the attackers moved in for the kill.

"Give me covering fire." Mez shouted above the cacophony of the ongoing firefight.

One of the team threw a smoke grenade into the road, to help cover their escape.

Vehicle lights appeared behind the defending soldiers.

"Fuck that's all we need, watch your arcs." Called Mez

"It's only the old dear we passed earlier." Snapper replied, but still keeping the slow moving Nova in his sights.

"Run back and tell her to get down, and we will rally back on you."

As Mez was shouting his orders one gunman fired a long burst through the smoke, smashing into the ruined G Wagon.

"Move now" Mez was trying to put his aim on to the rushing silhouette, he was quick and willow thin. Several bullets ricocheted off the road by his feet, but none stopped him.

The crew from the G Wagon screamed at Ms McGochan to get out of her vehicle and take cover. The old school teacher appeared to be frozen in terror after stalling her car.

The young pursuer had reached the stricken Mercedes-Benz and changed the magazine on his rifle, just like his Da had shown him. He was ecstatic; behind him he could hear his Da shouting JoJo! He peaked around the side of a smoking vehicle and spotted a group of men around another car.

"Da the fuckers have got another car." He shouted back

before unleashing another burst towards the driver side. It delighted him when the windscreen exploded into a million pieces. The men stood at the sides of the vehicle ran for their lives, one was carrying a man over his shoulder.

"They are on the run, Da." The adolescent man shouted as again he bound forward to kill any remaining soldiers at the next car. The helmet was bouncing on his head as he ran.

Withdrawing in contact carrying a casualty was a drill which the five Operators had practiced many times in training at their secret range in the Hollow, but doing it for real whilst under fire and being pursued by a savage enemy was a different matter. After ten minutes of bobbing and weaving, Mez called a rally point by the gate leading to an open field. Jacko was cold and white, his body limp as Mez carefully laid him down.

The shooting behind them had stopped, just faint orange glows back down the hill and the smell of burning rubber and cordite in the air.

"Did anyone grab the trauma pack?"

"No point mate he's gone."

Peewee was breathless when he finally caught up with his son.

"You ok Joseph, no injuries?"

Joseph Kelly was sat at the side of the road; rifle discarded by his side, cradling the body of an old woman. Her grey hair was matted with congealed blood. The helmet was lopsided on his head. Tears rolled down his face. "Da I've murdered Ms McGochan! She was my teacher in little school."

CHAPTER THIRTEEN

Derry

Secrillo had been nervous throughout his journey over to the west. He had managed a brief stop to make a call to his handlers on the way. They were very interested to find out what was going on and did their best to reassure him he would not be walking into a trap.

"We've got nothing to suggest you've been rumbled and if anything happens in Londonderry, we know before the Provo's do." Bernie also suggested that he would probably be promoted rather that 'nutted.'

Victor was also unsettled with the news from his handler that Bonner had been found dead in the boot of his car in the hills above Holywood. Throat cut and a savage beating, they had told him. The prods had got to him first; he thought. I wouldn't have prolonged the agony, a quick confession that a bullet to the back of the head.

It was uncannily quiet; hardly anyone was on the streets, not even the grey police vehicles or army foot patrols. His suspicions were raised further when he crossed the Craigavon Bridge without seeing another driver on the road. He hoped that Bernie hadn't made some stupid call and got every peeler and squaddie returned to camp. The big wigs at the Sinn Fein would scratch their heads how this man from Belfast had been given a free passage.

Secrillo turned the Golf into the Bogside estate: the brown roofs, dirty cream walls and rubbish on the streets screamed degeneration. No wonder this was the birthplace of the troubles. The Republican heartland which had been left to fester; whilst the loyalist enclaves across the Foyle were given government handouts to rejuvenate. They had sown the seeds of injustice and inequality in Derry.

The only hints of colour were from the occasional mural painted on the side of a house or neglected row of shops. Scenes showing staved men clutching filthy blankets or local warriors shot down in their prime by the forces of occupation.

Secrillo parked the car close to the football ground at Celtic Park, and then made his way down the lines of terraced houses to number fifteen. A group of men wearing black bomber jackets eyed him suspiciously. It was a warm June evening, yet Victor was feeling deathly cold.

"You Secrillo?" A thick-set man asked.

Secrillo looked into the man's eyes, they were dark and serious, no funny remarks to this guy he thought.

"Yeh, that's me brother."

"I'm not your fucking brother; now get your arse upstairs important people are waiting on you."

The guy giving Vic orders was familiar. He couldn't place him, but he knew they had met before.

The Mechanic's Farm, Tullydonnel, County Louth

Only a few miles west from Secrillo's nervous climb up the stairs of Cable Street, high-powered vehicles were racing to infiltrate the Southern Ireland at an illegal crossing point.

Operators from Charlie Team, North Detachment SSU had been tasked to conduct a close target reconnaissance of a farm complex over the border in Tullydonnel. Narrow roads and poor mapping had hampered their progress to reach the drop off point.

The four vehicles had manoeuvred into a small copse of trees off the N53 Concession Road. The relative safety of the border was a mere three hundred meters up the hill to their left. Sergeant Major Ben Clarke spoke in hush tones as he checked that he had loaded a round into the chamber of his H&K53. Around him the three other members of the recce team checked their night vision goggles and jumped up and down to ensure there were no rattles or loose equipment.

Sergeant Lorna "lol" Campbell and Corporal Paul Morris were to remain with the vehicles, acting as a quick reaction force, should the need arise. Their only cover was to act as if they were a courting couple should anyone see them.

"Ok guys we've done this a hundred times before, never in a foreign country it's true, but we all know the drills. Don't get caught in and out and then home for tea and medals."

Andy Holden, a Royal Marine Corporal, led the insertion at a brisk pace, only slowing down as he approached a stream or black thorn hedge, which surrounded almost every field. The ground soon changed from well-tended pasture to bogy marsh land with sparse clumps of trees which gave the invaders more cover from any potential guards.

Noise was now a problem with foot movement causing the inevitable squelching sounds of men carrying heavy equipment through a peat bog. Andy gave the hand signal to halt, as everyone behind went into all round defence scanning the countryside for any movement he crawled forward to a fallen tree and looked towards the Mechanic's farm. Five minutes later he returned to the group.

"Looks like they are still working in the complex Ben, lots of movement and banging. The place is lit up like a night match at Wembley so anyone in the area won't have any night vision. There's a line of trees to our right just over the track and lots of grey shadows, I think they might be more vehicles."

"Excellent shout mate, quick plan guys. Pete and Dillon check out the vehicles in the wood line. If you can put a tracker on one, it might give us a steer later on. Me and Andy will try to get a good look into the complex see who's working and what they are working on. If the shit hits the fan, this will be our rally point."

The team split with Andy leading towards the growing activity at the complex, and Pete Smallwood a former Army chef from Rochdale cautiously moving towards the dark shadows in the tree line.

It took a painstaking twenty minutes for Andy and Ben to

reach the back of a large barn. The corrugated iron acting as a wall for the barn was old and neglected; in some places, the metal sheets had fallen away, giving the two operators easy access.

Across the fields Pete and Dillon had carefully crossed the track and were now within touching distance of the large black shapes. Dillon kneeled and scanned the area as Pete ducked under a tarpaulin. Pete appeared to be from view for an age. The movement of the cover and his reappearance made Dillon jump.

"There's Toyota pickup under there with a recoilless gun on the back. It must be 120mm calibre at least. It's been in action as well I've pocketed a number of empty cases they look like AK rounds to me."

Andy slowly crawled into the barn, underneath a parked tractor and slurry tanker. Ben was at his heel. From his position Andy could see several men working on vehicles in a large concrete barn on the opposite side of the yard. Welding work was being completed on some vehicles and a forge was being used to realign bent metal. Andy felt Ben pull on his boot and he turned to look into his blackened face.

Ben was rubbing his fingers together and smelling them. He then pointed to a damp patch beneath the slurry tank. Andy reached down and felt the ground. It was sticky. The liquid was still dripping, so he reached up and touched the leak before bringing his gloved finger to his nose. The smell was unquestionably gasoline, but its consistency was all wrong as it was tacky. He dared a lick, and then turned to Ben.

"The fuckers have mixed icing sugar with the fuel, poor man's napalm." He whispered.

A tall skinny man stood in the middle of the yard directing operations. Men kept approaching him, then scurrying back to their task after seeking his advice. Andy took out the camera from his chest rig and took a few snaps. Ben crawled up to Andy's side.

"Who's the fucker directing traffic mate?"

Andy framed the tall guy for one last shot. The mop of ebony hair exploding from beneath a dirty, oily baseball cap, greasy blue overalls and the permanent cigarette hanging from a lopsided mouth, it had to be The Mechanic.

"After looking at the players list South Det sent us, I would say that he is the owner of this gaff, Danny O'Hare."

"We need to get a shifty on mate, I don't want to be south of the border when the sun comes up."

"Are you fuckin Dracula or something? It looks like all the gash from the wagons are being placed by the cattle shed to our left. It might be worth a nosy."

In the middle of the yard, a volunteer approached The Mechanic "Danny this radio has got a hole in it, have we got a replacement?" O'Hare placed another cigarette in his mouth and pointed him towards the cowsheds.

"Throw the broken one in the shed, and get a fresh one out of the container." Danny shook his head. Over the last few weeks he had looked at each truck as his own personal vehicle. He had spent hours creating and manufacturing brackets and stands which individualised each one. He was proud of them, but they had been returned to him in shit state. Bullet holes, twisted metal and mechanical failures.

"Let's track this dude; he's taking a vehicle radio towards the sheds." Ben and Andy slowly crawled out of the barn and kept a close eye on his movements away from the spotlights of the yard towards the darkened area of the animal compartments.

There was a clunking of metal as the volunteer appeared to throw the large dark box into the first open door. Ben then watched as he entered a blue ISO container, appearing only seconds later with a similar dark box.

Inch by inch the recce crew crawled towards the door. After checking that the volunteer was walking back towards the activity he sneaked into the shed appearing a few moments later with the dark green metal box.

"What the fuck is that?"

"A radio I thought it would look good in the Phoenix Club! Look its gash so they probably won't miss it."

"We'll put it in the club after the bleeps have checked it out, now wait here while I check that container."

Ben looked towards the floodlight area, and then darted into the container.

Holden kept observing O'Hare. He was unquestionably the kingpin at the yard. Another much larger volunteer approached The Mechanic "Danny another problem, one of the machine guns got a bullet through the side and it's knackered, have we got a spare?"

"Fuckin Brit's breaking my toys, Yeh get one out of the container, but put the gun to one side I will see if I can fix it."

"It looks banjaxed to me, but yous are the Mechanic." Tobias Timbrenan threw the machine gun to the floor. It had looked like a kid's toy in his massive hands. Standing at well over six feet tall and weighing over twenty stones, they had given him the nickname 'Mountain' because the other volunteers estimated he was taller than Slieve Gullion.

Andy looked towards the growing shadow which was stretching further past his feet. He quickly glanced around the corner of the shed and spotted a giant slowly walking towards his position.

"Get the fuck outta there Ben, you have enormous company." Andy whispered into the microphone of his personal radio.

No reply, fuck had Ben heard the warning? His commander would be trapped in a confined space with a person bearing a close resemblance to King Kong only much uglier and larger. Andy moved into the cover of some bushes, keeping his Colt Commando rifle trained on the monster as it entered the container, which now looked tiny.

Seconds turned into minutes as the sounds of heavy boxes being dropped, and footsteps on the metallic floor. After an age the giant reappeared carrying a new machine gun still covered in a greaseproof wrapping.

"Is it clear?" Ben asked on the radio.

"Move now." Andy ordered as Ben sprinted out of the door.

They spoke no words as they extracted back through the rally point, picking up the waiting Pete and Dillon, then further on to the emergency rendezvous where they lay down to observe if they were being followed.

"What the fuck are you lugging Andy?" Dillon asked

"A radio base station and its fuckin heavy. What did you two get?"

"I've got pictures of some other kind of radios which were left on the vehicles, cartridge cases and I put a tracker on one pickup." Pete whispered.

"Not bad for a fuckin Slop Jockey. I photographed loads of stuff hidden under blankets and tarps in an ISO container. Some guy disturbed me so I had to hide at the back until he fucked off, but whilst he was looking in boxes I found some paperwork all in Chinese. But it might help the Int boys build the picture. Now let's get out of here before I turn into dust."

"The only dust around here is in your wallet Ben, you tight arse." Andy fired back as he set his compass towards the extraction point.

Derry

Secrillo exited Cable Street with his head in a spin. He had remembered the angry man who had stopped him earlier, Ciaran Rock was the officer in command of the Derry Brigade and often acted as personal security for senior members of the organisation. As he drank his cup of tea whilst being introduced to a who's who of Republican bigwigs he had remembered Rock, and also that he should have been in Belfast helping the most recently deceased Mr Bonner.

The Adjutant General James McElwaine, a balding East Tyrone stalwart of the movement, had given a vitriol speech about the attempted coup by certain members of the Army Council and General Headquarters. He then read out a list of names which had been declared at an extraordinary meeting of the General Army Convention as being traitors. By order of the Army Executive these 'Traitors' were to be stood down from their posts and executed.

The executions were to be carried out immediately by Secrillo and members of his loyal Civil Administration Unit from Belfast.

Rebels murdering rebels; Secrillo smiled at the irony. An hour away from Derry, Secrillo found a deserted phone box to call his handlers.

"Hi its Bernie, spill the beans have you been promoted?"

"No, they have given me a job, well several jobs really and I might need some inside help. They have ordered me to kill most of the Army Council and members of the headquarters."

The line went silent.

"Hello Bernie, are you still there? Do you understand Jimmy McElwaine wants me to cut off the head of this serpent? There has been a coup and they want them all dead."

"Who's on the list?" Bernie asked after starting the tape

recorder.

"Who's not on the fuckin list you should ask. The top jockey is the Chief of Staff Padraig McSweeny then there's James Fagan he's Quarter-Master General, that fucker Sean McLarty who's now running Northern Command he's a dead man walking. They even want me to whack Charlie Griffin. He's 75 years old, grand auld fella he's in charge of Southern Command. They said he's complicit because he's given some of his volunteers to the fight in South Armagh."

Over the next few minutes, Secrillo gave names of men who were in line to be executed. In the background, FRU analysts were checking every name and referencing their future potential either dead or alive.

"Hold on Vic say that name again." Bernie almost dropped the phone.

"Are yous fuckin deaf? Head of Operations, second in command of Northern Command Paul Kelly."

"They want Peewee dead?"

West Belfast

Unlike Londonderry, Belfast had been a hive of activity. A wave of shootings and bombings aimed against the Loyalist leadership and members of Unionist political parties had been carried out overnight. Close quarter assassinations and under car booby traps had ensured that officers from the RUC had been stretched to the very limit. The police service was further stretched because of the Army deploying a vast quantity of men and equipment into holding areas, in readiness to retake South Armagh.

Police analysts had initially reasoned that the upsurge in violence was merely retaliation after the Loughinisland massacre in which six Roman Catholics were gunned down and a further five were wounded as they sat watching the Republic of Ireland and Italy match in the World Cup. The latest atrocities had shown that the attacks were calculated and specifically targeted against members of the combined Loyalist command.

Mr Woodrow was sat in the front passenger seat of the Lancia Delta, watching the front and side doors of the Rock Bar on the Falls Road. It appeared many of the locals were celebrating the IRA's recent successes in South Armagh and against the leaders of Ulster Unionism. The beer was flowing and songs of rebellion being sung as Mr Woodrow exited the vehicle and waved a newspaper above his head before briskly walking back towards Donegal Road. Woodrow was followed a pace behind by the vehicle's driver who, upon leaving the car had flicked a switch to start a parkway time which in five minutes would detonate the fifty pounds of energel explosives 'stolen' from the quarries above Antrim.

A moment later a screech of breaks from a Volvo 960 and Austin Montego, figures debussed in a well-rehearsed routine taking up fire positions opposite the revellers outside of the brightly lit bar. Bystanders' gaped open-mouthed as the darkly dressed intruders knelt in formation, balaclavas hiding their features.

A flash like a light bulb went off then the rushing sound as a rocket-propelled grenade hit the front door of the bar sending people sprawling. Incessant gunfire started, raking the outside of the pub and any flesh and blood which'd chanced to be in the way.

"Move,"

In the blink of an eye two men ran forward and lobbed hand grenades in through the glassless frames. Deafening booms then screams as the clientele within the bar were hit with razor sharp shards of piano wire, killing and maiming many.

"Withdraw" the assailants calmly turned to their left and jogged on to St James Road towards the safety of the Village, a protestant heartland.

The sirens of the emergency services could just be heard as the victims had gathered their senses and try to help the injured. Salvation was nearby just as the Lancia exploded into a million pieces.

CHAPTER FOURTEEN

Tuesday 28th June 1994

Harcourt Street, Dublin

"Dan this information has come right from the very top; I mean the Taoiseach himself who's has been given the nod by his counterpart over the Irish Sea. There will be a meeting of the top IRA boys in The Doheny & Nesbitt School of Economics.' We need to get our arses moving as they are getting together tomorrow night so the clock is against us." Chief Superintendent Louis Range was red faced and sweating as he had just rushed back from a meeting with Colonel Simon O'Malley the head of J2 the national intelligence service of Ireland at McKee Barracks.

"Aar Tango Squad are on standby already I think someone at J2 has tipped them off that something's brewing. Have they have given us the authority to deploy the Ghost Team?"

"Yes, take it as red that we can do whatever we want on this operation."

"So we won't be opening a disclosure book on this Boss?"

"Nothing attributed to the Garda Síochána; all products get sealed in an envelope and handed over to J2 no questions asked Danny Boy."

Renowned landmarks surrounded the Doheny & Nessbit Victorian public house on Baggot Street in Lower Dublin such as The Dáil, Grafton Street, Trinity College, and Lansdowne Road. It was a popular meeting place for politicians, bankers and well-to-do tourists.

The covert entry to the premises had been eventful because of the lock picker being unable to break through the main door. A quick retreat and further consultation with the floor plans indicated that access may be gained through a skylight. The next question was how to reach the skylight. The problem was solved when the lock picker quickly entered the nearby bank and disable the alarm system.

"Only in Dublin could it be harder to break into a pub than a bank." He laughed. Four hours later the upstairs meeting room of Doheny & Nessbit was ready to be covertly monitored.

Macau

The rainy season had started in earnest in Macau; the rising humidity levels of the previous month had given an early indication of the forthcoming deluge. The foggy morning had been driven away by the climbing temperature, which was even before midday in the high seventies. Suzanne Walker Johns and her close protection team had only been in the city for a day, but had already completed a reconnaissance of the Hotel Lisboa and a home address of Steve Ho. Accompanying Suzanne was Lee Yung from the Organised Crime & Triad Bureau. Yung had been flattered when approached by Suzanne to travel with her on an all-expenses paid trip to the Las Vegas of Asia.

Unusually Yung had turned up late for their pre-arranged breakfast in the Sofitel Ponte 16 hotel on the eastern bank of the Pearl River. Suzanne was about to tuck into her eggs Benedict when Yung arrived at her table.

"I must apologise for my punctuality Suzanne, but I have been on the phone to a contact of mine in the SIED who has made a few calls on my behalf and arranged a meeting this afternoon with our friend Mr Ho."

The Portuguese foreign intelligence Serviço de Informações Estratégicas de Defesa still kept a close eye on the colony, often picking up worthwhile strategic information.

"Mr Ho has been told we are a British delegation interested in property development in the Far East market. He has agreed to meet us at a restaurant, Fat Siu Lau, on the Rua da Felicidade. This area had a seedy past as it was one of Macau's many red-light streets. It's probably the reason Steve Ho chose the establishment."

After breakfast Suzanne and Yeung walked around the Ruins of St. Paul's Cathedral, whilst her security team located and swept the area around the meeting place.

On arrival at the meeting Walker Johns was immediately impressed by the remarkable black mahogany door with brass encrusted Chinese symbols and large smiling Buddha. The door framed by marble columns was set into white thick walls and covered by a terracotta awning. The white walls stood out from the dark narrow streets which were littered with many shops and eateries.

Sat at one of the many dark wooden tables was Steve Ho wearing a dark blue linen suit, starched white shirt and red tie. He looked up and registered the recent arrivals as they walked towards him.

Ho stood to greet his guests reaching out his heavily tattooed right hand "Nǐhǎo ma? Hello, how are you?"

"Hái hǎo pretty good, Wǒ jiào Suzanne Walker Johns Mr Ho."

"There is no need to speak in Chinese Suzanne, I can speak several European languages if you prefer, and please call me Steve,"

"Thank you Steve, this is Mr Lee Yung, one of my business advisors."

"A business advisor without a briefcase I see, and you both recognised me the moment you stepped into the restaurant, very enterprising that you seem to both know me. Your researchers' have done well, even though I can only recollect having my picture taken only once for my passport. I take it that the company you represent is British Intelligence and Mr Yung is an associate from the twenty third floor of Arsenal House in Hong Kong."

"Steve your perception is remarkable; perhaps that's why you have stayed off our radar for so long. Can we talk over lunch

I'm famished?" Suzanne flashed one of her disarming smiles as she picked up a menu from the recently arrived waiter.

"Fat Siu Lau is still run by the same family who founded it nearly a century ago: it's famous for its signature dish 'shek ki' roasted pigeon." Ho advised.

"That sounds charming, I will also have the Portuguese salty fish ball as an appetiser. I love the old-world charm and ambiance of this restaurant Steve, well done for choosing such a pleasant setting."

"Steve or should I call you Sun Yee On? That is your actual name, I take it. You are a very influential member of the Wo Shing Wo and a close advisor to the Dragon Head, Lee Yip Wong I believe. It came to my attention that your daughter Yu Yan Wu and her boyfriend Liu Zhau died in Belfast after an arson attack on a takeaway in the city. You did mention to Mr Wong that Yu Yan Wu was your daughter, didn't you?" Asked Yung.

Ho was no longer smiling; beads of sweat ran from his brow, his fists had tightened.

"Portugal is on friendly terms with the United Kingdom. It requires our economic assistance and tourism to survive. Macau remains a Portuguese territory; therefore, it is not beyond the realms of fantasy that the government would grant us a few favours." Suzanne stated.

"Is this woman threatening me?"

"I'm afraid she is, and she's very good at it, so listen carefully." Smiled Yung.

The still beaming Suzanne carried on, "We guarantee that you will be persona non grata from the western world. No matter what false passports you try to use. We also ensure you that the Portuguese authorities deport you back to China, which I am sure will not be very pleasant. We will also send an emissary to talk to Mr Lee Yip Wong to inform him of your deception. I take it from your silence that you never mentioned that this whole shenanigan was all to do with revenge for your daughter's death at the hands of Irish paramilitaries."

"So lady, you seem to have backed me into a corner." Ho was visibly squirming in his chair.

"Steve on the contrary, I do not wish to do that. Rats when backed into a corner are liable to strike out and be uncooperative. I have come to you with an offer, a business opportunity we could say. All I want to know is what arrangements you have made with your Irish friends, and how we can work together once this misunderstanding between your organisation and my country has been sorted out. Now let's have food and you can tell me all about your meetings with Mr Fagan, the arms shipments and your visit to a certain farm in Ireland."

South Belfast

The entrance to the old Black Mountain quarry in Hannahstown was dark and deserted. The workmen had long since left after a hard day's labour crushing rocks to be used in the road construction and building industries throughout the Province.

The isolated spot had been chosen as a clandestine meeting place by the FRU operators for its remoteness. Secrillo had been waiting half an hour in the dark, waiting for the appearance of his handlers. The taxi's heater, which only appeared to have two settings, Baltic cold and molten hot, had given up the ghost which made the windscreen quickly mist up. Secrillo shivered, it was a mixture of the falling temperature and his anxiety, which was not assisted by his diminishing vision of his surroundings.

Victor's mind wandered back in time to his first execution less than a mile from where he was parked, Thomas Malvern from the New Lodge, a tough old bastard who took a real beating from Vic and five other members of the Civil Administration Unit. They used metal baseball bats and breeze blocks to systematically assault the fifty-five-year-old grandfather. After five hours of questioning, Malvern refused to admit he had betrayed the organisation. He could remember the man's screams as one of the more exuberant members of the team took out a hand drill and revolved the handle as Vic and the others held the man face down into the abandoned garage floor.

Malvern begged his captors for mercy as the sharp drill bit worked its way through the tibial nerve and into his meniscus.

"Just tell us who you're working for and why you blabbed about the hide in Hillman Street. We have two young volunteers in the Kesh because of you. Admit you're a fuckin tout and we will put you out of your misery, nice and quick."

"I'm no tout I keep telling you cunts, I was rescuing members of the community from the prods when yous fuckers were in your Da's ballbag." Malvern spat back between broken teeth.

"So if you're not the tout it's your wife or your son Liam. Who's it going to be? Make your choice because somebody's getting nutted for losing our equipment and good men."

Malvern was finally broken; he could take the bruises, the smashed bones, the burns they would eventually heal, but he could never let the same injuries be inflicted on his youngest son Liam or his childhood sweetheart Deirdre.

"Ok I confess I'm your tout, I spoke to some Special Branch man in Tennent Street, now put me out of my fuckin misery."

They left it to Victor, the junior member of the execution team, to carry out the ultimate act. Even as he was about to die the abductors played a final macabre joke.

"Ask him to say the contrition then pull the trigger." The

leader ordered as he handed Secrillo an old Luger pistol.

A bag had been placed over Malvern's head and they had forced him to lean against a wall. Blood was oozing from the drilled hole in his knee, and his body was trembling.

"Say the act of contrition; it will be your last words before I execute you."

The beaten man sobbed as he tried to find the words. His mind was lost.

Victor looked for support from his leader, who just nodded. Secrillo stepped forward, placing the barrel of the pistol on to the back of the man's head, then pulled the trigger.

Secrillo momentarily flinched as the gun went pop, no recoil at all, the victim cried out shaking like a leaf and pissing himself at the same time. The assassin looked around in bewilderment at his team, who were in fits of laughter.

"Fuckin priceless, we took the bullet head out. We do it to all the junior apprentices, now cock the gun and do the fucker." It was a sick joke which Secrillo would use many times over the coming years.

Without further ado, Secrillo pulled back the toggle, forcing a new and complete bullet into the chamber.

"You fuckin cowards!" were Malvern's final defiant cry

Bang!

The white wall of the garage was splattered with blood.

"Give him a second one Vic; just to be sure, and then get the body in the car's boot, we'll dump him near the wood on the Upper Springfield Road. Tie a few wires to his arms. It will keep the crown forces busy in the cold and rain for a few hours. The rest of you clean this place up and pick up the empty shells I don't want the peelers finding any forensics to get us lifted."

Secrillo almost jumped out of his seat when the rear doors of his taxi simultaneously opened.

"Jesus Christ, where have you fuckers been? I've been here for hours waiting for you."

"Thirty minutes Vic don't exaggerate, and we've been watching you and the road every minute. Let's get down to business, I take it you have a little time?"

"No, I need to start work with my team down south, but I need to get through all the roadblocks. I've got a team of five boys that will travel with me in two separate cars, I will give you the details."

"So you're the avenging angel Victor, they will defiantly promote you after this."

"I need to get my team over the border tomorrow, we also need to have our tools with us, so I don't want any peelers, army or locally raised militia stopping us. Do you understand?"

"It's all been arranged squire; here are the details of a safe house you can all meet at in Strabane. Inside the coal shed are bags of Chinese weapons, ammunitions and grenades which we have recovered from hides in Belfast. We want you to make it look like this is a culling of dissidents by the dissidents so that Sinn Féin doesn't get involved in the bloodletting."

Victor couldn't believe what he was being told "But it was those bastards in their ivory towers which have ordered this operation, they don't want 'bloodletting' they want a fuckin genocide!"

"Calm down Vic, it's part of the bigger plan. Trust us and you will be well rewarded by us and also by your Republican friends. Remember, no Sinn Féin association; we need Gerry and Martin to able to raise their hands and say it was nothing to do with them just an internal feud."

Secrillo took the piece of paper and memorised the address before burning it.

"Good luck, Vic."

"Fuck yous." Secrillo shouted as he turned back on to the Upper Springfield Road.

Merrion Street, Dublin

"Colonel O'Malley to what do I owe the honour?" Albert Reynolds sat behind the large oak desk in his plush office on Merrion Street. His blue pin stripped jacket was hooked over a coat stand in the corner. "And would that be Louis Range with you?"

"It is Sir, now Chief Superintendent Louis Range who is in charge of the Garda Síochána Special Detective Unit. His team are helping us in the J2 with a very delicate problem we have encountered."

"Louis I remember the game against England in 1985 the referee was Clive Norling and gave you a right bollocking for the late tackle on Rob Andrew. Triple Crown winners, you're a national hero."

The Chief Superintendent looked a little bemused by the response of the Taoiseach.

"Thank you Sir, happy memories, but we have gained some vital information which needs your direct attention. A few days ago we received word from the British Foreign and Commonwealth Office that there was a secret meeting between some breakaway members of the Provisional Irish Republican Army at Doheny & Nessbit's, just a stone's throw from this office."

"Is that so, The English Prime Minister Mr Major had recently asked for greater lines of communication between his and our intelligence services."

O'Malley unlocked the brown leather briefcase chained to his wrist. Inside was a manila colour dossier with TOP SECRET written in large bright red lettering which he handed over to the country's leader.

"Very melodramatic Colonel." Reynolds commented.

"Sir inside is the transcript of a meeting attended by the Provisional's Chief of Staff Padraig McSweeny, his head of operations in the North Sean McLarty who has recently been released from our custody and the Quartermaster James Fagan. All well-known Republicans and with every right to walk our streets, I'm sure you would agree."

"And your point is Colonel?"

"My point is that joining them at the meeting was a friend of yours Liam Malloy the Secretary General of the Department of Defence, Ralph McGovern from your very own party Fianna Fáil and two senior ministers from the Deputy Director General of the Irish Prison Service and Department of Justice. There is no question that the Republican movement in the North has been consumed by a localised coup by some members of the Army Council and all the General HQ. Many people in the South have championed if not supported the actions of this breakaway group during the recent border attacks, but once you read the context of the conversations, you realise that they will not stop in the North. They also mention two Defence Force Brigade Commanders from the South and West that would be happy to commit their troops to overthrow your government."

"Oh, my god. This is preposterous, it's treason I tell you." Reynolds gasped.

Louis waited for his moment "Sir after the meeting my surveillance team followed the army officers to a second meeting with Major-General O'Hara at the museum in the General Post Office on O'Connell Street."

"Mike O'Hara is one of the conspirators?"

"I'm afraid so Sir."

Reynolds leaned back in his black leather chair; he appeared to be transfixed on a landscape painting affixed to the oak-panelled wall.

"How apt he met at the General Post Office, My party, Fianna Fáil was founded by Éamon de Valera, the name of which, when translated means 'Soldiers of Destiny.' On the 16 May 1926 de Valera and his supporters split from the anti-treaty wing of Sinn Féin on the issue of abstentionism. If what you tell me is correct Major-General O'Hara and associates are planning a coup of their own, one of which would be beneficial to our country or the United Kingdom. My first job is to find out just who my friends are, are you Colonel to find out just how deep this plot goes. I take it that all officers within J2 and the SDU are loyal to their government?"

"Yes Sir, there is no mention about any senior Garda officers, but it would appear that Ava Quinlon the Deputy Director General of the Irish Prison Service was responsible for the early release of Sean McLarty and through discreet enquiries we believe she is about to order the release of a dozen more highly dangerous Republican prisoners."

"I am in the most unfortunate position that I will have to share my dilemma to my opposite number across the Irish Sea. I want this stopped immediately, even if it means a purge on my own party and the institutions we hold most dear. Colonel work out a plan, knowing your background I take it you have put the Rangers on full alert."

"I have Sir, they don't know what for, but they are ready to go. We have been very lucky as Major-General O'Hara has not been in a position to be alerted to the Rangers operation on the west coast, but we can assume that if we spread the information any further, it will get back to him."

"Chief Superintendent, I watched you in awe at Lansdowne Road on many occasions. You made me proud to be Irish with your determination, I ask you once again to fight for your nation. Get me the evidence to bring these plotters to justice, and to you both trust no one in Dáil Éireann."

South Armagh

Peewee had thought long and hard about letting Manny visit his sick mother in Daisy Hill Hospital. It was a tough decision; the Brits still controlled Newry, and would probably reinforce the town to use as a launching area to re-take South Armagh. Manny had never interested the crown forces, so it was also conceivable that he could complete the visit and also scout around the town to see if there was a build-up of soldiers. Manny had fought and driven well over the last few days, he was loyal and he knew nothing about the plans of the flying column. If the peelers lifted him, what could he tell them, Peewee reasoned?

"Ok I've decided Manny. Jump in the BMW, but get changed out of your boiler suit first, then go home and take a hot bath."

"I don't stink that much, do I?" Manny looked tired and crestfallen.

"No, you fuckin eejit get rid of the forensics in case those black bastard peelers get ya. Now fuck off and see your Ma, then have a quick drive through town to see how many soldiers will be waiting for us when we attack Newry tomorrow."

Manny turned away to find a dry barn to dump his boiler suit and body armour. He smelt himself and he reeked of stale sweat. Two and a half days he had been on the go. His eyes burned and his ears had tinnitus from the gunfire, explosions and screaming. If this was war, you can keep it, he thought. Attack Newry, what was all that about? It was only last night that Peewee was telling Decers that the next target was the Fathom Line barracks. Newry heh! Fuckin guff he knew where the next attack would be.

Aldergrove Airport

The four Allison T56-A-15 turboprops of the C130 Hercules aircraft were still turning as the ramp was lowered and men carrying heavy Bergans disgorged from the rear. Tommy 'Time Bomb' Trainor had been waiting by the landing runway for less than ten minutes with a fleet of civilianised troop carriers.

Amongst the crowd of soldiers, Tommy recognised an old friend whom he'd shared a trench with during the defence phase of his Sergeant's course at Brecon.

"Darkie, here mate on me."

"Fuck me Tommy, I've been out of Province a year and you let it all go to rack and ruin. What's been going on?" WOII John 'Darkie' Phillips was a legend in the Special Air Service, awarded the Military Medal after five years undercover work in Tyrone and the Queens Gallantry Medal for shooting his way out of a PIRA ambush in the Bogside and saving a wounded colleague.

Darkie was given the nickname when he joined the Welsh Guards twenty years before. He had inherited his dark complexion and jet black hair from his Romany father.

"We were told you were bringing seventy blokes over, but it looks like you have the full Regiment here."

"When word got out that there would be a fight, everyone wanted to jump on the bandwagon. Some bods are support staff, but the rest are Blades, and they are ready to take the gloves off at last. I only flew back in from Norway with G Squadron this morning and the B Squadron Troop are all smiling after a few weeks skydiving in California."

"My job is to get you to a forward mounting base at

Portadown so you can be fully briefed and bomb up. My guys are over watching Peewee's farm, but apart from a fleeting appearance, he's out somewhere in the cuds."

"We all bombed up on the Herc mate, the loadmaster wasn't too happy when we were priming grenades in the back of his plane, but needs must. Oh, we have a stowaway this is Brad Powell, a former Rupert, but he's fairly average which is a compliment for an officer. He's a spook now, but one of the good guys."

"Hi Brad, I'm afraid it will be a tight squeeze."

"No dramas, as long as the former Marines don't call naked bar it will be fine. I need to ask a favour, buddy. Can you get me some uniform and one of your rifles I want to get into your OP watching the farm?"

Tommy removed his flat cap and closed his eyes. 'Fucking Rupert, he thought.'

Glosh Beach

There had been considerable movement to and from the beach all night. The Rangers mutually supporting OP's had been established and triggering the movements of men and equipment from the caches since last light. At midnight the signaller Nial White received a transmission from ARW HQ. After carefully decoding the message, he turned and woke his commander Nathaniel.

"Nat the National Surveillance Unit is now in the game. They have.set up a matrix of observation posts. The nearest one is located in an old water tower on Tallagh Hill, above Belmullett. Any movement away from the hides they will pick up."

Nathaniel had been in his warm sleeping bag for less than an hour. The news meant that things were hotting up as other

300

agencies were now being drafted in to support the mission.

"Any coffee left in the flask, Chalkie?" Nathaniel asked groggily.

"You had the last before I came on stag. Wait another message coming in; it's the boss wanting to speak to you."

Nathaniel crawled out into the crisp night air; above him was a cloudless sky. Millions of stars sparkled. The peninsula was almost free from light pollution and enabled viewers to pick out distant constellations.

"Charlie One things are now moving up a gear, will you be able to mount an aggressive option on our call?"

"An arrest option you want?" Nathaniel was curious about his commander's tone.

"Kill or capture, yes." Came the unnerving reply.

Nathaniel nearly dropped the headset he was pressing to his ear.

"What's going on Nat?" asked Chalkie.

"Someone has declared war on our own people." Nat muttered.

South Armagh

Peewee was busy; he had spent the morning with his son Joseph, out in the fields below the Fathom Line. Decers had found a suitable point to launch an attack on the Patrol Base, but they would require groundwork to bridge a roadside ditch and knock down the dry stone wall which lined Ferryhill Road.

"What's that thing Da?" Joseph pointed to a small pen on the edge of the wood line.

Peewee laughed "That my son is Pochin, Irish moonshine, and the beehive is firstly trying to disguise the illegal distillery from the Brit patrols and also for the mixture to be dripped through the honeycomb to make it more appetising. Wait till I find out who's been producing this without giving me an odd bottle." It was a lighter moment in what had been a demanding few days. Joseph could see that his father was exhausted.

"Come on JoJo, I've seen enough, your Uncle has done a grand job." Peewee patted his son on the wobbly helmet permanently attached to his head. The chinstrap swinging at least two inches below its intended position.

He suddenly realised that he hadn't eaten since the night of the Forkhill attack, and that now seemed a lifetime away. He looked at the boy clinging on a Chinese copy of an Armalite rifle and a British Army helmet precariously wobbling on his head. The body armour hung heavy on the lad's skinny frame, but at least it would give some protection.

Joseph had done well at the ambush, after the initial firefight he had joined Peewee and his followers in chasing a group of soldiers back up the road. His dad tried to slow him down as his youthful exuberance had taken control, running ahead of the pack and shooting like a Wildman. It was the last attack up the road when Joseph had become lost in the madness of war; he was brave enough, but not prepared to see the consequences of his actions.

Holding the body of Ms McGochan had brought the realities of his actions crashing down on his young shoulders.

TCG (S) Portadown

Joe gave his old friend a bearlike hug "Hello Brad, good to see you made it over, we need every help you can give us."

"The Squadron here have got a plan, but they will need back

up which I'm sure Seb will sort out. They have also got a surveillance aircraft on call, a Nimrod so they won't be going in blind unlike the unfortunate Victor One. Darkie and his boss will coordinate with Ulster Troop and get the wheels in motion once we get the details back from the aircraft. The other matter is I need to get into the Fusilier's OP over watching the farm. MI6 want me to be on the ground as an 'observer' just in case things go tits up."

"The COP lads are more than capable Brad."

"Wheels are in motion, I'm afraid. 6 want their asset out and I have been kindly loaned a uniform and one of those fuckin SA80 pea shooters. Patrols from Ulster Troop will meet me at the Vehicle Check Point and then we are meeting two of the COP OP team at an RV who will take me the rest of the way. They need a resupply so I'm not causing hassle."

Daisy Hill Hospital, Newry

Manny was in wonderful spirits as he got back into the BMW. His Ma looked great. The yellow tinge to her skin was disappearing, and the doctors were hopeful she would soon return home. He hated to admit it, but those Brits had probably saved her life. He was also happy to find a roll of used ten-pound notes in his mum's bedside locker. He gripped the steering wheel, then noticed the envelope. Inside was a handwritten note with the instructions Killeavy Old Church ASAP.

Manny guided the vehicle into the overgrown courtyard of the ruined church off the Ballintemple Road. He knew the place well as they had used it as a short term hide for weapons and explosives for several years.

As he got out of the car, he saw his two approaching handlers. "Yous two are taking a fuckin chance coming this far into South Armagh." He joked.

"How long have we got with you Manny?" The Geordie and obviously the senior handler asked.

"Not long Peewee wants me back tonight, and I have to get my clothes and armour from a farm in the south."

"Why tonight, Manny?" The Cockney questioned.

"I think there will be another attack. Peewee wanted me to look around Newry, because he said that's where the next attacks going to be."

"And what do you think?"

"Nah it's all guff, I overheard him telling Decers to check the area around the Fort on the Fathom Line. When I left the Mechanic's Farm they were filling up the big flame thrower towed by the tractor and a lorry with three Barrack Buster mortars on the back turned up."

Manny spent the next half hour describing in detail the attack on Forkhill and the commanders of each subsequent assault.

"So Decers led the attack on the tower above Forkhill?"

"Yes, he did. I think Peewee had told him a few weeks ago he would be the commander, because he was scouting around that area when we went to collect the first lot of guns."

Vince Hill looked at his partner, Steve Carter; both knew that Taylor had been recruited after the alleged scouting mission. Uncanny how it must have slipped his mind when questioned by his handlers Gary Grimshaw and Bex Hamilton.

"Look Manny, we hate to put you in this position, but you need to go back and drive Peewee. We can't have him suspect anything and change his plans."

"Look now I've told you all of this you will send in them murderers from the fuckin SAS and I will get whacked by them, or if I live my own side will smell a rat and I will get whacked by them so you need to get me out."

"No, that won't happen you need to trust us, and once this is over you will be on a plane with your Ma out of this country."

The Geordie's argument was logical and persuasive, even if it was a fucking risk.

"You've really got me by the bollocks, if it all goes wrong promise me you will look after my Ma."

The Geordie held out his hand and gave Manny two cigarette boxes.

"Put one of these under the BMW and the other under the vehicle you drive Peewee in. Both have powerful magnets so they won't drop off. These boxes are your lifeline as they are tracking devices so we can monitor wherever you go. The next time we speak this nightmare will be all over for you and you'll be free."

The Cockney put his hand on Manny's shoulder. "One last thing, when you start the attack do not under any circumstances get out of the vehicle. If you get stopped by the Army you give them the code word Orange, is that clear? Now fuck off to Peewee and good luck."

"I will need it." Manny replied as he returned to the BMW.

CHAPTER FIFTEEN

Friday 1st July 1994

TCG (S) Portadown

Ulster Troop gathered around the bird table, studying the air photographs provided by the Nimrod recognisance flight. Occasionally there banter would stop and they would rewind the videotape and compare the moving images with the pictures. Darkie appeared to be the main protagonist, throwing in little snippets of advice and information.

"What's going on Seb?" The COP commander Martin Jenkins was getting distracted. He was trying to get his head around the latest intelligence that Peewee's wife was an undercover agent and it would fall on his men with an attached MI5 officer to spirt her to safety if the shit hit the fan.

"They are having a big bun fight to see which troop gets to mount the ambush. The guys want some trigger time so nobody wants to be a cut off where they might not see any action. Although Darkie is not Ulster Troop they all respect him because of his in theatre experience." Seb explained.

Darkie broke away from the huddle "Right we have a plan, it's flexible but!"

"Oh, here comes the but Martin. And I suppose the flexible will entail us being able to shove our heads up our own arses Darkie?"

Darkie was grinning, "Oh, you've been listening in Seb. From the air recce it looks like Peewee has thinned out his manpower on the checkpoints to maybe four or five guys. The Victor One ambush point has only a handful of bods. The plan for them is to drop guys from Seven Troop B squadron off a few miles away and one by one we will clean them up. No dramas."

"I can get the remnants of the Victor teams to drop them off." Seb acknowledged.

"The second problem is the potential attack on the Fathom Line."

"FRU have been quick with their dissemination of this intelligence. They say that an attack in imminent and that their source is grade one."

"The insertion will be a problem as there are a few men picketing the top of the hill above Ferryhill Road. Our conclusion is that it's the same anti-aircraft team that fired on the Chinook crossing the Newry Canal. This nicely brings me on to the next problem, the Canal itself. Peewee has done his homework and knows that he needs to protect his right flank and deny us the use of the canal. He appears to have deployed a number of his men near the lock entrance to the canal and a strip of land further south towards Carlingford. Both are areas which we need to secure before ferrying troops across."

"I can get the rest of Martin's troops to watch the sites if need be."

"No need Seb G Squadron Boat Troop are deploying now to do that, but we will need to use Martin's troops later as cut-offs. The plan is that Boat Troop swimmers will cross and eliminate the threat on the far bank before we start pissing on Peewee's parade."

"We are also on a winner with the signals intelligence. The radio that was recovered from Tullydonnel was taken apart and reassembled now 14 Signals can eavesdrop on to the enemy's communications. We have also got transmissions from the beacons put on the pickup truck and the one deployed by the FRU agent Mr Orange. At least we will have a good idea if Peewee is on his way, even if he moves with radio silence. Oh, and Darkie a request from Arnott please don't shoot his agent."

"I will try my best boss." Darkie grinned.

East Belfast

Gary Andrews was a precocious eleven-year-old in the weeks leading up to the eleventh night he had become almost feral, returning home for food and sleep. He had helped the bigger boys unloading pallets and wood provided by the kindly strangers. All of them had been very chatty apart from the driver who never spoke a word.

The time of the fire lighting was almost upon them when the strangers returned with a number of old suites and chairs 'to save them going to the council tip.' Young Gary now had a bed for the night; he could remain close to his precious bonfire all night and guard it from the fuckin 'Taigs' that came from the Short Strand Estate.

It was close to two in the morning when the young child felt the warmth. Through tired eyes he saw the glow as his bonfire caught flame. From the darkness beyond the carefully pilled wooden tower, petrol bombs rained out into the night, aimed at the symbol of Loyalist domination. A petrol bomb was also thrown on to one of the vacant settees.

"Bastards, you fucking Catholic bastards." He cried as voices were heard behind him.

Young men partially dressed raced from their homes in the forlorn hope of saving their construction.

Young Gary picked up stones and raced after the fleeing Nationalist youths as he approached the burning sofa one of the vacuum flasks hidden in the arms exploded cutting the young child to ribbons. The half-dressed men stopped their chase by the blazing fire just as the bonfire detonated.

Dundalk

'Slim' Tim Flynn Secrillo spit into the Guinness glass he was holding, trying to remove an irksome stain in the bottom. The snug of the Lisdoo Arms was quiet when Secrillo entered. After only seeing the large barmen, he motioned to his waiting gang to remain outside.

"Remember me big fella."

Slim looked up in disdain, "Should I? You look like all the other fuckin Gringos that infest my bar."

Secrillo bit his tongue. "I was in here a few weeks ago with Mr McSweeny and I know that you are aware of him and what he does so first question is where is he and my second question is where is the big ginger fella that was also in here, they call him McLarty?"

"Yes I remember you, Ok I suppose if you're a friend of Mr McSweeny. If you need to speak to him, you need to ask his runner, Marie. She works on the counter at the petrol Station on Avenue Road. You can't miss her raven hair, a genuine beauty. The Boss lives outta town on the Blackrock Road, but I've not seen him for an age. As for the other fella, he's in and out all the time. He hangs around with the gang in the front room, so fuckin ask them." Slim again spit into the glass. The stain was long gone, but he wanted to show defiance.

"You've been helpful, Fat Boy!" Secrillo now had his business face on.

From behind his back he revealed a silenced Chinese pistol the first shot shattered the Guinness glass before embedding into the head of the shocked looking barman, who stumbled backwards before a second shot hit him in the throat. Secrillo looked over the solid Mahogany bar; blood was still pumping from a red hole in Flynn's neck as he slowly dropped to his knees.

The front room sounded lively, laughter, and chatter could be heard. Luckily Flynn had made no cries for help or brought the drinks optics on top of himself in his death throes. Secrillo walked back to the front door and ushered in his foot soldiers.

"You two dispose of the fat cunt behind the bar down the

cellar and be quiet about it. The rest of you I want you to go in to the front bar and order drinks."

"But you shot the barman, Vic!"

"And I will shoot you as well. I will act as the barman. There are a group of fellas in the front room that we need to capture and question."

South Armagh

Brad had been patrolling with the heavily laden soldiers from Ulster Troop. "You keeping with the pace Brad?" smiled Alfie Langer the troop's leader.

"It's like selection all over again Bud." He whispered as he felt another bead of sweat run down his back and down the crack of his arse. The new boots were busy breaking his feet in, leaving ever growing blisters on his heels. How he wished he'd had the foresight to wear his trusty German Para boots, they were heavy but fit like a glove.

Alfie led the snake of men to a stream junction and knelt. Without a sound, the individuals behind took up positions to cover any angle of attack.

An indistinct voice at the other side of the stream called "23"

All was hushed, then Alfie called back "27"

"Your maths is spot on" remarked a tall, gangly soldier as he jumped the stream.

"Eammon I'm the OP Second in Command, I believe you have a package for us."

Brad stepped forward "That would be me mate, we've also got more grub for you."

"Spotty dog, we like visitors bringing gifts. We've not seen much on the way here and no movement at the farm apart from the Bitch and her daughter. Peewee and Junior are still in the wind."

"No dramas, I'm ready to move when you are. Alfie and his team are going to snurgle into the patrol base, then set up a few surprises for Farmer Kelly and his crew."

Brad shook Alfie's hand then jumped the stream in pursuit of the tall skinny Corporal and his close protection Fusilier 'Wilky' Wilkinson.

Glosh Beach

Throughout the day more men and vehicles had been arriving on the windswept beach. By late afternoon the OP's started reporting that there were now twelve vehicles lined up in a convoy and preparing to leave.

J2 had passed on the message to Chief Superintendent Louis Range, who gave orders for the National Surveillance Unit to deploy into position to follow the shipment. O'Malley had also called for backup from the Emergency Response Unit, the Garda's elite tactical unit.

Static observation posts chattered as the line of vehicles crossed the small bridge at Belmullet. As the convoy passed a road junction, unfamiliar voices spoke up informing Range of the current progress and location.

Francie Molloy, the driver of the lead vehicle at the head of the convoy, was getting bored. He'd made the journey to the hides in the Trista Bog a dozen times. He wanted to stay on the beach and play with the new guns, which he had been lugging around. Just beyond the next bend was the turning on to the Srahataggle Road. His thought of having a brew and a sandwich with his brother evaporated when he drove into the police roadblock. Heavily armed coppers wearing black balaclavas swarmed over the vehicles, smashing windscreens and dragging out the drivers and passengers, dumping them in the damp ditch at the side of the carriageway.

O'Malley immediately gave the order for Nathan and his team to move to a blocking position on the isthmus. Within an hour SDU detectives led by Inspector Joseph Guilfoyle were on the beach arresting anyone in sight.

O'Malley sat back and looked across at the policeman sat beside him, Superintendent Dan Currie had just informed him that James Fagan had been arrested on the beach and was saying nothing.

"So we have the Quartermaster of the IRA and many of his cohorts in custody, and a substantial amount of weapons and explosives from large hides in Co Mayo."

"Aar that's right Colonel." Dan agreed.

"Well now comes the hard part, we will now arrest some of the most respected members of the Irish government and defence force. I need to get all the ARW teams back in and ready to go for the next phase of this operation. I'm going to require the services of the world's biggest albino."

Belfast

The Chief Constable was incandescent with rage. Beside him stood a forlorn Chief Superintendent Stan Lafferty, his eyes red and wet. "Most of the Bomb Disposal Units have been deployed to Armagh, so it will take time to get them back to the city along with the officers are down there on standby."

"Was the Minister any help, Sir?"

"He looked like I had crapped in his in tray when I told him we need to stop the bonfires and marches, but he has advised us to use all TV and radio stations to broadcast a Province wide threat warning not to light any fires. How the hell did this happen without us knowing Stan?"

"I'm sure it is linked to the events down South, but my major worry now is that we are getting reports that Loyalists in Scotland are mobilising to come over in greater number than usual."

"Doomsday?"

"Yes Sir, I think Ulster Resistance has pressed the red button."

"Four children and five adults dead, plus a dozen injured. What in god's mind were these animals thinking Stan?"

The Bay of Biscay

The Tungting, a 20,000 ton bulk carrier, had enjoyed an uneventful trip via Cape Horn. The crossing of a calm, but foggy Bay of Biscay had left the Captain Huang Bohai feeling relaxed. Only he and his loadmaster knew about the three hundred tons of weapons and explosives concealed under the grain in the hold.

Over the horizon, but shadowing the Tungting progress of the ships course was a naval task force comprising the LÉ Eithne an Irish Patrol vessel and the current flagship of the Naval Service, who had rendezvoused with the British Type 23 'Duke' class frigate HMS Argyll and the Commando Assault Ship HMS Fearless.

Fearless had been busy supporting the sea training phase of naval officer training at the Britannia Royal Naval College when an emergency notice from the Admiralty sent her to a position on the Celtic Sea west of the Scilly Isles. Lurking under the water was the last ship of the task force, HMS Vanguard, a Ballistic missile submarine who had immediately set sail from Faslane upon receiving the order.

A British Sea King helicopter hovered over the landing pad of

Fearless, inching its way slowly on to the grey deck. After a quick thumbs up from the loadmaster, several people jumped out and were ushered to the open hanger.

Major Berness Kerr from Irish Intelligence and Major Mike the commander of the ARW Special Operations Maritime Task Unit took off their life jackets and were greeted by a small but powerfully built man who offered his hand to the new arrivals.

"Hi Major Rob Thompson C Squadron SBS, Berness and Mike I'm guessing. Oh, and I should introduce you to your host, Captain Matthew Ghan, who is in charge of HMS Fearless. The two scoundrels lurking behind are Staff Sargent Kev McKenna and Corporal George Kirkham, who are on my team."

The introductions were cut short by the arrival of a Dauphin helicopter carrying Commodore Eugene Brackly and the Captain of the LÉ Eithne Earnest Kavanagh. Captain Ghan led the assembled through a labyrinth of corridors until they reached the Officers Mess. After the ubiquitous teas and coffees were served, Eugene Brackly reiterated the need for the overall chain of command to be headed by Commodore Niall Given based at the Naval Headquarters in Haulbowline, with full support from the Naval Intelligence Cell.

Once the sensitivities of sovereignty and decision making were out of the way the mood around the table became a little more relaxed as each commander discussed the structure of their forces and the capabilities which would enhance the mission. After a few hours everybody seemed to be in agreement, Ghan rose to his feet "Ok just to summarise what we have discussed. The command from Commodore Given will be made once we satisfy him that the ship has altered course and is making its way east of the Black Rock Lighthouse. When you get the word to go four SC's, from Z Squadron in Vanguard will covertly board the Tungting and hold the entry point. They specialise in underwater attack and insertion using swimmer delivery vehicles, so it makes sense to use them to ensure we get a covert entry before it all goes loud."

"SC's?" Berness asked.

"I'm sorry, I should say Swimmer Canoeists it's the badge our SBS guys wear, I think they only wear them to piss the SAS off. Once they are on board, a joint assault force of SBS and ARW will board by sea and an ARW team will fast rope by helicopter to assault the bridge. The intelligence we have is that the sailors on board will not put up a fight and probably don't know what the real cargo is. Once the ship is clear a helicopter from Fearless will drop off Police and Ammunition Technical Officers to start the judicial process."

There were nods of agreements all around the table. Brackly cleared his throat. "Ladies and Gentlemen, at its present speed and course the Tungting will approach Black Rock at approximately 23:00 hours. I suggest we now report back to our respective chains of command and await the next move. I'm assured that should the ship get into the landing site, the only greeters will be a number of heavily armed Garda."

Dundalk

Secrillo stood behind the counter of the Lisdoo Arms; apart from the gaggle of bodies from McLarty's team, the bar was quiet. In the corner a few old timers were watching the racing from Chepstow. One by one members of the Civil Administration Unit entered and ordered a drink before taking a strategic position behind the unsuspecting loudmouths.

Thomas Dexter stood up from the group and took every bodies order before approaching the bar. He looked at Secrillo and appeared to be puzzled.

"Where's the fat fucker?" he asked.

"No need to be nasty fella, so he's got a thyroid problem who cares."

"What the fuck are you going on about; do you know who we are? We are McLarty's Crew so get us some fuckin drinks ya fuckin prick."

Secrillo smiled and looked at the former farmhand from Cappagh.

"Thanks."

Dexter tried to comprehend what the barman was thanking him for. "Thanks for fuckin what?"

"Thanks for admitting yours and your friend's guilt. Gentlemen, you may now arrest these cunts. Take them out of the back door. Bag and tie them and we will take them out to the interrogation."

There was a scrapping of chairs and Secrillo's unit jumped to their feet brandishing machine guns and pistols. Minutes later the bar was clear apart from the old boys who continued to watch the racing. Secrillo had gathered all of his team's glasses and put them into the wash basin behind the bar.

"What the fuck are you doing here?"

Secrillo spun to see McLarty striding into the bar, his eyes darting around the room looking for his support. Seeing Secrillo behind the bar, he immediately sensed danger and grabbed a Colt 45 pistol from his waistband. Secrillo had been caught completely off guard with no time to grab the silenced Type 77 pistol he carried in a pancake holster on his hip.

He didn't hear the shot, but the force of it threw him back into a tray of freshly washed pint glasses and dropped him on to his back over the cellar trap door.

McLarty had hit him square in the chest and was happy that

he had put an end to the Chief Executioner it satisfied him that Secrillo got it first. He was in line for the 'good news' anyway Secrillo and the old guard would be collateral damage once the revolution began. He began laughing, "Victor, you got your P45 first." He goaded.

The mad Belfast man grabbed one of the open-mouthed old men.

"Where are my guys you auld fool?" he screamed as he shock the old man by his lapel.

The old man looked in terror, then pointed towards the bar.

McLarty looked over his right shoulder wide eyed as he saw Secrillo standing behind the bar, very much alive with a pistol pointing directly at his head.

"Amazing this bullet-proof vest Sean. Pity you were too stupid to wear one, but you always thought you were fuckin bulletproof. By the order of the Army Executive, I am here to arrest you and question your actions."

"You haven't got the bollocks......" were the last words uttered by Sean McLarty as the 7.62mm bullet hit him square in the forehead killing him instantly.

FRU, Lisburn

"So Manny has provided us with the lowdown of how it all unfolded." Corporal Rebecca Hamilton was in the FRU intelligence cell reading the recently produced report from Emanuel Holmes's handlers.

"Look Bex I shouldn't be showing you this, but I thought it might help you get some leverage if you get a meeting Declan Taylor." Malcom Russo reasoned.

"That's great, thanks Mal. So Manny is certain that Decers led the attack on the R23 tower above Forkhill, and that he had been conducting reconnaissance on it for several days prior to that."

Russo didn't notice that Hamilton was squeezing her knuckles until they were white.

"That's correct, but promise me you won't mention this to the boss until you get proper confirmation."

"Hey no dramas, thanks for the help." Hamilton turned away before the tears began.

Alpha One

The car sped on to the driveway of the farm, loose stone chips and gravel were displaced as the car came to a halt. "Joseph get a quick wash I'll get your Ma to make us some food before we get ready for tonight."

"So you're fuckin back." Eileen stood defiantly at the backdoor, arms folded, her left eye still showing the bruise inflicted by her husband's fist hours before.

"We're back for just a few minutes so get some food on for me and the boy or you'll get more of a hiding. I don't need your fuckin hassle at the moment. I will sort out some peace with you once I've smashed the Brits."

"Paul Patrick Kelly, you need to catch yourself on. It's all over the tele and radio. It's one thing killing soldiers, but those in Belfast were kids. One of them was only eleven. Have you lost your fuckin mind?"

Peewee stepped back. Kids were not part of the plan. Belfast was Bonner and McLarty's show, not his.

"It's also been on the Irish news that the guards have found tons of weapons and explosives on a beach. I suppose that's got fuck all to do with you as well."

Peewee's mind was in a spin. He didn't need any more weapons for the attack on the Fathom Line, but he would need resupplies to hold off the forthcoming onslaught by the crown forces, once they started moving towards the border.

"JoJo, forget the food we're going,"

Eileen looked behind; Joseph was stood in the doorway holding his sister Mairéad's hand, they were both crying; he was whispering into his sister's ear, trying to unburden himself. Joseph looked much older than the last time his mother had seen him. His gaze was blank and unfocused; the last threads of his humanity were being slowly detached.

She tried to put her arms around him and hold him, but he brushed past her.

"I'm sorry Mommy, I didn't know. It was..." He was desperately trying to explain something, maybe even trying to get some forgiveness, she thought.

Tears were in his eyes as he dawdled back towards the vehicle to join his father.

Eileen ran towards the car, but two shots ricocheting by her feet stopped her in her tracks.

"One more step woman and it will be the last one you ever make. He's a man now, so he's with me. I will sort you out when I get home." Peewee started the car and sped off.

Eileen was on her knees, oblivious of the sharp stones cutting into her knees. She sobbed uncontrollably. Mairéad joined her and flung her arms around her neck tightly.

"Mommy don't be cross with JoJo, he said he didn't mean to kill her, it was an accident."

It took an age for the child's words to sink in. "Kill who?"

TCG (S) Portadown

Seb barged into the Chief Superintendent's office, making him jump. "Joe the OP has reported seeing Peewee and his son briefly return to Alpha One. It looks like a disagreement took place and Peewee fired two shots towards Eileen."

"Is she OK?"

"Well, I bet she's shaken. The COP lads seem to think they were warning shots. He was so close he could have easily killed her. He just got the boy back and sped off towards Dungooly."

"And where is Mrs Kelly now?"

"She's taken the daughter and parked near to St Patrick's Church in Dromintee. She went into the church with the daughter, then came out without. It's a long distance from the tower on Jonesborough Hill, but they say she appears to be shopping."

Dromintee

Eileen had been shaking since leaving the farm. Beside her, Mairéad bombarded her with a fusillade of questions. After bumping into Mrs Maguire at the church, she had left her daughter in the care of the child's former Sunday school teacher. Men dressed in black suits stood smoking outside the office of McCreesh & Sons, the local funeral directors. She smiled as she walked by. One man acknowledged her.

"A sad day Mrs Kelly."

"Why would that be?" Eileen enquired.

"We're expecting the body of Ms McGochan. Everybody around is saying that the SAS executed her."

Eileen nodded and tried to calm her racing heart. A voice in her head was screaming 'remember your training, remain calm and composed' She was sure that her cover had not been blown. If Peewee knew she would have been dead already or tied to a chair in a damp barn awaiting torture. Her head cleared. After buying groceries at the local shop she asked for change so she could call her sick sister in Wythenshawe then made her way to the phone on Finnegan Road to inform her support team she and her daughter required immediate extraction. She was quick to the point.

"Anything else." The voice at the other end of the line asked.

"Something is going down tonight. I've seen him like this when he's under stress. Don't ask me where or what, but it's a big job tonight, and he's taking our son with him." She placed down the phone and sobbed for the first time in years.

South Armagh

Seven Troop had been ferried to forward mounting bases throughout the day, some by Q Car to the west of Newtownhamilton and Cullyhanna, others by patrols from Corry Square in Newry or the Permanent Vehicle Checkpoint at Cloughoge. The threat from Surface to Air Missiles was still high, which was backed up by the latest pictures taken by the Nimrod reconnaissance flight.

Seven One had made excellent progress from Cloughoge and established a forward operating base at Golf Zero One, the communications and command centre high on Slieve Gullion. Even on their high perch the smell of decomposing bodies could be sniffed in the light breeze. Ratu Tupou shook his head and turned his back. His oppo Trooper Ben Nash looked at him for guidance.

"What a stink 'Ratty' smells like a cow has died."

"Sega, no that's not dead cattle, but dead tagine, men. It smells like Bosnia, my friend."

Nash was new to the Regiment still in his probationary

period, the big Fijian Corporal was a seasoned veteran and B Squadron stalwart. He had immediately taken the fresh-faced, inexperienced man under his wing.

"Do you think it's the bodies of the Victor team we can smell?" He asked that, wished he hadn't.

The Fijian didn't talk, just did a double eyebrow raise. Nash had been around Ratty long enough to know that this was the Fijian for yes.

Newry Canal

Darkie and Tommy 'Time Bomb' Trainor were sweating after unloading the heavy assault boats and hiding them in the quarry a short distance from the Warrenpoint Road, which was the start line for the crossing of the Newry River. Fusiliers and Troopers had worked in unison to lift the boats from the trucks parked in a barn off the Aghnamoira Road, then follow the wood line to reach the now deserted quarry. The news an attack on Romeo One Seven, the Fathom Line patrol base, was now imminent was no surprise as the groups split into two crossing parties.

Darkie took Tommy to one side "This is 'Ski' Lampowski and Steve Richards, both are from Boat Troop and will deal with any 'obstacles' on the other bank. Both are carrying silenced H&K MP5SD submachine guns. Once they flash the torch get your boats in the water and get paddling. Ski and Ritchie will be dressed by then and lead you up the hill to One Seven. As soon as it gets dark some of the boys, I sent to the Patrol Base with Brad will sneak out and put a few surprises in the gorse lines that Peewee's boys will try to hide in. Make sure you go to the north of the camp or you might end up tripping over things you don't want to know about."

"Sounds like a plan mate. I will call you once we are in the cut off position. What about the SAM team on the hill, though?"

"Leave that to us, I've got a few of the racing snakes from Air Troop going to sort them out before moving back to the ambush site! Sorry I meant hard arrest area." Both men chuckled as Darkie placed his day sack over his shoulder and jogged off to re-join his men.

Blackrock Road, Dundalk

There hadn't been a struggle; McSweeny had opened the front door, oblivious to the danger. The secret door knock that set him at ease had been quickly extracted from Marie O'Hanlon with little coxing. After being abducted from the petrol station she had been blindfolded and tied before being driven to a large bricked hut, which was once part of an old army rifle range.

Even though blindfolded Marie could feel the terror. None of her captors had spoken a word. They had moved her forcibly and controlled along a corridor until they forced her to sit. They cut the rope around her wrist, only to be replaced by plastic tie grips which fastened her to the wooden chair. Only when she was immobile was her hood removed.

As her eyes became accustomed to the light, she saw a tall bald-headed man standing before her. She sensed that the other men were now standing behind her. The bald man cleared his throat, "Marie O'Hanlon by orders of the Adjutant General of Óglaigh na hÉireann you are to be interrogated and court marshalled. Failure to co-operate with me and you will be deemed an enemy of the organisation and executed just like your friends here." The man pointed towards a pile in the corner.

Marie had paid no attention to her surroundings, just focusing on her inquisitor. She then picked out the grotesque shapes of mangled bodies. Something dropped into her lap from a person stood directly behind her. She screamed in horror as a human eyeball rolled on her knees. The eyeball fell to the floor, but was replaced by a finger, then a toe. A man was giggling behind her.

"You will co-operate Marie or my men will start cutting off pieces of you. Let's begin with pulling your fingernails out, Leno pass me the pliers."

Secrillo was soon on his way towards his major target, Padraig McSweeny, the head of the Army Council. Marie, through her sobs, had told her captors McSweeny's location, the secret knock code and also informed that he was alone, having despatched his bodyguard to the fight in the north that very night.

Victor had chosen one of his most trusted lieutenants to accompany him, but before leaving he addressed the assembled men. "Our work in the south is only just beginning. Me and Darragh will take another scalp. As a present you can all have a little fun with that pretty colleen. Once you've finished with her she gets topped and thrown into the pit with them other fellas. Don't forget to put lime over their bodies." The follower's cheers were ringing in his ears as he strode out to the waiting car

McSweeny's face was a bloody pulp, nose broken and eyes almost closed shut. They had nailed his hands to the oak dining table, his feet to the floor.

The man was dearly holding on to life, he groaned, "Do you want my confession?"

"No Padraig, I've already passed judgement on you, but I need to know who else is involved in your little escapade, no loose ends."

"It was only me Victor you have my word. My plan I got the members of the council involved, they were only following my orders."

Victor smiled and gingerly rubbed the bruise in the centre of his chest.

"I'd like to believe to Padraig, but you're a fuckin nobody.
Who set up the introduction to the Chinese and who in God's
name let that fuckin loon McLarty out of Portlaoise Prison?
Anyway, while you are thinking up a lie to answer me, how
about a cuppa?" Secrillo nodded.

The captive man then felt the searing heat as a kettle of
scalding water was poured slowly over his back. His screams
ruptured blood vessels in his throat, such was his pain.
Blisters immediately formed as his skin contracted.
McSweeny was going into shock when a second wave, this
time icy water, hit him.

"We can play this game all day Padraig, or I could use these."

Secrillo placed bolt cutters on the table. Even through his
battered eyes, McSweeny could see they had smudges of
blood on the blades.

"I will first start with your bollocks..."

"No, I'll tell you everything, but please finish me quick and
don't shoot me in the face for my family's sake Secrillo."

Secrillo nodded and listened to the condemned man's full
confession.

Dublin

O'Malley was beckoned into the Prime Minister's. A number
of advisors surrounded him. Reynolds rose and shook the
soldier's hand firmly.

"Colonel thank you for planning this onerous task, but
considering recent intelligence I have just received from the
British Prime Minister I must ask you to cast your net even
wider."

"What seems to be the problem Sir?"

"I have it on very good authority that our very own Office Foreign Affairs and members of the Labour Party are also in collusion with rebels along with a leading academic Professor Shamus Donal. You will need to act fast, what resources do you require?"

"Where have the British got that information from?"

"Colonel, I did not ask and if I am honest I do not wish to know."

Belfast

Chief Superintendent Stan Lafferty almost knocked the Chief Constable off his feet as he tried to enter his office.

"What the hell is going on, Stan? Compose yourself."

Lafferty had sprinted up the stairs from his office within Tasking and Coordination Group East. Gathering what breath he had left, he told his commander. "Army intelligence has found out all the other booby trapped bomb sites, and the location of the bomb making factory. I'm getting teams together to make the arrests and informing local divisions to cordon off the bonfire and await the bomb disposal trucks."

"How the hell have they got that intelligence so quickly?"

"I'm not asking questions Sir, I'm just glad they have given us the information. It has to be a source at the highest level, but thank god he's on our side."

CHAPTER SIXTEEN

Monday 4th July 1994

The Mechanic's Farm Tullydonnel, Co Louth

Peewee was deep in thought. The news from Belfast had been a shock, but he reasoned that the crown forces would have to send soldiers and policemen back up to the city, giving him an even greater chance of victory. He had received no reports of helicopter flights further north than Newry and no more convoys of undercover soldiers. He decided that the Fathom Line attack would go ahead as he had planned. Sure it was those Jackeen city boys that fucked up in

The yard at Tullydonnel was busy as vehicles were brought in between the barns and loaded with weapons and ammunition. The volunteers were running from shed to shed whilst the Mechanic barked orders with the ever present fag stuck in the corner of his mouth. Beside his vehicle lay Joseph, sleeping fitfully, his arms cradling the assault rifle his father had given him the day before. In the driver's seat sat Manny, who appeared to be nervous, He had been fidgeting with the engine, then crawling underneath the vehicle to check the suspension, now he was tapping on the steering wheel like it was a bodhrán drum.

"For fuck's sake Manny will yous calm down, you're getting on my wick." Peewee was trying to relax and run all the consequences through his mind. Although he had brought most of his men back to Tullydonnel, he was confident that the three road blocks in Cullyhanna, Silverbridge and Dromintee would stop any Brit attempt to infiltrate back South and flank his next attack. He was also happy that the anti-helicopter missiles that had done so well stopping reinforcements flying into Crossmaglen and over the Newry Canal remained in place. Even the men over watching the Canal had reported back that they had seen no military vehicles moving towards Newry along the Warrenpoint Road. As Peewee pushed back in his seat to ponder further a small black box only a foot beneath his backside was transmitting his location.

Newry Canal

Fusilier John Bennett could feel the warm sun burning the back of his neck; He took a mental note to give himself a bollock later for not applying cam cream to his only exposed part of his body. His spotter Stu Taylor lay motionless by his side, his eye glued to the aperture of the M49 Bariner spotting scope, His right hand moved slightly to adjust the tripod before resuming his visual of the three men sat four hundred meters away on the other side of the Newry river in the car park of Victoria Lock, the inlet of the Newry Canal.

Bennett was observing through the sight of his L96 sniper rifle. The 6x42 Schmidt & Bender fast reflex telescopic sight had been a superb choice by the rifle maker, Accuracy International, in pairing it with the best rifle in the world.

"I could drop all three before they got back to the car, Stu." Bennett whispered.

"I'm sure you could mate, but you would fuck it up for the Blades crossing further downstream. We carry on with Time bomb's orders, observe and report."

A mile upstream, Darkie was being updated by his sniper team.

"What do you mean there are only two of them? The recce flight shows four."

"I'm telling you Darkie, we've not seen the other two for two hours now. Maybe they have got their heads down in the scrub. The two we have a bead on are nonchalantly walking through the silver birch and gorse like a Sunday school outing. We even brought up the thermal image sights, but still a blank. The car is still in place, just two missing Tangos."

Black Rock

"Sir Vanguard is reporting that Tungting is listing to port."

Captain Matthew Ghan looked at his Executive Officer in amazement

Huang Bohai the Captain of the Tungting was born and raised in the Pearl River Delta of Guangdong, standing at over six feet tall he was a giant compared to the average male in his home country. As the ship altered course into the Porcupine Seabight following a course along the Slyne Trough Bohai scanned the horizon for the Black Rock Lighthouse, which had been described to him as the "one that looks like a volcano".

The crew were happy that they had reached calmer waters than the storms they had encountered rounding Cape Horn. Now bright sunshine, a gentle breeze and an almost wave less sea welcomed them towards their landing point. The sun had started to drop towards the North-West horizon when Bohai received the message from his master back in China. His large forehead was furrowed as he gathered the ship's crew together on the bridge.

Ghan had just finished on the sat phone to the joint operations room at Haulbowline Island in Cork Harbour.

He looked at his Executive Officer "There are reports that the Tungting is asking for help, is that correct?"

"Worse than that Sir, Vanguard is reporting they are manning the lifeboats."

"What's going on?" before Ghan's question could be answered, the radio sparked into life.

MAYDAY, MAYDAY, MAYDAY

THIS IS CHINESE BULK CARRIER TANGTING

HELPME, HELPME, HELPME

IMO 9743781 CALLSIGN CHN 3HL

"My god, get the Sea Kings prepared and in the air. I want the Captain on my ship ASAP."

"He got his men to board the lifeboats before sending the Mayday alarm Sir. It appears he's had orders to scupper his ship and all the evidence." Reasoned the Executive Officer.

MAYDAY, CHINESE BULK CARRIER TANGTING,

IMO 9743781 CALLSIGN CHN 3HL

MY POSITION IS 24° 02'.52.7N 010° 21'.00.54W from Black Rock.

I AM SINKING

I REQUIRE IMMEDIATE ASSISTANCE

FIFTEEN PERSONS ON BOARD, ABANDONING TO LIFE BOAT

OVER

Macau

Suzanne Walker Johns and Lee Yeung were sat at the sumptuous bar of the Hotel Lisboa. It was approaching two in the morning when Steve Ho re-joined them both in the deserted saloon. Only hours after Suzanne had made a toast to future business, 'Ganbei' replied both men. The Baijiu sorghum wine, as intoxicating as tequila, appeared to be taking a hold of the two visitors.

"It is done Suzanne; the shipment is heading five hundred meters to the bottom of the sea."

The MI6 agent giggled, "Well, let's drink to that."

"I am afraid that you have put me in a precarious position, Suzanne. My employer will need an explanation."

Suzanne called over the waiter, "Three of your best Shui Jing Fang." She turned to Ho and smiled.

"Steve, why are you worried about the boss, when you ARE the boss?"

Ho took the drink and wondered if this was some kind of English riddle."

Lee Yeung was laughing, "Mr Ho, we must have forgotten to tell you. Fifteen minutes ago Lee Yip Wong, former Dragon Head of the Wo Shing Wo was arrested and is facing quite a lengthy jail sentence. It looks like you are the new boss."

"Well, Mr Dragon Head are you now interested in aligning with UKPLC?"

Ho raised his glass and shouted 'Ganbei.'

South Armagh

All over South Armagh men were busy checking equipment, weapons and testing communications on their personnel Racal PRM-4515 Cougar radio sets. Two vehicles with remnants of Victor One commanded by Lee 'Mez' Mereday had driven out of Corry Square and held up in a layby near to the Cloughoge Golf Club.

Mez was more than happy to be a 'tethered goat' as the commander of call sign 72 Johnny Rathbone had detailed his task.

"All you need to do is drop us off a mile down the road. When we give you the shout drive down the Dromintee Road, all calm and collected like, until they stop you, wait till the fucker approaches and pop the flash bangs and get into cover. We will do the rest." Johnny explained like it was a walk in the park.

In the back of both Q cars were two heavily armed soldiers from Seven Troop, only disguised by heavy jackets over their combat clothing. The remainder of Air Troop, B Squadron had split into two further patrols, 71 high on Slieve Gullion commanded by Ratu 'Ratty' Tupou and 73 who had been earlier covertly dropped off at an old wood yard on the Cullyhanna Road.

Just as the sun was setting HQ transmitted a message "All call signs this is zero Op Hydra teams to deploy to objective areas." The troops acknowledged the transmission about to move and the over watch towers. Ratty looked over to the new Trooper. "No rattles or shine check now." He ordered as he walked towards the other members of his team 'Wild Bill' Brooks and Harry Ashford, both well-seasoned men.

"Op Payback is on guys." Both smiled.

"I thought Darkie said it was Op Hydra Ratty?" Ben asked.

"After what they did to the Victor team, it's now Op Payback, fuck what the head shed calls it lad." Joked Wild Bill in his deep West Country twang.

Nash was nervous and thinking of ways to not show out to his friends.

"Ratty, why do the old sweats call you F NOB?"

The big Fijian picked up the GPMG machine gun and slung it over his shoulder his face was a beaming smile "You have been listening in to them two old bastards' boy?" He was laughing.

"After I passed my probation I was sent to B Squadron, I broke my leg playing for the Pilgrims Rugby team. A few weeks later the boys ended up at Princess Gate, and I was stuck just doing admin for the assault team. My Fijian brothers Tom and Jim went in and I was the Fijian Not on the Balcony so F NOB. Operation Nimrod was probably the most written about Special Forces attack ever, but hardly any fucker wrote about these Irish bastards killing one of officers three days before. Just you remember that when you have to pull the trigger tonight."

"Big boy's rules Nasher and don't forget." Wild Bill pipped in. The team nodded their heads in agreement.

Bennett had carefully wrapped the telescopic sight and placed it safely into his daysack a CWS night sight with freshly inserted new batteries had been placed upon the sniper rifle. In the growing gloom the two divers had made their way across the Warrenpoint Road and hidden themselves in bushes at the edge of the Newry River, from the new spot they could see that the falling tide had presented them with another problem. Before reaching the water, the pair would have to slide over two hundred meters of thick glutinous mud. On the plus side, the swim was now only one hundred meters, but the crossing of the mud would be noisy and leave them perilously exposed until they reached the safety of the water. Even the sniper team on the home bank wouldn't be helpful, if the gunmen remained near the car park of Victoria Lock as the effective range of the sniper's night sight was only three hundred meters added to the fact that they could not chance using an infra-red beam in case it was spotted by the waiting sentries with their own night vision equipment.

With his left hand Bennett knurled the night sight dial to focus in on the movement on the far bank. He scanned, looking for the tell-tale signs of movement; the x 4 magnification was not helping the sniper much, as trees with low-hanging branches had reduced the amount of ambient light in the car park.

The green picture suddenly glowed as one man on the far bank lit a cigarette.

"Three on a match" Bennett smiled his white teeth

highlighted against the blackness of his camouflaged face, referring to the old Crimea War story that the third soldier to use the match would be the one shot by the waiting sniper.

Less than a mile downstream Darkie had been giving a final briefing to his divers Phil Sturdivant and Alex 'Geordie' Brown. Still worried about the missing two tangos, he had asked for local knowledge from the intelligence section back in Portadown. He was quite surprised to find out that on the far side of the spit of land held by the two patrolling gunmen was Patsy's Parlur lounge bar, a local drinking place frequented by Newry IRA men who didn't want to be troubled by Peelers or soldiers. He had seen the building on his map but assumed it to be a dwelling.

"Assumptions, eh! Mother of all fuck up's Darkie." Geordie commented.

"Get your fat arse into that dry suit, you Geordie maggot. Phil, don't forget to check he's got his boots on the right feet when you get to the other side." Geordie slipped him the bone sign and walked towards the river bank. The SAS swimmers only had two hundred meters of swimming and unlike their colleagues trying to get to Victoria Lock, no mud flats to negotiate.

Ski Lampowski was the first to reach the lock and slowly swam into the mouth to find the metal steps leading to the car park. Over the Cougar radio Stu Taylor was giving enhanced commentary about the lack of movements from the waiting piquets Steve Richards was soon at the bottom of the steps with his swim mate, both pointing their silenced HK rifle towards the rim of the canal.

"No further movement, both Tangos are in or around the area of the vehicle which is Twelve o'clock from your exit point."

Ski nodded at his partner, and then pulled himself clear of the water. He hung above the canal to allow any noisy drips to run off his dry suit before climbing the remaining steps.

After peeking over the top to orientate himself, he crawled over the top and commenced watching the two men laughing and joking by the small dark hatchback car. The green light from Ski's night vision goggles showed that both men were either stupid or incompetent. The new song by Blur was blasting the car radio. Occasionally the picket stood outside of the car would flash a torch in the general direction of the canal.

Bennett kept his eyes peeled on the area of the vehicle, then two dull flashes in his sight picture. The radio silence was broken by Ski "Tangos One and Two confirmed KIA prepare for a home run."

"Home Run." Stu replied then turned to Tommy "Let's get paddling."

Further downstream the Boat Troop swimmers had made good progress making the crossing, but upon landing had struggled to make a stealthy approach through the dense yellow gorse bushes which covered the scrub land. Phil Sturdivant had taken up a fire position at the base of a silver birch tree which provided suitable cover. Sturdivant heard a twig snap in the distance, the sound carried in the still night air. The hiding trooper then felt the vibrations on the ground, he looked towards the river, silhouetted was a huge shape carrying a machine gun. From out of the darkness a monster arrived in the shape of six foot seven Eammon 'The big fella' Dore. In his tree like arms he cradled a Type 80 general purpose machine gun. A linked belt of fifty 7.62mm rounds swung casually as he patrolled. He had been walking all day. The other three morons from the Free State had pissed him off, two had fucked off to the pub and stayed there and the other one Robert "The Italian" Hennessey was asleep in the back of the van. The Big Fella was raging; when he got back to Peewee, he would beat some discipline into the jokers from Southern Command. As he was considering which nose to break first, he noticed something wet and glistening on the ground by an old tree. He turned to investigate, raising the heavy machine gun to his shoulder.

PHAT!

Big Fella's head exploded like a watermelon being struck with a cricket bat. Like a giant Red Wood tree, the giant's body started the wobble, and then lean before finally crashing down inches from hiding Sturdivant.

In the darkness, he could make out the smiling face of Geordie.

"You left that a bit late!"

"Nah, I just wanted to see you shit ya sen marra." He joked.

Minutes later darkie received the call "Far bank clear Tangos Three to Six all KIA. Prepare to move to Home Run."

Phil and Geordie had little problem over powering the final three sentries as one was snoring in the back of the blue transit van whilst they had shot the other pair as they fell over the fence into the scrub land after staggering out of the pub.

Johnny Rathbone was concentrating on the radio traffic from the two units crossing the canal and relaying it to the people in the cars which had hidden up beyond their intended spot and found a secluded track off the Bernish Road.

"Both teams have given Home Run, they will have a boat race across the river now. I'd estimate another two hours before we move forward, mate." Mez in the front passenger seat looked down at the car bag by his feet. The folding stock of the HK53 machine gun with two magazines clipped together was ready and waiting for any sudden surprises.

"When we get to the ambush site, don't go rogue on us. Stick to the plan and just deploy the flash bangs, we will do the rest. We know what they did to your crew, so let us handle it. No cowboy stuff." Mez and his driver Frankie Hewitt nodded in unison.

Ben Nash had set off at a lightning pace, using lights from the villages of Mullaghbawn and Silverbridge as a quick reference. After carefully crossing the Cashel Road, they made their way into a large field and wormed their way around the fishing pond until they reached the steep bank of Silverbridge Road.

"Ratty, why have we brought a Baby Blade out with us? He's just done selection, fuckin speed of a gazelle, slow it down fella, the bad guys won't go away." Wild Bill panted.

After a brief rest, Ratty led his team forward towards the enemy's blocking position. As he approached the junction with Glenmore Road, the big Fijian gave the hand signal to halt. Voices could be heard on the wind, Ratty pointed at the young Trooper and placed a hand on his head, the universal sign for 'Come to me.' Ninety minutes had slowly passed before the two returned to the waiting Wild Bill and Harry Ashford. While Ben kept a lookout, Ratty whispered the plan to the two waiting men.

"One man is on the vehicle with a heavy machine gun, facing up Glenmore, and one guy stopping cars on Glenmore another on Silverbridge Road. The forth one is getting his napper down in the bus shelter. Attack will be like we planned from South to North. You know your targets so we will move into position when we get the shout. All gave him the thumbs up. The plan was classis Special Forces 'KISS' Keep It Simple Stupid.

Call Sign 73 had made steady progress hedge hopping and ditch jumping from their hide in the wood yard. The only casualty so far were Craig McSwann's ripped combat pants and John Docker's busted nose after falling off a barbed wire fence. Surprisingly, it was the Aussie McSwann who was bleating the most. "What the fucks wrong Swanny? You've only ripped your fuckin kecks man, the Docs got a broken nose, and he's not crying." Sargent Alan Shirwell, the team leader asked.

"Al it's not the ripped pants mate, I just don't want to go to war with my bollocks swinging."

"Better put some cam cream on the fuckers then." Joked, Simon De Velda, a big South African.

After completing a full circle of the village, all four patrol members entered the graveyard of St Patrick's Church. Parked on the driveway was a dark Transit Van, one of the many stolen by Manny in the weeks leading up to the attacks.

Liam Crossen had seen the young 'Donald' Pleasance grow and develop over the last few days. Gone were the stupid questions, the nervousness and wanting to check on his mother. Donald would become an exceptional asset to the Cullyhanna Gun Club. Crossen lifted his feet to rest on the parcel shelf of the van. His active service unit had been given the 'Gun Club' moniker by the Brits, May 1990 on the Slatequarry Road he remembered. One woman in the village said she thought she had seen soldiers hiding around the old Quarry, and the Cullyhanna boys did the rest. The news later reported that a Sargent from a Scottish Regiment had been killed, but Crossen and the rest believed that was a lie. Sure the shooting went on for ages they must have been SAS commandos, and everyone in the bar afterwards said they had shot a Brit so at least ten were dead. Another thought entered his head. Tomorrow was the anniversary of his father's death. He set his mind that he would visit the grave when he took over from Donald on watch and say a silent prayer.

Newry Estuary

After checking the bodies, Ski Lampowski and Steve Richards had quickly changed out of their dry suits and recovered their belt kits from the dry bags they had towed behind as they crossed the canal. Behind them they could hear faint splashing noises as the Fusiliers paddled across the water as the tide began to rise.

The Fusiliers raced ashore and moved into a defence position as the boat was securely tied to the bank.

After a quick head count Tommy squeezed Ski's shoulder who immediately stood and walked off towards the dark steep wooded hill followed by the recent arrivals. The column snaked silently along a firebreak between the pine trees, gaining height with every step. Every fifteen minutes Ski halted and kneeled, each man behind him mirrored his stance and scanned their arcs, whilst opening their mouths and listening for any noise on the gentle breeze. A cloudless sky chilled the night air as the trees became sparser, giving way to larger areas of heathland. Below the marching, the moonlight shimmered off the water in the estuary below and reflected off ancient granite stones protruding from the heather beside the trail.

Up ahead a bright red light was visible on top of the radio mast of the Fathom Line patrol base 'Romeo One Seven.'

Tommy gave Ski the thumbs up and led the COP soldiers to the north of the base, crossing the Upper Fathom Road before turning south to use the old dry stone wall flanking Ferryhill Road as concealment to reach the western cut off position.

After watching the last Fusilier disappear into the distance Ski and Steve Richards re-entered the wood line, silently hand railing the road until they found a suitable spot to observe the road and fulfil their mission as the north road cut-offs.

TCG (S) Portadown

Martin Jenkins was carefully listening in to the reports of the of his men's progress. He turned and gave Seb a nod. "We're in position on the lower slope."

Seb immediately acknowledged him and stuck his head through the serving hatch type aperture. In the room next door was the operations room for Special Forces. A mirror image of the COP room apart from large monitors displaying a live feed from carefully concealed cameras hidden in the heather on the hill facing Romeo One Seven, and a thermal image picture being beamed from a Nimrod spy plane, well out of earshot of people on the ground.

Seb looked around, signallers were sat in concentration, headsets draped over their ears. The Squadron Sargent Major Damo Twizzle was in conversation with the Squadron Second in Command Robbie McDermott. Finally he set eyes on the man he was looking for. "Hamish, how's Darkie doing?"

Major Hamish McLeod MC looked over his copy of Ulysses. Every six foot five inches of the man screamed officer in the Foot Guards. He pushed his spectacles on to his receding hairline and pinched the bridge of his nose.

"I now know why this book was officially banned in England in 1929."

"Why's that Boss?" his Sargent Major asked.

"Because my Kiwi friend, it's bloody awful."

Damo smiled and went back to haranguing McDermott.

"Well Seb, you know Darkie better than me, he likes to leave things till the last moment. His last transmission was they had some problems getting to the wood, and then the wood was dense."

"Well, he needs to get a shifty on because I'm getting word from the technical people that Peewee's convoy is on the move south of the border, but slowly heading towards the Fathom Line."

"I'll get Damo to give him a kick up the backside. The other patrols are all in position and reporting that the illegal road blocks are thumb up bum and completely switched off."

Seb thought about the comment. "Maybe Peewee has only taken his best guys, leaving the chaff to do the shitty jobs. It's possible they have switched off because they are not on the big job."

"Or they are so supremely confident in Peewee's ability, they have become bulletproof."

Fathom Line

It had been a slow start once all the Ambush team had assembled on the scrubland. The four chosen men from G Squadron Air Troop carrying Heckler & Koch MP5SD Silenced Submachine Guns had disappeared into the shadows to stop any disruption by the anti-aircraft missile crew hiding in the bracken above Ferryhill Road. Darkie had whispered In Jerry St John's ear as he led the four-man patrol away, "If I don't see you in Hell, I will see you in Hereford."

Darkie was pushed for time. Sneaking past the white pebble dashed walls and grey slate roof of Patsy's Parlur lounge bar had taken an age, then trying to find the forestry track shown on the map proved to even worse. The issued maps were old and what had appeared to be an evenly spaced plantation was now old and almost impenetrable in the dark.

"Top cover secured three Tangos KIA." Jerry's cockney voice.

"How the fuck did you get up there so quick, we are stuck trying to get through the wood." Darkie questioned.

"Fuck that mate, one hundred meters up the road there's a

track to a farm, but it's a derelict now, ten minutes to your position if you jog you fat bastard."

"Have you found their radio?"

"Yes, Jock's manning it and will give rapid tones if anyone calls. Hopefully, they will think its bad comms or the batteries are going."

Kilcurly Crossroads.

Peewee's convoy had been staidly tracing the line of the border since departing the Mechanic's yard. Before leaving, he had told Decers to check all the check points before meeting him on the hill across from the army base.

He turned to his driver and gave him a playful punch on the shoulder. "Notice anything Manny?" He smiled.

Manny wondered if it was another one of Peewee's trick questions. "Should I?"

"No helicopters, pull over we're meeting someone at the crossroads."

In the distance, a vehicle's lights flashed. Manny stopped in front of the line of vehicles.

"Come with me and pull your balaclava down." Peewee ordered.

Both men got out of the 4x4, leaving Joseph to man grenade launcher on the back.

A man also wearing a balaclava and holding a rifle stood at the side of the red DAF tipper truck. Manny recognised the voice behind the mask as Arthur O'Donnell from Crossmaglen.

"Does he know what he has to do?" Peewee asked.

"Yes, but you might want to make the point again."

Peewee stepped up on the wheel of the lorry and put his head into the cab. He looked at the driver chained to his seat.

"Are you Dennis Kennedy, from Adagavoyle Road?"

The man was weeping and nodded his head.

"Now Dennis, you know we mean business, your wife and children are under arrest until you carry out this minor job. Am I clear so far?"

Kennedy gave another nod of acknowledgement.

"Drive to Kilnasaggart Bridge and park directly beneath the railway line. We will make a phone call to the Crown Forces to rescue you. You have not been booby trapped and the timer will not go off until you are well clear. Nod if you understand my instructions."

The man complied

"Now off you go, my men will be watching so don't fuck it up. Once we are happy I will release your family, now do your job for the cause."

Peewee jumped off the truck and marched back towards his vehicle.

"What was all that about Peewee?"

"An added fuck off pill for the politicians on both sides of the border." He smirked.

"Who will ring the bomb warning in?"

Peewee looked at his driver, "Nobody!"

Fathom Line

Darkie heard the tractor straining to get up the steep road, burdened by the heavy slurry bowser it had taken an age to appear in the waiting soldier's Kite Sight. Behind the tractor was a van which pulled into the side a few meters inside the Irish border. Ominous shadows appeared from the van and moved up the tarmac road.

In Darkie's ear the southern road cut off only fifty meters inside Northern Ireland gave six clicks of the radio presell.

Darkie whispered to the Machine gunners flanking him, "Six Tangos, hold your fire."

Over the next hour the six men with the help of the tractor's dozer blade pulled down the dry stone wall on the opposite side of the road. The work team, using the debris filled in the ditch to create a bridge into the fields beyond.

Once constructed the tractor and slurry trailer continued up the road towards the cut off manned by Ski and Steve.

"Flame tractor towards North road cut off." Darkie whispered.

The six men retreated to their van, and then moved it to block the newly constructed gateway.

The men in the ambush position focused intently on the six men just a road's width away. They appeared disciplined and organised, unlike their friends lying dead by the side of the river. One man broke away from the group carrying a long rifle. He jogged up the road towards the camp.

The southern cut off began giving rapid clicks on the radio, a warning. The ambush team could then hear the vehicles; the men by the gateway also heard the noise and responded immediately by moving their van to clear a space for the approaching fleet.

"Turn in here to your left, Manny." Peewee instructed.

Peewee's mood had changed. For the last ten minutes he had been trying to radio the men watching the Newry River and canal to no avail. He'd also tried to speak to his missile men at the top of the hill, but all he got was static and a series of clicks. Even his most trusted Lieutenant Decers wasn't answering his radio. He threw down the handset in disgust, "Fuckin imbeciles." he cursed under his breath.

TCG (S) Portadown

All the commanders were gathered around the bird table. Seb was looking around. "If you're waiting for Joe, he's rushed away to answer an urgent call in his office."

"No dramas Herbie, you can back brief him when he gets back. I just want to bring everyone up to speed with the state of play. Kris, can you kick us off with what's happening at One Seven."

"Last night we inserted Alfie Langer's Ulster Troop into the camp and withdrew the green troops. They have laid several PAD mines and remote ground sensors in the bushes we expect to the attackers to form up in. The technical boys from NISS have also placed out ground cameras which are showing movement of individuals, but as yet not deploying to attack positions; however a sniper has shot out the mast security cameras, which was also a prelude to the Forkhill attack. Finally, we have been told by intelligence sources that Peewee's vehicle is in situ."

Martin raised his hand, "I can concur with that. My troops have seen a number of vehicles slowly move into what they are describing as a line of departure. All engines are off. One of my snipers, who has watched Kelly for months has given a positive identification of Kelly and said that his vehicle is at the rear of the T shaped formation they have settled into." Jenkins pointed at the map on the table to indicate the position of the attackers.

McLeod studied the map carefully, "Buggers are going to use that small track as a reference point to lead them towards the base." The assembled commanders looked at him. "Once the operation goes noisy, I think a few more than expected will run down the hill towards your team Martin, ah well no plan survives first contact and all that."

Joe entered the room shaking his head. "I've just had the word from London, they have requested Backlash, Brad and the COP boys need to extract the agent immediately."

"When was that called in, my troops saw her make a call from the phone box in Dromintee this afternoon?"

"Good question Martin, I'm afraid, red tape and passing communications from one intelligence service to another and department to department has not been robust. Where is she?"

"At the farm with the daughter, probably shitting herself waiting for her husband to return and murder her."

"Well, give the order and get her out."

As Jenkins turned to open the operational package above the briefing map, the radio burst into life.

"Boss the OP and Romeo Two One are reporting a massive explosion about a mile West of Jonesborough."

CHAPTER SEVENTEEN

Tuesday 5th July 1994

Kilnasaggart Bridge

The lights of the red DAF truck illuminated the grey stone arch of Kilnasaggart Bridge as it descended the narrow road. Kennedy had fully expected to be stopped by waiting soldiers, promised by the men wearing black balaclavas. Dennis, a devout Catholic, had never committed a crime, spoken to the Forces of the Crown or assisted the Republican movement. His only misconduct was to tend an injured soldier shot on his doorstep; it was a Christian act on the spur of the moment. He'd placed a tea towel on the dying solder's head, after being shot by a sniper. After that one incident the community shunned him, work as a lorry driver became scarce, he even considered leaving South Armagh. Now he was chained to a wheel of a truck on a delivery of who knows what to a railway bridge in the middle of nowhere.

In the back of the truck was over three thousand pounds of homemade explosive and initiation pack of Chinese commercial explosive connected to a radio-controlled receiver.

Peewee had directed Manny to a position behind the lead vehicles of the flying column. He looked at the one-to-one radio in his lap and pushed the key. The signal flashed to the receiver, over four miles away in a millisecond, instructing the radio-controlled improvised explosive device to arm the bomb and start the trigger sequence. A red LED flashlight on the truck's dashboard illuminated and began flashing. The warm glow made Kennedy jump in his seat; he looked at the controls to ensure he had not touched the hazard warning lights or indicators in his nervousness. A cold realisation dawned on him about another chained man he had read about in years before, an attack on the Killeen check point only four years before. The IRA had tied the man into his delivery van and told him to drive to the checkpoint where the soldiers would cut him free he was only 'delivering' the bomb. He thought hard and remembered the young soldiers name Smith, Cyril Smith, he was an Irishmen, but how did they describe the bomb? Yes, that was it the word they used was proxy......

TCG (S) Portadown

"Is everyone OK, Corporal Boreman? I need a sitrep ASAP." demanded an anxious Martin Jenkins.

"The guys in the OP felt the ground shake, but they are all fine. The cut off group gave a no change and have gone back to radio silence so the main reporting is from Romeo Two One. Del has done a rough estimate and thinks the bomb has gone off in the area of Kilnasaggart Bridge."

Joe had stepped into the back of the room and immediately picked up on the implications of the explosion. "Herbie check the train times for the Dublin to Belfast service. It's another diversion, gentlemen."

"That's a bold statement Joe, how do you know?"

"Ah Peewee you are a riddle, wrapped in a mystery, inside an enigma." He laughed.

"I love that statement, it was one of Churchill's don't you know. He's trying to draw more soldiers out of the camp so he has less to fight. He's also sending a message to the Free State if he can bomb a railway line over here he can also do it down there. This boy is a maverick all right. Ask for permission to instigate Hydra once Peewee makes his move. I will push the police support units down to Newry; we'll need a lot of officers on the ground after this. I will also let our friends in the Garda know about the Tullydonnel Farm. We can't deal with that place, but I'm sure Dan Currie will be eager to nab those wee bastards."

South Armagh

Mez had instructed his driver to pull into the layby off the Dromintee Road over two hours ago. The heavily armed men in the back had disappeared into the darkness; he was feeling exposed and nervous, not helped by the colossal explosion towards the border. Without thinking, he tapped the waiting machine gun with the toe of his boot. Over his earpiece, he heard Johnny Rathbone whisper that his team was in position.

Fathom Line

Bennett slowly and meticulously cut the loophole which would become the aperture for the muzzle of his L96 sniper rifle. Bennett had been a sniper for six of his ten years' service; a quick pull through of the barrel to ensure that no dampness had entered the barrel during the stalk into position and he was happy. Beside Bennett his spotter, Stu Taylor busied himself setting up the Bariner spotting scope and judging distances to several key reference points. Each reference point was carefully marked on to a range card which was placed into a waterproof cover and sat between the sniper and his spotter.

Once all was in order they both changed into the camouflage quilted suits, which would make laying on the cold damp ground more bearable.

Both men lay motionless, mouths open, trying to catch any faint nose which would show the forward movement of the enemy. From their position they could cover the western side of the envisaged attack on to the patrol base. Unsighted to them both behind a dry stone wall on the Fathom Road was Ulster Troop who would provide the primary ambush site at the exit on to Ferryhill Road.

The gorse bush in the corner of the field junction was approximately three hundred meters from the small knoll on which they had observed Peewee conduct his ground recce. The bush gave good concealment from view, but damn little protection from bullets or rockets.

It was Taylor who first heard the vehicle engines cough and splutter into life. Peewee was on the move.

TCG (S) Portadown

Joe rang the office of the Special Detective Unit in Dublin; he hoped that the duty night detective could pass a message on to his friend Superintendent Dan Currie warning him about the activities at a certain farm on his side of the border.

"Aar Joe, what is it, we're kinda busy right now?"

"Jesus I nearly dropped the phone, are you on nights or something?"

"Aar no, and I can't say much, but the things you told us have triggered something over here so it's all hands to the pump. Every available officer from SDU is here getting a briefing, so I gotta dash."

"Before you go write this address down and get some of your boys to search the place, you will find a few weapons and get some arrests."

As he put the receiver down Seb dashed into the office. "It's beginning; we've had the good to go from command."

Joe followed the young officer back to the operations room and watched him as he picked up the radio handset. He looked towards Joe, who nodded.

"All call signs this is Zero Stand By Stand By!" he waited, the silence hung in the air.

A distant voice on the radio reported "Bravo One is on the move."

"Op Hydra is Go Go Go!"

South Armagh

Ski nudged his partner and pointed in the direction of the road as it sloped to the south. Out of the darkness chugged a Massey Ferguson 390 tractor straining against the gradient. As the vehicle approached the crest it pulled over towards the trees, the driver closing down the engine. A man jumped from the footplate and began to work on an attachment on the Slurry Tanker. The man was grumbling as he tried to turn something over. They could hear the sound of metal on metal before a small jockey motor erupted into life. Both soldiers in the cut off observed closely the men only a few meters away from their hiding place, their night sights giving them a green zombie like appearance.

Richards reached into his chest rig, feeling for the rounded base of the 'Willie Pete' white phosphorus grenade. After ensuring the split pin's arms were straightened and still retaining the fly of leaver, he gently placed the old but deadly object to his side.

They had split the forward line of Flying Column either side of an old, partially overgrown track. All the vehicles drove slowly, to avoid revving engines. The left hand column slowly drifted away down the hill, coming into the killing area of the hiding Fusiliers in the western cut off. Occasionally a vehicle would scrape along a tree branch or heather bush and there would be a muttered curse as wheels dropped into invisible pot holes.

After fifteen minutes of slow and ponderous movement, Peewee was happy with the position he had previously chosen behind the gorse bushes just below the crest of the hill directly opposite the patrol base.

From their fire position Bennett and Taylor had monitored and reported the unhurried advance. Peewee moved from the front passenger seat to take up position at the rear of his vehicle behind a thick stubby weapon. Beside him was another volunteer. Through the Bariner scope the other person was a small and slim figure, but Bennett could tell from his night sight that the figure was a young man holding on to the arm of Peewee for balance.

Call sign 71 had almost been on top of the check point team when they opened fire, Ratty disposing of the man behind the heavy machine gun with one shot of his German made G3 rifle. Ben Nash had fired a burst from his Colt Commando at the figure resting in the bus shelter. He sprinted across the road to look at the body hanging half out of the blue sleeping bag. It was the first time he had seen death close at hand.

Wild Bill had shot the other two men standing in the road before his partner Ashford, could get a shot off.

Wild Bill strode over to Nash, "Big boys' rules Nasher old son. Welcome to the Squadron." He said as he gave the new Trooper's shoulder a squeeze.

The four-man patrol hiding in the graveyard of St Patrick's Church in Cullyhanna had seen a young man carrying an assault rifle walking along the main road. The guard appeared to be fairly switched on and disciplined, walking along slowly and observing his arcs as he patrolled. The man then returned to the van and woke up a second person before getting into the rear of the vehicle.

Shirwell looked at the Trooper closest to him and mouthed "Stag Change"

Docker passed the message down the line as all four trained their rifles on the new sentry.

Liam Crossen was still sleepy, and his back ached from the uncomfortable position he had taken up in the front of the van. He had a piss by the wall of the church, and then said a quick Hail Mary for his sin. After a quick walk along Tullynavall Road he looked across to the orange street lights of the St Patrick's estate. On the horizon a faint glow appeared. Crossen turned and passed his make shift home; Donald was already snoring in the back. Ten minutes and those Brits will get a real wake-up call, he thought, as he stepped his way amongst the gravestones towards his father's resting place. There was a movement by one of the stones then a faint flash, Liam Crossen fell dead.

The sharp whip lash noise seemed to be part of a dream Donald was then weightless, he was flying, but the dream suddenly became a nightmare as his head was rammed into the tarmac road. A knee pressed hard into the small of his back, taking the wind out of his lungs. The unseen demons forced his arms behind his back before something was wrapped around his wrists and pulled tight, cutting off the circulation to his hands. The demons then thrust a bag over his bald head as he hyperventilated.

Someone with the strength of a giant yanked him to his feet before slamming his head into the side of the van, then forcing him to kneel.

"Stay calm Sunny, you're in the bag. Thank your lucky stars you're not your mucker with no fuckin face." The voice was menacing, foreign, possibly South African.

Mez finally got the order to move. Out of all the anti-ambushes, this was the most dangerous one. Frankie Hewitt looked at him, "Are you sure about this mate?"

Mez clenched his teeth and nodded. "Let's do it." He called as he removed the HK 53 and placed it on to his lap.

Johnny Rathbone saw the headlights of the saloon as it slowly made its way South on the Dromintee Road, his team had identified four men at the roadblock one of whom was stood on the back of a Toyota pickup with a huge black anti-aircraft gun.

The site they had chosen was a split crossroads with the Dromintee major road and secondary Ballintemple and Aghadavoyle roads. Johnny had smiled after he had completed the recce of the area. Whoever was the commander was no tactician, too few men to cover too large an area. They were all split up with communication done by shouting. The only mutual support would come from the large gun on top of the pickup.

The grey saloon crested the hill, driving at a moderate speed; up ahead a figure in the road was circling a torch light to instruct the driver to stop. Beyond the figure, a road sign showed the direction to the local GAA club.

In his ear piece Johnny heard Mez counting down the distance to the stop.

The fields to the left of the car were open and filled with dozing sheep, separated from the highway by a thin line of neatly trimmed bushes, on the driver's side large trees and dense foliage lined the road. The outline of the man in the road became clearer; he was wearing a balaclava and a black boiler suit. A sign over his shoulder indicated left and Jonesborough two miles.

"Stand By, Stand By." Mez whispered into the dashboard microphone.

The car rolled to a halt about ten meters from the road guard.

Fuckin ejit, the man in the balaclava thought as he walked towards the headlights. It annoyed Paul Gerrity, he had shown the driver where he wanted him to stop "Switch them fuckin lights out he shouted." As he nonchalantly walked towards the car. His night vision was now ruined; thank god it would soon by daybreak. He blinked as he was part way along the vehicle bonnet and tried to see if he recognised who was inside the motor. Young fella driver, hands on the wheel, passenger black thing in his arms!

Mez screamed "UP" and let loose a burst of automatic fire through the windscreen from the HK53, the 5.56mm rounds hitting Gerrity in the throat then head, killing him instantly. Frankie flicked a hidden switch, immediately deploying the flash bangs underneath the vehicle. There was a blinding flash, then a further three loud cracks as Johnny Rathbone's patrol disposed of the three remaining members of the roadblock. Men with blackened faces emerged from the roadside. The engagement lasted a matter of seconds, clinical and precise.

Rathbone approached the vehicle and snatched opened the door for Mez,

"I thought I explained the plan in full you Muppet! We do the malleting you just provide the distraction."

"Sorry Mate but..." Mez started trying to explain.

"Don't be sorry to me, say sorry to Billy here, he had that Tango in his sights for two hours and you whacked him first."

The SAS Sergeant looked down at the body in the road. "Good grouping, though. I take it you noticed he was wearing body armour, so you went for the noggin?"

Mez shook his head. "What fucking body armour?"

"You lucky fucker, anyway, job done." Rathbone turned away and reported over the radio that four more Tangos lay dead.

The men from the van that had constructed the bridge into the field had been called forward by Peewee, their job was to put suppressing fire down at the two towers as the vehicles drove forward through the line of gorse to their firing line.

The men walked forward slowly, shoulder to shoulder in the distance a number of shots could be heard. "Sounds like the

Dromintee road block have found more SAS." Alfie
McGaught whispered to his partner Tobias Timbrenan. As
they hit thicker patches of gorse Tobias snagged his boot on
an object which immediately snapped. Peewee felt the hot
ball bearings flying passed his exposed position before he
heard the blast as the PAD mine exploded. A second mine
detonated quickly followed by a third. Some vehicles were
smoking, volunteers were screaming as they rushed to help
limbless friends caught in the first salvo.

As the flame tractor tried to advance a small metallic object
flew from the wood side landing beneath the trailer. Eleven
ounces of white phosphorus turned the vehicle and crew into
a fireball.

Peewee saw the huge fireball erupt beyond the trees to his
right. In the rising flames he saw the look of fear in his son's
eyes. Machine gun fire from Peewee's left brought him back
to reality; he had walked into a trap.

He called out on the radio for support from the mortar team
who were supposedly in a position on the hill with the Anti-
Aircraft missile men, but all four lay dead, the heavy mortar
tube not even set up, after stumbling into the four waiting
men from Air Troop and their silenced machine pistols.

Bennett slowed his breathing down the inverted V of the
night sight gently rose and fell the waves became more
shallow as the experienced sniper took up the first trigger
pressure before releasing the shot.

Peewee felt the kick in his chest which sent him barrelling
over the side; Joseph had felt the round zipping past his nose
like a fire fly prior to hitting his father. Stu followed up by
launching a light armour rocket into the back of Peewee's
truck, showering Joseph with red hot pieces of metal in his
back and legs.

"Manny, get the boy and get out of the ambush area." Peewee
shouted whilst trying to regain his feet.

In the confusion the volunteers turned to run down the hill, but were met with a withering hail of gunfire as Tommy Trainor directed his GPMG gunners to engage the fleeing volunteers.

Some vehicles were luckier and bumped their way back to the improvised bridge only to drive head on into the waiting guns of G Squadron. Tracer rounds smashed into the remnants of the Flying Column and Troopers fired 40mm grenades from M203 underslung launchers.

Manny threw his pickup into reverse, screaming at Peewee to jump on the back. Joseph vaulted from the rear to help his father; behind him as Taylor fired a second rocket.

Unlike his first shot, Stu had miscalculated the new range which went below his intended target. The missile skimmed the chassis of the vehicle, hitting the heather on the far side which triggered the piezoelectric fuse to detonate the primary warhead charge, instantaneously sending pieces of the missile's copper liner far and wide.

The blast lifted the bleeding boy off his feet as his father disappeared in a cloud of smoke, dirt and heather.

Manny continued reversing "JoJo get in." he screamed above to sound of the increasing machine gun fire.

"I'm not leaving my Da." The boy sobbed.

In a panic Manny jumped from his vehicle and ran to the patch where he had last seen Peewee. The air stank of explosives and burnt flesh, Manny stumbled upon something on the ground, he reached down and picked up a leg. He then heard Joseph's voice in the bracken. As the smoke cleared, he could see the adolescent boy cradling his father's head in his arms. "Help him." He demanded.

Peewee lay there barely conscious, body armour blown off, and both legs gone. The boy tried to drag him away, which only made the dying man moan. Peewee reached out and put his arm around his son's head, drawing him closer so he could whisper in his ear, "Tiocfaidh ár lá."38

"Manny take him away, please." Peewee croaked whilst spitting out blood.

"No Da." The boy was crying as Manny threw him into the pickup and drove away from the ambush. A single pistol round went off behind the bouncing vehicle; neither Joseph nor Manny looked back. Paul Patrick Kelly was dead.

Manny placed an arm around the sobbing boy who was bleeding from cuts on his back and legs. "JoJo I will get you to a hospital in the free State then back to your Ma. Just remember what your Da did, in the future people will compare him to Finn McCool the giant, a true warrior and defender of the Irish." Manny was also trying to fight back the tears, in his heart he knew he had betrayed Peewee and all of his friends who now lay dead or dying behind him.

Steve looked down at the charred remains of the two terrorist and winced at the smell. "Burning flesh, horrible smell." He commented as he turned to his partner, Ski.

"Vey apt really, taking them both out with a Willie Pete. I bet you didn't know that white phosphorus was first used by Irish nationalist arsonists in the 19th century."

Steve gave Ski a mystified look "Are you auditioning for the Shit and Shovel Corps or Mastermind." He laughed.

All over the hillside the shooting had stopped. In the breaking light no movement could be seen, although cries and screams could be heard in the vegetation.

Manny pulled the pickup to a sharp halt. The exit back on to Ferryhill Road was blocked by smouldering vehicles; bodies were draped grotesquely over the bodywork. Manny scanned for an escape when he felt the icy steel of a rifle barrel poke

38 Our Day will Come

into his ear. On seeing the soldiers Joseph leapt from the front seat to avenge the death of his father only to receive a punch in the face which sent him dizzy.

A burly SAS soldier with a large handlebar moustache covered in camouflage cream dragged Manny from the driver's seat.

"And what's your name?" The voice was dispassionate.

Manny's mind was racing. He should let the soldier shoot him and leave his body in the heather like his comrades. Racked with guilt, he tried to remember the word given to him by his handlers.

The world finally came to him. It was the ultimate betrayal he would never become one of the South Armagh martyrs, but a figure of hate, forever condemned to a life of fear. "I am Orange."

The big soldier dragged him to one side. "I thought it was you, Manny, Mr Agent Orange himself."

"That's right." Manny agreed and was then led off towards the woods, "What about the boy?" He asked over his shoulder.

"That's for the RUC to decide."

The SAS Trooper leading many to the woods turned to the big Sargent Major.

"Is this fucker going to get the good news in the woods Darkie?"

"No Geordie it's his lucky day, he's flying out club class when the first chopper arrives, unlike young Peewee here who will visit Castlereagh."

Alpha One

Eileen had been looking out of the kitchen window all night, her eyes switched from the gateway to the farm then to the two small bags waiting by the door. She checked her watch again. Her head was pounding; they said on the phone they would come; they had always said they would endeavour to rescue her. She had been a good loyal servant, seventeen years playing the role as the female lead of this long running soap opera. She admitted to herself that in the last few years she had been dropped to playing minor supporting roles as the leading actor had become so consumed in his precious war.

Over the years she had bonded with her husband Paul, they did have a certain chemistry. She tried to comprehend the feelings she held for the man, was it love, friendship or was he just 'the job.' In truth she had loved the adrenaline of being so close to a dangerous man and learning his secrets before informing on him. She always doubted he would ever suspect her, never dreaming that he was sleeping with a British Spy, but those surges were few and far between, she believed that was why she took up the chance to have an affair with Declan Taylor, against the orders of her controllers. The sex was wonderful, but the exhilaration of not being exposed even better.

Paul had previously never threatened her with violence, they had massive bust ups, some in public, but she always appeared to win, not now though. She was scared; the look in his eyes when he took Joseph and punched her told her that his desire for power had finally engulfed him. He was forever lost to her. She hoped that her son would return unharmed and Peewee return dead on his shield. Her husband now believed he was either invincible or on a suicide mission.

"Is JoJo coming with us Mommy?" Mairéad voice sounded tired and worried.

She took the child's head in her arms and pulled her close. "I hope so my love, now try to sleep, I will wake you when the taxi comes to take us to the plane. We will soon be with your

Auntie Elizabeth." Yet another lie, she hatred herself. How was she going to explain this to the children? The nagging voice again awoke in the back of her mind questioning if she would ever see Joseph again.

She fought back the tears as she saw the car headlights approaching the gateway.

Decers had immediately ignored the order from Peewee and driven to the one place he felt safe. He was convinced that this was one attack too many; the Brits were not stupid and Peewee had started believing in his own legend.

After ditching the boiler suit and body armour, he prowled the confined space of the caravan, trying to think of a plan to save himself. His future life would forever be away from South Armagh as the finger of suspicion would be pointed at him as a surviving volunteer. He couldn't go on the run with Bridget and the kids. God, he could never prise her out of the door, anyway. The idea then struck him; he would take Eileen and run. If Peewee survived, he could say he was protecting the matriarch of his family. Failing that, he could contact his handlers and arrange an escape to the mainland. Eileen would be useful to them, he reasoned. She must know all about Peewee's activities. A gigantic explosion shook him, it was time to move Decers was in a more positive frame of mind as he threw the Type 56C short-barrel carbine into the passenger seat and shoved a bayonet into the thigh pocket of his cargo pants. He looked in the rear-view mirror at the caravan as he drove at speed towards the main road. As he drove passed the still smoking ruins of the barracks at Forkhill, a blinding flash followed by a rising fireball appeared over the wooded hill where the Tievecrom Tower once stood. Peewee had walked into trouble, big trouble.

Alpha One

Brad and all the members of the observation post were wide awake, the explosion from Kilnasaggart reminding them of their own mortality. Corporal Eammon Mulready looked at the monitor in the waterproof Peli case for signs of movement at Alpha. Other farmers had left their homesteads and walked to the main road to see what the disturbance was, but nothing from the targeted address.

To his left the new guy Brad was sat up in his sleeping bag spooning the last mouthful of bacon and beans boil in the bag ration into his hungry mouth. "Tastes better with chilli mate." He commented.

"Mull the Boss is on the blower, he said to ask the attached guy about Op Backlash and it's a go." Lance Corporal Steve Hills looked at Mull in puzzlement "What the fook is Backlash?"

Brad Powell almost chocked on a piece of bacon rind at the word.

"We're on boys; I need some bods to get me down to the farm pronto. Our job is to rescue Eileen and her kids. She feels they have compromised her and needs to extract. Eileen Kelly is a deep undercover agent."

The OP crew were silent, heads shook in disablement.

"You're chuffin telling me that the Bitch, someone we have had the pleasure of watching, and taking abuse from for the last eighteen months is one of ours?" Hill's was incredulous at the latest information.

Mull chipped in "Ok so she on our side, and shit me what a game she's played, not only fooling every British squaddie and copper but also the leader of the Provo's. Thing is Brad, where are we going to take her? Back up here? The nearest patrol base or have you got a fold out hele landing pad in your bergan?"

"Anywhere to safety first which means north of the border,

further exfiltration will be off the cuff.”

“You sound like my Directing Staff at Brecon. Right Hilly you’re with me and Brad, Snapper and Reeves give us top cover while Dougie and Flan pack things up. If all goes to rat shit we might need a quick bug out.”

The three men felt good to be stood upright in the crisp night air, the first flecks of the new day were just becoming visible.

“Order of march: me Brad then Hilly. Take our time and no engagements, you understand that big man?” Hilly smiled.

“Mull we’ve got lights towards Alpha One.”

“Fuck that bollocks then follow me.” Mul turned and ran downhill.

Eileen shouted down the corridor to Mairéad, the escape was about to begin, the young girl appeared carrying a favourite doll in her hand as a car screeched to a halt outside, it sent stone chippings flying. Eileen heard a door slam and footsteps towards the door; instinctively she lifted her daughter then reached for the bags by the kitchen door. The door flew open, knocking the bags sideways. In the frame stood Decers, a small machine gun slung over his shoulder.

“Eileen, come on let’s make a run for it, get away from this madness. I think Peewee and the boys have walked into a trap, I’ve heard the shooting, it sounds like they’ve been set up.”

She was frozen. Why did they send him? What about Joseph was he in the ambush with his father?

“You’re our escape? Who sent you,” she questioned.

“Yes, it looks like you were waiting anyway, your bags are already packed.”

“But they never said that you would come, I didn’t even know you were on our side. I thought it would be the Army.”

"Army! What the fuck are you going on about?" Declan couldn't understand his lover's conversation and then saw movement through the window over her shoulder.

His mouth was wide open in disbelief. "Fuckin Brits, it's you..... You're the traitor, you told them about us, and you told them about tonight's attack, you cold-hearted Bitch." He shouted as he raised the stubby machine gun to his shoulder.

"Mommy No." Mairéad shrieked and squeezed her mother.

The glass window behind the girl shattered as a bullet from Mull's rifle aimed its way towards the angry figure holding the small carbine in the kitchen. Decers felt the searing red hot poker as it broke his clavicle, making him drop the gun. In slow motion, the weapon fell to the stone kitchen floor before bouncing up. The force of the fall was significantly strong enough to release the safety sear from its protective hold of the weapons firing mechanism and hammer. Three rounds spewed from the muzzle in rapid succession before it fell quiet.

Decers in agony saw Eileen being flung away from him, and the little girl tumbling from her mother's arms to the ground screaming. Self-preservation took over as Decers charged out of the door, running towards his car. A flurry of shots ricocheted between his feet and hit the wheel of his getaway vehicle. He ran faster, his right arm dangling limp and lifeless by his side. The pickup was no longer an option; he scanned the yard for an escape before he felt a mule kick to the jaw, which sent him sprawling on to the gravel.

His jaw hung loose on to his left shoulder, his mouth open and gapping. Dazed, his survival instinct spurred him on. His right ear was deaf; blood was flowing from the hole where his right cheek used to be. He fought against the black waves of unconsciousness which would engulf him if he let it. By the road he saw a child's bike and sat astride it, propelling himself along using both feet as the handlebars supported his ever growing limp body. There was a car headlight up ahead. His mind was tiring, surly the Brits couldn't chase him this far into the south. He crashed into the car with the blue flashing lights, hitting the tarmac hard. His loose jaw flapping held on only by skin and sinew.

A face looked down at him.

"Is that you, Declan Taylor?" The voice was distant, but familiar. An older man wearing a peaked cap. Then everything went black.

"Brad we have a fuckin problem here." Mull shouted.

Brad ran back to the kitchen to find Mulready trying to stem the flow of blood from the young child. A loose round had hit her in the abdomen, beside her Eileen was screaming in pain, arterial bleeding pumping from her Femoral Artery.

"I've done a quick triage Eileen has been clipped in the artery, luckily its cut not severed I need you to push the artery against bone until I can grab the clamps out of my trauma pack. Hilly local protection and quickly pick up the brass we fired."

"We've got blue lights about a click up the road Mull." Hills replied as he switched on a powerful torch to pick up the discarded shell casings.

"What about the young kid?" Brad asked.

"Took one to the gut, I can't find an exit wound, but fuck knows what damage it's done to her vital organs. Both need medevac ASAP, but we happen to be in a foreign country." Mull finally clamped the source of the spraying blood and wrapped the wound before applying a tourniquet and inject her with his own morphine syrette. The ten milligrams of battlefield analgesia slowly eased Eileen's agony.

Brad looked around and saw the keys to the Range Rover. "How are they doing?"

"Not too good, the kid is still breathing, but her pulse is

getting weaker and she looks ashen. We need to get the fuck out of Dodge before that blue light gets any closer."

"This is a mad idea, but probably the only chance they will have. Me and Hills will load them up in her car. Radio Portadown tell them we are driving to Daisy Hill Hospital and will need doctors and a security detail ready."

"What about the roadblocks?"

"Hope and pray that the Troop have done their job."

Dublin

People all over Southern Ireland were waking up to the disturbing news that an attempted coup had been thwarted. It had been too early in the morning to make the papers, but front page headliners were being hastily substituted and latest editions pumped out to all kiosks throughout the country.

The televisions were in full swing, parading so called 'experts' discussing their opinions on Anti-Terrorism, policing and government.

Sargent Major Albie Docherty grinned at the news feed on the television placed up high on the operations room wall. "Feckin experts Ex means former, and a Spurt is a drip under pressure."

Simon O'Malley looked up from the report he was reading, "I suppose your next gag is that opinions are like arseholes, everybody has one."

"Something like that." Docherty grinned.

"So come on Albie, what did those politicians say when you burst through their doors?"

"Pass the feckin toilet roll, I think. Anyway, they were soon talking like burst arseholes, dubbing in all of their co-conspirators. The Guards are going to be busy." He managed to say before shoving another chicken leg into his mouth.

The plan had been simple, In the West men from the Special Operations Maritime Task Unit, who had boated up the River Shannon had quickly subdued the Military Police guard force on the gates of Custume Barracks in Athlone. Brigadier General Hugh Cullen along with a Colonel and four Lieutenant Colonels were quickly detained before being handed over to the Garda.

In the South, Blue team from Special Operations Task Unit had climbed the wall on Pope's Hill at the Southern Brigade headquarters at Collins Barracks in Cork and quickly made the arrests of Brigadier General Arthur Munro, Two Colonel's, one Lieutenant Colonel and three Majors.

Danny Breverty gave Simon a nod. "Just receiving word from Red team, Nathaniel Heggerty is saying they have caught ten men at the farm address we got from the SDU. He's asking for the Garda as they have uncovered a substantial amount of weapons and equipment. No shots fired, they all gave themselves up."

A studio presenter cut from his questioning of yet another 'expert' to a news reporter standing outside Leinster House. The Seat of the Irish Parliament appeared on screen, bright in the sunshine, two tricolour flags were slowly flickering in the minimal waft of warm air; both were at half-mast above the four granite columns

"The Taoiseach will give a press conference this afternoon."

Albie laughed, "I bet he feckin will."

EPILOGUE

October 1994

Stormont, Belfast

Seb broke the cover of the treeline, crossed the pristine lawns and was immediately engulfed by the storm which had started as a light drizzle when he started his morning run. The weather had suddenly become more akin to monsoon time in Java than an Ulster autumn. Red and brown leaves displaced from their trees danced in the wind as the tall officer pushed on.

As he reached the tarmac road, he turned right up the hill and pumped his legs and arms in a final defiant sprint towards an imaginary finish line. The soleus muscles in his calves were on fire, he tried his best to ignore the grating in his right knee, protected only by a flimsy Tubigrip sleeve as he pushed on up the ever increasing gradient towards the monument, for the fifth time that morning. The increasing wind drove the rain droplets hard into his exposed face and legs. He felt like he was being whipped by nettles as he pushed himself further.

He stretched out his hands and finally grabbed the granite plinth. Instinctively he looked down at his watch and quickly estimated that the ten miles had been completed far quicker than he had expected. He reached back into his nylon rucksack and fished out his flask of water. He rinsed his mouth and spat it out instantly, before taking a huge gulp. The cool water calmed his breathing as his heart rate fell. Not bad for an old man, he thought, not as fit as I was on the hills phase, but nobody every regained that level of fitness once selection was over. He looked up at the twelve foot statue and the four bronze plates detailing the political life of the Ulster politician. Chiselled into the stone was his name CARSON, the man's right arm rising into the ever greying Belfast sky as raindrops dripped from the effigy's nose.

Beyond, the light emanating from the Portland limestone walls of Stormont, the beating heart of Loyalist rule, appeared to highlight the bronze man on top of his icy stone platform.

Seb returned to searching his bag and found a banana, he remembered the Fusilier COP boys laughing at him one night after eating his third ration pack in a row, whilst his eyes were glued to the pictures being fed back from a lonely observation post in South Armagh. "Food is fuel, never to be enjoyed." He lectured the giggling soldiers.

He looked back down the hill towards the car park. Neatly manicured lawns which would have graced The Oval flanked the road on either side. He stretched his long legs, trying to push the lactic acid from his muscles, and then slowly jogged back towards the car. His overlong hair was wet and matted against his face; water squelched in his Hi Tec Silver Shadow trainers and his parachute silk hooded running top was cold and clung to his body. As he slowly picked up pace, he played back the events since that fateful early morning call from Big Joe in February. A lot of things had changed since that call, people had changed and people had died.

The last two days had reminded him of Exercise Pilgrims Progress, the combat survival phase of selection. After being captured Seb had endured seventy-two hours of stress positions, sensory deprivation and man handling. In between they had interrogated him on four separate occasions, each one using a unique approach, but each with the same goal, to break him and make him talk. The board of enquiry he had just been subjected to was just the same apart from he had to answer the board's questions, precisely and succinctly. At least during interrogation he only had to repeat his name, rank and number or 'I cannot answer that question Sir.' For the last forty-eight hours he had been bombarded with questions, on his combat estimate, decision-making process and man management by a group of staff officers with no comprehension of the black side of the war in Ulster. None of them even acknowledge that it was a war that had taken place. Internal security, my arse! Don't make me laugh.

Even when he tried to explain that there had been a mini invasion on the United Kingdom, in which soldiers, barracks and aircraft had been destroyed they looked at him blankly.

The changes had begun almost immediately as helicopters and vehicles ferried the soldiers back to Portadown to be met directly by the flying lawyer and RMP Special Investigation Branch. He smiled as he remembered the young Fusilier sniper remonstrating with the RMP Corporal who wanted to take his beloved rifle before he had a chance to clean it and Darkie shouting to everyone within earshot "Tell them fuck all, we've signed the Official Secrets Act. Monkey bastards!"

The mood in the briefing room was solemn whilst the Brigadier in command of JCUNI gave his customary well done everybody and pats on the back to all speech. Even crates of Bushmills and beer didn't lift the mood, fighting men huddled together shaking their heads, the young SSU Corporal, Mereday sat looking aimlessly out into space holding a full can of beer in his shaking hands and tears welling up in his eyes. The only cheering was from the signals and police staff that had never set foot outside of Portadown.

Seb remembered thinking that the pat on the back was merely a recce for the knife, which was quick to follow.

The mood hadn't lifted a week later when he had accompanied Joe and his officers on a visit to the whiskey factory with their colleagues from south of the border. They too appeared in limbo. One guy Simon had told Seb that his country wished to pull a cloak over recent history; Fianna Gael and Fianna Fai'l had begun an alliance to ensure that Sinn Fein would never take control of the Oireachtas.

One of the Garda Superintendents had spoken of an avenging angel stalking their country. For the last few days his officers had found mutilated bodies from Dundalk to Dublin. The victims all had one commonality, they were all staunch Republicans.

The real hammer blow had come when Joe had taken him to one side and told him he was going to take early retirement. The Chief Constable had told him he would be awarded the

Queens Police Medal in the next honours list. Weeks later Seb walked along the narrow lanes of Dundonald Cemetery as Herbie Grey along with his colleagues carried Joe's coffin to his final resting place. His guardian angel could not save him from the cancer which killed him.

The offices at Portadown now seemed empty; Joe left a big void in more ways than one. His replacement was a career copper, not a thief catcher, only there to get a few management ticks before moving up the promotion ladder. Within days he had sent Joe's men packing back to divisions throughout the Province, replacing them with yes men and bean counters who could only work when being micro managed or were more 'community focused.'

Seb's wing man Sergeant Major Kris Derbyshire had moved back up to the SSU in the Hanger to take over as Operations Officer after the dismissal of both Major Julian Clemont and Sargent Major Colin Armstrong. Even the Fusiliers COP had left the Province, replaced by a Yorkshire Regiment; the new Platoon Commander was a keen fella, but couldn't match the recently departed Martin Jenkins who was dynamic, meticulous and a demon drinker.

The August peace agreement, when the Provisional IRA announced a cessation of military operations, had come like a thunderbolt. The men of peace had won the day, but at what cost. Operation Hydra had been an enormous success; the military action on the ground had eradicated the hardline foot soldiers, leaving inexperienced volunteers to take their place.

At an extraordinary General Army Convention. The remnants of the Army Executive had called to order the Army Council and GHQ before standing them down. Further Court Martials were undertaken. Victor Secrillo was exonerated and promoted to 'Adjutant General.' A few villains had slipped the net, some by accident some by choice, but what really mattered was that the path was now clear for the Republican politicians to take the lead.

Seb had argued strongly that this was a rocky road, which would lead to even more antagonism of the Loyalist community. "There's more honesty in a terrorist carrying an AK47 than a whinging politician." He remembered telling his inquisitors'.

Captain Peter Arnott the head of the FRU had scoffed. "Look at the big picture." After the dust settled, now Arnott and several members of his staff had been placed on the honours list whilst the more deserving received nothing. They were the actual people the board of enquiry should have been questioning; without doubt they held back vital intelligence which would have saved countless lives. No Arnott and his cronies played god instead of providing good and timely, actionable intelligence.

There were the dead and injured on both sides, and communities that would never heal or trust again. There was also the collateral damage done to an MI6 deep undercover agent that needed to reintegrate back into her own life along with a daughter who would always be scarred and a son that would never understand his mother's actions if he ever was ever released from prison.

On another continent a young Republican spy, unable to return to his homeland, would forever looking over his shoulder and shying away from strangers whilst looking after his ailing mother.

Seb reached the car, they made his mind up, he'd had his fill of the mob, sunnier climbs awaited him. Cedric had phoned him from London telling him not to make any rash decisions as he was in line to become the next Officer Commanding A Squadron, but his mind was made up. He'd stay in touch with the community, but not be part of it any longer.

Our Lady of Lourdes Convent, County Louth

Decers eyes blinked at the bright pen light held by the Nun.

She came more into focus, young, a little plump and the glasses didn't flatter her at all, but then again she was a bride of God.

The pain in Decers left shoulder was immense as he tried to rise. His mouth was closed solid. He tried to run his tongue over his teeth, some were serrated, others missing completely. His mind was trying to recall how he had come to be lying in a hard bed with fresh clean sheets.

The Nun reached for the glass of water by his bedside and eased a straw through his swollen lips

"Mr Taylor you cannot talk, your jaws are wired shut. I am Sister Marie Carmel, a Novice here at Our Lady of Lourdes Convent in County Louth. A policeman, Garda Jacobs, brought you here for safety. Your body has suffered terrible wounds; you've been in an induced coma for many days."

That was the trigger for the memories to flood back. He remembered being in the kitchen with Eileen and her daughter when the soldiers burst in. He scrunched up his eyes when he saw the bullets hit the child and Eileen. He felt betrayed by his former lover; she had put the Brits on to him, got him into a world of trouble.

Throughout the day Nuns attended to Decers dressings and replaced the IV drip in his right hand. Sleep came in fits and starts. The recollection of his last moments with Eileen disgusted him. The memory was destroying him.

Decers awoke to find his room dark apart from a small bedside lamp, which gave out barely enough light to illuminate his bed. The earlier sunshine which had been cascading through the window was long gone, replaced by the steady thump of rain.

In the dim glow of the light Decers could see another Nun sat beside him, head in her hands as if in prayer. Somehow this Nun seemed more familiar even behind the clinical mask she wore. The pale complexion, freckles and those inviting deep blue eyes. He knew her, but from where. He had never knowingly dated a Nun, but there was always a first time.

The Nun rose to her feet and took a glasses case from her pocket, inside the case was a syringe which she screwed into the medication administration port before squeezing the clear liquid into the tubing. She held his gaze before removing her mask, flecks of her auburn hair fell from the wimple and veil covering her head revealing Decers former handler Corporal Rebecca Hamilton.

"Remember me Declan?" The blue eyes were sinister and blazing.

His eyes twitched he was paralysed with fear.

"Were there a few things you forgot to tell me when I first recruited you?"

His eyes gave him away as he scanned towards the door in the vain hope that one of the other Nuns might walk in and save him from the beautiful, but deadly assassin.

"You didn't mention that you had been told to scout the small tower on Tievecrom Hill above Forkhill, or that you would lead an attack on that site."

Decers was trying to scream for help, but only a low pitch whine was audible.

"You butchered four outstanding men in that tower. You left mothers' without sons, wives without husbands, kids without fathers and a sister without her big brother. Your actions left four children without a father." She stared at him. My brother Corporal Chico Hamilton B Company, The Royal Anglian Regiment Commander of Tievecrom Tower, murdered by you.

He was trying to say the word sorry as the warm glow started rising along his right arm. The glow turned into a burning sensation; he turned to look at the affected arm to see if she was holding a naked flame to his skin.

"Before I joined the army, I was a chemistry student and trained as a pharmacist. Fascinating subject, especially when you see what affect some local plants, when mixed correctly can do to a human body. Take your right arm, for example."

Decers looked in horror as he the blood in his veins became molten hot.

"Near my home there's a wild growing plant called Wolf's-bane. It's exquisite with its pretty dark semi-saturated blue-purple colours. I first looked at the plant after brushing against it as a child and it giving me a severe irritation. As a student I studied it more and found out that a herbal decoction made from the roots makes Aconite. A deadly drug which leads to a combination of neurological, cardiovascular, and gastrointestinal breakdowns in the human body."

Decers entire body was now on fire, but his face and upper torso had become numb, his eyes rolled and become unfocussed.

Nausea began in his stomach, followed by bile being forced into his mouth. Spurts pushed through the few gaps in his mouth, the remainder were sucked back down his throat drowning him in a torrent of his own vomit. The agony increased as he felt another wave of spew, his heart beating to a maximum. Just as he lost consciousness he saw the ginger haired Nun close the door as she left his room.

Belfast

John Joseph 'JoJo' Kelly slowly rose to his feet. His white shirt clung to the new dressing which covered the wounds on his back and his black trousers hid the thick dressings on his upper legs. No longer was JoJo Kelly a child. In the weeks since he had been incarcerated to recover from his injuries in Woburn House detention centre, many events had occurred. Word soon spread amongst the other offenders that a 'special' prisoner was on the wings.

Young Loyalist, still furious at the cowardly bonfire attacks, sought revenge. After a severe beating in the washroom and being slashed in a stairwell, the authorities desperately looked for a secure place to rehouse the young Kelly. Before they could move him four Protestant teenagers buggered the sobbing youth in the laundrette.

Eventually Joseph transferred to Hydebank Wood with a new identity. Not only had JoJo lost his father, but his mother and young sister had disappeared off the face of the earth. His only family was his Aunt Bridget Taylor, who was still in mourning after the death of her husband Declan.

Now JoJo stood awaiting sentencing by Sir Ian Ridgway looked down from his lofted position. Earlier attempts by JoJo's defence council for the trial to be held in a Youth Court had been immediately thrown out, as was his solicitor's pleas not to use the crimes of the father against the child.

The Diplock Crown Court took only a week to declare that Kelly Junior was guilty of the common law offences of seven counts of murder, the statutory offences of position of explosives and firearms, terrorism offences and being a member of a prescribed organisation.

In his summing up Sir Ian took a while to explain to the young defendant and the news reporters in the gallery that the crimes put before him were of the gravest he had ever had to make a judgement upon. Each were heinous attempts to destroy the very fabric of society, and therefore he was forced to seek special powers from the Law Lords before recommending that Kelly would receive an 'indeterminate' prison sentence of no less than twenty years. The harshest sentence ever given to a youth in the history of the United Kingdom.

The judge retired to his chambers; it had been an interminable day, and he was relishing the drive back to Tandragee from the Crumlin Road in Belfast. He removed his short bench wig and placed it on the stand before locking it into a wooden box. He removed his scarlet robes with grey silk facings and brushed the flecks of dandruff from the shoulders before hanging it on a heavy wooden hanger. He reflected on his days' work and smiled contentedly. A knock on the door disturbed his thoughts. He opened the door to find a smartly dressed middle-aged in tweed. The man was fit looking for his age; his eyes were quick and observant. "Sir Ian I heard your wonderful summing up and the sentencing, so I have brought a bottle of Dom Pérignon."

"Thank you, Graham; I hope our mutual friend the Reverend is happy?"

"Indeed, he is and asks us to join him at the Reform Club later."

"So what's the toast?" The judge asked.

The man in the tweed suit raised his glass "Resistance." Graham replied.

Macau 1995

The Philippine Airlines Boeing 737 from Manila landed on the baking hot runway of Macau International Airport. The humidity even within the air-conditioned marble walls of the arrivals lounge was oppressive. The fat man strode towards passport control, his short sleeve white shirt already dripping with sweat. A slim, statuesque Chinese woman held a piece of paper above her head with the name CHARLES WHEELER written upon it in large black stencilled letters. Beside her stood a small, stocky man, immaculately dressed in a grey suit. He thrust out his heavily tattooed hand with a missing finger to great the new arrival.

"Hello Mr Wheeler, good to meet you again, welcome to Macau. I have booked you into a suite at the Hotel Lisboa. Two of my best girls are waiting for you to help you relax."

The heavy man smiled "Thank you Mr Ho."

"Please, Charlie, call me Steve. Once you are refreshed, I will take you to dinner, I have some friends who are dying to meet you. I believe they have a business proposal they wish to offer you."

Wheeler looked sheepish. He stood head and shoulders above the Dragonhead who stood before him.

"Mr Ho, Steve I'm sorry about what happened in Belfast a few years back, it was some kinda misunderstanding about them Chinese kids getting burned alive. The fella that did it was called Bonner, and we brought him to justice, if you know what I mean Sir."

High in the gantry above, Lee Yung fired off a few more pictures with his Cannon A1 Camera. In his right ear he was listening to the grovelling Loyalist.

"He's taken the bait, Suzanne." He informed the elegant woman by his side.

She raised her sunglasses to the top of her head. She put her lips next to Yung's ear and whispered, "Ne ad ludos rursus incipere."

"What's that?"

"Have you never heard of Latin before? It means let the games begin again. Now let's see if our new portly friend can point us toward Ulster Resistance and their links to the upper echelons of British society."

ABOUT THE AUTHOR

Howard Lycett served in the Second Battalion the Royal Regiment of Fusiliers for 24 years, completing two extended tours of Northern Ireland.

His first book Fusilier is an account of his army career, and looks at the fun and comradery experienced by a band of brothers on operational tours.

Stories about patrolling the streets of war torn Belfast to conducting some of the longest running covert observation missions ever carried out in the province.

He is a strong supporter of the Royal British Legion and other military causes.